To John

God Bless

Vic Cassiozzi

THE ELIJAH CHRONICLES

THE ELIJAH CHRONICLES

A Dangerous Challenge Pits An Entire Kingdom Against One Fearless Prophet

Vic Cassizzi

ALEXANDER BOOKS

Founded
332 B.C.

abooks.com

Alexander, North Carolina

Publisher: Ralph Roberts

Editor: Pat Roberts

Cover Design: Ralph Roberts
Interior Design & Electronic Page Assembly: **WorldComm**®
Copyright ©2001 Vic Cassizzi

10 9 8 7 6 5 4 3 2 1

Library of Congress Cataloging-in-Publication Data

Cassizzi, Vic, 1947-
    The Elijah chronicles: a dangerous challenge pits an entire kingdom
    against one fearless prophet / by Vic Cassizzi
       p. cm.
    ISBN 1-57090-100-7
    1. Elijah (Biblical prophet)--Fiction. 2. Bible. O.T.--History of Biblical
    events--Fiction 3. Prophets--Fiction.   I. Title.

PS3553.A8115 E45 200
813'.6--dc21

00-57630
CIP

The author and publisher have made every effort in the preparation of this book to ensure the accuracy of the information. However, the information in this book is sold without warranty, either express or implied. Neither the author nor Alexander Books™ will be liable for any damages caused or alleged to be caused directly, indirectly, incidentally, or consequentially by the information in this book.

The opinions expressed in this book are solely those of the author and are not necessarily those of Alexander Books™.

Trademarks: Names of products mentioned in this book known to be a, or suspected of being trademarks or service marks are capitalized. The usage of a trademark or service mark in this book should not be regarded as affecting the validity of any trademark or service mark.

Alexander Books™—a division of Creativity, Inc.—is a full–service publisher located at 65 Macedonia Road, Alexander NC 28701. Phone (828) 252–9515, Fax (828) 255–8719. For orders only: 1-800-472-0438. Visa and MasterCard accepted.

Alexander Books™ is distributed to the trade by Midpoint Trade Books, Inc., 27 West 20th Street, New York NY 10011, (212) 727-0190, (212) 727-0195 fax.

This book is also available on the internet at **abooks.com**. Set your browser to http://www.abooks.com and enjoy the many fine values available there.

From the Author

Elijah has intrigued me from the first time I read about the prophet in the scriptures. Over and over I read the few lines in the Bible that told of his exploits, and was amazed how little background there was about him.

What kind of childhood and training or tragedy and suffering, did it take to produce a man with such trust in his creator? He seemed as elusive as a mirage.

From the desire to know more about the man behind the miracles, I began to envision circumstances that might have made him who he was. Either by the Spirit, or by imagination, scenes came to mind, which, by the grace of God, I have put down on paper for the inspiration and pleasure of the reader, and for the glory of God.

Often while writing this novel, I felt the wonderful presence of the Spirit of God. I pray that the reader may feel that same presence.

—Vic Cassizzi

Acknowledgments

The author gratefully acknowledges all who assisted in the writing of this novel, and especially thanks:

Ann Putnam
Allen Dunn
Nelson Walden

*And gives very special gratitude to **Harley Dunn**, whose encouragement and support through the long process of writing, editing, and proofing for publication has made this book possible.*

Smoke drifted upward into the night carrying glowing sparks from the campfire. The young man was entranced, as he watched them float skyward and fade into the night, like the haunting melodies of these strange Eastern people. His thoughts returned to the moment, as another slave girl began to dance to the sensuous music. This one caught his attention like no girl or woman ever had before. Her long silken hair swayed with each enthralling move and the shimmering orange light of the fire caressed one side of her body and danced with her, while the silver light of the moon outlined the other.

These magical nights came only once a year for Elijah, who sat among the men of the caravan and the merchants that came to trade with them. The young woman dancing appeared to be about nineteen or twenty, the most beautiful creature he'd ever seen. He wondered how she came to be a slave. Was she born into slavery, or was she perhaps taken captive in some distant land? How high might one have to bid to purchase a slave of such remarkable beauty?

She moved in an increasingly erotic fashion to tempt Elijah. Judging by his clothing, he was from a wealthy family and could easily pay her price. She was intrigued by his piercing blue eyes, made to seem even bluer by his tanned face and dark hair. He was handsome and appeared very innocent, the sort who would make a kind master and possibly even elevate her to the status of a wife if she pleased him.

Earlier in the evening when this young man at the side of an elderly companion entered their camp and passed by the slave tent she had been peering through a narrow opening where the tent flap didn't meet the side. The opening was less than the width of her eye.

She knew that he had felt her gaze when he stopped a few feet away and looked directly at her. That was when she first saw his blue eyes. She had never seen blue eyes before she was brought to Israel. She had been told that people with blue eyes could see into your soul. Maybe it was true because he seemed to know where her stare came from but as she danced she hoped that it wasn't true. If he knew what evil had brought her into bondage he most surely wouldn't be interested in her.

Each year Elijah made this trip with his father to rendezvous with the caravans in the valley of Megiddo where they would stay and trade for several days. There had always been dancing slave women but he had never seen one to compare with the one he was watching now, or perhaps he had been too young to notice before. At night they danced to show their beauty and desirability and would be sold the following day.

The beautiful young woman seemed to be dancing only for Elijah and made him feel special, as though some unspoken, unseen language was passing between them. Her inviting eyes met his, unlike the Hebrew women of his homeland of Gad, who were not allowed to look into the eye of any man outside their own family.

Slaves were in abundance and the merchants were more interested in trading for silver, frankincense, colorful linen or silk, and some for opium and other potent compounds made of ingredients kept secret. They were involved in bargaining talks and hardly noticed the intoxicating dancer. Elijah became so captivated by her he hadn't noticed that he was the only one watching. He felt a twinge of guilt for watching and wondered why. He was nineteen, and his father hadn't called him away as he had in previous years, even though in previous years he had never taken such notice of one particular slave woman.

Uncertain of how much time had elapsed, Elijah suddenly realized that he hadn't seen his father in a while and looked around, hoping that his father hadn't seen him either. Relieved that he was nowhere to be seen, he turned back to the girl who moved rhythmically to the music. There were many caravans camped in the valley this time of year, but Elijah was glad they had chosen this one tonight.

"She is beautiful, is she not?" His father's gentle, powerful voice drowned out the musical instruments. Startled, Elijah turned to see his father standing behind him. His father watched his face carefully in the flickering light of the campfire, "I've not always been an old man, you know. I understand what you are feeling."

"She is the most beautiful thing I've ever seen. I think she has stolen my heart," Elijah answered. He looked at the dancer again, then back at his father. "You know, Father, you could use another servant. What do you think her price tomorrow will be?"

"She would not be a bargain for you, even if I would allow such a thing. Her owner's servants are watching you even now from the shadows outside the light of the fire. They see the look on your face as she dances, and they will not forget come tomorrow's bidding. You are not the first young man they have set this trap for. She is like the lamb that baits the lion trap.

"A woman like that is capable of destroying a good man, particularly a young naive one like you."

Embarrassed by his father's words and his own inexperience, he lowered his head as he looked around. A shadowy figure watched him from beyond the corner of the slave women's tent.

Less confident now, Elijah continued, "But her eyes are so kind and warm. I don't believe there is any evil in her. I don't believe she could ever do any harm to me." A moment later he added, "Or to anyone."

"No? Before you become so sure, let me tell you about her.

"I inquired of the Assyrian who will auction her tomorrow. He is the servant of her owner, the man sitting over there bargaining with the opium sellers.

"She was the only wife of a nobleman, a man not yet thirty, a wealthy man. She was caught in the act of adultery with one of the servants. The servant was put to death, a horrible death I understand. She was sold into slavery because her husband still loved her and couldn't bear to see her die."

The words of his father were like a knife piercing his heart. Could he have misjudged this beautiful creature so completely?

"I didn't stop you from watching her because it's time for you to learn about the wickedness in the hearts of men, Elijah. You know the Law of Moses better than anyone I've ever known. You have a natural understanding for it, but in the ways of the world you are quite innocent, and I will not always be here to protect you."

Elijah's attention had been divided between his father and the woman, but now he turned to see if he could read something in his father's eyes that wasn't being said. He had to stand to get a closer look in the dim light of the dying campfire. His father's hair and beard seemed whiter than he had ever seen them before and his eyes looked very tired. Their gazes locked for a moment before he spoke again. "Elijah, in the last nineteen years I have seen many things in dreams about you. You are called of Yahweh and must keep yourself unspotted by the world."

There was a long pause, as they seemed to look into each other's souls. "Never repeat what I am about to tell you, and know that it's not meant to hurt you, but you are old enough now to hear the truth. Your mother was just like this beautiful young woman who seems to have stolen your heart." He studied Elijah for a long moment as he let his words sink in. "If you can be destroyed, separated from your destiny, it will be by a woman."

The woman sensed that she was the topic of their discussion and danced closer, hoping they were debating on the price they would bid for her at tomorrow's slave auction. She was able to pull Elijah's attention back to her when he realized that she was much closer than before. She began to spin in a small circle in front of him. With the words of his father's warning still echoing in his mind he watched, but her spell had been broken for the moment.

A man clapped his hands twice and the music stopped. A moment later the beautiful young woman ended her dance and spoke to Elijah in an Arabic dialect common in Gilead, one that he understood. "Did you like my dance? It was for you." She smiled then turned and ran.

Elijah turned back to his father and asked, "Can we stay until the slaves are auctioned tomorrow?"

His father nodded a concerned reluctant approval. "It will only bring you pain, but if that is what you want we will stay."

Elijah slept little that night. Images of the woman crept into his mind each time his eyes closed. He wished the night would hurry past so he could see her again, yet at the same time he was filled with anxiety knowing that she could never belong to him. So many mixed feelings and the words about his mother added greatly to his turmoil. Exhaustion finally overtook him just before dawn and he slept, only to be awakened a short time later by the morning's activities outside his tent.

By the time they had eaten, the crowds were already gathering and the traffic was heavy leading up into the city of Megiddo, a short distance above the caravans encamped in the valley below. For the few weeks after harvest virtually anything one might want or need could be found in the markets of Megiddo. New caravans from the east on their way to Egypt arrived daily. Hobbled camels grazed in the open areas among the black tents to the south.

Merchants, vendors, the wealthy and beggars all mingled together. The smell of roasting lamb or goat, mixed with the smoke and the smells of faraway places floated on the dusty air. The buzz of the milling crowd was punctuated by vendors, calling to passers-by the type of wares being offered.

Camels, horses, and slaves were all sold in like manner. The cries of vendors would gather crowds about them in circular islands of humanity. The vendors then extolled the virtues of a particular horse, the strong back of a male slave, or perhaps the great beauty of a woman bought in some faraway place. The vendor would then take bids from the people around him until one came close to his price. The buyer and seller would then grasp hands with a tight grip and would argue sometimes for more than an hour over the last few pieces of silver or even the small copper wedges. People gathered around would move on to more interesting sights if it looked as though the arguing was going to last for a while. With some of the merchants it was a game, since the one to release his hold first agreed to the other's price.

Elijah stood in the hot sun through the morning, until the slave woman he had been waiting to see was brought out from a nearby tent. She was paraded in a circle before the bidding began. Elijah stepped back into the crowd to keep from being seen by her. He was afraid that she would look to him to redeem her. His embarrassment for her mixed with jealousy as the slave handlers disrobed her in front of the crowd of leering men. She looked around, her eyes darting through the crowd as the bidding began. She found him through a very small opening between the men that he had retreated behind. Her eyes rested on him and a small light of hope came back to her face.

As the bidding continued without Elijah's participation the expectant look on her face turned to dismay. Her price rose until any moment she knew her master would clasp hands with one of the bidders. Then it would be too late for the young man that she had pinned her hopes on to bid for her. With her eyes she was now pleading for him to make an offer.

Elijah pushed his way to the front but was helpless to do anything. Though he was never without silver, he carried nothing close to the bids that were being made. He had a great inheritance that had been left to him but it was in land, sheep, and goats, and was back in Gilead.

Suddenly a priest of Moloch, wearing a bright scarlet robe and the customary sash and headdress of white and gold, stepped forward and took the hand of the auctioneer. It was only a token grip of hands, for he was willing to pay the seller's price and released his hold in less than a minute. The priest often purchased women from slave traders to make into temple prostitutes, but to find one of such great beauty was rare. The priest smiled at the thought of introducing this young woman into temple service.

This was the worst possible outcome Elijah could have imagined. He dropped his face into his hands for a moment and the young woman began to cry uncontrollably as she was forced back the way she came and another woman was brought out to be sold.

Since the days of Moses many of the Hebrews had accepted the worship of pagan gods where temple prostitutes were sometimes elevated next to deity. But Elijah couldn't see it that way. To him it was a fate far worse than death.

Feeling the greatest despair he had ever known, Elijah made his way back to his father's tent, fell to one of the mats and lay there. The woman with whom he had made this bond, something he could not yet understand, would be forced to become a temple prostitute.

Elijah couldn't remember his mother and had never experienced any real feelings for her until this moment. He suddenly realized that this girl and his mother may have fallen into the same snare in life. What had his father meant when he said his mother was like the dancer? He had always seen her as the woman who abandoned him as a child, but now he wondered. How could he have these feelings for this girl and resent his mother? Was his mother's pain as great as that of this beautiful young woman? Her tears and the look in her eyes were burned deep into his soul.

Elijah smashed his fist into the mat. "Damn this Moloch!"

His father came in at nightfall carrying bread, wine and a roast of lamb. "Maybe it wasn't a good thing that we stayed. Tomorrow at daylight we'll leave." Elijah didn't answer.

"Eat with me and we'll talk," said his father. Elijah would rather have died than to disrespect his father, whom he considered to be the kindest, most god-like man in the world, the one person he loved most. He sat up and said, "Thank you, you're too kind to me. I don't deserve this."

"Neither of us deserve the good things Yahweh has given to us but it gets even better. I've brought the most wonderful date and fig cakes I think I've ever tasted."

His father sang a short psalm of thanksgiving before they began to eat. There were several minutes of silence before Elijah spoke what was on his mind. "The beautiful dancer was bought by a priest of Moloch."

"That's unfortunate," came the reply that wasn't as complete as Elijah had hoped for.

After a few more minutes of quiet he said, "You could have used another servant."

"I have all the servants that I need, and I would not have trusted that woman near you. I want you to have a wife who will always be at your side. You know the story of Potiphar's wife. If a man chooses wisely he'll never be faced with a situation like that."

"And what of my mother?"

His father looked at Elijah thoughtfully before he spoke. "Well, as you know, she was my brother's wife. I fathered you by her to produce heirs to my brother after he died, according to the Law of Moses, and the custom of our people. I really didn't know her well. Later, when she ran away, back to Moab, I went to find her, since she was my brother's wife, and your mother.

"It was then that I learned that she had been bought out of slavery by my brother for a great sum of silver, many times more than the dancer brought today. How my brother even met her is more than I can understand.

"The women of Tishbeh shunned your mother because she was from Moab, and would taunt her when she went to the well or to the market. As you know, our people have an unreasoning hatred for the people of Moab. I have never been able to understand this, since King David's great grandmother, Ruth, was a Moabitess. She married Boaz of Bethlehem, in the land of Judah, very much like your mother married my brother. The people of Judah accepted her then, but things are very different today. Your mother was miserable here in Tishbeh.

"My wife loved your mother, but even she could not stop the rumors that kept coming up about her past. My brother never told us of her past, or that he had bought her freedom. I searched for her throughout Moab, but when I learned that she had gone back to the life she had lived before she met my brother, I stopped looking for her.

"I have never told this to anyone until now, and you will be wise to never repeat this, in fairness to your mother, and to my brother, whose name you bear. There are whirlwinds in life that catch us up like the desert wind, and take us where we don't want to go.

"My brother and your mother were not too unlike you and this dancer. In other times and circumstances this might have been different for you, just as it could have been different for your mother. She was not someone to hate, Elijah. She was caught up in circumstances larger and stronger than she was, like the serpent catches the rabbit.

"Your brothers resent you because of her, because she was a Moabitess, and because your inheritance through my brother is equal to all of theirs put together. Plus, as my son you have an inheritance from me equal to each of theirs.

"My son, you have a large inheritance to tempt those who are jealous of you. When I am gone you can trust your brother Eliab. He is honest and will look out for your interests. The others will change when they see in you the man that I see."

Elijah was quiet as he thought on what had been told to him.

His father reached over to him with a date cake. "Reveal to no one that you know these things about your mother." He waited for a minute, then added, "You were raised by a woman who loved you more than her own sons."

Another minute passed before he began to tell Elijah what he had planned to keep secret until arrangements had been finalized. "I have talked to a man about his daughter for your wife. She is very beautiful, but she is young yet. In a few years, when you are ready, she will be seventeen.

When spring arrives, I will go and pay her dowry and sign a contract on your behalf."

He took a bite of one of the cakes and chewed for a minute before continuing. "Believe me, she will become as beautiful as the slave girl. And she has been raised in a home that respects and honors Yahweh."

Elijah, still grieving over the slave girl, didn't brighten up as much as his father had wished, but asked, "Have I ever seen her?"

"No, my son, she is not from Tishbeh."

Elijah was torn between the exciting news of his impending engagement, and the brief, but tragic encounter with the slave girl. For two months afterward, Elijah was tormented by memories of the young slave woman, but the unexpected death of his father put her out of his mind. Now all he cared to remember were the years he had spent at his father's side, the lessons on the law he had taught him, and their last long conversation as they had returned to Tishbeh from Megiddo. Elijah had nervously looked forward to spring, but he never met the young woman that his father was going to arrange for him to marry.

In those days, the divided tribes of the Hebrews were at war. The long sought promised land had been divided into two kingdoms. Asa ruled the southern kingdom of Judah and Elah ruled the northern kingdom of Israel.

In the twenty and seventh year of Asa, King of Judah, Zimri, commander of half the war chariots of Israel, conspired against King Elah of Israel and slew him and his household. Zimri took the throne and proclaimed himself king in Tirzah, the capital city. When Omri, commander of the rest of the chariots of Israel, heard of the treason of Zimri he assembled his troops and besieged the city. Zimri, defeated and cut off from his forces, rather than surrender, burned the palace down around himself. He had reigned only seven days. The acts of Zimri are recorded in the book of the kings of Israel.

Four years of civil war ensued. Omri's forces prevailed in the thirty and first year of Asa, King of Judah. Thus began Omri to reign over Israel. It was in those days that Yahweh began to raise up a prophet to judge the land.

****

Breathlessly, Elijah made his way out of the murky water of the Jordan and pulled up the steep muddy bank holding a tree branch. Eight of his friends were still splashing and fighting over a round piece of wood wrapped in rawhide, the ball that was the focal point of their game. "Aaaah! Elijah, come on back."

Elijah looked back and said, "I've been in the water long enough. I'm cold and tired. Besides, the sides are even now."

"Johanan stood the last watch over the sheep last night, but he's still willing to play. And Joshua is only fifteen, he can't keep up."

Johanan spoke up, "Let him rest. We'll do fine without him for a while."

Johanan knew that Elijah had other things on his mind and had only stopped on their journey home from the sheep market and played this long at their urging. He knew that Elijah felt the resentment from his brothers even more since his father's death, and was still grieving. He was also afraid that Elijah wasn't content in Tishbeh any longer.

Once he was at the top of the riverbank Elijah dropped to his knees in the sand. Beads of cold water covered his body and dripped from the hair that hung in curls about his face and neck. He shivered and hugged himself for warmth.

As he slowly warmed in the rays of sun filtering through the scattered rain clouds gathering overhead, he began to focus on the game still taking place in the river. The object was to keep the ball away from the opposing side as long as possible and the game became quite rough at times. All but a couple of the young men were about his age, around twenty, with the youngest two being fifteen and seventeen. Though they always insisted that he join them in their games or contests, Johanan was his only true friend. For some reason that he couldn't understand he was unable to feel close to anyone but his father, who was now gone, and Johanan who had been his friend his whole life.

Later as Elijah and Johanan walked along, Elijah confided in him. "I'm leaving Tishbeh."

In a scolding tone Johanan answered, "Why would you do that? The land you own is here, ...and your family."

"Here, my life is already planned for me, but I really don't fit into that life. I don't know where I belong, but I know it isn't here. I have studied the law like everyone else, but I know there is more to Yahweh than the law. My life doesn't leave room for me to find the God of David and the friend of Abraham that I sense in the Scriptures. I see it in the mountains and the hills around me that He has created, but I don't see it in the life of people that I know here. It's like we have taken the Law of Moses and used it to hide God in a wineskin, where we can pour Him out when we want to. Surely there is someone, somewhere, who can help me find this truth; who can tell me what this fire in my bones means."

Elijah looked anxiously at his friend Johanan, suddenly afraid that he had said too much, but his friend only appeared perplexed.

"Elijah, you are..." he hesitated. Johanan didn't want to offend his friend, but he felt that this was somehow a moment of great importance, and that he must tell Elijah what he had always known, but had never said.

"Elijah, you are different. You are not like other people, here or anywhere else. For reasons that you or I may never know, Yahweh has made your thoughts different from those of other men.

"But that doesn't mean you have to leave, you can live here. We'll do things together like we always have! It will be a great life! We'll marry beautiful women, and our children can play together. Elijah, it will be good, you'll see.

"You're rich, you have everything here that any man could ever want. You could even buy that temple slave that you were so taken with last year," Johanan went on. But as his words tumbled out, he knew that somehow, something had already changed. Maybe the very act of saying these things had sealed the course that Elijah would pursue.

Elijah was quiet, as his thoughts went back to the events of last year that now seemed so long ago. They walked along in silence for a time.

"What does Eliab say about you leaving?" Johanan finally asked.

"He doesn't approve, but he will take care of the land and flocks until I return. He thinks that maybe I just need some time away. He's made arrangements for me to continue my studies in Jericho. Tell me, do you think Yahweh chooses a man to be a prophet or do you think a man can choose to be a prophet himself?"

They walked along quietly for a few minutes before Johanan answered. "Well, if Yahweh speaks through him then he is chosen, if he doesn't then he isn't, and he has chosen himself."

That came as a revelation to Elijah who suddenly realized how simple the answer was. "I want Yahweh to speak to me and through me more than anything in the world. What if he doesn't?"

"Then you will have to raise flocks of sheep and children and be content to be rich. That isn't so bad, is it?"

As night fell over Tishbeh, the young men walked the quiet road that would soon lead Elijah to most of the cities of Israel, to the great teachers, and to a quest that would take a lifetime and beyond.

****

In a small village near Jerusalem, a scribe picked up his pen and began to write what he had been turning over in his mind for many years.

"These, the words of Jehew the seer, the son of Hanani; having finished the acts of Jehoshaphat the King of Judah, as I was directed, am now led by the Spirit of Elohim to write of the life of Elijah the prophet, and of the awesome events that surrounded him as he followed the call of our great God Yahweh, Creator of the Universe.

"These remarkable events would not have been believed, except they were witnessed by large multitudes of the people of Israel. I too witnessed many of these wondrous works and am therefore compelled to preserve this account for all generations, up until the time of the end.

"Knowing Elijah as well as any one could know him, perhaps with the exception of Delah, who had the privilege of living in close quarters with him for two years, and Elisha to whom Elijah's mantle and anointing were left, it is reasonable that Yahweh Elohim has chosen me to chronicle the acts of that prophet.

"I had the honor of hearing him teach at The School many times, and talked with him at length on more than a few occasions. Much of this story was written by Elijah himself, who entrusted me with the prophecies and revelations that were given to him.

"During his time among us he grew into the relationship with Yahweh Elohim that he was destined for, unlike many that I have seen who fell by the wayside. Elisha said that in the last years Elijah was so consumed to know Elohim, that there was no vanity left in him, and the things that we count so dear of the treasures of earth came to mean less than nothing to Elijah.

"I traveled to Zarephath to meet Delah, the widow who shared her home with Elijah for several years. I went to learn what she knew of him, and of the details of the death of her son and how Elijah raised him from the dead. It was apparent that she saw him as a man and not as an angel sent to earth, as some believe him to be. She knew him to be a humorous man, a side that I never knew. To me he seemed too serious, as though he felt responsible in some way for the infidelity of Israel to Yahweh.

"Before anyone had heard of Elijah, I knew he was special, called of God, and anointed with the Spirit of God. But I was not aware of just how great the power of his anointing was until later."

Jehew's pen scratched across the parchment in the dimly lit room, as his mind began to picture the events of the life of the man Elijah. He raised his head and looked out the single open window in the small room. For a moment he watched as the patches of white clouds against the blue sky moved in his direction, to be obscured from sight by the walls that surrounded him. "Elijah came and left like one of those clouds," he said to himself. A revelation struck him as clearly as that open window. As those clouds will surely rain back upon the earth, Elijah will return. "Elijah will be sent back one day," Jehew said aloud. As suddenly as he saw that truth, he was also made aware that to seek greater insight into Elijah's return would be fruitless, for that revelation was not for his generation, but for a generation yet centuries away.

Jehew put the pen into the ink and continued his account.

Elijah remained among the prophets in Jericho only a few months, long enough to learn that the false doctrine proclaiming that Ashtoreth, an ancient pagan goddess, was the queen of heaven and the bride of Yahweh, had been accepted by many of the people there. He spent the subsequent years traveling over Israel, searching for true teachings, and taking an account of the believers that had remained true to the Law of Moses.

The faithful were few. Most of Israel had become Baal worshipers, believing he was the principal god of heaven and the nether world. Some had accepted Moloch or some lesser god and among those that worshipped Yahweh, most believed He ruled the universe jointly with his queen, Ashtoreth. Most often Ashtoreth was believed to be the wife of Baal, but there were as many different beliefs circulating as there were cities and hamlets in Israel.

A new doctrine that was spreading across the land was that there had been a war in heaven among the gods, and that Baal had triumphed and was therefore the most powerful and important god to appease. Human sacrifice had become as common as it had been in Canaan when Yahweh destroyed the people with plagues and sent Israel to conquer them. Some idols required the sacrifice of young virgins, for others the highest sacrifice was the offering of small children, about the age of four. The worship of Baal required many human sacrifices of children and virgins, and many people even offered themselves, having been taught that they would be given a higher rank in the after life.

Elijah searched throughout the land for teachers of the law of the God of his fathers. When he found one he would spend months, sometimes a year or more studying and learning from them. He was surprised to find some of these wise men among the nomadic Ishmaelites. They lived by the Law of Moses and the Abrahamic covenant more closely than any of the Hebrew tribes Elijah had encountered. Elijah remained with one of them for nine months on the edge of the desert, studying with a wise man who reminded him so much of his father that he sometimes thought his heart would burst. During this stay with the Ishmaelites, he felt a compulsion, unlike any other he had ever experienced, to go to Samaria.

On the three-day journey, Elijah continually questioned why he felt he must go to this pagan place, but against all logic, he knew he had to make the journey. Samaria was a new city, built by King Omri to honor himself, and it was widely known that he was a Baal worshiper and had built an altar to him in the palace. Yet, Elijah felt that he had to make this journey.

In the third year of King Omri of Israel's reign, to form an alliance with Zidon, he arranged a marriage between his son, Ahab, and Jezebel, the daughter of King Ethbaal of Zidon. The palace of Samaria was under construction, and though the capital wouldn't be moved there from Tirzah for three years, the marriage ritual was carried out in the splendid hall of the new palace.

The new palace was even more heavily fortified than the rebuilt palace of Tirzah. It was austere, reflecting the military background of Omri, but there were lavishly decorated banqueting rooms used for entertaining heads of state, like the one used the night of the wedding feast.

King Omri and King Ethbaal were seated together at the head of the room. Jezebel sat to the left of her father Ethbaal while Ahab sat to the right of King Omri. Ahab had only met Jezebel a few days before this, his wedding night, and could hardly take his eyes off her. He could see her clearly, as was customary, and was almost jealous when a servant stepped between them. She made sure that their eyes met often, speaking of pleasures to come.

Jezebel was a master of conveying thoughts with a glance. She could say with a look what written pages could never convey. At seventeen, she had the wit and wiles that others strive a lifetime for and never achieve. She had an aura that made those around her certain that she was attuned to, or knew something they didn't.

To be a wedding guest of King Omri was a great honor, but the opportunity to see the fabled beauty of Jezebel was to be especially treasured. Her beauty was renowned, her skin very light, her long bluish black hair was braided into a bun the night of her wedding. There was something so seductive about Jezebel that everyone wanted to be near her, not just in a sensual way, but a spellbinding, mystical attraction.

The black in the center of her dark eyes could be cold and deep and many were uncomfortable, even fearful, when looking into them.

A thousand people were gathered in this great hall for the wedding of Ahab and Jezebel. The ceiling was thirty cubits high, supported by huge columns. The walls were decorated with banners, each to commemorate one of Omri's victories. The great Omri had never been defeated, and his name struck fear into the hearts of his enemies, for he was without mercy. Many a foe died a slow terrible death at his hand.

It was for this reason that Zimri, Omri's competitor for the throne of Israel, killed himself after losing the battle between he and Omri at Tirzah. So great was his fear of Omri's revenge that he burned the palace down around himself at Tirzah, burning himself to death, rather than surrender to Omri.

Omri attributed his great success in battle to the demon god Baal; therefore Baal's image dominated the room.

As the time was nearing for Ahab to rise in view of the great company of guests and escort Jezebel from the room in their sight, she was studying his handsome features and planning her controlling spell. In fact she was planning a strategy by which to get her way for the rest of her life. She was not under any false illusion; she knew that the measure of her influence would be limited in part by his own will power, but she was sure that she would get most of what she wanted.

She was glad that Ahab was handsome, "very handsome," she thought. His hair and beard were dark with reddish highlights, his eyes were hazel, he had a strong slender nose with typical Hebrew features like those associated with the tribe of Dan. His teeth were white and even, and he stood several inches taller than the average man. She felt more than just a little smug knowing that he would someday be king and that she would be able to influence him. And no matter how many other wives he took she would be the queen.

There was so much noise and motion in the room with the servants carrying food and drink, and the many conversations, that only Ahab noticed when she stood and moved among the servants to the doorway where Tamara, her servant and seeress, stood. Wherever Jezebel was, Tamara was always nearby.

Jezebel borrowed a small blade from Tamara, pulled a few strands of her hair from the long braided bun on the back of her head, and cut them. "Weave these into the bed covering in the bridal chamber, and hurry. The time is near." With those orders Tamara hurried away and Jezebel returned to her place.

Tamara was the same age as Jezebel, born of a slave family of King Ethbaal. The astrologers said that the wisdom of the gods would speak through her, and because of the nearness of her birth to Jezebel's she was to be Jezebel's helper through this life. She was born only minutes after Jezebel. The conjunction of the planets was rare and powerful the night they were born. Because Tamara was to be Jezebel's counselor for the rest of her life, a special ceremony was given for her at age eleven. Baal was entreated on her behalf. Another child was offered as a sacrifice in her place, at which time Baal was to give her special gifts as a seeress.

Jezebel relied on her constantly and would have been lost without her, but there was one problem. Tamara was as beautiful as the princess, and had that very rare golden hair, rumored to be more common to peoples of the far north. Jezebel would let no one admire her for even a moment, for when she suspected that Tamara got a glance that she didn't, Tamara would be sent immediately on some errand out of sight. Because she was a slave she was never allowed to wear any of the face colors that fine ladies wore and Jezebel felt that difference gave her the edge. Openly she would never have admitted that she was sometimes jealous of the beauty of a slave. Tamara's eyes were dark blue and she was slightly taller than her mistress.

Jezebel turned her attention to the image of Baal and the activity of the priests preparing to make sacrifices on behalf of the new couple, once they entered the bridal chamber. Her thoughts drifted back to the sacrifice made for Tamara and her when they were eleven, a ritual that had never been performed before, but one Baal had instructed them to do. A Syrian girl, as close to their own age as could be found, was placed on a stone altar in a temple in Zidon. Arteries in her neck and arms were cut ever so slightly to cause her to bleed slowly to death. The rectangular altar had grooves carved into it, all leading to the front center where a golden bowl caught the rivulets of blood. Jezebel and Tamara watched the child's eyes grow slowly dim and glaze as her life drained away. When the girl's eyes were set like stone, she and Tamara drank from the bowl of gold; her life. The remaining blood was then sprinkled on Tamara.

The room became still and quiet and Jezebel was suddenly pulled back to the present. King Omri was standing. His fine royal robe and white hair distinguished him from everyone else. The multitude stood as he intoned, "O great Baal, pre-eminent among the gods," he lifted his golden cup to the image of Baal as he spoke. "For our victories and for our prosperity, and for uniting the Kingdom of Zidon and the Kingdom of Israel, we honor you. Let our children's children for a thousand generations rule over Israel, and may they all give homage to you, O great Baal."

Night fell when Elijah was only a few hours from the city but he pushed on. The half moon moved in and out of the clouds as he walked the darkened road. Like all the young men of Gilead, his early years had been spent in the fields at night guarding the family's flocks. There had been times that he had sensed danger and felt a twinge of fear, but for the most part he was comfortable with the dark. And yet there was something strange about this night that made him uneasy. He was feeling a kind of fear he had never known before, vaguely familiar, but more powerful than anything he had ever experienced. Several times he looked over his shoulder to find an empty road behind him.

From the corner of his eye he caught the movement of something in the shadows. He stopped and watched and listened and quieted his own breathing. He stepped into the shadow of the trees and waited for his eyes to focus in the even darker night. With his staff he probed the blackness that was beyond his ability to penetrate but there wasn't anything there. After nearly half an hour of motionless pensive anticipation he stepped back into the road and continued but couldn't shake the feeling that someone was behind him.

Elijah was glad when he reached an area of long sloping treeless hills that allowed him to see a great distance in every direction. For a few minutes he felt more comfortable until the distant shadows seemed to begin to move. The feeling that he wasn't alone returned. It was unmistakable. Elijah knew he wasn't alone, that he was in the presence of something truly evil. He continued along in the silent darkness as his eyes began to burn from straining to see into the night. He closed them tightly to moisten and rest them for a few seconds but quickly opened them again when he saw an angry monstrous face glaring at him through closed eyelids. A cold chill ran over him as he quickly turned in all directions. Nothing was there.

Never so alert as he was now with all of his senses on edge, Elijah's heart pumped hard and his stride picked up. Without breaking into a run he moved swiftly toward Samaria and was glad when the lamps and torches along the city wall came into view. At first the knowledge that people were nearby gave him a measure of comfort, but as he approached Samaria the intimidating evil presence seemed to be growing stronger. Something was terribly wrong, but what was it?

Camped at the foot of the hill on which Samaria stood was a caravan that reminded Elijah of the Ishmaelites with whom he had been dwelling. Elijah made his way toward the camped caravan, remembering something he had once witnessed among the Ishmaelites. A mad man had been brought to their camp to be delivered by the elders. The chief elder was a very wise man of God, one who was widely known among the nomadic tribes for his understanding of such matters. The mad man was dragged into the tent of meeting bound and screaming. His eyes were wild, like those of a wounded animal. Fascinated, Elijah sat with the younger men of the tribe who were sometimes allowed to observe such rites as a teaching process. Expecting a ritual of exorcism, Elijah was somewhat surprised when the musicians began to play their harps and lyres as the elders began to sing, "Holy is the name of Yahweh, great are the works of El Shaddai. He delivers the weak from the oppressor and the humble he exalts above the mighty. His name is hallowed and strikes fear in the hearts of the fallen ones, the angels of Lucifer that left their place among the Seraphim."

The fallen ones! Elijah suddenly realized that he was now in the presence of a host of the fallen ones. He finally recognized the fear that he had been feeling, and felt a flood of joy as he remembered how the mad man had been released from the power of the ones who had once dwelt among the angels. The man screamed in agony as the elders worshiped the God of Abraham, then he became still. His eyes returned to normal and a few minutes later he began to worship the God who had set him free. Daily the worship continued, until the spiritual gate through which the demon entered the man's soul had been sealed.

That was an experience Elijah would never forget. He had called the ancient elder aside and asked how the mad man had been delivered without an incantation that invoked the name of Yahweh and cast out the evil spirit, as Elijah had always imagined an exorcism. The wise seer explained, "Like an adoring child is loved by his father Yahweh appears in the praises of his children. He loved to walk with Adam in the cool of the day. Nothing evil can abide in that presence, the source of the light of all creation."

The wise one had looked directly into Elijah's eyes as he said, "It is not a great mystery. As the night flees from the rising sun, darkness cannot abide in the light of Yahweh's presence. The demon fled from that presence and, as long as the man abides in the Law of God and remembers how he was delivered, he will never be bound again.

"My son, exorcisms in the way you were expecting are very dangerous, releasing great and powerful forces that you cannot resist. Never put yourself between Yahweh Elohim and the fallen ones. Keep Yahweh between you and the evil one. The rabbit who stands between the hunter and the lion gets shot through with the arrow. Do not call out demons so that they may devour you. Praise our God from your heart, and His glory will surround you. Then demons will flee from His presence."

Elijah would try this knowledge to bind the evil host that had now come against him. He was aware that the presence of evil was stronger than ever and to close his eyes for even an instant conjured up nightmarish images. "Yahweh El Shaddai, there is no name like the name of the God of Abraham. It was You that formed the earth and stars with Your word and measured the seas in the palm of Your hand. The Glory of all things belongs to You. You defend the defenseless who call to You, and You alone are my shield."

Elijah had never felt such power before. He stopped and dropped his staff and bag and cloak, then lifted his hands toward heaven and sang aloud with renewed energy. "O Great God of my fathers, I lift my hands to worship and bow my heart before you." Tears burst from his eyes as he became aware that the power now present was a thousand times greater than the power that had made him afraid. He sensed that victory was on his side. He knelt in the road as the tears of joy streamed down his face. It was the greatest anointing Elijah had ever experienced. As he sang louder than before a dog began to bark then another answered the call of the first. Elijah sang even louder, "Let everything that has breath praise Yahweh Elohim."

After a few minutes Elijah looked again at the city. This time he saw something that he wouldn't have believed had he not seen it himself. He didn't know if it was a vision or some other apparition, since he had never seen a vision before.

Elijah blinked his eyes several times. Dozens of plumes of smoke were rising from Samaria as they would from any city that time of the evening, from cooking ovens or fires for light or warmth. The smoke was gathering into a cloud above the city and hanging there, but what he saw in the cloud was the ghostly image of snakes writhing in a gnarled tangle like they would in the spring time when they came alive again in their dens. The serpents were writhing in pain and striking at one another. It was a sight that frightened Elijah. His heart pounded hard as he wondered if this had something to do with his coming here.

As he stood and continued, he discovered that when he praised Yahweh it caused the serpents terrible pain. When he stopped, some would slither down the plumes of smoke into the city. Elijah wondered if his senses had left him and he had gone mad. He thought, "I don't feel mad." Then he asked himself, "Would a mad man know that he was mad?" He couldn't answer that question with any certainty.

The vision of serpents went away, but the great cloud of smoke remained. As Elijah surveyed this scene, a large camel caravan approached the city, accompanied by a contingent of King Omri's mounted guard. Elijah moved close enough to overhear part of the shouted conversation between the guards of the approaching caravan and the captain of the guard on the wall. "We overtook the bandits and have rescued the prince's caravan bringing gifts to the wedding celebration," shouted the commander down below. "Open quickly, lest we incur the wrath of the king for being so late!" The captain of the guard ordered the gate opened.

Elijah stepped into the shadows, moved close to the caravan and took hold of the harness of one of the camels. There was only one driver for every three to four camels, so he passed as a driver and entered the city at the side of one of the lumbering animals. Once inside he stole away into the shadows. He had done something he would never have contemplated doing before. Why was he here? For what reason had he been led to come to this evil place?

****

Omri turned to King Ethbaal, who arose, took Jezebel by the arm, and escorted her over to Ahab. She wrapped her arm in Ahab's, and he escorted her from the room, followed by their families, musicians and hundreds of guests. Through the long hallway to the bridal chamber, Jezebel was filled with a joy and pride she had never known before. She drank in the envy of the maidens who would have done anything to trade places with her.

She looked up at Ahab, then back at the merriment that followed them. Suddenly the smile left her face and for a moment she was gripped in a powerful presence that engulfed her in a cold chill, a feeling she had never experienced before. Her eyes searched frantically for Tamara for some kind of assurance. Tamara wasn't there. At that moment Tamara was leaving the bridal chamber where she had carried out the order to weave her mistress's hair into the bed covering. The same powerful presence that engulfed Jezebel also gripped her. She was virtually paralyzed for several moments.

Neither woman knew where this strange presence emanated from, but at that moment the elusive figure of Elijah slipped from shadow to shadow, following the caravan to the center of the city. He watched from outside the torch-lit square in front of King Omri's palace as the camels were made to kneel on the flagstones near the entrance. Dusty carpets that covered the animals great packs were removed. It was obvious from the way the goods were handled that this was not ordinary merchandise. Small chests, rolls of fine silks and other objects were carefully handed to the masters of the caravan. The great care with which these items were handled, as well as the large quantity of seemingly very valuable things made Elijah curious. What was going on here tonight? Whose wedding was this, to command such a tribute?

As Elijah pondered these things, the animals were unloaded, then removed from view at the insistence of the captain of the palace guard. The camels were led around the north side of the palace to a stable within the palace grounds. Elijah too, went down the side street for fear of being discovered, as the guards' attention was no longer diverted by the riches they had just seen.

After the camels were out of sight within the stable gate Elijah found himself alone in the dark street. As he turned to leave he caught the smell of sweet incense, then saw the light of torches approaching from a narrow alleyway. He again ducked into the shadows as a procession of the priests of Baal, carrying several young boys around four or five years of age, stepped into the side street and crossed over to a narrow entrance nearly hidden in the courtyard wall. The smell of the sweet incense turned vile in his nostrils as he realized that this was a sacrificial procession on the way to some bloody ritual in the palace.

As Elijah stepped back into the side courtyard to keep from being seen, he felt that he had stepped into the very den of the serpents coiled above the city. "Yahweh Elohim," he prayed, "Take your sword and end the lives of these killers of small children now!" Elijah began again to worship and praise God in the darkened courtyard across from the palace.

A large black raven screamed and streaked from atop the wall surrounding the priest's quarters as the power of Yahweh filled and surrounded Elijah praying in the courtyard. Fear struck the guards surrounding the palace as they watched, startled, as the screaming raven disappeared into the dark cloud above the palace.

Many others in the palace at that same moment felt the strange presence that Jezebel and Tamara felt. Zohelethbal, the high priest of Baal, as well as other priests and many of the guests were affected, but none so dramatically as Jezebel and Tamara.

Mentally, Jezebel reeled under this strange power. Ahab could see that something was wrong and turned to her with concern. "Perhaps it's the wine," she answered, before he could ask. She would have collapsed if Ahab had not steadied her with his strong arms. With a great force of will she rallied her composure enough to continue on to the bridal chamber. Once the door was closed behind them, the procession returned to the great hall.

Influenced by the customary sacrifice of children by the Zidonians, Omri had begun to practice human sacrifice, believing that human sacrifice was greater than that of animals to appease the gods. Literally every occasion was dedicated to Baal and, for fear of offending the devil, the altars became stained with the blood of children. That night was no different. As the feasting was going on, the priests were preparing to offer the sacrifice of the innocent.

Three bound, frightened children were placed in the midst of the orgiastic ritual before the altar of the demon god. Temple prostitutes danced before the idol, passing near, then touching the terrified children. When Zohelethbal placed the dagger against the throat of the first child, the child fainted from fear. A moment later, the life's blood gushed from the child's throat. The terror in the other children's eyes fed the frenzy of the priests and temple dancers to an even higher level. Blood from the priest's bodies began to cover the floor as they sliced fine lines back and forth across their own bodies with razor sharp blades.

As the tumultuous festivities reached an intoxicating height, the temple prostitutes led the multitude into the orgy worship of Baal. Many, made drunk by the lust of their fleshly pleasure, were deceived of reason and natural affection, and sent for their own children to appease Baal.

Before the night was through, the floor and the altar were deep in blood, and seven children had lost their lives, most given over by their parents.

Tamara spent the night in her room burning incense as she prayed to Baal. Cold chills caused her hands to tremble and though she remained wrapped in a blanket she couldn't shake the chills. Before dawn she saw in a vision a man holding a net full of serpents that he cast into a fire. It didn't make sense. It didn't relate to anything she could think of and troubled her greatly. Then she saw something even more troubling. A giant in golden armor stood with a drawn sword outside the palace wall in the courtyard next to the priest's quarters.

Though she wasn't allowed to travel outside what had become Jezebel's quarters, Tamara knew that the princess would approve if she went to the tower overlooking the area she had seen in her vision. In fact, if Jezebel knew, she would be angry if she didn't investigate something this important, so Tamara ran from her room toward the north end of the palace. The guards recognized her and let her pass as she entered the tower. She rushed up the steps and was breathless when she found a long narrow vertical window made for archers. Far below in the dim light she could make out only the outline of an average looking man as he knelt on both knees with his hands stretched skyward. What a strange thing she thought with her gaze transfixed on the shadowy figure, but the great presence that she had felt the night before gripped her again. She could hardly stand and braced herself against the wall.

As the black of the long night began to change to the purple of predawn, Elijah felt someone's eyes on him. He rose to his feet and looked in every direction, then finally rested his gaze on the narrow tower window, but couldn't see beyond the gray stone exterior. After a few moments he turned and slipped from the courtyard, back toward the gate of the city. He was exhausted, as if he had been wrestling with the thick darkness all night.

Tamara watched as Elijah made his way down the narrow street. The greater the distance between them grew, the less she felt the strange presence.

The encounter with a presence Tamara never knew existed before that night left her shaken. She sought Baal for answers but her god was silent. Three days after her wedding Jezebel slipped away from Ahab to counsel with Tamara. She walked with Tamara into the hall of the wedding feast. As they stood on the bloodstained stone floor before the Image of Baal, Jezebel said, "A mighty presence engulfed the palace as Ahab and I were on the way to the wedding chamber. Were you able to discern what descended upon us?"

Tamara looked down as she thought, trying to find words to explain what she had felt. She looked back at Jezebel when she began to answer. "It's hard to describe, but it was an adversary of Baal."

Jezebel quickly interrupted, "Who was it?"

"It may have been one of the ancient gods of this land returning to make war with Baal and his sons, but I don't know who exactly. I spent the night praying to Baal, but he did not answer."

Jezebel answered, "You must be right. There must have been a war taking place in the realm of the gods. We must find out what happened! If it was one of the old gods that was conquered by Baal in the great war, which god was it?"

Tamara turned to Jezebel, "There is more. There was a man, an ordinary looking man, kneeling beside the priest's quarters that morning, just before dawn. He was not a priest of Baal."

In just a little over a year Jezebel bore her first child, a daughter she named Athaliah.

"When Yahweh speaks to a prophet, His voice is like the fingers of a skilled musician on the strings of a nevel. If the instrument is tuned, it will send a clear note and will resonate that note in harmony with the other notes and will create a melody. You are the instruments of Yahweh's choosing. Your spirit is your eye to the chief musician. You have two responsibilities, to stay in tune, and to keep your eyes on the chief musician. If you fail to do either of these, you will be of no use in creating the music that delights Yahweh."

The young would-be prophets were entranced by Elijah as he stood before them. His words were as spellbinding and piercing as his gaze into them. He knew that the young prophets would understand the analogy he was giving them, since many of them were musicians.

The scribe Jehew and the prophet Micaiah began this school of the prophets. Jehew had been educated at the school of the prophets at Naioth in Ramah, the school most respected by the prophets, the school that was begun by Samuel himself. Jehew felt they had lost the great presence of God that they had begun with under Samuel's direction. In the early days, there were times when men passing the school at Naioth would fall to their faces weeping because of their transgressions, convicted by the presence of Yahweh.

There was the time King Saul sent soldiers to capture David, who had fled there to take refuge from the king. The Spirit of Yahweh came upon them and they wept, repented, and prophesied. The king also went to Naioth to capture David, fell under the power of the Spirit of God, and was unable to lay a hand upon him. He also wept and prophesied.

Both Jehew and Micaiah believed that through total abandonment to Yahweh, that same power would be restored to the prophets, and then they would have a real voice in Israel. This was their third year, and Yahweh was manifesting His presence in a way that had not been seen since the early days of Solomon's temple.

As Samuel taught at Ramah, that the Spirit of prophecy would come upon them through worship, Jehew now taught this generation of prophets. Sometimes the music was spontaneous, directed by the Spirit of Yahweh, and would engulf them suddenly like an early morning fog blowing in from the sea, yet it was invisible. Each person knew when the Spirit came upon him, and would begin to sing and find his instrument of music, as though the chief musician had given him the signal to begin.

As Jehew watched Elijah teach the young prophets, his thoughts drifted back to the time when the coming of Elijah was foretold. On that day, beneath the shade of the mountain against the western sun, nearly a hundred young prophets either sang or danced or played one of a dozen instruments of music. The conditions were right, for with the first line of the first song came the presence of Elohim.

"Thy presence, Oh Elohim, is like a drink of cold water in the desert. Elohim, you are like the warmth of the sun in the winter, and in your presence is a joy greater than the joy of a bridegroom on the day of his wedding."

The music ebbed, making room for Micaiah to walk into their midst. "Behold, tomorrow Yahweh is sending a chosen vessel to you, Elijah. And, like his name, he has made Yahweh his God. The God of Abraham is raising him up to be a sword in His hand, to cut away the leprosy of wickedness from Israel. Yahweh is bringing him here to impart to the sons of the prophets that which He bestowed within him."

The following day, as one or another would remember the prophecy, they would glance down the hillside and across the plain toward the Jordan to see if someone was coming. It was again late afternoon in the shade of the mountain as Jehew read aloud from the first book of Moses. Thirty students sitting on benches before tables were transcribing the script as the prophet read, when in the distance a lone figure came into view.

Jehew continued to stand before the scribes holding the scroll, reading, but glanced across the wide expanse to keep track of the advance of this man whose coming had been foretold.

Eventually the solitary figure began his ascent up the long hill and dropped out of Jehew's sight. A short time later he cleared the rise and walked onto the plateau where the school stood. He came near to where Jehew stood, but waited in silence until he finished and acknowledged him.

At a convenient point, Jehew stopped reading and looked up at Elijah. "Peace to you, son of Abraham."

The greeting puzzled Elijah. How did this man know that he was a son of Abraham? But Elijah had heard enough about the famous Jehew to recognize him. He assumed Jehew's keen discernment revealed that he had descended from Abraham.

"And peace to you, Jehew, prophet to kings."

"And how would you know me, sir?" Jehew asked.

"Everyone in Israel knows Jehew, the prophet who prophesied to King Baasha. Yahweh has let none of your words fall to the ground. That is why I am here; to be taught of you, if you will accept me as your student."

"No, my son, that is not why you are here. You are here to teach, Elijah."

"I don't understand," Elijah stammered. "How did you know my name?"

"Elohim has foretold your coming. Your teaching by man is complete. From now on, your training will come from Elohim." Jehew turned back to the class and, with a movement of his head, indicated to one of the young men to come to the front. The young scribe hurried to Jehew. "Continue to read where I left off," Jehew said, as he handed him the scroll. He then turned back to Elijah. "We have many things to talk about. Let's sit over there in the shade of that tree," he said, as he moved towards a low hanging tree on the side of the hill. Elijah had to take several quick steps to catch up.

They walked in silence for a minute, then as Jehew found a comfortable seat beneath the tree, he asked, "Where are you from, Elijah?"

"Tishbeh, of Gilead. I am of the tribe of Gad," Elijah answered as he found a place to sit near Jehew.

"Elijah; Yah is God. Is that not the meaning of your name?" Elijah nodded, but before he could say anything, Jehew continued. "Elohim told us your name yesterday. Where did you learn the law?"

"My father was a judge and a teacher, and his father before him, and his father before him was Gad, the seer of Gilead, who was adviser to King David."

"Yes, I have read of Gad, seer of Gilead. Samuel wrote of him, and I read often of the acts of King David recorded by your grandfather." Jehew stopped, then added slowly, "He was a great musician." He paused again. "If you stay here long, you will find out that we love music as much as King David did. Your great-grandfather was with King David a long time. He changed the course of Israel."

"I have heard many wonderful things about Gad from my grandfather, who was taught by him beside the sons of King David."

"So you are a seer," Jehew said approvingly.

"I would to God that it were so. From the time I was a boy listening to my grandfather, I've never wanted anything more." Jehew detected a note of despair in his voice.

"Your testing is not over yet. Elohim has great things for you, but with great things come great trials of faith. The greater the trial, the greater the reward. Without tests, faith wouldn't be needed. No matter what it is you want of Elohim, you must never give up. Never!" There was silence for a few moments before Jehew asked, "You have no wife?"

"The desire for a wife is the second strongest desire I have in my life."

"Then why do you not have one? A handsome man like you, with a heritage as rich as yours, you shouldn't have trouble finding a wife."

"My father never made arrangements for a wife for me. Now I don't know where I belong. He had chosen a woman for me, but he died before he ever told me who she was. How could I bring a woman into that kind of confusion?"

"Perhaps things won't be like that much longer." Jehew stood up. "Come with me. I must introduce you to Micaiah. He will be disappointed that I didn't call him the moment you arrived. Everyone has been waiting to see what kind of man you would be, since your coming was foretold by Elohim."

As they walked back to find Micaiah, Jehew, to change the subject to a brighter note, said, "David said of the men of Gad, that they were mighty men, fit to make war, as fierce as lions and as swift as the wild deer. Could that be true, as your great-grandfather, who was named after the patriarch of your tribe, recorded it?"

"It is true," Elijah answered with enough confidence to convince Jehew that he truly believed it, and with a little bit of pride. After a minute he added, "King David made them captains over his army."

Elijah stayed and taught at the school for the following year and came to love Jehew as a father, and to respect Micaiah as a man who truly knew the voice of Yahweh. Micaiah was approximately his own age, but Elijah felt that he was far advanced over himself in the things of the spirit.

Elijah didn't teach often. He spent most of his time in the hills, waiting for Yahweh to give him a message to bring back to the students. Sometimes he would be gone for days. Jehew allowed him special freedoms because he knew that a greater purpose awaited him, and this was just another step in his preparation. There were times when he would teach all day long and into the night.

There was a certain fulfillment in teaching these young men who were hungry to know Yahweh but he still wasn't content. When most men had already found their places in life, Elijah, in his early thirties, was still looking for what God wanted of him. He had not found in the letter of the law the kind of fulfillment that he knew was to be found in Yahweh Himself. He had gone as far as he knew how and was looking for a door that would take him all the way to El Shaddai. He often thought that if he had been born a priest of the tribe of Levi and could enter the Holy of Holies, he might find there the water that would quench his never-ending thirst.

One evening as the sun was setting, Elijah, Micaiah, and Jehew sat on a bench watching the sun slowly disappear behind the distant mountain range. The sun reflected a pink glow onto the light colored limestone walls of the school; a large unrefined structure built by the students and prophets who sought after Elohim there. Several smaller buildings were used as dormitories. The three men sat quietly, enjoying the last rays of the sun. A soft melody was being strummed on a lyre until other musicians tuning their lyres or nevels interrupted it. Others were gathering wood and preparing goats for roasting over the fire. As the pink glow faded into a bluish twilight, someone began to sing one of the most often sung psalms of David.

"Make a joyful sound unto Yahweh, all lands of the earth. Serve Him with gladness: come before his presence with singing."

Elijah could feel the presence of Elohim in the music and knew that this was going to be one of those special times when Elohim would come down and rejoice with them. It was at sacred times like this that the most poignant prophecies, profound insights into the Scriptures and revelations, were given.

The feeling of the presence of Yahweh grew until Elijah could not contain himself and began to sing along. "Enter into His gates with thanksgiving, and into His courts with praise; be thankful unto Him, and bless His Holy name."

"Yea, Elohim, has come down to be with His people this night, to refresh them and strengthen them for the battles that lie ahead," Micaiah prophesied as the Spirit of Yahweh surged through his body.

Feeling the urgency of the moment, Jehew, filled with emotion that reflected in his voice, said, "I must have my desk brought out. There will be much to record this night." He rose to his feet and started towards the main building, gathering several young men with him as he passed through the crowd.

They sang and worshipped for hours then ate. After the meal, they danced arm in arm around the fire, singing until the Spirit of Elohim moved them to prophesy, one taking up where another left off. What unfolded was a detailed description of the persecution that was to come upon the true worshipers of Elohim, and was even now looming over them, ready to be unleashed like a flash flood in the desert after a summer cloud burst.

Jehew sat at his desk, scratching across the parchments as quickly as he could in the firelight. Even with torches and lanterns, the light was not quite adequate to do the job easily. By his side were two student scribes, Zechariah, his son and the other, one of the most accomplished students. Each would hold in his mind as much of a prophecy as he could until Jehew would tap them for confirmation of what he was putting down with his pen.

In the gray light of early dawn, before the sun's first rays began to overtake the flickering images produced by the fire, Micaiah stood in the midst of the congregation. A hush fell over the gathering, for everyone knew that when Micaiah stood, Yahweh was about to speak in force.

"Elohim has spoken. 'A great persecution will arise against His people. From the throne of Ahab, a sword will go out beyond the borders of Israel to destroy every prophet and priest of mine who will not bow to the image of Baal. Strengthen those who are about to perish. Great joy awaits them in my presence.'"

When he finished speaking there was a long hush that fell over the gathering. There were so many questions to be answered. How to prepare for such tribulation, and Ahab was not yet king. Then slowly the low hum of voices asking questions of one another began to grow.

To quiet the crowd, Micaiah raised his arms. Again a holy hush fell over them all. "That is all I know, all that Elohim has given to me."

As quickly as the presence of Elohim descended upon them the previous evening, His presence lifted after Micaiah had spoken. From that day on, they kept close track of the events taking place in Samaria. They knew that the day Ahab became king, the fulfillment of that prophecy would not be far behind.

Tamara sat at a table inhaling a mixture of thick blue incense smoke. Her eyes were glassed over, and she could hardly focus on Jezebel when she raised up to look at the princess who sat across the table from her. Several times Jezebel coughed, though she wasn't in the direct flow of smoke. She had to turn aside for a breath of fresh air and was reluctant to turn back into the strong incense odor.

Aware that she hadn't been as precise in her predictions as she had been before coming to Israel, and of Jezebel's growing frustration with her, she had concocted the most powerful mixture of incense she had ever dared to put together, against Eber's advice. The mixture, Eber had warned, could take her to a realm that she might find impossible to return from.

Tamara inhaled deeply, desperate for a sign or vision to appease Jezebel. Death was preferable to the way Jezebel would make her feel if she didn't produce something to satisfy her with. Jezebel would curse at her and belittle her until she felt as low as the dust on Jezebel's sandal.

Tamara had never had to move into the spirit realm where a battle raged before coming to Israel. Raised to believe that Baal was the most powerful of all the gods, she was unaware of the source of the opposition, but the battle that raged indicated that there was one more powerful. What she was sensing she would not dare say. "If Baal would only speak to me," she half thought and half prayed.

"Tell me what you discern." Jezebel's demand, sounding as though it came through a tunnel, broke into Tamara's dazed mind.

"I see the gods of Egypt bow to Baal, and all the gods of heaven and earth bow down to Baal. I see the great Baal lifting you up in his hand to exalt you, Princess."

Jezebel knew that most of what Tamara had just said was contrived and that added to her frustration. "You know what I want to know," Jezebel stated with a cold gaze at Tamara. "How long before Ahab is king?"

Tamara was glad she couldn't focus clearly into Jezebel's cold eyes. "The stars and all signs agree that the time for Ahab to be king is close."

"How long can that old man live? We know it can't be much longer. Omri is old, too old!" Enraged, Jezebel screamed, "When, when, when? I want an exact time!"

"It will be soon, but I will continue to seek Baal to see if he will give the day," Tamara answered apologetically. Jezebel had never before treated her so badly as she had since she married Ahab and came to Samaria. Tamara knew that Jezebel hated the kind of cowering she was doing before her, but she seemed to have no choice. One slip of the tongue could cost her life.

"I should sell you at the next slave auction, you worthless little dog," Jezebel scowled at her.

"I serve you faithfully. I live to serve you, but the gods reveal only what they want us to know." Tamara hesitated as an idea struck her. "There are battles taking place in the spirit world that make it hard for me to hear what the great god Baal is saying. If you could make a great sacrifice, or build a great image to Baal, maybe he would be pleased, and it would clear the air and the heavens of all of this confusion."

Jezebel answered, "I also have had trouble in the spirit world since we came to this place. Perhaps what you suggest is correct." Jezebel stood to her feet.

That evening, when Ahab returned to the palace, Jezebel was waiting for him. As captain of the army of Israel, he had very little time for her and she resented it, but never displayed anything but adoration for him. Jezebel bowed to the floor as Ahab entered the palace with his first officer at his side.

"My lord Ahab, I beg an audience with you," Jezebel said with her face to the floor.

"I am your husband, not a god," Ahab said as he lifted her to her feet.

"You are the prince of Israel and will one day be the king, and to me, you are a god."

Ahab turned to his first officer. "Leave us, please." With that the officer turned and walked out.

Jezebel placed her arm around Ahab's waist as they strolled down the long corridor towards his quarters. "My lord, let me have this evening with you, I pray."

"I have never known the kind of pleasure I find in your arms," said

Ahab. "Yes, please stay the night." His hand was already caressing the soft skin of her shoulder.

As Ahab closed the door to his quarters behind them, Jezebel took him by the hand and pulled him over to a chair. He sat down as Jezebel got on her knees at his feet and began to loosen his sandals.

"My lord," Jezebel began as she laid her head on Ahab's knee. "Would you build a temple for me, for my god Baal? The nearest temple of Baal is back in my homeland, Zidon."

"My beautiful, charming wife, the worshipers of Baal in Israel offer their sacrifices in the groves, in the high places. There is an altar to Baal here in the palace and there is a temple of Baal in Megiddo."

Softly Jezebel answered, "Baal is my god and I don't see how he could be pleased when the God, Yahweh, has the glorious temple of Solomon to dwell in. Build a temple for my god, for me." With a pouting look she added, "I have heard of the temple at Megiddo. It's old, and small, and hardly qualifies as a temple at all."

"I am only the captain of my father's army. I can do nothing."

"You will be king one day. Promise me that, in that day, you will begin a house for Baal, a house more glorious than Solomon's temple."

Ahab pulled her to her feet and onto his lap. "In the day that I become king, I will build you a temple, and it will be more glorious than Solomon's temple, I promise. Until then, if you wish to sacrifice at Megiddo, I will assign to you a platoon of fifty men to guard and escort you wherever you go."

Jezebel stood up and pulled Ahab to his feet. "Come to bed, my love."

Ahab was a willing slave to Jezebel's charms and loved her with great passion. King Omri had given Ahab the Mount of Jezreel to build a palace of his own. Ahab had begun a palace there that he would give to Jezebel, and dedicate it to his love for her.

Tamara lay prostrate before the image of Baal all that night, and the following morning found her again breathing an even stronger mixture of incense. She refused to eat until Baal spoke to her. She continued this pattern of lying before Baal's image every night and inhaling incense day after day until Jezebel saw that she was destroying herself. Jezebel forced Tamara to eat to regain her strength, then they would travel to Meggido. There they would sacrifice to Baal, performing a ritual that Tamara hadn't used since they came to Israel, a ritual that had never failed to gain the favor of the gods and sometimes even Baal, the lord of the gods.

Months before, Jezebel's chief eunuch, Eber, had sent to Egypt, Syria, and the mountains of Lebanon for the precious herbs needed for the incense and ointments to perform the different rituals of Ashtoreth and Baal. The local priests had most of the many ingredients needed, but Eber was a master of the apothecaries' art, far more skilled than the priests and magicians in Israel. He had been a captive from the east country, where live the people of the slanted eyes. Captured while he was a magician's apprentice, he was sold several times. Because of his small stature and strange language, he was considered to be of little value until, in Phoenicia, his ability in the magical arts was learned. Jezebel brought him with her to Israel and, because of his great skill and loyalty to her, she gave him authority over the other eunuchs, and allowed him greater freedom.

Eber's formulas were known only to him. He required ingredients that were more difficult to come by, and more expensive, than other wizards of the apothecary arts. He worked with the dried innards of certain types of fish, morels from the mountains of Lebanon, the dried juice of the orange flower of Syria and other plants that grew in the waters of the great sea. He imported the roots of the desert thistle of Egypt and a hundred other herbs that were unknown in Israel.

The fermentation of the potion was completed by the time the last ingredient, the morels, arrived and it was less than a week until the full moon, the only time this ceremony was allowed. Eber added the final ingredients to the greenish mixture, contained in a large urn, less than an hour before Jezebel's caravan departed for Megiddo.

Jezebel had never participated in these rites, but had been with Tamara through them several times before they came to Israel. After each ritual Tamara would have insight into questions they sought answers for, and would tell of extraordinary experiences of communing with the gods and traveling with them to other lands, not of this world but of theirs. Jezebel envied Tamara for that, and for her superior ability in manipulating the elements by the power of the gods. This time, wherever Tamara's spirit soared, Jezebel would go with her.

Accompanied by the fifty-man platoon and their captain's chariot, Jezebel took with her thirty handmaids and ten eunuchs who would care for them while they were in the world of the gods. Her son, Ahaziah, six months old, was left in Samaria with his nurse, who suckled him. The caravan arrived in Megiddo after a long day of travel. Jezebel was pleased to find the city to be modern and accommodations in the royal house as fine as those of Samaria.

She met with Zohelethbal, the high priest of the temple at Megiddo, to discuss preparations for the ceremony, one with which he wasn't familiar. She was greatly impressed with Zohelethbal's knowledge of other rituals that produced similar results.

On the morning of the full moon, preparations began with the sacrifice of a bullock on the altar that stood twenty cubits in front of the porch of the small temple. Smoke from the sacrifice ascended upward most of the day as the priests, wearing only loin cloths, danced to the constant ancient rhythm of the drum and halil pipe. Over and over, the instruments noted out the same haunting melody. The priests drank of opiate-spiked wine, then with lances began to slice into the flesh of their chests and abdomens as they danced. Within the temple, Eber's mixture of incense burned on altars at each side of an image of Baal. It was an image only as tall as a man, one that Jezebel thought might not be powerful enough for what she wanted from her deity.

Three sacred children, boys between the ages of three and four, born of temple prostitutes, were being bathed and anointed with perfumed oil. They would be the greatest and most expensive sacrifice that could be offered. A priest stood atop the highest tower of the city, waiting to signal with the trumpeting sound of a ram's horn the sighting of the full moon, the signal to place the first sacrifice on the altar that stood in front of Baal's image. When the moon could be seen on the horizon through a window at the east side of the building, directly opposite the idol, it would also shine into the eyes of Baal. That was when the first sacrifice would be made. As the moon climbed into the night sky, its reflection would move downward to strike the altar and the last sacrifice. If the three children were not sacrificed by the time the moon's reflection passed the altar, the entire ceremony had to be stopped. After each bled to death on the altar, their bodies would be burned on the altar of sacrifice in front of the temple.

Jezebel and Tamara lay on couches in one of the side chambers of the temple. Each wore only a loincloth between her legs that draped to the knees both in the front and back and was held in place by a blue linen cord. Their heads were spinning from the spiked wine as they were attended by the handmaids. Eber's secret green ointment was applied to the bodies of the two women from their faces to their feet.

The rhythmic melody that had not deviated since it began that morning seemed to them to be in harmony with the beating of their own hearts. When the last sacrifice was taken from the altar and placed on the sacred fire of Baal, they were led into the room of the image where they danced sensuously for his pleasure. Present with them in the room, watching, were the ten eunuchs, the thirty handmaids and Zohelethbal, the high priest.

Though Jezebel had never danced at one of these rituals before, her movements were more erotic than those of Tamara, and her rhythmic gyrations as sensual as those of the best temple prostitutes, Zohelethbal thought. At any other time he would have participated in a dance like this which normally led into orgy worship of Baal, but she was a princess, and unless he was invited to participate, initiating such a move could cost him his life. Tamara entered the world of the gods and collapsed to the stone. Alone before the idol of Baal, Jezebel danced with renewed energy and collapsed several hours later.

As the women fell, they were picked up, more ointment was applied to them, and they were placed into beds where they would remain for days while their spirits communed with the gods. If Baal were pleased with the dance, and the sacrifices, he would manifest himself to one or both of them. Two of the handmaids stood watch over each woman continuously. There were times when each woman would ask for water. Water would be given to her, then she would return to the world of the gods. On the third day, Jezebel got up from the bed and stood staring blankly out the single small window in the room. When she turned back, her eyes didn't focus on either of the servants, but gazed in one direction, then another, where there was nothing but stone walls. Her mind was able to focus on how terrible she must have appeared with the dried green ointment flaking away from her face and body, and demanded that she be bathed. When she had been bathed, she asked to be clothed in her purple gown and robe.

From that day she believed she was the incarnation of Baal's queen, Ashtoreth, and that Baal had given her a greater knowledge of the apothecaries' art than Eber. Afterward, she knew Eber didn't possess any magical ability, which he claimed to add to his potions as no one else could. For the next two days she remained in the world of the gods, seeing nothing of the world around her except when she needed something, and sat at a table drawing diagrams of a temple that only a skilled architect could have drawn or understood. From that day, whenever she spoke of Baal, she would mention how gloriously beautiful he was.

Several times in her delirium, Tamara called out to Baal. On the fifth day she was bathed and came back to her body. Jezebel was very pleased with her experience, but never felt the need to repeat the ritual. Baal had conversed with her face to face and chosen her to be his bride on the earth. Tamara had witnessed the communion between Baal and Jezebel, but he hadn't spoken to her. She knew he was angry with her over her inquiries about Yahweh Elohim and had relegated her to a spiritual realm below him, and to lesser gods.

One thing that Jezebel didn't receive was the knowledge of when Ahab would become king and she the queen. That question was even more important to her, now that she knew the spirit of a goddess lived in her, and that the spirit was the great queen of heaven, Ashtoreth.

When they returned to Samaria she again put pressure on Tamara to give her a time. Jezebel prayed and sacrificed to Baal, but he was silent. Over the following months Tamara fasted until her health began to fail. Jezebel could see that she had lost a considerable amount of weight and her eyes had become dark and sunken into her skull. She could only go for short periods without breaking into a coughing spasm.

Sitting across the table from Tamara one afternoon, as Tamara inhaled the sacred incense smoke, Jezebel's heart was moved with compassion. She relied on Tamara more than she wanted to admit to herself. For the first time in her life she realized how much she needed her. Tamara inhaled deeply then broke into one of her coughing spasms.

Between coughs she tried to speak what she thought was one of the most important things that had been revealed to her in weeks, so important that she couldn't wait until the coughing was over. "Cough, cough, The great Baal, cough, cough, has shown to me, cough, cough, cough, I have seen the de-, cough, cough, death of Omri." The coughing stopped but her breathing was so labored she had a difficult time getting the rest of the revelation out. "Within..." She took several deep breaths before she could continue, "...a month, Omri will be dead." She rested a few moments. "Before the new moon."

It was the news she had been waiting to hear, but now it didn't seem that important. Jezebel did not know how to react to the feeling of compassion. From the time she was a small child, she had been around the sacrifice of other children. Many of them had been her age, some older, some younger. The only life she had come to value was her own, but now something inside her placed a value on the life of her adviser and slave, Tamara. They had grown up together and had been taught by the same teachers. No one knew either of them as well as they knew each other. And though Tamara had to remain a virgin for Baal, when they were just girls they had at times exchanged secret desires for romance with some prince riding in from the desert on a swift black Egyptian charger. The revelation was important but it was overshadowed by this sorrow for Tamara.

Reacting to this strange feeling that also brought with it confusion, Jezebel struck the bowl of smoldering incense sending it crashing across the room. "This cursed smoke is killing you."

"Baal is calling for you to be the high priestess of Ashtoreth, and you are to build him a temple." Tamara panted out, then slumped back in her chair exhausted. This was a confirmation for Jezebel, and she knew that Tamara must have received it from the gods since she hadn't told her all that Baal had revealed to her. Jezebel knew the price Tamara had paid for this revelation was high.

"You are killing yourself, you are killing yourself!" Jezebel screamed.

"Let me be the next sacrifice you offer to Baal, Oh great princess and priestess of Baal's queen," Tamara coughed out before she fell from her chair to the floor unconscious.

"Eber!" Jezebel shouted as she left the room. Afraid of her own feelings, she went into the gray stone corridor without looking to see if Tamara was alive, for fear that she wasn't.

"Eber, Eber!" she continued to shout. Eber, who was never more than an earshot away, came running.

"Mistress," Eber bowed quickly.

"It's Tamara. She's lying on the floor. See to her!" Jezebel ordered. She stood impatiently waiting as Eber rushed into the room.

He reappeared a few minutes later carrying Tamara in his arms. "She is alive, but she is very sick."

"Take her to my chambers, then bring the physician." As he started away she shouted, "Hurry!" Taking short quick steps, the little man half ran down the corridor with Tamara's limp body hanging from his arms. Jezebel did everything in her power to bring Tamara back to health and, except for the shortness of breath that she had until the day she died, she did recover.

It was two days until the new moon and Jezebel doubted the prediction of Tamara. Omri seemed as healthy as a lion that morning as Jezebel watched him from a window high up in the east-end of the palace overlooking the parade grounds. The top edge of the orange disk of the sun was beginning to peer over the horizon. "Oh great Baal, from your chariot of the sun, empower me to do your bidding, god among the gods," she prayed.

Omri walked through the ranks formed by the legion of newly trained troops standing at attention on either side. Their numbers were six thousand two hundred in all. Ahab and two generals escorted the king through the battalions. "Not since the days of Solomon has Israel had an army as powerful as the one it now has," Omri boasted, as he walked along exhibiting the demeanor of a general rather than that of a king. With his golden breastplate and gold studded harness, he could never play the part of the general that he once was to these men who knew him only as king.

"Ahab!" Omri spoke to his son in the tone of the commander that he was. "This is the twentieth legion, is it not?"

"Yes sir! The best trained soldiers in the world, Sir," Ahab answered, sounding more like an officer than a son. That is the way it had always been between them.

Omri talked as he walked along, stopping to inspect the armor clad soldiers up close every ten to twenty yards. "The tension between us and Judah has continued to be strong since the days of Baasha. He continually instigated war with them. King Asa hasn't forgotten that, but he has been content to let it rest. I have word that he has taken ill and cannot get up from his bed. Should his son, Jehoshaphat, be seated on the throne soon, we don't know what course he will take. I am told that he is a brilliant strategist. I feel that we should strengthen the border against Judah." Omri paused to look at a soldier for a moment then continued. "Perhaps Jehoshaphat may be more aggressive than Asa. We will increase the troops by ten legions, then Judah wouldn't dare go to war against us. And we will reclaim the cities of Ephraim that Asa took from Israel when Baasha was king."

Omri stopped in front of a soldier. "Stand forth, soldier!" Omri commanded.

The young soldier took one step forward. The two generals looked at one another, then towards Ahab. Ahab shrugged. He didn't know what was about to take place any more than they did. Jezebel shifted her position at the window to see better, but to no avail, since Omri's back was to her.

"Defensive stance!" Omri ordered the soldier.

The young soldier planted his feet, drew his sword, and positioned his shield. "That is correct," Omri commended him.

Omri turned to one of the generals, "Have the archers target this man." He then turned to Ahab, "Would you say that's two hundred cubits to the company of bow men?"

"Perhaps a little more," Ahab replied.

The first general shouted to the commanding officer of the company, "Bow defense position!" The officer repeated the order with a thundering command, "Bow defense position!"

The company of troops made a wall with their shields to deflect the arrows, an exercise they had become accustomed to during training and Ahab was confident that they would impress his father now. Omri interrupted, "Not the company, this one soldier."

"Formation attention!" the general ordered and that order was echoed by the company officer.

The company of troops lowered their shields and stood at attention.

"Soldier, here in the center, take a bow defense position," the general ordered the young soldier, knowing that a man with one shield was not as protected as the whole company was behind a wall of shields. The general was impressed, along with the others, when he saw how well the soldier tucked himself behind his shield. With his head between his knees and with his right arm under his left leg, he held the shield to his left side and braced it with his left forearm.

The king, Ahab, and the second general stepped to one side where the second general ordered, "The king's defense!" Every soldier in the army knew the meaning of that command. It meant to surround the king and die if necessary to protect him. Instantly a wall of men and shields surrounded them.

The other general stayed in the open where he could supervise. He motioned for one of the aids that had been at attention far behind, but where he could be called upon if necessary. In a rapid run, the aid reached the general who gave him a command to take to the officer commanding the company of Simeon archers. All companies were arranged according to tribe, a tradition begun by Solomon to help keep unity within the ranks, a tradition that King Omri found effective because the tribes were clannish. They fought to protect each other, and for the name and glory of the tribe. The general had chosen the Simeon archers because they were the finest in the world, seemingly born with a natural talent for the bow.

Jezebel could see the runner leave the general's side and end up at the company of Simeon archers, and wondered what was taking place. The company of archers moved into position facing the lone target.

The voice of the officer over the archers echoed off of the palace wall "Ready!.......Ho!" Five hundred arrows were released with deadly accuracy. The thunderous impact of the arrows driving into the shield knocked the soldier to the ground and arrows glanced off in many directions, some, driving into the standing formations on either side. The man who was targeted scrambled back to his feet unscathed.

One of the arrows found its way through the first row of soldiers and into the neck of one the troops in the second row. He fell forward to the ground between the two men in front of him. Another arrow had gone through the ankle of one of the men still standing at attention on the first row and had stopped with a third of the arrow through the back of the ankle.

King Omri stepped between two of the men that had shielded him, into the clear, and strode over to the soldier with the arrow through his ankle. "Remove the arrow from this formation," Omri ordered.

The soldier stooped down, laid his shield on the ground, took hold of the feathered end of the arrow with both hands and snapped it in half. He then reached around to the pointed end of the arrow and, without flinching, pulled it through his ankle. He picked up his shield and stood back to attention.

"Step out here, soldier," Omri ordered the injured man, then turned to the soldier who had been targeted, standing with hundreds of arrows lying around him. "Defend yourself against this man."

The two soldiers drew their swords and began to slowly circle one another as though they were doing some strange dance of death, each looking into the eyes of the other for any kind of signal that the other was about to strike. At that moment they knew this would be a fight to the death. Suddenly the swords began to clash as though an invisible signal had been given to them at the same time. As suddenly as they began to clash, they abated momentarily, then the clash of iron began to ring again. The soldier with the injured ankle faked a blow to his opponent's right, throwing him off guard. He then thrust forward. The other soldier was able to dodge the full impact of the blade but sustained a small flesh wound on his side, under his right arm. He knew that before he could regain his balance he would be open for another encounter with the blade at any place his adversary chose to stab him.

"Halt! Halt!" Omri stopped the fight. "Not like that. Give me the sword." Omri took the sword from the man who had just made the thrust. "When you thrust, you must thrust with the shoulder with the weight of your body behind it." Omri demonstrated the technique he was explaining. He made one thrust slowly then another more rapidly. "Like that," he said, with his arm still extended. Then without warning, the sword dropped from King Omri's outstretched hand and he fell heavily to the ground. Startled and dismayed, Ahab and the officers rushed to the king. For a moment there was a gurgling sound coming from his throat, then he lay perfectly still as his skin turned an unnatural gray color.

Stooping down beside his father, Ahab slowly realized that the king was dead.

One of the other generals first spoke the words, "King Omri is dead." Then looking across the body of Omri to Ahab, he said, "Prince Ahab, you are now King. Long live King Ahab."

Inside the upper window, Jezebel saw everything that had transpired and already knew that Omri was dead. "It's time for my breakfast. I think I'll have raisin cakes," she said to herself.

Elijah's eyes were fixed in a distant gaze to the east over the Jordan River valley. He sat on an outcrop of rock on a high ridge near the school. His mind was drifting through his knowledge of the days when the tabernacle was still in Shiloh. The Ark of the Covenant was there from the time of Joshua until the days of Samuel, when Eli was high priest. He often walked over the same ground where the tabernacle once stood, where Yahweh Elohim once dwelt. Only a few people lived there now, the rest lay in ruin.

If only he had been born a priest, one who could enter into the Holy place and speak to Yahweh Elohim face to face as Moses had. The thought sent a chill through his body and he quivered slightly. By the law he could never have been a priest, and he wondered if he could ever be to Yahweh what he wanted to be. Many times in the past few months his search had felt useless. Maybe he should give up his quest to know Yahweh, for it seemed that his continual plea was going unheard.

"Elijah!" He recognized Zechariah's young voice calling and turned to see Jehew's youngest son running up the steep path in his direction. Panting hard, the fourteen-year-old was able to get out the words between breaths as he collapsed to the ground, "The King... Omri is dead."

"Slow down, rest a minute. What are you trying to say?" Elijah wasn't sure that he had heard clearly.

Zechariah lay there for a minute trying to regain his breath before attempting to repeat the news. "King Omri is dead. He died two days ago."

"So now it begins," Elijah said softly.

Zechariah sat up in the grass just below the three-foot rock where

Elijah was sitting. "And Micaiah is going to Samaria. He said that Yahweh is sending him there."

"When is he leaving?"

"He is preparing now."

"How did you know where to find me?" Elijah asked.

"When you're around, you're always up here at first light."

Elijah slid from the rock. "Come, let's go, I must leave with Micaiah. I'll go with him part of the way."

An hour later, Elijah and Micaiah were walking north on a narrow path along the steep slope of Mount Ebal. They would stay the night in the small village of Tirzah, where Micaiah had family.

"What is your reason for going to Samaria?" Micaiah asked, glancing back over his shoulder at Elijah who was following close behind, since the path wasn't wide enough for them to walk abreast.

"From Tirzah I'm going to Gilead. I must warn my family of the persecution that is to arise, now that Ahab is king. They will probably go to Judah." They walked along in silence for another minute before Elijah added, "Since King Asa has done away with all idolatry in Judah and decreed that the nation must worship Yahweh Elohim, it will be the only safe place for God's people. Ahab will be afraid of going back to war with Judah. They did not prevail before and they cannot prevail now; Yahweh is with Judah."

From Tirzah, where he parted from Micaiah the next morning, it was a day's journey to the Jordan River, where nightfall found Elijah making camp. He was tired from the two-day walk in the heat of summer, but he couldn't find sleep. He spent the night watching the reflection of the full moon slowly cross the water of the Jordan. The apostate condition of Israel troubled him so that he rarely had a full night's sleep anymore, but now something in his spirit was troubling him that he couldn't quite define. He didn't know how it could be, but he was beginning to feel that he would be the instrument in the hand of Yahweh that would prevent the total destruction of Israel. He searched every possibility that his mind could conceive but didn't see how he, as limited as he was, could ever be that useful.

"Oh Elohim, make your will known," he prayed as the moon was disappearing in the west. Despairingly, he sat for a few minutes longer, then prayed again. "Help me to put these troubling thoughts aside, for I am so weary in body."

Before the sun appeared in the east, a thin mist was drifting upward from the surface of the river when Elijah stood up and began to gather his things. He looked back at the river, hesitated a minute, then dropped off his clothes and dove into the water. "Whoo!" he yelled when he surfaced.

The water was cold. His voice echoed against the high cliffs on either side of the river. He suddenly felt a freedom. For the first time in years his mind was on something besides his quest for Elohim, and it felt good. He realized that he had been trying so hard to find God that he might have been unavailable for God to find him. After all, God was everywhere.

He swam for a good part of the morning, and would have stayed longer but wanted to reach Tishbeh before dark. An hour before sunset Elijah entered the small village, two dozen homes spread out over a long high slope overlooking the Jordan valley to the west, all families of shepherds, and all of them Gadites. Except for the very youngest, those that had been born in the last five or six years since he had been gone, he knew them all.

Elijah felt a certain pride as he looked at the familiar houses which sat near the road. These people were all faithful believers in Yahweh Elohim. Since the days of Gad, the seer, all the men of Tishbeh had been taught the law and commandments, and how to read, by the sons of Gad. And now that responsibility fell upon the shoulders of his brother, Eliab, since their father had died.

The territories of Gad, Reuben, and Manesseh made up the eastern boundaries of Israel and, because they were east of the Jordan, were not well protected by the armies of Israel. The men of Gad were taught how to defend themselves by their fathers, each generation training the next. Shepherds in the fields learned to wield a sword or use the bow or sling. Two of the eleven mighty captains of David's army were of the tribe of Gad, and had come from this, Elijah's home, and from his own family. Their story was more than a hundred fifty years old, but they had become legends, and again he felt a sense of pride as he remembered his heritage.

Elijah smile changed to a frown, as a darker thought crossed his mind. If Micaiah's prophecy was right, these people would die for their faith. He knew that they would never deny their God if persecution came. "No walls," he thought. They won't stand a chance if Ahab decides to come against them. Tishbeh, like many rural communities in this remote area of Israel, had no fortified central area. "They will have to flee to Judah if it comes to war with Ahab," thought Elijah.

There were a few craftsmen and artisans along the road, a potter, a carpenter, a silver smith and others. Elijah watched each one carefully as he passed, hoping that a familiar face would appear. By the iron furnace of the smithy's shop stood Johanan, his closest friend from childhood. Elijah watched Johanan pump the great bellows that heated the iron and marveled at how powerful his friend had become. He remembered how they had played and worked in that very shop as children, when they weren't taking their turn in the fields watching the flocks.

It was evident that Johanan felt Elijah's stare, for he turned to see

Elijah watching him from the road some thirty yards away. He stared back for a moment before he recognized his old friend. It was the thick hair that first gave him away. Even at twenty-one, the last time Johanan had seen him, Elijah had more hair than any man he had ever known.

"Elijah!" Johanan shouted and began at half gallop towards him, limping on the right side. Elijah met him half way with a bear hug. Johanan lifted Elijah off of the ground for a moment, then set him down. "Where have you been for so long, my friend?"

"The last time I was back to visit, you had been forced into Omri's army," Elijah answered, then added, "and it looks as though you fared well."

"Not as well as it might appear." Johanan lifted the right side of the leather skirt that he wore to reveal a hideous scar that ran from his groin up to the hip then around his side to his buttock. He turned to expose another scar beneath his left shoulder blade the size of two hands. It looked as though the flesh had been torn away and grew back deformed in welts. "I was run down by a Moabite chariot on the field of battle. But even worse than that, we were made to do things that I have nightmares about even now. Things to our own countrymen, things that if I had to do again, I would make them put me to death instead."

"That's all over now. Elohim forgave King David, did he not?" Elijah hesitated then added, "Ahab is going to be Israel's worst enemy, and we must prepare the families of Gad; Elohim has warned us of what is to come."

"Has my friend reached his dream of becoming a seer?" Johanan asked.

"No, that is the word that Elohim has spoken through the prophet, Micaiah. I have been teaching at the school of Jehew, though."

"Jehew must put a lot of trust in you to let you teach."

"He is the same kind of man my father was. That reminds me. How is my brother Eliab?"

"He is the closest thing to a true priest in Israel. The people come to him to judge matters of the law, and he teaches the young men the law. He reminds me of your father when we were boys. He even looks like him."

"What of my other brothers?"

"Their flocks have grown large and so have their families. There is some bad news. Three of your nephews have been forced into service in Israel's army, the same as I was." Johanan put his hand on Elijah's shoulder. "Come on, let me walk you to Eliab's house." They turned to walk back to the road. "Will you be staying long?"

"Maybe for the rest of my life, or maybe I'll go on to Judah to escape the persecution of Ahab."

"If you should stay you can work with me at the forge. Your brother's house is full. You can stay with my family and me. And another thing, it's time you find a wife and settle down." Fearing that he might have spoken out of turn, Johanan added, "You don't have a wife, do you?"

"No, I don't have a wife," Elijah answered. "And Eliab would be offended if I didn't stay with them, but I would like to work with the forge again, even if it's just for a short time."

Elijah couldn't have had a better welcome home than to see Johanan after so many years. All of Elijah's brothers had been much older, so Johanan had been closer than his brothers.

It took Elijah a week to become reacquainted with family and friends. Every night was a feast in honor of the brother who had returned.

Eliab called a meeting of the men and elders of Gad. It took a week for them to arrive from the most remote areas. Armed with bows and slings and some with swords, more than five hundred men sat on the pastoral hillside with Eliab standing before them at a lower level. "Men of Gad, I've called you together to hear the words of a prophet of Israel, witnessed by my brother, Elijah, who is known by some of you."

Eliab stepped aside and Elijah stood before the audience of warriors. "Brothers, kinsmen, I witnessed the words of Yahweh through the prophet Micaiah, a man who's name will be recorded with the great prophets of Israel." He paused, looking around at the lined faces of the elders before he continued, "What I repeat to you now is treason."

Elijah took a moment to gather his thoughts, and to let the significance of his opening statement sink in. "Great persecution is going to come from the throne of Ahab, against the true worshipers of Yahweh. I don't know how or why, but I know the words of Micaiah are sure. I was with him at the school of Jehew for more than a year, and Jehew bears witness to his words. You have all heard of Jehew and how Elohim has let none of his words fall to the ground."

A powerful-looking young man who sat a few feet in front of Elijah spoke up, "We can defend ourselves against Ahab."

"Can you put together an army of a thousand thousand? Ahab has more than that," Elijah answered. "What is the largest army Gad can raise, forty or fifty thousand men? Some of you would be fighting against sons and brothers."

A wise looking gray-haired elder stood. "What would you propose that we do?" he asked.

"Micaiah's prophecy said that the faithful worshipers of Elohim would suffer at the hand of Ahab. Elohim would not have given us this warning unless He wanted to spare us. We could find protection in Judah under King Asa."

"Judah is not at peace with Israel. Many of us have left the men of Judah lying in their own blood on the field of battle," the gray-haired elder answered. "I for one believe this word that you speak. Ahab has begun a temple for Baal in Samaria, a temple that will rival the temple of Solomon in Jerusalem." The news of a temple being built for Baal struck a chord in Elijah's spirit. The elder continued, "I have just come from Samaria and have seen it with my own eyes." He paused a moment. "The things you say must be weighed, but we can not leave our homes and flocks until we know more certainly about the intentions of Ahab."

Everyone agreed that they had too much to lose to leave it all behind and flee to Judah just yet. They would stay informed of what was taking place in Samaria, and when persecution seemed imminent, they would decide what measures to take. But for now it was a time for feasting and singing, as was always the case when this many of the tribe of Gad came together in one place. In a gathering of this size there were many relatives and friends, and many of the men had brought their wives or sons, or both.

Though Micaiah's prophecy was on everyone's mind and lips, they played for two days, the same as they would have at any other time. Elijah was amazed at how skilled the young men were when competing with the javelin, the sling and the bow, as he watched with the rest. He had once been the fastest runner in Gad, and when it came time to race he was compelled to join in. He was beat out by one young runner an arm's length in front of him. Elijah couldn't remember when he had been so burden free.

For the next year Elijah was content to work with Johanan as a smith. It was toward the end of that year when news came that King Asa of Judah had died and that Jehoshaphat now sat on his throne. Everyone in Israel now wondered if that would mean a renewed warfare between Israel and Judah. It meant little to Elijah who knew that the real enemy of Israel would be Ahab. Every sunset found Elijah walking in the hills praying for his people.

"Elijah!" Johanan called one morning. Elijah stood before the anvil, holding a piece of white-hot iron in place with tongs as he struck the metal again and again, carefully shaping it into a strong gate hinge. "Elijah!" Johanan repeated, as he worked on another project next to him.

Elijah turned to Johanan. "Did you say something?"

"Where has your mind been all morning?" Johanan seemed a bit impatient. "You've been here more than a year now and things have gone very well for you. Have you thought any more about a wife?"

"I think about it all the time," he answered, then added, "but I don't have money for a dowry without dividing the herds of Eliab, and I don't want to do that just now. I'm feeling restless, like there is something I should be doing for Yahweh."

"Ah, my wife has a young sister, seventeen and very beautiful, and she has a head on her shoulders. She was betrothed, but he was killed in battle several months ago. And I have put aside a good bit of money that I would like to give you for a dowry. Besides, my father-in-law is more interested in finding a good husband for Adah than in a dowry."

"I've never even seen her."

"Believe me, when you do, you will beg me to give you the money for a dowry. She is not going to be available for very long, she's beautiful."

"You've heard me say it many times. Great persecution is going to come from King Ahab, and maybe I'm wrong, but I can't help feeling that I'm going to be involved somehow."

"If it's going to happen, what difference would it make if you had a wife?" Johanan retorted.

"I could make her a widow at a time when she would need someone most."

"You meet her," Johanan said more softly than he had just spoken. "If you don't like her, I will keep my mouth shut. If you do, you accept the money. And at least no one else can have her, and if you change your mind and must leave, well, a little money is lost." Johanan stepped closer to Elijah, "My oldest and best friend, you need a wife."

"And I want one. Remember when we were young, the way we talked of women, we bordered on the profane. And though we didn't say all that we thought, you knew what I was thinking and I knew what was in your mind." Elijah looked at the iron that had grown cold on the anvil. "Now look! I've got to heat it all over again. What I was saying is that I haven't changed that much, I just don't allow myself to think about such things."

"Why not? What is wrong with love between a man and his wife?"

"Nothing. How would any of us get here if not for that? When a man doesn't have a wife, it is sinful to think about such things." Elijah's voice rose in defense, then he added. "And what makes you think that a young beautiful woman would be interested in an old man like me?"

"You're not an old man, and besides, I've already told her about you," Johanan said as he reached and plucked several hairs from Elijah's beard, "You handsome ape." Just as quickly Elijah grabbed his face where the plucked hair had caused a moment of pain. Johanan added, "You have a large inheritance of land that you've never claimed and flocks that belonged to your father and, with a woman as beautiful as Adah, you would have everything that a man could want."

"I will meet her, and if I like her then I'll borrow the money from you for the dowry."

"Ah!" Johanan shouted then began to sing "nah, nah, nah," to a familiar wedding song, as he danced around. In tune he added the words as he sang, "You will not borrow the money, it is a gift from Elohim. He has told me in my spirit to give it to you, in His name."

Johanan made arrangements for his sister-in-law, Adah, to come for a visit. She lived in Zarathan, and it took a month to make arrangements and find a time when she could make the trip.

Early one morning Johanan was late arriving at the forge. Elijah already had the fire going when Johanan came rushing in. "We will not be working today. Your young bride arrived late last evening."

"She's not my bride yet! And may never be."

"I have met her and I know that she is the right one for you. Come with me, you will meet her right now." As they turned to leave, Johanan, practically pushing Elijah in front of him, said, "You must use your best behavior. Two of her brothers escorted her here and they will be looking you over very carefully." Suddenly he stopped. "You cannot meet her wearing those dirty leather kilts and apron," Johanan sighed. "We must go to your brother's and get you something to wear."

A few minutes later they were at Eliab's house with Elijah's sister-in-law excitedly rushing around trying to prepare Elijah to meet the woman they hoped would become his wife. Eliab gave him a new tunic and robe.

"Before you put that on, sit down outside under the tree. I'll be right out. We've got to cut some of that hair," his sister-in-law ordered. She painstakingly cut Elijah's long hair into a neat even shape. When she had finished, his hair and beard were shorter than they had been at any time in his adult life. They all thought that he was very handsome, though no one said anything, for fear of embarrassing him by reminding him of how hairy he was, a fact that he was aware of more than anyone else.

When Elijah and Johanan finally arrived at Johanan's house, Johanan's wife and her sister Adah were sitting beneath a clump of trees where a small spring bubbled through the surface of the ground and trickled into a small pool too wide to step across. The water ran from the lower end of the pool through the trees down the hill a short distance where it was channeled into a garden. Large stones had been arranged by the pool to make a sitting area. "Adah, this is my good friend Elijah," Johanan said as they approached and the women stood.

Struck my Adah's beauty, it took Elijah several seconds to find words. Adah, sensing his awkwardness, eased his tension by opening a dialogue between them. "You are Elijah. I've been told that you are a prophet."

In those first moments he studied her face, her soft-looking olive skin, large brown eyes, full lips, small feminine nose, and the warm brown hair that framed the upper half of her face. She was far more beautiful than the weeks of Johanan's describing her could have ever made him believe.

"I have looked forward to meeting you, but no, I am not a prophet. I am a teacher, but since I was a boy I've wanted nothing more than to be able to hear the voice of Elohim like Jehew has heard Him."

Johanan interrupted, "In the last year I have learned more about Elohim from this man than in all my years before, and just the things he feels are prophetic."

Adah stepped closer to Elijah and looked into his eyes. For a moment he felt uncomfortable, but a warmth, a compassion, something he had never known before flowed through her to him. Was this wonderful thing that he had missed out on until now, love? How could it be? They had just met, and yet there was something that he couldn't deny.

Continuing to peer into his face with a look of wonderment on hers, she said, "There is a fire in your eyes that I have never seen before." Being more forward than would have been considered respectable at this point, she raised her right hand up and touched him on the cheek. "You are truly a man of God, a prophet of Yahweh Elohim."

She could not have known how badly Elijah needed to hear those words. They could have come from Jehew, or Micaiah, or his brother Eliab, but they came from this beautiful woman whom he had beheld for the first time only moments before. She said it in a way that no one else on earth could have.

Johanan looked at his wife who stared with amazement at her sister. She had never known Adah to be so perceptive, or so forward, or to be so immediately drawn to anyone.

Johanan broke the spell for the moment. "I must introduce you to her brothers who will chaperon this day."

After the introductions, they were left alone beneath the canopy of trees. Her brothers were within sight, but far enough away to give them privacy to talk.

Elijah never had a more attentive audience as he found himself talking about what occupied his mind most, Elohim. She was quick to understand and already knew more than most women. There were periods where nothing was being said, but they were comfortable just listening to the trickle of water over the rocks. He knew in the first moments after he laid eyes on her that he wanted her for a wife, but the longer they were together this first day the more complete his life felt.

They were interrupted in the late afternoon, when Johanan and his wife brought out a meal and shared it with them. When they had finished eating, Elijah and Johanan looked at each other, each knowing what the other was thinking. They stood up together. "We must be going now," Johanan said as Elijah nodded a regretful good-bye.

"Is she not everything that I said she was?" Johanan asked, after they were out of sight.

"She is, she is all that you said she would be. I will give as much as it takes from my inheritance of the flocks to pay her dowry, but I must know what she thinks of me."

"You will do no such thing. It is my gift to you, my friend." Johanan turned and took Elijah by the shoulders. "You will accept this or you will offend me."

He held him at arm's length a moment. "Her father has already agreed to terms, provided you like her; and they are fair. And you would have to be as dumb as the iron you pound on each day not to know that she is holding her breath, praying that you will pay her dowry. You are right for each other." Johanan smiled, "We will send the dowry back with her brothers in the morning and you will have no more chaperon, then you will have to answer only to my wife."

The law had been fulfilled. Adah was his but he would not take her to wife until he had a house, as was customary. Though Adah hadn't said anything about it, he knew that she was looking forward to a wedding but would have been overjoyed to have been taken by him at any time.

Elijah had purpose, and hope, and dreams, as he daily worked on constructing a home with the help of friends and nephews. His brothers divided him a portion of land next to Tishbeh where he could be near Eliab. His portion was not as large as theirs but it was some of the best in the country, and they gave him his portion of the flocks that their father had left to him. He hired nephews to tend his flocks. He found little time to pray with so much going on, and the evenings that he once spent seeking Elohim were now being spent at Johanan's with Adah.

On an afternoon when Johanan reclined on a mat in the small court of his home, snacking on dried fruit as the women prepared a meal, his wife interrupted her heavy eyed husband. "Johanan," she said softly. He looked up to see her and Adah standing over him. When she had his attention she continued, "I know only a little of the story of Elijah, but you grew up with him. Adah has sensed some things about him that I think you might be able to explain."

Johanan looked at Adah and said, "He is an unusual man, but an exceptional one. Sit, and tell me what you want to know." Adah sat down, and his wife busied herself at the court oven, close enough to listen.

Adah said, "Elijah is different from his brothers, and, except for Eliab, I wouldn't have known they were brothers. They don't look much like brothers, and why has Elijah been so reluctant to accept any part of his inheritance? Eliab is always trying to give him more and more, as if he's trying to make up for something."

Slowly Johanan answered, "That's very perceptive. Eliab was never quite like the other brothers, but even he didn't like Elijah when they were younger." He looked down as he thought for a few moments. "Do you know of the law regarding the death of a brother who has no children?" he asked as he looked back at Adah.

Adah shook her head. "No," she answered.

"I wouldn't have known about that law either if I had never known Elijah. Their father's brother brought a Moabite woman here to Tishbeh. The family learned that she had been a harlot, but he took her to wife anyway. I've been told that she was very beautiful. From what I know of him, he was a rebel. No one in Tishbeh approved, especially the family. Theirs was a noble family, one that produced many leaders. It was a disgrace to them.

"He took sick and languished away for more than a year before he died. Hilkaih, Elijah's father, the oldest son of his family, and a teacher and judge of Gad, took her to raise up an heir to his brother's name, according to the law. That meant that Elijah would receive the inheritance left to the father he was born for, and an inheritance with the sons of Hilkaih. Hilkaih was already old when Elijah was born. His other sons, Elijah's brothers, were grown.

"Since he was born of the Moabitess, his brothers resented him and felt that he didn't deserve an inheritance in the land of Gad at all. She was never accepted in Tishbeh. The women scorned her. In those days the fighting between Moab and Israel was fierce, until Omri subdued them. And you know about the wars since then, when they've tried to break free from Israel." Johanan took a deep breath and sighed before continuing, "She was very unhappy.

"After the birth of Elijah, Hilkaih never went in to her again, but he was old. She ran away and left him when Elijah was three or four. She must have known that it would be better for him if he were left with Hilkaih. She went back to Moab. No one knows what became of her. Elijah doesn't know that she had been a harlot. No one has ever told him. He is so sensitive that it would only cause him more grief.

"Elijah was raised by Hilkaih and his first wife. He became their favorite. If that wasn't enough to make his brothers angry, Elijah was one of the smartest young men in the entire tribe of Gad, seemingly able to accomplish anything. He could out run or out wrestle anyone in Gilead. He had no friends but me, and yet he was so kind to everyone.

"From the beginning he had a natural grasp of the Law of Moses, but he was never content with that. He felt that the real nature of Yahweh eluded him, and he left here to find whatever it was that only he knew would satisfy his hunger.

"His brothers already had their inheritance when Hilkaih died. Eliab tried to make Elijah take his portion but Elijah, afraid of offending his brothers, refused to accept any of it until he met you. If he accepted all that is truly his, he would be a very wealthy man, but he won't."

They sat in silence as Adah took a few moments to absorb it all. "I thank you for sharing this great confidence with me. I will never tell him about his mother," she vowed as she stood to resume her duties.

The house was a fine house, one to be admired, Elijah thought one evening as he was finishing the day's work on the roof. Everyone had already gone. He knew that he was late getting to Johanan's, but with a little extra time it could be ready by tomorrow evening. He would present it to Adah on their wedding day. He didn't want her to see it before then.

"Elijah!" The voice that called his name was not the voice of a man. It was like silent thunder that shook him to the core of his being. He almost fell, like a man in an earthquake. Then there was a silence so great that he strained to hear something, anything. He stood motionless, listening, his heart pounding, the veins in his neck throbbing to the beat of his heart. It was Elohim! He knew it, but now he wasn't sure that he wanted to hear what Elohim might say.

Time stood still until Johanan grabbed him from behind. "What is wrong? Didn't you hear me call?"

Elijah turned to face Johanan and shook his head for fear that he might burst into tears if he tried to speak. He realized that the sun had been down for more than an hour.

"The women are waiting for us."

The two women looked worried as Johanan entered the house with Elijah behind him. "He was still working on the roof," Johanan explained.

"You must be very tired," Adah's soft voice purred as she met Elijah and touched his face with her hand like she had the first day. The moment their eyes met she knew that something had changed.

That evening as they dined, Elijah could find nothing to talk about. If Adah hadn't suspected before, she was sure now that something had happened.

The next morning before the sun had lighted the path enough to see clearly, Elijah was back up on the roof to petition Elohim. He had only begun to pray when the powerful, silent voice of God again shook him to the core of his being, leaving him weak and trembling, too shaky to get to his feet from his prayerful position on his knees.

Elijah had never seen or experienced anything like this at the school.

The voice of Yahweh wasn't anything like he had expected, but what He said without words was unmistakable. Elijah was shaken by the message given to him. He had been hoping for this all his life, but he wasn't expecting to start with a prophecy to the king of Israel. Did Yahweh really mean for him to deliver a message to Ahab? He knew it was so, but still he wondered; why would Yahweh choose him for such an important undertaking?

All that he was able to do was roll over onto his back. He opened his eyes to look skyward, and was surprised to see Adah kneeling by him. She touched his lips with the tips of her fingers. "Don't say anything. I know. Elohim is sending you away. I knew it last night when I looked into your eyes." She stroked his brow for several minutes until he could speak again.

"I didn't know that it would happen like this," he said with much regret. Tears streamed down his face.

"You must go, for Israel is depending on you." Her heart resisted, but her mind knew that he was important to Yahweh and to Israel. Somehow she had always known.

"I don't know what's going to happen but when it's all over, I will find you," he promised.

"I have spent the night crying to God, and the only thing I know for certain is that things will never be the same for us again after today. Today is the day He is sending you away." Silent tears now streamed down her cheek.

Elijah sat up and faced her. "This house, the flocks, I will have Eliab sell them for you. You must promise me that you will take the money and go to Judah." He waited for her promise then said it again, "promise."

"I promise," she answered, then leaned over and kissed him. He could see the hurt in her eyes, and then he felt her tears on his lip. It was the only kiss Elijah had ever known, and the feel of it was burned into his mind forever. Trying to hold back all of the pain was useless anymore. Adah broke into uncontrollable weeping, got up and ran across the roof. His last memory was of her disappearing down the steps.

Careful not to step on a slippery stone on the river's muddy bottom, Elijah eased into the Jordan. As the cold water grew deeper he raised the wool bag he was carrying onto his shoulder. The early rains had caused the river to swell, and the normally gentle current was stronger than Elijah had realized. It was pushing him at an angle, and each time he took a step the water would force his foot to settle onto the stream bed a quarter step down stream. He had to lead with his left leg, as the water would have thrown him off balance if he had lifted his foot on the side against the river's force. He then dragged his right foot behind, trying to keep his balance.

He knew that he was in trouble when he stepped into a hole up to his chest and couldn't get enough of a foothold to remain standing. Suddenly he was riding in the water's flow downstream, and as he struggled to remain upright, he lost his hold on the bag. It was swept away from him. As he turned to see where the current was carrying his belongings, he realized that his water-soaked robe was too heavy to swim in, and was pulling him under.

Elijah tried to remove the robe, but it was clinging to him. He nearly had it over one shoulder when he was pulled under. Desperately, he fought his way to the surface. He was able to get his lungs partially filled with air an instant before he was pulled under again. It was strange that, in the seconds that followed beneath the surface of the muddy water, he remembered sitting with Adah by the pool at Johanan's. As he struggled to free himself from the cloak, he could see it as clearly as if he were there. For an instant it seemed more real than the dangerous currents that held him tightly in the river's grip.

He was rammed into a boulder that rose from the bottom and didn't know what happened until he suddenly broke the surface of the water.

Somehow the heavy water-logged robe came off and he began to swim toward the shore. Elijah was caught in a water eddy that forced him into a willow tree growing out over the water. He caught hold of its trunk and held on for a minute, then with more effort than he would have believed he could muster, he pulled himself to shore with one of its branches and fell onto the sandy bank, exhausted.

He remained there only long enough to catch his breath, for just below him, tangled in another clump of limbs, was his bag. It had been washed into another tree, along with several logs. Elijah wanted to rest for a moment and savor the joy of just being alive after nearly drowning, but he had to recover his bag, or he would not be able to survive in this land. Without it, he would have neither money nor provisions.

When his mission was over, he would find Adah again and live to have many children, Elijah fantasized, as he lay on the ground after recovering his bag. In his bag he had a change of garment, a small knife and a purse with enough silver to live on for three months.

Later in the afternoon he was filled with apprehension as he walked towards Samaria. It comforted him, knowing that he could return and reclaim what he had left. The only thing that sustained him through the two-day walk was the fire of Elohim that burned inside his soul. When grief for what he left behind began to overtake him, the fire to do what God had called him to do would come alive. It was like pouring lamp oil onto a fire that had burned down to a barely visible flicker. He didn't know what the word was specifically, but he knew that he carried it and he knew he was to confront King Ahab.

Just east of Samaria, Elijah neared the summit of a high hill overlooking a wide valley. Across the valley he could see the city of Samaria and the colossal structure of Ahab's renowned ivory palace. From that great distance, still unfinished, Elijah perceived that it was by far the greatest structure he had ever seen. Far down into the valley below Elijah saw something else taking place. Thousands of men and beasts of burden were laboring along the road northward, moving giant blocks of stone. He made his way down the slope, studying the scene before him as he went. It reminded him of something he had seen many times as a boy and had once sat for hours watching, a living chain of ants carrying away figs that had fallen from a tree, a bit at a time.

He was following a path that intersected the road at a point where thousands of Moabite men, slaves taken in the Moabite war, labored under the taskmaster's whip. They had rebelled against the high tribute placed on them by King Omri and increased by Ahab. Ahab had subdued the rebellion and had enslaved enough of them to ensure their submission, and to complete his palace and temple to Baal. News of these events had reached Tishbeh, but the scale of the captivity of Moab hadn't been apparent to Elijah until now.

The slaves pulled a twenty-cubit segment of a pillar that was about five cubits thick. It lay on a wooden sled of squared beams a cubit thick. Men laid round beams a half cubit thick in front of the sled for it to roll on, while more than a thousand others either pushed or pulled. Long ropes, thicker than a man's arm, stretched out in front of the stone a tenth of a mile. For every few men, there was a whip-man driving them forward.

Here and there to the side of the road stood travelers who were forced to make way for the stone. As far as he could see in either direction, men and beasts labored, moving stones and timbers. A half-mile up the road, he could see another stone that looked to be as large as this one. Standing far enough back to be out of the way, Elijah watched and listened as the ropes creaked, the whips cracked, and the taskmasters called out orders.

Down the road to the south a different kind of movement caught Elijah's attention. A soldier rode up the road. As he passed, the slaves cleared the way then fell to the ground prostrate. The soldiers bowed to one knee or stood to attention depending upon rank. Far behind the rider, something else was moving in his direction. The outline of a royal carriage appeared over the disarray of materials and men spread alongside the road. As the carriage moved rapidly in his direction, he could see that it was borne on the shoulders of more than twenty men, and escorted by several chariots and thirty or forty footmen.

Three people could be seen in the partially open carriage, two women and a boy perhaps four years old, Elijah guessed. This was his first glimpse of her, but he knew instinctively that one of the women was the queen. "Jezebel," he said to himself, as he bowed to one knee along with the other onlookers.

When the carriage reached him it had to leave the road on the far side of the now silent pillar, and slowed from a rapid pace to a crawl because of the rough terrain. His head was partly bowed, but he peeked from under his brow and for one instant he saw Jezebel's eyes before the carriage disappeared behind the pillar. The hair stood up on the back of his neck. "Her eyes are a like looking into a well," he thought. "A deep, evil well."

Elijah shook his head to free his mind of the image. He was glad to be out in the sunshine.

Within the carriage Jezebel turned her gaze from the giant stone toward Tamara who sat across from her. Their eyes locked for several moments. Something had reached into their spirits and grabbed their attention, turning them from the physical world to the spirit world.

They both felt the presence. It was like a powerful supernatural force had bound the powers that governed their lives. To anyone else it would have been like suddenly losing the sense of sight or hearing. Tamara took hold of her head and bowed over to her knees. Jezebel ordered, "Lower the carriage."

The order was repeated by a soldier on horseback, "Halt! Lower the carriage." When the carriage was settled, Jezebel stepped out. The slaves who carried it fell to the ground. Tamara cautiously followed Jezebel, leaving little Ahaziah, Jezebel's son, behind in the carriage to romp from seat to seat. Jezebel looked in one direction then another. Elijah was not visible from that side of the giant pillar. Jezebel walked out in front of the carriage, but still could not see anything out of the ordinary.

With a clear impression that he should begin worshipping God, Elijah began to sing praises in his heart. "I bless your holy name Yahweh Elohim. Great and wondrous are all the works of your hand, oh my God."

Jezebel trembled as she searched frantically in one direction, then another. To the mounted soldier, it was obvious that something was wrong. He slid from his horse, rushed to her side and bowed. Restrained by fear of death for touching the queen, he offered, "Your Highness, how may I assist you?"

Jezebel leaned onto his shoulder to keep from falling to the ground. "Help me to the carriage. Take me from this place!" Tamara had already gotten back onto the carriage and was weeping tears of fear when the soldier helped Jezebel back. "Tamara! Stop those tears!" Jezebel demanded. As the platform was hoisted back into the air, she said, "We must find out what this thing is."

"I felt it the night of your wedding. That night I thought I was dying."

"I also felt it that night," Jezebel answered.

When the carriage moved past, Elijah was the first one in his vicinity to stand. He watched the carriage move swiftly in the direction of the temple. When it was nearly out of sight, he continued on to Samaria.

Elijah looked for his friend Micaiah in Samaria. When he couldn't find him, Elijah assumed that he had returned to Tirzah. He found an inn near the palace and for several days Elijah watched the construction of the palace, waiting for instructions from Elohim. Each day the army of slaves carted blocks of white marble through the palace gates to finish the interior. The new palace was being built around Omri's older, much smaller, fortress, and from what Elijah could see, would be very opulent.

Ahab wasn't in Israel at the time, but had gone to Assyria to attempt an alliance with King Shalmaneser III. Elijah knew that he had been sent to Samaria, but the circumstances weren't falling into place and he didn't have enough money to live at an inn for very long.

Elijah was becoming very anxious about his mission in Samaria. To occupy his mind, and his time, he went to see something he had only heard about. An hour's walk west of Samaria was the largest iron works in the world, where they fashioned tools of war. Hundreds of smiths worked the forges as slaves unloaded large ox drawn carts of ore.

He walked through the array of work, where he saw racks of swords and spears still unfinished, and hundreds of iron chariots in different stages of completion. The chariot wheels were done with such precision that he wondered if he could do such work with the same skill. Hammers rang or thudded on new iron depending on how hot it was, and the familiar smell of the furnace filled the air. It was apparent that Ahab was preparing for war. Israel already boasted of more than two thousand chariots and there were at least a thousand more being fashioned here.

A stir began at one end of the complex and spread in his direction. Messengers ran from forge to forge. As they neared Elijah, he overheard part of what was being delivered. Ahab had returned, and they were being forewarned of an inspection tomorrow by the king.

Suddenly an approaching guard a few feet in front of him confronted Elijah. The guard had his sword drawn at his side. "This is off limits. What are you doing here? What is your origin?"

"I'm of the sons of Gad, of the city of Tishbeh." Elijah was sure that he needed to be very precise. The guard didn't look like he knew the meaning of mercy or patience. At that moment a richly dressed man with a scribe following at his side stepped up to Elijah's right rear. His presence was given away by the guard's glance in his direction.

"Sir Obadiah," the guard greeted with respect. Elijah knew he was in the presence of someone of authority.

"I'll take care of this," Obadiah replied. The guard turned and left them, then Obadiah said to Elijah, "I thought you might be in trouble when I saw the guard approach you. They kill trespassers on the spot if they suspect them of being spies. I saw you walk across here. I sense that you're not a spy, but you shouldn't let that guard see you here again. What's your name?"

"Elijah, of Tishbeh, of Gad. Thank you, sir. I have worked as a smith and wanted to see this great marvel."

"Go on, be gone. If the overseer knew you were a smith, you would be put to work for the king and the glory of Israel," Obadiah ordered with a half smile and a shake of the head. He watched Elijah for a long minute as he made his way out of the area through the veil of smoke. He felt somehow connected to the young man walking away.

When Elijah inquired about the king, he found out that Ahab had already returned to the palace and left again to inspect the temple of Baal.

"Maybe today is the day," he thought as he walked towards the temple, knowing that it would be after dark by the time he reached the site.

Elijah began studying over in his mind what he knew of Jezebel. The picture of her in her carriage that day on the road wouldn't leave his mind. Their eyes never met, but he did see hers from a distance and they troubled him. There was perhaps more determination in her than he had ever seen in anyone. He didn't know that she had stopped the carriage that day to find him. All he knew was that a commotion had taken place on the other side of that great section of a pillar.

She was high priestess of Ashtoreth, the Phoenician goddess, which meant that she would preside over the worship orgies. Elijah wondered how that would work with her also being the queen. Would she possibly participate? It was already widespread knowledge that she hated the true God, the God of Israel, Yahweh Elohim. Why, he wondered, when she believed in all the gods of the Canaanites and Phoenicians? Maybe because it had been the belief of many Israelites, that Yahweh was the only God, and she wanted that belief stamped out in Israel.

Elijah passed a city of tents where the priests of Baal and Ashtoreth, guards and slaves, were living until the Temple of Baal and houses for the priests were complete. It was dark when Elijah reached the base of the temple mount where the road forked. The branch that led to the temple wound gradually upward along the ridge to the east. It was a long walk to where the road leveled out onto a plateau.

There in the distance stood the nearly completed temple of Baal. Closer to him were two rows of pillars, reaching twenty cubits into the air and standing thirty cubits apart, with a fifteen cubit high image of the goddess Ashtoreth standing at the east end of the rows. Before the image was an altar, and in front of the altar was a skillfully woven tapestry with images of men and women engaging in acts of prostitution. The tapestry was draped over poles, making a canopy. It was well lit by fires burning in iron basins between each pillar. Two larger fires burned at each side of the image. A dozen priests were putting the finishing touches on the unholy setting in front of Elijah. The sound of a hammer, driving a stake into one corner of the tapestry to hold the tent-like structure in place, reverberated from the side of the temple.

Elijah's eyes turned to the temple in front of him, as he slowly walked past the asherah. It was four or five times larger than Solomon's temple in Jerusalem. In his quest to find Yahweh Elohim, he had gone to Jerusalem several years before and had left still unfulfilled. Solomon's temple was much more detailed, with intricate carvings, but was dwarfed by this temple of Baal.

The segment of pillar that he had seen on the road into Samaria made the base of one of the two pillars that stood on the porch in front of the massive doors that led to the interior. Workmen were working through the night by the light of fires that circled the building.

On the north side of the temple Elijah saw what he had been looking for, the royal tents of the king. Jezebel lived on the temple site to make sure that every detail was exact. Everyone knew that she had used her influence as queen to force her acceptance as high priestess. She was the voice of Ashtoreth, and was considered to speak on behalf of Baal at times. Zohelethbal, the high priest of Baal, was afraid to cross her and agreed that whatever her whims, they were the will of Baal.

Elijah could see twenty or more tents and dozens of fires and torches that lit the night around the camp of Ahab on a plateau below the temple mount. He studied the layout of the camp as he made his way along a parallel ridge. Somehow he had to get close enough to the King to deliver the word of Yahweh but he needed a way of escape once he fulfilled his task.

Within one of the tents Ahab and Jezebel dined alone. She held a fascination for him that none of his other wives could. No other woman pleased him the way that she did and she had occupied Ahab's mind more than anything else in his absence. The dedication of the temple was only a few days away. She knew that Ahab didn't put a great deal of faith in any god and wanted to take the opportunity to influence him. She figured that it would give her even more power if she, through Baal, could hold sway over the king.

Two servants brought trays of meticulously prepared delicacies of pheasant and lamb, melon and fruit and fig cakes. As they were leaving a third servant brought a golden flagon of wine, the second of the evening.

Jezebel said, "My lord, Ahab," her voice was soft and sensuous. "I am very pleased with the temple. It is more glorious than anything in Zidon. Surely the Temple of Solomon in Jerusalem couldn't be as beautiful, and I've been told that this temple is many times larger than Solomon's. Baal will exalt you above all the kings of the earth." Jezebel paused to wait for a response.

"There are many powerful nations I would have to conquer before that would happen," Ahab answered, as he held a whole baked pheasant in his hands and broke it into two pieces.

"I have never seen you bow to any god," said Jezebel as she held up her cup to be refilled by the servant. "Do you give homage to any of the gods?"

Ahab, who was lying on his side, rolled onto his back and looked up at Jezebel who sat at his head, leaning against a large pillow. "Which of the gods can do the most good for me?" He paused a moment, "Or harm?"

"What do you believe?" Jezebel asked hoping to find some ground to promote Baal.

"Ashtoreth is but a goddess. Chemosh, the god of Moab, cannot be very powerful. My father conquered Moab many years ago, and it is Moabite slaves that build this temple to Baal." Ahab stopped to think a moment before he continued. "The people of Ammon worship Milcom, and they are a weak people. King Asa and Jehoshaphat, his son, worship the old God of Israel, Yahweh and they are powerful. But Asa must have displeased Yahweh because he died of a terrible disease. Or maybe he would have died anyway and his God had nothing to do with it." Ahab rolled back onto his side and took a long drink from his cup before he continued, "Maybe the things that happen, that the priests say are from god, whichever god they represent, would have happened anyway. My father, the greatest king to ever live, worshipped Baal and Ashtoreth, and the great Solomon worshipped all the gods. Which is the greatest god? I don't know!"

Ahab broke off a pheasant leg and began to eat as he continued, "I've just come from Assyria where King Shalmaneser the Third worships a god called Ashram, and Shalmaneser is a powerful king."

Jezebel replied, "Baal rides the chariot of the sun. What god can be more powerful than that?" and a moment later added, "What god can cast down spears of light to the earth and kill men and cattle at his will? Lightning is a creation of Baal. How else can it be explained? And earthquakes, what could make the earth to quake but the power of a god?"

"It is true that lightning and earthquakes are beyond the realm of the natural, but couldn't one of the other gods cast a spear of light or cause the earth to tremble as well as Baal? The priests of each god claim that their god was responsible for some flood or earthquake. Not all gods are responsible for the same thing." Ahab's voice grew to a note of anger. "With my own eyes I have never seen proof that any god has power except the god or gods that casts the lightning to earth or makes the earth to tremble, and which god is that?"

****

In the dark moonless night, Elijah made his way to an elevated knoll slightly higher than the royal tents of Ahab. He watched the fires and torches of the camp and awaited the word from Yahweh.

After Ahab's last statement Jezebel sat in silence for several minutes, slowly eating from the food in front of them. Ahab finished the wine in his cup and poured another. Jezebel clapped her hands and a servant rushed in. "Bring Tamara here to me!" she ordered.

"My lord Ahab, Baal is the god of the sun and lightning and of fire. He sends the rains to water the ground to those who honor him and he withholds the rains from those who fail to appease him." There was a long minute of silence that was broken by Tamara's entrance into the room.

"My Lord, your Highness," she greeted them as she dropped to her knees and bowed her head to the ground.

"Who is pre-eminent among the gods? Tamara, the power of Baal lives within you. Show the king the power of Baal."

In only a few moments Tamara was entranced, her eyes fixed as the pupils enlarged then slowly contracted to only a barely perceptible dot then opened again to cover the color of her eyes with blackness. She rose to her feet and moved swiftly to the flagon of wine and picked it up. She poured a little of the wine into an oil lamp that sat on the mat in the midst of the platters and trays of food in front of Ahab and Jezebel. The flame shot up four feet into the air.

Ahab was unimpressed. He had seen strong wine burn before. Tamara began to pray, "Great Baal, accept this offering at my hand and bring glory to your name. You alone are king among the gods."

The room was lit with numerous lamp stands. Tamara sat the wine on the floor and extended her right hand towards one of the lamps. "From your chariot of the sun, extinguish the light of this lamp." The flame of the lamp went out, then all of the lamps on that side of the tent flickered and died. The flames of all of the rest of the lamps in the room rose seven to ten inches and whipped back and forth as though they were in a desert wind.

Ahab was still unimpressed and a bit annoyed. He had seen magicians do similar tricks at the royal banquets of the Pharaohs of Egypt. There were several moments of silence before Tamara spoke again, praising Baal. "You bury the sun in the sea each night and cause it to rise from the desert each morning. Renew the fire of the lamps again, Lord Baal." Every lamp burst into flames. Tamara turned and bowed to the king, then to the queen.

"Perhaps you can blow flames out of your mouth like the magicians do," Ahab chided, then took another drink from his cup. At his comment Jezebel lowered her eyes and replied, "Baal can do much more than just make the lamps to die."

At the queen's comment, Tamara picked up the flagon of wine, moved closer to Ahab and offered to refill his cup. Cautiously he extended it toward her. She filled his cup to nearly overflowing. Ahab had to hold it carefully, as he took a sip to keep from spilling any of the wine.

Then Tamara reached into the flagon and paused for a long moment. When she pulled her hand back through the opening she was holding a thick gray desert viper between her thumb and forefinger. The writhing snake was more than a cubit in length. The viper quickly wrapped itself around Tamara's wrist as she released her hold on the snake's head. Ahab sat up straight, holding his breath. He had seen men die within a few minutes of being bitten by this type of viper. He was even more astounded when Tamara turned the jar up side down and more vipers fell from the jar onto the mat in front of them. Six, ten, more than the flagon could have held.

The serpents lay there in a writhing pile for a few moments, then began to slither out into the room. Ahab jumped to his feet and backed away from the pillows and trays of food where he could cautiously observe every direction.

Jezebel could see the alarm on Ahab's face and ordered, "Tamara, it is enough."

Slowly Tamara sank to her knees with the flagon on the floor in front of her, then she began to chant. Slowly the snakes turned back toward her and crawled back into the jar, one at a time. Then she pulled the one that was working its way up her arm off and placed it back into the container.

Jezebel stood and walked to where Ahab stood. "I didn't mean to alarm you."

Ahab's breathing slowly came back to normal. "They are deadly, I've seen this type of viper before and what it can do to a man."

"We were safe," Jezebel answered. Then she turned to Tamara and softly ordered, "You may return to your tent." Then she held her arm out toward Ahab, motioning back toward the pillows as she said, "Return to the soft pillows with me." Ahab cautiously picked up the pillows, looking under them before he sat down again.

Before Tamara reached the doorway, Ahab and Jezebel heard her let out a sigh, "No!" They turned to see her drop to her knees, then double up on the mat that covered the tent floor. Jezebel felt the presence and looked around. All the lamps in the room flickered again, as though they were in the wind, and Jezebel felt something like a cool breeze brush against her face. A chill ran through her body as she tried to stand. Her legs trembled under her and she fell into the pillow that she had been lying on.

Ahab jumped to his feet then knelt by Jezebel, "What is happening?"

"Lord Baal, help me!" Her plea brought a greater trembling to her body.

Ahab clapped his hands and a servant rushed in. "Summon the physicians!" he shouted.

Several minutes earlier Elijah had a moment of supernatural insight. He had not been sent to deliver a message to Ahab, but to begin a war, a war that was to be fought in the heavens. However it was played out on earth, it would be won or lost in the spirit realm. For a few moments he could see it so clearly, more clearly than words could have conveyed, and a joy he couldn't contain flooded his being. Just above a whisper, he began to worship Yahweh.

"Oh God of Abraham, let me be a weapon in your hand. I give my life to you, use me to bring glory to your great name. You that keep covenant with man. Your word is faithful and true, you fight for the souls of Israel because of your promise to Abraham. Keep me that I shall not fail. Your love is better than the love of women. I praise you that you have chosen me to serve you."

Elijah felt the presence of Yahweh like he had never felt it before. He continued to sing his prayer for more than half an hour, and when the presence of God lifted, he began his long walk back to Samaria.

Inside Ahab's tent, three physicians attempted to determine what was ailing Jezebel and Tamara, and each step that Elijah took away from there, the trembling they were experiencing abated by that much. By the time Elijah was a half mile away, they had recovered.

"You silly physicians, you know nothing at all!" Jezebel lashed out when she was able to sit up and speak. "If you knew anything of the gods, you would know that the gods are doing battle."

Tamara came over to sit next to Jezebel, but wasn't about to say what she knew, and what she was sure Jezebel would never admit. There was a God much more powerful than Baal. His very presence would make Baal tremble and plead to be spared the agony that His presence brought.

"The great Baal has triumphed. You see how we have recovered," Jezebel boasted.

The following days Jezebel spent most of her time selecting children and young women, virgins, for sacrifice at the dedication of the temple. Most of them were from Syrian and Moabite captives, but a large number were from Israel. Parents who wanted to be blessed by Baal offered their children to be sacrificed. Slave traders, seizing the opportunity to sell slave children at a high profit, came from surrounding countries to sell their commodity to Jezebel and Zohelethbal, the high priest.

Obadiah, Ahab's steward, responsible for all accounting of taxes and money spent in Israel, had never liked Jezebel, and in the days preceding the dedication of the temple, he came to despise her. One afternoon he would have driven a spear through her heart if he could have escaped into the desert. A Hebrew family was brought before Jezebel. A husband and wife and five children, two sons and three daughters, sold into slavery for a debt they couldn't pay.

With the king's two sons at her side, Ahaziah the eldest, six, two years older than Jehoram the younger, Jezebel dickered with the slave trader. The eldest child of the slave family was a fourteen year old son. A strong handsome lad, Obadiah thought, as he watched the scene before him unfold and felt his heart begin to ache as though they were his own children.

Jezebel bought the son to be made a eunuch to serve her as long as he lived. She enjoyed playing with people, inflicting emotional pain and delighted in watching physical suffering. The other children were designated as sacrifices to Baal and Ashtoreth. There was a girl of thirteen, another one twelve, a boy of seven, and a four year old girl. Obadiah knew the two oldest girls would be raped to death before the idol of Ashtoreth, and the two youngest would be slain and their bodies burned to satisfy Baal's thirst for blood.

Obadiah glanced toward Zohelethbal, who sat on one side of the room, to see a look of approval on his face as he looked over the two oldest girls. Jezebel sensed what Obadiah felt and smiled at him mockingly.

Jezebel stroked the head of Ahaziah, as she turned the parents away to be sold elsewhere, heartbroken at the fate of their children. The four year old clung to her mother, crying hysterically, and had to be torn away from her by one of the guards. Every member of the family was crying uncontrollably as the guards brutally shoved the parents from the room.

From that day on, Obadiah prayed for the demise of Jezebel. He knew that her blood ran cold and mercy didn't exist in her.

****

Within the great temple of Baal, his priests danced before the twenty-cubit idol in a frenzied act of sacrifice, slashing themselves until blood ran down their bodies and covered the floor. Jezebel watched from an elevated position built for the high priest and priestess, across from the idol. There was room for four thousand worshipers in the temple. This was the first day of the dedication week of the temple.

Four hundred and fifty was the sacred number of priests of the temple and four hundred was the sacred number of priests of the Asherah and the goddess Ashtoreth. Only the priests of Baal cut themselves with knives and twenty of them bled to death that week. Baal and Ashtoreth had to be worshipped together to ensure the spring rains and bountiful crops. She was his queen and Jezebel believed that she was the incarnation of the goddess.

To the right of the image of Baal was a lesser statue of Ashtoreth and on the left was a pit where the flesh of human sacrifices was burned. In front of Baal was a large rectangular stone where the sacrifices were made.

On the outside of the temple, oxen and sheep were offered on altars located around the temple. It looked like most of Israel had moved into temporary shelters in the valley below to participate in the week long dedication. The worshipers of the two deities were given a concoction to drink that would bring them to the brink of insanity and the loss of all inhibitions.

On the altar of Ashtoreth young virgins, most of them barely in their teens, were repeatedly raped, then finally bludgeoned or hacked to death and their bodies burned. A thousand died that week as men and women committed every sexual act known. There were two hundred priestesses that led men into things they would have never been bold enough to do on their own. Another two thousand children died on the altar of Baal, as their bodies were burned one after another. Their flesh burned night and day for the entire week.

Elijah spent the week walking in the hills near Samaria, praying. It was during those days that it became clear to him that he was to confront Ahab on his way back to Samaria from the temple dedication. Elijah found a place where the road cut along the steepest slope of the mountain and dropped off to the west, too steep for a horse to follow if he should need to flee. He wore a short tunic with a wide leather belt and carried a small knife in the belt. What little else he owned was left at the inn.

He spent the night on the hillside above the road in prayer. It was during the night that Yahweh revealed his plan. God had been unwilling to judge Israel as severely as He was about to, until Israel had fallen to the depth of depravity that they had in the past week.

Elijah's mind was illuminated during the night and he saw things the way Yahweh Elohim saw them. The children who had died were Yahweh's children, and had only been entrusted to the parents for an instant of time. Elijah felt the heart of God, and marveled that the creator of all things would grieve.

Now that Elijah knew what God felt, his commitment to Him was cemented forever. Israel had failed to listen to the multitude of prophets Yahweh had sent to them, and now He was going to judge them and prove the many idols to be as helpless as the stones from which they were carved.

The sun had risen two hours into the sky when Elijah spotted

Ahab's caravan still more than a mile away. There were two horsemen out front, followed by four chariots. Ahab was in the lead with an ornately decorated golden chariot. Behind the chariots came Jezebel's carriage that rode on the shoulders of twenty finely dressed slaves. Her personal guard walked to the front and rear, followed by a wagon for the king's two sons and their nurses. At the rear was a detachment of fifty foot soldiers.

As they unhurriedly approached, Elijah's heart began to pound. He prayed in a whisper, "Yahweh, cover me with yourself." After the two horsemen passed, he knelt on one knee by the road and waited for Ahab's chariot a hundred yards further back.

Within Jezebel's carriage Tamara began to tremble. She looked at Jezebel, who was also feeling the strange sensation.

"What is this thing?" Jezebel was almost pleading.

"It is the old God of the Hebrews," Tamara answered to Jezebel's obvious dislike.

"Baal is with us. There is no god greater than Baal. And when was the last time anyone saw that God? Baal is the god of Israel now. No one in Israel goes to Jerusalem to worship anymore." Jezebel, feeling the power of Yahweh, defended Baal.

"I have felt this strange thing since before daylight and now it is very close." Frantically Tamara began to plead, "Your Highness, we must not provoke this God. I fear that he can do us great harm." When Jezebel didn't respond with a rebuke, she continued, "After He touched us before, I began to ask questions about Him. There was a time that He destroyed every nation that opposed Israel. He even rained stones from heaven on the enemies of Israel."

"There is no god greater than Baal. If the gods shall war, Baal will triumph. Baal will protect me. The spirit of Ashtoreth, his bride, lives in me," Jezebel boasted, but Tamara knew that she had doubts.

At that moment Elijah stepped into the road about fifty feet in front of Ahab's chariot. The driver continued forward and Elijah began to wave his arms to halt the horses. As the team of matching whites became agitated and slowed, the reins tightened and pulled them to a stop with Elijah standing directly in front of them. Though Ahab didn't seem to be in any danger, a chariot pulled up on each side of the king. An archer in each leveled an arrow at Elijah. Behind Ahab, the caravan stopped. Jezebel ordered her carriage down and, followed by her guard, began to make her way to the front. The driver of Ahab's chariot said in a sharp tone, "Do you not bow before the king?"

Elijah bowed slightly, "I am Elijah, servant of Yahweh Elohim, the God of Abraham, the God of Israel, before whom I stand. This is the word of the true God of Israel. There shall neither be dew nor rain these next years but according to my word." He could see the queen peering at him from between the chariots. At that moment the two horsemen that had been out front came galloping up behind him.

"It is Baal that brings the rain!" Jezebel spat back, but inside she feared the power of the presence that rested on Elijah.

"You are a prophet of Yahweh," Ahab stated and let it settle for a moment before he ordered, "Seize him!"

Elijah was over the side of the road and running down the steep slope before anyone began to move in his direction. The guard in the chariot on that side shot an arrow at Elijah but Elijah's sudden bolt had startled the horses and caused the chariot to jerk. Before he could reload the bow, Elijah had disappeared behind the brush that cluttered the mountain.

"After him!" Ahab shouted. The foot platoon and the horsemen went over the side after Elijah.

Jezebel turned to the officer of her personal guard and ordered, "You men also, after him!" Another dozen men leaped down the steep rocky hillside.

The terrain proved too steep and rough for the horses. Most of them fell headlong downward. The footmen with their armor and weapons were no match for Elijah, who had already reached the valley below. Several of the men reached the bottom uninjured and began across the flat land after him. Those who began to peel off their armor and drop their weapons held up under the rapid pace much longer. Finally, near death, the last soldier collapsed. He had lasted ten miles into the chase.

When Elijah knew that he was in the clear and couldn't see anyone behind him, he slowed to a trot. He panted hard and the sweat ran in rivers down his beard.

"Elijah, turn back eastward, and hide by the brook Cherith that is before Jordan. You shall drink of the brook and I have commanded the ravens to feed you there." Did the voice come from within or without? He couldn't tell but it was the voice of Elohim and it was clear.

The soldiers returned to Ahab. Several had been injured and one horseman killed on the steep mountainside. Their captain bowed by Ahab's chariot. "My lord, he escaped. He had no armor to carry."

"It is of no consequence. He was nothing but a madman," Ahab answered.

Jezebel, still standing where she had watched the chase down the side of the mountain, said, "My lord king, these men who returned uninjured shouldn't have given up the chase until they brought this Elijah back. They must be punished."

Ahab, wanting to appear as strong as Jezebel, agreed. "And they will be," he said, even though he knew that the men hadn't stood a chance, racing against a swift runner without weapons or armor.

Except for the men who had been injured on the mountain, the rest would later be tied to poles and whipped into unconsciousness.

Ahab sent men into every city and village searching for Elijah. A decree was issued that anyone hiding or withholding information about where Elijah was would be put to death, and their families sold into slavery.

The issue with Elijah at the moment was only a distraction for King Ahab. Israel had prospered so greatly that Ahab had built a second palace for Jezebel in one of the most beautiful places in the land, Jezreel. It was only a fraction of the size of the fortified palace in Samaria, but every detail was exquisitely done, and there was a splendid long range view of the plain toward Jordan.

Naboth, a local land owner, had refused to sell an adjoining vineyard to Ahab, one he wanted for a garden for Jezebel, otherwise Ahab thought the place perfect for his queen. Ahab surprised Jezebel with the palace on her birthday, two weeks after the encounter with Elijah.

As the daylight was fading, Elijah kept looking over his shoulder, suspecting that the king's troops might be tracking him. He traveled through the night, resting only once under a low-growing tree, where he could watch the route he had traveled. It was the following evening when he reached the mouth of the brook Cherith where it emptied into the Jordan River in Gilead.

Exhausted from the two-day trek, he collapsed to the ground as night fell and slept in the sand until morning. He had been too tired to care the night before, and the short tunic lying beneath him hadn't been sufficient to keep his body from the uncomfortable sand that was clinging to him when he awoke.

With a clawing hunger inside, he bathed in the river then began his ascent alongside the cascading brook. In a short while he moved out away from the brook and the heavy foliage that obscured the vista over the gorge where the brook and Jordan River met. Above there, the brook leveled into a tranquil flowing stream and beyond that the water cut through seventy-foot canyon walls where it ran from pool to pool. It was along the north wall that Elijah found a natural shelter carved into the rock by centuries of the brook's flow. There was a cavity under a ledge high enough for a man to stand with ease. It went back eight to ten feet and was fifteen feet wide. In front of the opening was a sandy bank, sloping down to a pool deeper than his height.

Feeling weak, Elijah took a seat in the warm sand by the stream and rested for a long while. He relived his life from the time he had returned to Tishbeh. Precisely when it happened he couldn't determine, but at some point during the past two years was when his life seemed to begin. Everything before that seemed like the life of another person. His mind drifted through everything he could remember about Adah, her smile, her voice, and the things they had dreamed together. He remembered his old friend Johanan and smiled at some of the funny things Johanan had joked about. The memories brought heartache with them, but they were memories he would often relive to keep them alive.

Yahweh had answered his prayer, and though he didn't feel any different, Yahweh had used him to prophesy to a king, he was a prophet. He would never forget how real the presence of Yahweh had been the night before he had confronted Ahab. How swiftly life can change directions, he thought, then realized that several hours had passed.

He stood to his feet and began to scavenge along the stream for driftwood that had piled up during the spring rains when the brook rushed in torrents. At the base of every tree along the bank and behind every large boulder there were piles of wood. He made many trips up and down the stream, dragging drift wood limbs back each time.

He was returning once again with his arms burdened with wood, when he saw two ravens on top of a nearly flat waist-high boulder at the edge of the water. The way they were squawking, Elijah thought they must have been fighting. Then he remembered the words that God had spoken to him, and repeated them out loud. "I have commanded the ravens to feed you there." He thought about it for a minute, then asked himself, "What does that mean?" He dropped the wood he was carrying and walked down to see the ravens that were making a fuss with their shrill squawks. They flew when he came near, but lying where they had been was a cake of bread and several chunks of raw mutton that had been carved with a sharp knife. Elijah looked up to see more than a dozen ravens flying overhead. "Where could this have come from?"

He took his knife and carved some thin chips from a piece of dry cedar he had found and, with a piece of flint, started a fire. He leaned against the rock cliff as he sat holding the meat over the fire at the end of a stick. As the long shadows stretched across the narrow canyon, fireflies began to dot the branches of a willow across the stream. Stars began to appear in the blue evening sky as he ate.

In the morning, a short while after daylight, the ravens returned to the same stone with the identical meal that they had brought the evening before. Elijah couldn't imagine where the ravens could be bringing the food from, and was even more amazed when they appeared again that evening with the same meal. They flew away when he came near, but morning and evening every day they came with the same gifts.

During the first few days, Elijah walled up the front of the small cave with stone, using clay as mortar. At one end he left an opening in the top of the wall for smoke to escape, and a small doorway at the other. He used split reeds to weave a door, and, in the same fashion, wove a mat that covered the entire floor. It made a small but comfortable room where he would spend an unknown number of months.

The days of summer shortened into autumn, and autumn into winter. From the day that he had confronted Ahab, not a single cloud appeared in the sky, and the brook was only half of what it would normally have been.

Elijah never knew where the meat and bread came from, but as the days passed, the ebony colored birds began to accept his presence like he was one of their young. He often fed them from his hand. One night when he had fallen asleep by a fire next to the brook, he was awakened the following morning by one of the ravens standing on his chest. It was as though the bird was concerned because he wasn't moving.

Daily he spent time praying for Israel, but he occupied most of his time working with his hands. He made a couple of earthen pots and baked them and spent days carving a bow but didn't have any sinew to braid into a bowstring. He fashioned a flute from river reeds. Several times he hiked up or down stream to the springs that fed the brook or to the Jordan River that the brook fed into.

Eight months had passed when Elijah became convinced that Israel wouldn't survive much longer without rain. He began to plead with Yahweh to change the hearts of the people, before the nation was beyond recovery, but the God that gave the land to the children of Abraham was silent.

Daily he swam in the pool by his cave shelter until the winter chill made it too uncomfortable. Then he would venture into the cold waters only on the warmer days. Most evenings would find Elijah sitting by a fire, meditating or singing one of the hundreds of psalms that he had committed to memory. Sometimes he danced around the fire as they had at the school locked arm in arm, but now he was alone.

At the palace in Samaria, Obadiah was taking inventory of the palace stores in the court where the roasting pits and bread ovens produced the large meals for the royal court. A dozen bread ovens sat at one end of the court, and the roasting pits at the other. An arbor covered a spiral stone stairway that led down to a deep well. There was a large gate that led to another court, and from there another led through a fortified, heavily guarded gate in the palace wall. Carts of wood, partially dressed beef and sheep, ground meal, pheasants, doves, fruits and melons were continually rolling through the palace gate.

A scribe walked at his side and made notes as Obadiah dictated. As the servants prepared large trays of meats and breads, he saw several ravens swoop down and steal what they could as a dozen others of their kind circled overhead. Amazed at the sight, Obadiah asked his assistant, "Did you see that?"

"See what?" was the reply.

Suddenly Obadiah had the impression not to do or say anything about what he had seen. His beliefs, a mixture of the Law of Moses and legends of Yahweh that had been told to him by his grandfather, lent to the feeling that the birds might be on some divine mission. How that could be he didn't understand, but he had learned to follow his intuition.

The following morning, he was watching for them on the chance that they would return. They arrived at a time when they could steal unguarded food with the greatest ease. From then on, Obadiah watched the birds return each morning and found that the servants who worked in the court were not able to see this intriguing oddity. Were they blinded to it, and why was he allowed to see?

Obadiah respected Yahweh because of his early childhood teaching, and desired to know the truth about Yahweh and the other gods. Was it true that there were many gods? Was Ashtoreth the queen of Yahweh, or was she the queen of Baal? Had Yahweh been defeated by Baal? What he had seen of the cruel child sacrifices the priests of Baal and Ashtoreth offered to their idols caused him to secretly resent the ones that worshipped those gods.

From the early days of King Asa, Judah had returned to their faith in one God, Yahweh Elohim. And now Judah was prospering, while Israel was being destroyed by a drought that Baal seemed helpless to counter. A drought prophesied by a man that he had once met, Elijah, prophet of Yahweh, a man whose name and whose God were becoming well known in Israel because of the drought. A man that King Ahab had committed all available resources to find.

When Ahab's search for Elijah failed, Jezebel called a meeting of the highest-ranking priests of Baal and Ashtoreth. There were more than a hundred seated in the circular temple chamber before a throne-like chair that the queen sat upon. She stood to her feet. "We have built a glorious temple to Baal and his queen, and there has never been a sacrifice made to the great Baal like the one we made to him, and continue to make daily. Why is the great Baal not bringing the rain to the land?"

Zohelethbal, who was standing to the side of the room, stepped closer to Jezebel. "We have already discussed this, Your Highness, and we agree that Lord Baal is displeased. There is a sect in Israel proclaiming that Baal is not a god at all, and that Yahweh is the only God. Baal must be worshipped above all gods, or he will not hear our prayers. Was it not a prophet of Yahweh who declared that the old God of Israel would bring drought upon this land that Baal has made so great among the nations? And wouldn't only an evil god bring such a plague upon the land?"

"What do you propose, Lord Zohelethbal?" Jezebel asked, hoping that he would have the answer.

"If the king would send troops throughout the land to rout out those who deny Baal, then Baal would answer our prayers," said Zohelethbal convincingly. "Go to Zidon and to your father, Ethbaal. Many Israelites are fleeing the drought there. Go into every city in Israel, and into all nations that worship Baal like your homeland, with priests and images of Baal. Everyone who refuses to bow to his image, put to death. Then Baal will be pleased and bring the rains again to Israel."

After a moment of thought, Jezebel replied, "The king will do as you suggest. He is perplexed as to what to do, and every day the drought continues, the nation becomes weaker. Israel cannot continue to sustain its army, and if Moab should become allied with Syria, we wouldn't be able to hold back a rebellion. I will talk to the king, and before this day is over your plan will be implemented."

After conferring with Jezebel on the advice of the high priest, King Ahab issued the orders and, as the army and priests began to organize, Obadiah got word of the decree. He knew that the true worshipers of Yahweh were about to suffer the worst persecution since the days of slavery in Egypt, and maybe even more.

In Ahab's search for Elijah, two things were learned about the before unknown prophet. In Elijah's introduction to Ahab he had told him that he was a Tishbite. From that it was learned that he was from the tribe of Gad, and that he was a friend of the school of Jehew, the scribe, renowned prophet and teacher. Obadiah knew that he must warn Jehew.

After ordering his horse saddled and brought to him, Obadiah rode through the palace gates and galloped through the streets of Samaria. Though he had never been to the school, he knew the vicinity. He rode hard for several hours and, as the daylight began to fade, he spotted, in the sunset's reflection, a white limestone structure high on a hill in front of him and knew that it was his destination.

His lathered horse panted hard as he reached the plateau and Obadiah pulled him to a halt. He had been spotted before he reached the school, and was greeted by Jehew and a dozen students. "I've come to speak to Jehew, the seer," he half shouted.

"I am Jehew," the distinguished, graying Jehew answered.

"I am Obadiah, the king's steward. The king has decreed, at Jezebel's urging, every person who will not bow to the image of Baal shall be put to death." Sensing the horse's need for rest, Obadiah climbed down as he continued. "The army was here before, looking for Elijah, was it not?"

"Several months ago," answered Jehew.

"They will be here again by tomorrow. This time they will be looking for an excuse to kill the worshipers of Yahweh Elohim, unless you bow to and kiss the image of Baal. You must worship Baal to be spared."

"Everyone here is prepared to die for the God we serve." Seeing the horse labor for each breath, Jehew offered, "Let one of the young men walk your horse until he cools down and give him some water. He's not fit to carry you back just now."

One of the young men took the horse's reins as Obadiah walked with Jehew. "Bring some bread and wine," Jehew ordered another student.

"You must send word to the family of Elijah in Tishbeh," Obadiah's voice carried a note of the authority he was use to wielding.

"Do you know Elijah?" Jehew hoped to hear that he did and that he was alive somewhere.

"I've only met him once. No, I don't know him."

They walked to a bench and sat down as the sun was disappearing behind a distant chain of mountains. "Why would the king's steward be interested in warning us?"

"I know some of the history of Israel, and I believe the stories of how the God of Abraham delivered and saved Israel over and over again. I am returning to the faith I knew as a boy, and I've seen what Yahweh has done for Judah. The king believes that you, or his family in Tishbeh, have been hiding Elijah, or know where he is. That is where he will send the troops first, but all of Israel will be put to the test. Everyone will have to bow to Baal or die."

Jehew replied, "Yahweh warned us of this tribulation more than two years ago. We've been waiting for this day, and praying for the strength to remain faithful."

"There are caves at the south end of the Sea of Chinneroth, in the hills to the east. If you will take one hundred of the most faithful of Yahweh's there, I will provide food for you until this is over. I may be able to bring food for a hundred but no more than that."

"Why would you do that?" Jehew questioned.

"Perhaps Yahweh won't hold me accountable for serving such a wicked king, although Jezebel is behind most of the wickedness that takes place." Obadiah had many questions that he wanted answered about Yahweh, but remembered the urgency of the situation. "You must prepare to leave, and move quickly!

"From where the sea flows into the Jordan, travel due east for one hour and wait there. In three days I will have supplies sent to you there and a map to the caves." He stood up just as one of the students brought the bread and wine. He gulped down a cup of wine, then called for his horse.

After Obadiah left, Jehew sent his son, Zechariah, to Tishbeh to warn Elijah's family, as he led a hundred faithful believers northeast towards the caves.

The following day, a detachment of fifty foot soldiers and a mounted captain arrived at the school with six priests carrying an idol of Baal on their shoulders. It was too quiet. The captain, thinking it might be an ambush of rebel forces, ordered the men to stand ready. He divided them in half and ordered the buildings searched as the rest stood guard. When he was satisfied that there wasn't anyone there, he ordered everything burned.

Throughout Israel the worship of Yahweh Elohim had been so incorporated into Baal and Ashtoreth worship, along with many other idols, that most people welcomed the opportunity to bow before the images that were brought into their villages. They believed that to kiss Baal's image would bring blessings. Twenty images of Baal, each two cubits high and carried on the shoulders of six priests, were sent in different directions throughout the land. There was a priest in front and another behind, carrying censers that wafted a thin smoke as they walked. Each idol was accompanied by a detachment of fifty foot-soldiers and a mounted captain, as they went from village to village.

Zechariah, on horseback, reached Tishbeh a few hours before the army and the idol of Baal. Johanan was working at his smith shop when he heard the pounding hooves approaching. He stepped from the shop into the edge of the road as the rider pulled his horse to a halt.

"Is this Tishbeh?" Zechariah shouted.

Uncertain of the young rider's intention, Johanan nodded slowly as he studied the condition of the horse that was breathing out blood with each hard breath the animal released.

"Would you be the smith, the friend of Elijah?"

When Johanan heard the name of his boyhood friend that had become a legend, he lowered his guard. "Yes, I'm a friend of Elijah. Is something wrong?"

"The army of Ahab can't be too far behind me. They're coming here to find Elijah and will torture the last person, even to the children, until someone gives him up to them. And throughout Israel, everyone that refuses to bow to the image of Baal will die." Zechariah took a quick breath then continued. "Elijah has told me about you and his father, and about Tishbeh. Will you warn his brothers?"

Johanan was already removing his apron as he answered, "Yes! Yes! I will warn them. Quickly get down from your horse."

"No, I must return home, my father has instructed me to take my mother and flee to Judah."

"You have killed your horse, he's dying. He won't live through the night. Leave him here and I'll put him down." Johanan raised his arm and pointed up the road. "You run up the road, just beyond the palms you'll come to the house of Eliab, Elijah's brother. He'll have another horse for you. Tell him what you've told me. Elijah warned us that a time like this was coming."

Zechariah jumped down from his horse and saw the blood coming from the horse's nostrils as it struggled for each breath. "Oh no. I'm sorry I rode you so hard." He turned to Johanan and asked, "Will you put him down after I leave?"

"Yes, but we must hurry. I must warn the people of Tishbeh." Zechariah ran up the road as Johanan found a dagger.

When Ahab received word that Tishbeh had been found deserted he sent a second detachment there with orders to destroy the hamlet. After Tishbeh had been burned the remaining walls were pulled to the ground. What remained of Tishbeh were piles of smoldering rubble.

Thousands of faithful Israelites hid in the mountains of Israel, while others, forced to leave because of the drought, fled into the surrounding countries. In the days and weeks that followed, thousands of Israelites were put to the sword, and many more publicly burned alive as examples. Their children were offered as sacrifices to Baal, and young virgins raped to death before the Ashtoreth idol. It didn't matter what a person believed. As long as they were willing to bow down to and kiss the image of Baal, they were spared. Many believers of Yahweh, when faced with death, bowed to the image.

The beat of the drums had sounded so steadily over the months that it seemed to replace real thoughts with mindless responses to the beat. Over a hundred priests danced before the image of Baal in the temple. Their feet were red with the wet blood that covered the stone floor. More blood ran from their backs and chests from sacrificial wounds they had inflicted upon themselves and each other, as offerings to the gold and stone idol.

Jezebel sat on a throne next to her god the way she sat next to Ahab when he was seated on his throne. The worship of Baal never stopped as sacrifices were offered one after another.

Frustrated by her inability to move Baal to send rain, Jezebel went about on the verge of exploding into a rage at any added discomfort of mind or soul or body. Judah, the only nation in all the world which clung to the notion that there was only one God, and that was the old Hebrew God, Yahweh Elohim, was the only place east of Egypt unaffected by the drought. As far as she knew, everyone in Israel had bowed down and kissed Baal's image, and still there was no rain. Famine and drought were ravaging Zidon, her homeland, as severely as Israel and Baal was pre-eminent among the gods there.

Jezebel stood to her feet. Everyone in the temple bowed to the floor. The music stopped. A hissing sound of the burning body of an infant on the altar and the crackling wood beneath were the only sounds that could be heard for a long minute before she spoke. "It has come to me that Lord Baal is waiting for the supreme sacrifice. The willing sacrifice of ten priests." She looked around at the hundreds of people there with her eyes resting for an instant on certain priests. "Which of you will sacrifice yourselves to Lord Baal for his glory, and for the redemption of Israel?"

Several moments passed, then one young priest, his naked body half covered in blood, stood to his feet. A moment later another stood then another and another until there were six naked men standing. "Lord Baal will be appeased with no less than ten willing sacrifices." Jezebel's voice echoed through the great hall. A minute passed, then another stood. Angrily she stormed, "This lack of faith is the very reason Baal has withheld the spring rains and the winter rains! You are ignorant, for you could be dining with the gods this very night! If Baal would allow me to, I would offer myself for the good of Israel!" Another stood, then another, until fourteen priests were standing.

Through the night and next day they were burned on the altar, and another week followed without rain.

Jezebel was lying upon her plush bed with her firstborn, her daughter, Athaliah, lying snuggled up to her left side as she pondered the plight of Israel.

Unable to reconcile the facts with her beliefs, she began to feel the most frightening thing that had ever come into her mind. If she were the incarnation of Ashtoreth, Baal's queen, and with all of her heart she knew that she was, then Baal had to be foremost in her life. The only person she had ever had any real feeling for until Athaliah had been born was Tamara. She began to realize that Athaliah had come to mean more to her than perhaps even Baal. Was Baal angry with her and demanding that Athaliah be sacrificed to him? "No! Baal is my only love!" her mind shouted as she shoved the child away from her.

She took delight in her sons but she had made the mistake of loving her daughter more than Baal. In that moment she cut the bonds of love that extended to Athaliah. Maybe the child would not have to be sacrificed if she sacrificed her in her own heart.

Athaliah began to cry and reached for her mother, only to be pushed away again. At that moment a servant came into the room carrying a tray of dates, figs and raisin cakes with honey.

Sharing the sweet cakes most days had become one of Jezebel's favorite things, but she determined that it would never happen again. "You feed her," she ordered the servant as she got up from the bed.

"Eber!" she shouted. In a few moments the eunuch entered the room. "Ready my carriage and get Tamara."

To appease Baal, she and Tamara lay on the bloodstained stone floor in the temple before his image through the night. By morning she had again convinced herself that the fault for the drought was with the believers of Yahweh Elohim. "Elijah!" her voice reverberated through the massive pillars that lined the great hall as she walked the length of the cavernous room.

Raised a Phoenician princess, Jezebel's maternal grandmother had been Hebrew, of the tribe of Asher. Because of that, she had grown up with an awareness of the pockets of Hebrews that still survived in Zidon. Her people had mostly assimilated Asher, the tribe that had once conquered her land, but there were a few Hebrews that could still trace their ancestors back to Abraham.

Among those fragmented groups in Zidon was the only place on earth Elijah could be. Ahab had searched the world looking for him, except for Zidon. He couldn't openly send troops into Judah looking for Elijah, but Ahab had secretly sent many of his puppet prophets there to find him. Among the Hebrews in Zidon was where he must be, Jezebel convinced herself.

"Eber," she said to the sleepy servant sitting on the temple porch leaning against a pillar. He had waited the night there for her, with two guards that now stood to attention when Jezebel exited.

Like Eber, the guards had been slumped against the entrance until the queen arrived. They stood nervously now, hoping Jezebel hadn't seen them. She had been violently unpredictable for the past several months. Only last week, the sergeant at arms was disemboweled and left hanging upside down to die for sparing the life of a young guard who had fallen asleep at his post. Fortunately, she was focused on other things this day.

"Yes, Your Highness," Eber struggled to his feet and bowed.

"Ready my carriage, and bring a scribe."

A few minutes later she was seated on the temple porch dictating a letter to her father. "Noble King Ethbaal. Live long and find favor with the great Baal. You know that Baal has withheld the rains from our lands. It is because there is a sect of Hebrews living among us who deny his greatness. It is the sect that holds to the notion that the old God of the Hebrews, Yahweh Elohim, is the only God. Until the land is purged of this fallacy, Baal will maintain his anger.

"It is also believed that the fugitive Elijah, whom you know about, and who, as you know, caused this drought, is hid out among that sect in Zidon. Father, I respectfully request troops to accompany the priests and image of Baal throughout Zidon to purge the land, just as Israel has been purged, to appease Baal's anger." Before she got out the last line Tamara stepped up onto the porch.

"He is not in Zidon, but here in Israel."

Jezebel was taken aback at Tamara's forwardness in interrupting her. "I have prayed the night at the feet of Baal and I believe that he has shown me where this false prophet is."

"I know for certain that he is here in Israel," Tamara said with less concern for Jezebel's anger than with what she was convinced was the truth.

"I am high priestess of Ashtoreth. Should Baal choose to reveal anything, it would be to me before anyone." Jezebel rose to her feet with fire burning in her eyes. She began to tremble with anger before pulling herself together.

"I will call a council of the priests to meet on the next new moon. We will see whom the gods speak through. And if they have shown you that Elijah is indeed here in Israel, then they will tell you where. Nonetheless, Zidon will be purged of heresy."

Tamara already knew what the outcome of the council on the new moon would be and looked forward to being freed from Jezebel. She gave Jezebel one last defiant look, then turned and walked away.

Tamara had been nearly as close to little Athaliah as Jezebel. Tamara had longed for something she could never be, a mother. As a seeress of Baal, she had to remain a virgin, and if Baal should ever choose to take her virginity, she had to be pure. That was the way half men, half gods came to be; men that ruled the world, that couldn't be beaten or overthrown, that became gods when they died.

Tamara was beginning to abandon many of her beliefs based on her experiences with the supernatural powers. She could not say so, but there was a God in Israel that dwarfed Baal. There were times when she could see into that realm, and Baal quaked with fear, just at the coming presence of that strange God, the old God of the Hebrews.

In the few weeks before the new moon, she filled her life with Athaliah. She took her for walks in the gardens of Jezreel. That seemed to be the only beautiful place left on earth. Jezebel had her gardens watered while cattle were dying by the thousands throughout the land.

Every moment that Tamara could steal Athaliah away from her nursemaids, they spent together. It was as though she was trying to make up for what she had missed in life. Daily, they shared fig and raisin cakes beneath the shade of a sprawling fig tree that dominated a corner of the garden. Many times she caught a glimpse of Jezebel watching them from a tower in the palace that overlooked the garden. She knew that Jezebel despised Athaliah's growing affection for her, but she didn't care and would continue until Jezebel stopped them.

Athaliah was spoiled, but Tamara was so filled with love for the child that she hardly noticed. She was bright and Tamara could feel that she had a good heart if only someone would take the time to develop it. She had a lifetime of love stored up with no place to let it out until now, and it was all bestowed on the daughter of Ahab and Jezebel.

Within a few days after King Ethbaal answered Jezebel's letter giving her permission to eradicate Yahweh worship from Zidon, priests carrying images of Baal, accompanied by troops of Zidon, made their way beyond the northern border of Israel that divided what was left of the tribe of Asher.

Within the country there were many believers in Yahweh Elohim, but none to the exclusion of Baal and other gods until they reached the city of Zarephath. People were driven from their homes into the street, where they were given a chance to bow before Baal and kiss his image. Scores of men and women died rather than kiss the idol. Many were tortured for information about Elijah before being thrust through with sword or spear. To die for what they believed was one thing, but many couldn't endure the pain of a glowing brand thrust onto their flesh and begged for mercy, then gave up the names of the leaders of their faith. Everyone knew of the man Elijah but none had ever seen him.

Of the leaders of the faith, one name repeated several times was Azor, a ship builder who lived against the northeastern wall of the city. Azor had brought the teachings of Yahweh from Judah.

Hoping to find information about Elijah, they left off purging the city and went directly to the house of Azor. He was home in observance of the Sabbath, when he heard a loud banging at the gate. He rushed into the small court and opened the gate cautiously. Two soldiers shoved their way in and made way for their captain.

"Are you Azor?" the officer asked, as he looked around the small, well-maintained court.

"Yes, I am, and why are you here?" demanded Azor.

Delah, along with their eleven-year-old son, Isaac, and a female servant, stepped from the house into the edge of the court.

"We are looking for a fugitive named Elijah, and a sect of Hebrews who are perverting the worship of Baal. We've learned that you are one of the leaders of these people who deny the deity of Baal."

Azor, knowing that any honest answer would be wrong, hesitated for a moment. "Do you know that I am the king's master shipbuilder?"

"It doesn't matter to me who you are. I have orders to put to the sword anyone who refuses to bow to Baal." The officer turned to his men, "Have the priests bring in the image of Baal."

With the image sitting near the center of the court, Azor was forced close to it. Delah rushed to Azor. "Please do what they ask," she pleaded.

"I cannot," Azor answered, as he looked into her eyes a moment before embracing her. "Yahweh will take care of you," he whispered into her ear.

"Take the boy into the house," the officer ordered one of his men. The soldier receiving the order walked over to Isaac and shoved him and the servant into the house.

"No!" Isaac shouted. A second later the butt of the soldier's sword knocked him unconscious. The servant knelt beside Isaac as the soldier returned to the court.

"You can bow to Baal and live, or die here in front of your wife." Vexed in soul from murdering, the officer hoped Azor would bow to Baal and live.

"Please let her go inside," Azor pleaded.

"She must also bow or die," he answered.

Delah dropped to her knees in front of the image. "Please, let him live! I will worship Baal."

Azor reached down to pick her up but was shoved aside with a spear handle. When he tried again he was stopped by the point of the spear touching his midsection. "Delah, don't do it, please don't do it," he pleaded with her.

"If Baal is not appeased, the entire land will be decimated," the officer explained, hoping to change their minds. All morning he had been trying to talk people out of dying by bowing to Baal. The priests that stood by were amazed. Nowhere, not even in Israel, had there been this much resistance in one place.

"Baal cannot bring rain. The God of Abraham has brought this drought upon the land and only He will remove this plague when the people turn back to him. Judah is not experiencing drought. I've been there. Judah is flourishing and they worship the God of Abraham." Azor's argument was convincing, but the officer was afraid to even listen.

"I will worship and serve Baal," Delah pleaded through tears "Please, Azor, worship Baal. I don't want to live without you."

"You could still worship your God, if only you would give homage to Baal. Why don't you listen to her?" Seeing the conviction in Azor, he knew what the answer would be, but made the offer one last time. "The land, the people cannot survive any more of this plague. Seize him!" he ordered.

Two soldiers took hold of Azor and forced him to the ground as two others heated a brand in the flame of a torch. "What do you know about Elijah?" the officer demanded.

"I know who he is, he is the prophet of God! I've never met him though," Azor strained out. A sharp dagger cut Azor's tunic from the neck down, exposing his back. A moment later the hot iron seared into his flesh near his right shoulder blade. Azor inhaled deeply but never made a sound.

"Please!" Delah cried out as she wailed hysterically. She kissed the image of Baal then turned back and bowed at the feet of the officer. "Please."

The reheated brand was pressed into Azor's back a second time with the same results. Azor had earned the respect of the officer who was disgusted with what he had been ordered to do. "He doesn't deserve to die like that," he said, as he drew his sword and with a continuous stroke struck Azor in the back of the neck, nearly decapitating him.

"Bring out the servant," he ordered. When the servant was brought out, the officer asked, "Will you worship Baal?"

"Yes, I will bow to Baal," she whimpered.

"Then get out of here. Go somewhere else and bow to Baal." The servant ran from the court, and a minute later the priests and soldiers left leaving Delah lying on the ground by Azor's still body. She embraced him as she cried, finding it impossible to accept. "Is there no way to turn back time, or bring him back from the dead? How could this have happened," she tried to reason. "Why, oh Elohim, why?" she sobbed.

Upon receiving word of Azor's death, King Ethbaal dispatched a letter to Jezebel that read:

"Daughter, Queen of Israel, in your zeal to please Baal, Azor, my master shipbuilder has been put to death. He was the wisest and most skilled man I have ever known, and one of the most important to me at this time. Zidon has the swiftest ships and the greatest navy in the world. Azor deserves much of the credit for that. His work will continue without him, but in establishing an alliance with Judah, Azor is irreplaceable. King Jehoshaphat has plans to build a fleet of cargo ships. I loaned him the services of Azor who was in Judah designing and laying out plans for Jehoshaphat most of this past year. His death will not be taken lightly by Jehoshaphat.

"I was not aware of Azor's beliefs, but would have been willing to make atonement to Baal in his behalf at any cost.

"In questioning the men that were present at his execution, it is apparent that Azor established who he was, my master shipbuilder. For that, the captain in charge has been executed.

"For Azor's death, I expect compensation from Israel equal to Azor's value to me. A similar letter of my grievances is being dispatched to King Ahab."

When Ahab received Ethbaal's letter, he made a personal trip to Zidon. Israel needed the alliance with Zidon for protection of their northern border, and their navy for protection of Israel's coast. Whatever restitution would cost, Ahab was willing to pay.

****

Elijah had not set eyes on another human in more than a year, and he was feeling particularly lonely as night began to engulf him. The ravens stayed around most of the time now, and some he even recognized and called by the names he had given them. They always flew away as the darkness encroached.

Though he was having to travel farther to find fire wood now, he piled up a huge pile and built the largest fire he'd had. When the flames were dancing high above his head he began to sing and dance.

"Oh praise Yahweh, all nations; praise Him all people. For His merciful kindness is great toward us, and the truth of Yahweh is everlasting. Praise Yahweh. Oh, give thanks to Yahweh, for He is good, His mercy endures forever. Praise Yahweh." Each time the verse was repeated it became slightly faster. Elijah danced and sang and danced. He knew that the night was exceedingly dark but hadn't noticed that it was the new moon.

In the circular council chamber of the temple of Baal, Jezebel was in session with the high priests. She and Tamara were the only women present among the thirty priests and twenty musicians.

They sought answers to three questions. One had become a continuous cry, "Where is the rain?" The other questions they were seeking answers to were "Where is Elijah?" and "Would Baal choose to speak through Tamara, or through his queen, Jezebel?"

Before the great image of Baal in the next room, a child, a girl of four, was being slain to bring the favor of their god. Seated on steps in the council room, one, then another would stand and give voice to what they believed Baal wanted to speak through them. Each would drink from a mixture that was passed around again and again. Jezebel was seething with anger at how trite and commonplace each oration sounded. Each priest, trying to impress the rest, said nothing of real value. Slowly the priests stood and disrobed as they danced around the floor to the rhythmic beat of the music.

As usual they began to inflict bloody wounds with honed dagger blades to offer their blood to appease Baal. The already red stained floor became sticky as blood began to stream down their scarred bodies.

Zohelethbal stood, his eyes transfixed on a fire that burned at the side of Baal's image. The music died, and the bloody priests bowed to the floor. "I see ravens, black as pitch. I see them flying around the man called Elijah." He stood motionless, entranced, for several minutes then he continued, "He sings, Oh praise Yahweh."

Tamara, seated next to Jezebel, stood and continued where the high priest left off. "There is a fire." There was a long minute before she continued, "He is dancing and singing to his God."

Jezebel interrupted, "Where is he?"

At that moment Elijah, was distracted from his dance by a strong wind that rushed through the canyon, pulling the flames and sparks of the fire downstream. He stopped and listened to the wind howling against the cliffs. He had never seen the wind blow between the cliffs like that before. It brought with it an ominous feeling. After a few moments he chose to ignore it and began to dance again.

Tamara continued, "The wind of Baal has found Jezebel's enemy." Tamara's voice sharpened drastically, "The spirit of Baal is fleeing from the presence of spirit men surrounding him. They are mighty spirits; they are gods." Tamara turned and looked into Jezebel's eyes. The look frightened Jezebel. "You must not do any harm to this man Elijah."

Defiantly, Jezebel responded, "Elijah has brought much sorrow upon Israel."

Tamara's eyes widened, "He is no ordinary man. The earth would open up and swallow the person who would harm him." Tamara's voice began to quiver and she was barely able to get the words out, "I am afraid, for his God is God! We are the enemies of the true God. Yahweh El Shaddai is God."

With a violent, almost supernatural strength, Jezebel rose up in Tamara's face and slung her into the center of the room and onto the floor. "Seize her! She shall die before Baal this hour!"

Within moments Tamara was tied on the altar of Baal, with the knife of the priest poised to slit her throat. Jezebel, jealous of Tamara's ability to see into the realm of the gods, now wanted her dead at any cost. Even the remorse she would feel at the loss of her life-long companion would not stay her death.

"I knew I would die on the altar of Baal this night, but there were things revealed to me tonight that you do not know."

Jezebel motioned for the priest to hold back the blade another moment. "Jezebel, queen of devils, the generation of your children will be cut off and this great temple of Baal will be made level with the ground."

Jezebel staggered quickly back from the altar. Tamara had never been wrong.

She screamed, "You liar!" She took the dagger from the priest and was about to thrust it into Tamara's heart. As Tamara held up her hand to say one last thing, Jezebel hesitated again, with a slight hope that Tamara might plead for mercy and repent of her words.

"Death is preferable to sharing this life with you. I now sacrifice myself to the Almighty Yahweh." Jezebel trembled with anger as she delivered the knife into Tamara's chest with all her might and her life's blood gushed out. It took thirty seconds for Tamara's eyes to set, a sight that would haunt Jezebel for the rest of her life.

The priests placed Tamara's body on the fire of Baal. There was no orgy, no ritual, not even a chant, as would have been customary, depending upon the type of sacrifice that was being made. No one said a word. Tamara had been respected for her accuracy in prophecy.

"Get out, all of you!" Jezebel ordered. Feeling alone and regretful, she watched Tamara's body slowly disappear into the glowing coals until only her charred skeleton remained.

An ominous gray-brown dust cloud loomed above, dimming the noon sun to less than half its brightness. A dusty haze, pushed by a constant wind, swept the hills south of Samaria. Atop a methodically plodding humpback, Obadiah wrapped his face from the stinging sand as he led a camel caravan, followed by a train of ox drawn carts, south towards Ephraim. The fertile fields of Israel lay desolate like the Syrian Desert to the east, and the dwindling flocks and gaunt herds lay on the ground, or stood with their back sides to the wind.

Ahab had sent a letter to King Jehoshaphat asking for terms of trade. Jehoshaphat answered with a letter of passage, giving permission for King Ahab to trade with the area of south Ephraim controlled by Judah, but not within the borders of Judah itself. And, no armed Israelites were to attempt to pass into any territory belonging to Judah.

It was hard for Obadiah to understand why Jehoshaphat would allow any type of trade with the northern kingdom. The two countries had been at war for more than sixty years, since the reign of Rehoboam, the son of Solomon, and now, because of the drought, Judah was in a position to conquer Israel.

Judah was the only nation east of Egypt that had not been decimated by the drought, though Israel was the only one that had not received any rain. Because of the conditions that existed in Israel, the thousand thousand-man army had been reduced to only seventy thousand, and it was known that Judah maintained an army of more than eight hundred thousand, plus a militia of over a thousand thousand; enough to easily conquer them.

The caravan's military escort was left at Baal-Hazor, the last city of Israel that the train of camels, wagons and oxcarts passed through before they entered the Judean controlled territory of Ephraim. It was five miles from there to Ephron, a fortified city with a large garrison of Judean troops.

Obadiah was amazed at how quickly the barren ground turned to lush green pastures and leafed trees just beyond Baal-Hazor. There were numerous flocks from Israel grazing on the thick green grass between the fortified cities of Israel and the watch towers of Judah.

Watch towers within sight of one another stretched from city to city along the border. Each had vats of oil at the top that awaited a signal fire at the sighting of any invasion force. Within half an hour the entire country of Judah could know of an advancing army. At every city, and along the long expanses between cities, Judean troops were garrisoned.

As they crossed the border near Ephron, Obadiah was surprised that the troops that guarded the highway didn't stop them to question the purpose of such a large caravan marked with the king of Israel's banners. A dozen soldiers stood by the road and observed them closely as they passed, but nothing was spoken.

The small walled city of Ephron was dwarfed by the city of tents outside its walls. Obadiah saw caravans from Syria, Philistia, Zidon and Moab. Merchants were selling grains and fruits and melons, camels and oxen, sheep, mules and horses. It was like Megiddo had once been. Most of the livestock was being resold after being traded for grain. Judah was prospering greatly as a result of the drought upon the rest of the world. "This sight alone should be enough to convince anyone that Yahweh is God," Obadiah said aloud.

He spent the afternoon buying what grain he could, but most had already been sold. Obadiah was able to fill only a third of the king's carts and send them back to Samaria. He heard there was a chance that one of the largest farms in the country had not harvested all of their crops. Another day's journey west, beyond the next city, Beth-Horon, he would come to the farm of Eliphaz, but his sons could be found at the markets at Beth-Horon.

The following day as they neared the city of Beth-Horon, they found that it was clearly within the borders of Judah and had to camp on the Ephraim side of the border. The line between Ephraim and Judah was clearly marked by abandoned towers and fortifications that once separated the two. Obadiah walked alone into the city, unhindered. The market of Beth-Horon was as busy as the one in Ephron and another they had passed through in Zemeraim, a small city on the way to Beth-Horon, but the only foreign traders there were from countries allied to Judah. They were getting the choicest grain at the best price. A hundred caravans the size of his couldn't meet all of Israel's needs. Even so, he was finding it increasingly difficult to find enough grain to load one. When he inquired about the sons of Eliphaz, he was directed through the market street to a man with many carts loaded with sacks of grain. Obadiah would recognize him because he would be the man without a beard.

When Obadiah spotted the smooth face of Elisha he stood and watched him from a distance for a moment before approaching. He sensed something unusual about Elisha. It was the spirit within the man and he could feel it. He watched Elisha load heavy sacks of grain onto a cart that other men the same size would have found too heavy. Obadiah asked, "How do you do that with such ease?"

Surprised by the stranger's voice Elisha looked at him for a moment before answering. "I am a man thankful to be alive, and because of that I have worked harder than anyone else. The harder I worked the easier the work became. When you lift a sack a hundred times, it becomes heavier. When you lift a sack a thousand times, it becomes lighter." Elisha shouldered another bag of grain as though it were filled with straw.

"I am from Israel; Obadiah, governor of the house of King Ahab. We have need to buy grain from you. Would that be possible?"

"How do you know me?" Elisha asked.

"In Ephron, I was told that a man by the name of Eliphaz still had large amounts of grain left, and that his sons could be found here at the market."

"There are still a lot of stores of grain in Judah. It has mostly all been sold here on the border." Elisha paused from his work and looked at Obadiah for a moment, "I am the son of Shaphat, Eliphaz is my uncle.

Obadiah detected something in Elisha's accent that betrayed his origin. "Your accent betrays you. You are not from Ephraim but north Israel, maybe Manasseh."

"That's very perceptive, and very close. I am of the tribe of Issachar of Abel Meholah, below the Sea of Chinneroth. That's where my inheritance will be." At that moment there was the long low sound of a ram's horn. "We can do no business now until day after tomorrow. It's two hours until the beginning of the Sabbath."

A moment later Elisha added, "I have heard of you, Obadiah. You are a great man." That statement puzzled Obadiah. How or why would anyone know of him here, and if they had heard of the governor of the house of Ahab, why would that make him great? "What means of transporting grain do you have?" Elisha's voice brought his querying mind back to the task at hand.

"Across the border in Ephraim awaits a large caravan." Obadiah answered, then asked, "You are from Abel Meholah, how did you get here to Judah?"

"We couldn't survive in Israel any longer with the drought. We lost a third of our herds and came here to my uncle's, who had more land than he could till.

"You can stay at my uncle's house through the Sabbath. There will be bread and meat and your animals can graze. I know that there is no grass left to graze in Israel," said Elisha. "I'll get my mule and meet you at your caravan."

Elisha put the servants in charge of securing the grain before closing for the Sabbath. He and a younger cousin met Obadiah at the caravan thirty minutes later. Elisha rode alongside Obadiah, whose camel seemed agitated at having a mule at her side. She kept turning her head to bite Elisha's mule, and would have except for the sting of Obadiah's rod on the side of her muzzle.

Elisha looked up at Obadiah. "You are not obligated to buy grain from us, but you would not be able to buy grain anywhere in Judah until after the Sabbath anyway. I can give you the most reasonable price on grain of any one in Ephraim, provided your servants will help."

"What is your proposition?" Obadiah asked.

"Last year, because of the drought, we prospered above our greatest expectations. Merchants from all over the earth, it seemed, were here to buy. This year we planted every piece of ground that could be planted, expecting that some wouldn't make it like most years, too dry, too wet, too cool. There is always something, but not this year. It seems that every seed multiplied a thousand times. We've not been able to harvest it all. Some of it will ruin if it isn't harvested now. If you provide the men, we can load two, maybe three, caravans the size of yours, just from the unharvested grain. And, I see that you have many servants with you," said Elisha, as he turned and surveyed Obadiah's entourage behind them.

"And the price?" asked Obadiah thoughtfully. This seemed too good to be true after what he had seen on the border.

"My uncle has prospered greatly because of my business instincts and allows me to set the price. I'll sell it to you for half the price of grain anywhere. There is some barley left, and wheat in abundance. We also have wine and dried fruit." Elisha stopped for a moment as Obadiah's camel turned her head in his direction to be met with Obadiah's rod again. The camel snorted at the sting on her nose. "Ah! There is one thing that you should know before we reach my uncle's home. You are a worshiper of Yahweh, but some think that we are too strict in keeping the Sabbath. By the time we get there it will be the Sabbath. My father and uncle will not allow anyone to violate it. Neither you nor any of your servants will be allowed to do any work except to water the animals. You must not anger them by allowing what they forbid, or they will not allow you to buy one grain of wheat, even if you paid ten times the price. And, if you accept their hospitality you will be expected to go to Beth-Horon for the reading of the law tomorrow."

"My grandfather told me of Yahweh," said Obadiah. "He would sit and tell of the great things the God of Abraham did for our forefathers in Egypt, in the wilderness, and here in the Promised Land. When I was very young, Yahweh Elohim was the only God that I knew of, and I walked in fear of offending Him. Later as a young man I began to doubt. It seemed hard to know what the truth was, with so many gods being propagated in Israel. Many men that I thought were wise didn't believe in Yahweh."

Obadiah paused a moment then continued. "I was taught the Law of Moses and I cherish the memory of the stories that my grandfather told." Obadiah sighed, and paused again before continuing, "I have made some grave errors. I never told my two sons, who are about your age, the stories my grandfather told me and now they are Baal worshipers. What is your belief?"

Elisha listened, thoughtfully, then he said, "I owe my life to Yahweh. You see when I was young, maybe eleven or twelve, I was unconscious most of the time. Actually, it was more than a year. My father and mother petitioned the Almighty for my life, and a fever that would have killed anyone else, I survived. He spared me for His glory, and now I wait to see for what purpose I was spared."

"Do you have a wife?" asked Obadiah.

"I could not disgrace a woman by marrying her. I can't grow a beard, and a man without a beard is not a man." Elisha pulled the blue rope ajhal that held his kaffiyeh in place and removed the cloth from his head, revealing a completely bald head. "I can't grow hair anywhere except the thin brows above my eyes."

Obadiah felt embarrassed for Elisha and answered, "I don't know of another man that could lift those sacks of grain with as little effort as you. In strength you are more of a man than anyone I have ever seen." At that moment he had to tap the camel on the nose again as her head began to turn towards Elisha's mule.

They crossed the crest of a ridge and Obadiah pulled his camel to a halt. The caravan behind him stopped, but it took Elisha the length of his mule before he realized that they had come to a halt. Before Obadiah's eyes was a valley that stretched far to the north, covered with fields and woods like patches on a worn out garment. "Could the Garden of Eden have been any more beautiful?" he asked, almost to himself.

Elisha looked back. "Yahweh has blessed all of Judah like this. He has done this for a testimony to His people."

Obadiah nudged his dromedary into a walk and continued down the sloping road. Elisha fell in beside him again. "You said that tomorrow is the reading of the law. Does that occur every Sabbath?"

"And on Sabbath weeks it is read every day from dawn until midday," Elisha answered, then added, "King Jehoshaphat has sent elders and Levites throughout Judah to teach the people. And, while Jezebel thinks the worship of Yahweh has been suppressed in Israel, it is flourishing. It is spreading from the borders of Judah like the dust carried by the wind. And you, Obadiah, must be very careful. I have heard how you have hidden from Jezebel a hundred prophets of Yahweh and fed them. Too many people know, and sooner or later someone will tell Ahab or Jezebel."

Stunned for a moment, Obadiah asked, "How did so many people come to know about the prophets that are hidden?"

"To hide a hundred men that have families and no one find out? That would take a miracle as great as opening up the Red Sea."

For a moment Obadiah felt weak with fear, knowing the type of death that would await him if Jezebel should find out his secret. He had seen some of the prophets of Yahweh die by the sword without uttering a word of fear or regret, and admired them with the greatest respect. If he could die with that kind of honor and dignity for Yahweh, even the pain might be worth it. He took comfort in that thought and courage rose up within him. "I am ready to die if that is what Yahweh should want of me," he said. Even Obadiah couldn't believe the kind of boldness that he heard from his own lips.

"You are considered a hero here in Ephraim. I know that by now it must be difficult to find enough grain to feed a hundred men, and their families must be destitute by now. If you, Sir Obadiah, will allow me to help, I will give you all the grain you need to feed the worshipers of the Almighty Yahweh."

"The king doesn't know it, but he has been the major provider to the prophets," said Obadiah, with a wry grin.

Elisha laughed, "That's like Pharaoh raising Moses in his own house."

"After the drought, when you decide to return to Israel I can see that you get your land back. I have considerable influence with the king. I know that many that have left won't be welcome back, not without paying a very high tribute."

The home of Eliphaz was a walled enclosure fifteen cubits high, surrounded by palm trees. The outside walls were a hundred and fifty cubits square, with one large gate in the front and smaller gates on each end. Inside was a palace-like structure with a pool in the center of the court. It was not unlike the homes of the princes of Judah and Israel.

Since it was the Sabbath, the evening meal had been prepared before the trumpets of Judah sounded in the cities to usher in the Holy day. It was quiet and reverent, and everything that had to be done was accomplished with a minimum of effort.

It was a large gathering, with the sons of Eliphaz and the sons of Shaphat and their families. With the grandchildren, there were more than fifty present. At the end of the meal Shaphat called for the servants to bring and play the harps and flutes.

The likeness between Eliphaz and Shaphat was unmistakable. Both were leathery, brown-skinned men with typical Hebrew features. Shaphat was taller than his brother and his hair was snow white, while Eliphaz was only partially gray. Both men had piercing blue eyes, with faces framed by lines found only on men who smiled often, as they did that evening. Eliphaz's plump wife was nearly a mirror image of him, and Elisha revered them more than most subjects did the king. Shaphat asked Elisha to sing for them. Obadiah supposed that it must have been customary for him to do so, for the moment the harp sounded the first note he began.

"May God be merciful to us, and bless us, and cause his face to shine upon us, Selah," sang Elisha.

Before he had finished the first line, the melodious words sent chills over Obadiah. He had never heard a singer with a voice so rich, and powerful and clear. Elisha's voice without the accompaniment was the most beautiful music he had ever heard. The two harps and the two flutes enhanced the tones that reverberated from him, but there was something else, something almost tangible about the sound.

Obadiah had read these words of King David once or twice, but they had always seemed to be the words of a poet, not the warrior king of Israel. He knew they were songs, but he had never heard them sung before now. The words seemed to come alive as Elisha sang, causing something to rise up inside of Obadiah. He was so inspired that he wanted to break into song with praises to the Almighty Yahweh.

"Oh Yahweh, you have brought my soul from the grave; you have kept me alive that I should not go down to the pit.

"Sing unto Yahweh, all of his saints, and give thanks at the remembrance of his holiness."

Elisha sang long into the night and would have continued, but they had to rise early to go to Beth-Horon, for the reading of the law.

It seemed that Obadiah had just gotten to sleep when they were all awakened. The mules had been saddled when he and several of his men met with the family of Shaphat outside the gate. It was only a half hour to Beth-Horon, and they arrived as the sky in the east was turning pink with the rising of the sun.

The men of the region sat on the ground in front of a platform where a Levite read from the Book of Joshua. At the end of the reading a priest came to the platform and expounded on certain passages. At noon the men rejoined their wives and children, who had remained on the sides, or to the rear and sat under canopies, out of the sun.

From the grain offerings that came to the priests each week, bread had been baked and was served to everyone present. In the mid-afternoon, the Levitical law concerning the conduct of daily affairs was read. At the end of each law the priest would comment on how, or why, that law should, or could, be implemented, and how in previous generations, the people were punished when the law was ignored. The drought in Israel was mentioned many times as being the result of Baal worship, and failure to adhere to the law.

When evening came, ending the Sabbath, the people were reluctant to leave. Obadiah and Elisha, other members of the family, and some of Obadiah's company sat around a fire. Obadiah was listening to the politics and gossip that circulated when he heard the voices of hundreds of women singing worship songs. He looked towards Elisha, knowing that Elisha would tell him what it meant. Elisha understood and answered, "You will see."

The sound grew louder. Obadiah looked around, into the distant tents and campfires to see a multitude of women running, spinning and dancing as they sang. With each camp they passed, more women joined the throng.

"I will sing unto Yahweh, for he has triumphed gloriously: the horse and rider he has thrown into the sea."

Obadiah recognized the song of Miriam, as the women came dancing by their camp. Elisha shouted over the roar, "Many of the young women would like to catch the attention of a handsome young man. The rest are following the example of Miriam after Moses brought them through the Red Sea."

Throughout the camps harps and flutes began to accompany them. Many of the women carried timbrels. It was a melodious roar.

Elisha seemed a happy man, but Obadiah sensed a subtle pain inside him that had callused over. This wasn't the first time the virgins failed to look in his direction. Obadiah watched Elisha as he clapped his hands and sang along with the roar. He was a remarkable man. Obadiah admired and envied his simple faith and complete dedication to what he believed.

Obadiah had never felt so renewed as he did that night riding back with the words of the song of Miriam running through his mind.

The following morning the fields glistened with dew droplets reflecting the rays of the early morning sun as Obadiah and Elisha rode out to estimate the size of the ungathered wheat harvest. Obadiah couldn't remember the last time he had seen dew. It seemed to add to the bright feeling he was already experiencing.

The following week was spent reaping and threshing wheat. Obadiah returned to Samaria with the first caravan of twenty carts and fifteen camels laden with grain. The transition from Ephraim back into Israel and Samaria had the look and feel of being expelled from the garden of God, into the desert that Israel had become.

The closer they got to the city of Samaria, the more aware Obadiah became of the presence of something very evil. It was only a feeling, but it was something he had felt only vaguely before, almost like coming back into a room with a strong odor that you hadn't noticed until you went out and came back in again.

The atmosphere was still hazy with the blowing dust, and the country-side was virtually barren. There was a part of him that was glad for the drought. It was the famine that accompanied it that had given him a greater understanding of the God he had known as a boy.

Obadiah remembered the beautiful children he had seen that had been marked for death on the altars of Baal and Ashtoreth. It made his heart ache, and the greatest hatred he had ever known gripped him. Obadiah trembled with anger when he thought about the evil that Jezebel had brought to Israel.

The constellation Orion slowly passed through the night heavens as Elijah sat next to the streambed. Sleep eluded him as he pondered the plight of Israel and his own destiny. If he had counted correctly he had been there five hundred and thirty days. The brook was dry except for one small pool containing not much more than a pitcher of water. He prayed and listened for God to speak, but the only thing he heard was the rustle of the willow branches.

As the day was dawning, Elijah stood on a boulder in the middle of the streambed and remembered when water had rushed around both sides of the large stone. He lifted his hands towards heaven and prayed again. "O Mighty Yahweh, holy is your name. You are from everlasting to everlasting. Hear me, your servant. I am here at your direction and the water is gone. What would you have me to do?"

Elijah stood quietly with his hands stretched toward heaven for several minutes and still could hear nothing. The return of the ravens distracted him. They flew by and landed on the rock where they had delivered the bread and meat for more than a year and a half.

Elijah jumped down from the rock and went to prepare a meal, but as he stood by the flat stone looking at the bread and meat, he realized that the stone was shaped like an altar and thought it was strange that he hadn't noticed it until now.

He quickly gathered an armload of wood and laid it neatly on top of the stone. He lit a fire, and when it was blazing hot, he placed the bread and meat in the midst of the flames. "Oh mighty Yahweh, God of my fathers, accept this sacrifice at my hand and hear the prayer of your servant."

He took a pot that contained most of his water supply and held it above his head. "I have no wine or oil, my Lord Yahweh. Accept this water as a drink offering, as you did at the hands of King David." Elijah poured the water out upon the dry ground where the stream once ran.

A chill rushed through Elijah, and he knew that Elohim had heard. For several moments there was a stillness, as if time stood still. Then there was again a slight rustling of the willow leaves as its branches swayed. Yahweh had heard his prayer.

"Arise! Go to Zarephath, which belongs to Zidon, and dwell there. Behold, I have commanded a widow there to sustain you." The voice was as clear as if it had been audible.

Elijah gathered up only what he had arrived there with, as he thought about the voice. He then made his way along the dry stream bed, where the palms and oaks and willow trees were still green. When he moved out away from the stream bed, he found that the land was terribly barren, even worse than Elijah had imagined. A constant wind blew a thin dust across the barren ground.

A half day's travel north, he climbed a ridge and spotted a deserted military outpost. A lookout tower stood at the crest of the ridge, with an abandoned garrison in the valley below.

Elijah descended the steep slope to the compound. He had just stepped through the broken wall into a vacant stable behind the main building when, Bam! a loud thunderous noise startled him. He froze in place as he waited to hear anything that would reveal the source of the sound. A long minute later, Bam! he heard it again. Elijah eased out of the stable and circled the eight-foot clay brick wall. As he came around the front, near the entrance, the large wooden gate to a court blew open, then slammed shut again in the wind, Bam! Elijah breathed a sigh of relief.

Inside the compound he found a deep well that was dry. The pile of dirt by the well told him that whoever had been there had tried digging the well deeper when it ran dry, but it was obvious that their efforts had not been successful. Even the old olive trees by the barracks, whose roots went deep into the earth, were dead.

Suddenly a gust of wind blew a swirling cloud of stinging sand into his face. He pulled the mantle around his head and slipped into one of the buildings.

Elijah stepped back and caught his breath quickly. Lying on a straw bed to one side of the room was a human skeleton.

After standing there for a long minute, he moved closer and studied the remains of what had been a soldier of some rank, based upon the chain mail that rested upon his rib cage and the remains of sandals that lay beneath the bones of his feet. The skeleton's fingers were still wrapped around what looked like a dagger. Elijah thought that he might possibly have been a soldier that had been wounded in battle and was either left behind to die, or perhaps had escaped a lost battle and hidden from his pursuers. Or, this soldier may have simply been traveling alone and been thrown from his mount in this isolated place. Fatally injured, he may have taken refuge here. A thousand things might have brought him here, thought Elijah. Whatever had happened to him, Elijah hoped that he hadn't died alone.

Elijah found the stillness eerie as he moved closer, to see as clearly as the dim light filtering into the room would allow. Outside, the wind wailed a mournful sound as it blew around the end of the building. Elijah knelt to one knee as he studied the remains of this soldier. He would have avoided contact with the dead man at all costs, not wanting to make himself unclean, but it was too late. He had inadvertently stepped into the room before he saw the skeleton, so he was already unclean in the eyes of the Law.

Upon closer examination, he realized that the skeleton was not as ancient as it first appeared. Tell tale signs of the creatures of the desert were evident. The body of this soldier had sustained the insects and rodents of the desert until his skeleton was picked clean. Elijah shuddered at his own thoughts and drew his mantle closer about him.

He reached down, took the dagger by its point, and eased it from among the bones. He stood and turned into the slightly brighter light coming through the open door. The blade was honed very sharp, and the handle was gold with a blue sapphire imbedded in the hilt.

Elijah was uncomfortable standing there in the stillness. Something about this soldier, and his death in this lonely place, troubled his soul. Then, the gate slammed shut again, startling him. He stuck the dagger in his belt, then stepped quickly from the room into the wind, and continued on toward Zarephath.

A few minutes later, the stench of rotting flesh filled the air as he walked around the decaying carcasses of what had been sheep. If the rains began today, it would take years for Israel to recover, he thought. In a half-run, he moved away from the area to find air that he could inhale deeply again.

Elijah cut across the hills, away from any known road, so as not to meet anyone, and found water at the small lake of what had been the Sea of Chinneroth. Traveling along the east shore of the lake by night, he continued up the Jordan River, northward.

He had never been this far north and didn't know at what point to turn west, but he knew that when he did he would be without water. On the morning of the third day he came to another lake. At the north end of the lake were two streams running into the placid waters that filled the basin of what had been a much larger body of water.

Elijah followed the stream that ran from a westerly direction, keeping himself out of sight behind the natural cover along the river. On the opposite side of the shallow stream were many people dipping water from the river, filling barrels on carts. He passed several two-man irrigation wheels that could fill large vessels quickly.

By the end of the day he decided it was time to turn west toward the sea, but he would stay the night by the river. As he left the populated area behind, Elijah found a small secluded pool to bathe himself in. He felt renewed, and was glad to have washed away the feel and the thoughts of the abandoned outpost that was now far behind.

In the morning he drank as much as he could hold and soaked his tunic before continuing. Several hours later he came to a road and saw a lone figure in the distance walking towards him. It was an old man dressed in typical Zidonian apparel. The stranger was kind enough to give Elijah directions and drew a map to Zarephath on the dirt road.

It felt good to talk to another person after being alone for so long. Elijah was disappointed to learn that he was still a day's journey away. He hadn't eaten in four days, and wasn't sure that he could go that much further.

In the light of a nearly full moon, Elijah traveled an empty road, but before daylight the moon disappeared over the western horizon, and he found himself stumbling along in the dark.

He became too weary to go on and sat down to rest, against the bank on the upper side of the road. A few moments later he was asleep. It was light when he was awakened by the lowing of an ox pulling a passing cart. He opened his eyes to find the driver of the cart standing over him, looking down.

"How far to Zarephath?" Elijah asked, as his eyes focused on the driver.

"If you stand up, you can see it just up the road. I thought you might be dead lying there." The man reached down and helped Elijah to his feet.

"No, there is a lot of life left in me yet," Elijah answered, not very convincingly.

"If you are well, I must be on my way."

"Yes, thank you." Elijah started toward Zarephath as the cart headed in the other direction. He took about ten steps and stopped. His body swayed as his head reeled with dizziness. A minute passed before he was able to go on.

Tall green trees lined the road and shaded him from the morning sun as he approached the city. Groves of large ancient oaks extended out from both sides of the road. The city gate lay just ahead, but the need to rest was greater than his ability to continue. Elijah stepped from the road and walked toward a large spreading oak. As he was about to sit down against the tree, he saw a woman farther into the grove gathering small dead branches that had fallen from the trees. As he half fell to the ground, he caught her attention.

The woman looked toward Elijah. This stranger looked as though he might be in need of help. With her arms full of wood, she began to walk toward him as he called to her, "Would you bring me a little water, please?"

Realizing he needed water badly, she stopped for a moment, then turned toward the city gate as she called back, "I'll be only a few minutes."

As the woman was leaving, Elijah called to her again. "Would you have just a small piece of bread that I could eat?"

To keep from shouting, she laid down the bundle of wood and walked over to him. "As the Almighty Elohim lives, all I have is a hand full of meal and a little oil. I'm here gathering some wood to make one small cake for my son and me, then we shall starve to death," she said despondently.

She was very plain in her dress, but was an attractive woman who looked much like Adah might have looked in ten years, he thought. Suddenly, Elijah was aware of how much he must have looked like a poor beggar. His tunic was ragged and he hadn't trimmed his hair in weeks.

He sat up a little straighter and brushed the hair from his face. It took him a moment to find the words to answer. "Don't be afraid. Go and do as you've said, but first make a small cake of bread and bring it to me, then make some for yourself and your son." His voice deepened as his mind was instantly enlightened, and he felt the power of the Spirit of Yahweh rushing through him. The thought flashed through his mind: this is what Samson must have felt the moment before he pulled the posts and gates of the city out of the ground and carried them away on his shoulders.

"Thus says Yahweh Elohim, the El Shaddai of Israel; the barrel of meal shall not diminish, neither shall the cruse of oil run dry until the day Yahweh sends rain upon the land."

She had never heard a prophecy before, but she felt the power of the words. It seemed they were filled with a lightning that ran through her bones. She recognized the voice of God in the words of this wild looking man.

"You're him, you're the one," she stammered a moment, "E, El, Elijah!" There was a long moment as their eyes met. "I'll send Isaac, my son, with some water. Wait here! I'll be back as soon as I can." She turned and walked quickly toward the city gate.

Several minutes later, a boy who looked to be about eleven, carrying a clay bottle, came out of the city and looked around a few moments before he spotted Elijah and began walking briskly toward him. His pace slowed as he came near the prophet. Because of the boy's gaze, Elijah felt self-conscious, again realizing how he must look with the ragged clothes and shaggy hair. He rose to his feet. "You must be Isaac," he said to break the tension.

"Yes sir," Isaac answered slowly, as he handed him the bottle of water. He seemed to be anxious to get away from Elijah. "I have to bring wood so mother can cook," Isaac said, as he was edging away. Elijah knew that Isaac was torn between an obligation to be polite and a desire to escape from him and the awkward situation this posed. Elijah nodded, giving the boy tacit permission to go that relieved him of any responsibility to stay. Isaac turned and trotted away.

Elijah took a long drink from the earthen bottle, savored it for a moment, then took another long drink. As he let the water renew his strength, he looked around and spotted several pieces of wood. Elijah took another drink, then set the bottle by the tree before he stood up and began to gather broken branches.

Isaac quickly found the wood his mother had discarded, gathered it up and started walking toward the city. Looking back over his shoulder, he shouted, "You rest. I'll be back in a few minutes." Elijah gathered a large pile of branches, broke them into a usable size, then sat down to finish the water.

The next thing he knew, the widow was kneeling beside him. "Elijah," she tapped him on the arm, "Elijah," her soft voice interrupted his nap. When he opened his eyes, Isaac was standing at her side. On a cloth in her hand, she held a cake of bread. "Here, eat something."

He took the bread from her hand. "You are a widow," he half-asked, half-stated.

"Yes I am, but how would you know that?" she responded as she set another juglet of water beside him.

"Why did you bring this bread to me? Answer that and you will know how I knew that you are a widow."

"For days, I've had a strange feeling that someone was coming that I was to help, and that somehow Elohim was going to take care of my son and me. One of the last things my husband said to me was that Elohim would take care of me. His words have been going through my mind over and over again, for over a year now, but this morning when I looked into the barrel of meal, I lost hope."

"Was this the last of the meal?" Elijah nodded toward the bread.

"Yes, that was the last," she answered.

"Return to your house and bake two large cakes for you and Isaac, all that you can eat. When I finish eating this, Isaac and I will bring the wood that I've gathered to your house. What is your name?"

"Delah."

"It's a good name." He looked at her son. "So is Isaac. You're Hebrew?"

"Of the tribe of Asher." Delah stood up. "Come along when you're ready." She turned and walked a short distance with them watching her. It surprised them both when she broke into a run and continued through the city gate. Isaac and Elijah looked at one another and smiled.

Elijah broke the bread and offered half to Isaac. "Would you like part of this?"

"No, that's for you," said the boy. To keep from feeling awkward again, Isaac immediately began to look for more wood, as Elijah ate.

A short time later they were standing at the gate of the home of Delah and Isaac. Isaac banged at the door with the wood in his arms. Delah was smiling when she opened the gate. "There is plenty of bread for all of us." Elijah noticed that she had a man's robe in her hands. She had forgotten about the wood until she saw the load in their arms. "Isaac will show you where to put the wood." She followed them to a corner of the court where Isaac dropped the load of wood, followed by Elijah.

"This is for you," said the widow. She handed Elijah the robe when he had finished brushing the dust and chips of bark from his arms and chest. "It belonged to my husband, Azor. I made it for him. It's old, but I've sold everything else." Delah turned to Isaac, "Draw some water from the well, please."

When Isaac had left them she said to Elijah, "You must be more careful. You wouldn't be safe anywhere outside this house."

"Why?"

"Haven't you heard about the talent of gold Ahab has offered to anyone who knows where you are?"

"No, I've not seen another person in more than a year and a half, until yesterday. A talent of gold would make you very rich."

"Yes, it would, but I may be the only person in Israel or Zidon who wouldn't turn you over to King Ethbaal, or Ahab and Jezebel."

"You don't know me. Why would you pass up a chance to be rich for me?"

"I will die before I'll turn you in. You can trust that. Why do you think Elohim sent you here? I have prayed day after day that Elohim would give me another chance. It is his mercy to me that has brought you here.

"Most anyone in Zidon would kill all of us for a talent of gold. We must keep your hair cut close. They are looking for a hairy man, and it would help if you were to keep your beard trimmed close and shaped like the Zidonian men do. There is a room on the roof, there is a bed, and I have already taken water and a blanket up there for you."

"Is there something I could do to repay you?"

"We don't have any money, so I can't hire a teacher for Isaac. You can read, can't you?" asked Delah. "If you would teach him, that would be more than I could have hoped for, but just to be able to feed my son is more than enough payment." In that moment her face lit up. "Praise be to Elohim. When I came back earlier, a miracle happened. There was enough meal for us to have all the bread we could eat tonight." For a moment he saw tears come into her eyes, then she had a moment of doubt and asked, as she wiped them away with her hand, "There will be meal again for tomorrow, won't there?"

Elijah looked into her face, and could feel that she had gone through some terrible anguish. "If I am a prophet of Yahweh, there will be meal again for this evening and tomorrow, but each day leave just a little in the barrel," said the prophet. He looked at the widow. "And, I will teach Isaac to read."

Before the day was over, he had trimmed his hair and beard the way she suggested, and when he came down from the upper chamber that evening, the transformation was more than she could believe. Though Azor's robe was old, it had once been a fine garment, and looked good on Elijah. The three dined together, which wouldn't have been acceptable by the tradition of the elders, but Elijah couldn't think of any law that it violated, and she knew only a little of the law and none of the interpretation or traditions. How many were left in Israel who lived by them anyway, or who was there to be offended? Still, Elijah felt uncomfortable as they ate, and her constant stare in his direction didn't help. To most of the people in the region, Elijah had become a legend, and the stories that had been made up about him made him seem as elusive as the wind.

Isaac had seen how little bread flour had been in the barrel before Elijah arrived. He couldn't bring himself to accept the explanation that a miracle had taken place. Even if it was a miracle, how did it work? "How can Yahweh make something from nothing?" he asked, after spending most of the meal talking about it, trying to believe something his mind could not accept.

"Yahweh does not create something from nothing. When someone is able to accept that Yahweh is the creator of all things, and His words are the substance that all things are made from, then miracles are not so difficult to accept." It was clear to Delah that Elijah was using this example to teach Isaac about Yahweh, and her heart was glad to hear such things discussed in her home again.

Isaac couldn't accept Elijah's explanation, and was the first to look into the barrel of meal each morning, and, throughout the day, whenever he thought about it, he would take a peek at the meal. Sometimes it was nearly empty, and at other times there was enough for the day, but there was never enough for two days.

Except for the meals together, Delah kept to herself, and, though he taught Isaac daily, the boy remained coldly polite as though he were obeying some disagreeable rule. Most of Elijah's time was spent in his small room praying. He felt badly that the wood gathering was left to Isaac. His contribution was the meal that multiplied daily in the barrel, but that was a gift from Yahweh. Over the next few months, all the firewood that could be gathered easily was gone. Elijah then felt that the responsibility fell to him.

At the risk of being discovered, he began to go out for wood a couple of times a week. Accompanied by Isaac, he would leave before daylight so that no one would see him coming out of the home of the widow, Delah. But even after six months Isaac remained very cold to Elijah.

On one of their wood gathering trips, as Elijah was chopping up a small tree, he noticed Isaac carving on a piece of wood that was about two and a half cubits in length, and about the diameter of the boy's wrist.

Elijah decided to rest for a minute and stepped into the shade of the large green tree where they had placed two vessels of water and a bag of bread, and where Isaac sat working. Elijah observed him for several minutes until it became clear that he was attempting to carve a bow. Elijah asked anyway, hoping to start a conversation, "What are you making?"

Sounding as grown up as he could, Isaac answered, "A bow."

Not wanting to offend the boy, Elijah said very gently, "That's the wrong kind of wood for a bow."

Isaac looked up at Elijah. "What's wrong with this wood?"

"It isn't strong enough. It may not break the first time you pull on it, but it will break, and it doesn't have the power that a bow should have."

Angrily, Isaac flung the piece of wood twirling out into the sun. "My father was going to help me make a bow, but they killed him." He sat there seething for a few moments. "All he would have had to do was bow to Baal."

"I could help you make a bow," Elijah offered, trying to soothe his anger and sorry that he had intruded.

"No! I don't want your help. I know who you are and it's your fault." At that moment Isaac swung at a bee that had been buzzing around his head.

There was a minute of silence between them that made the hum coming from a hive within the tree louder than it really was, and very noticeable. Twice Elijah's height, where a broken limb had rotted away from the trunk, Elijah glanced up to see several of the bees floating around the entrance to the hive.

Looking back at Isaac, Elijah thought for a moment, "If Yahweh had told your father to go to the king and tell him that because he and the nation were so wicked, there wouldn't be any rain, would your father have done it?"

Isaac stared at Elijah without answering for several seconds. "Why did he have to die?" he shouted.

"I don't know. No one has ever told me how he died." Elijah relaxed slightly as he asked, "Why don't you tell me?"

"My father died because he wouldn't bow to Baal, and so did all the prophets in Israel, and anyone who wouldn't worship Baal, because of you."

"What about the thousands of children who have died on the altars of Baal and Ashtoreth, children just like you?" Elijah asked.

The boy was defiant. "And maybe that is why we've never had drought like this before. There is as much proof that Baal is a god as there is that Yahweh is a god." Isaac eyes teared as he choked and stammered for a moment with a lump in his throat.

"My father once believed that they were both gods until he went to Judah to build ships. If Yahweh is as great as my father believed he was and he did all those great things, like opening up the sea of Egypt, or making the sun and moon to stand still, why didn't he stop them from killing him?"

"That's a question I can't answer. Yahweh protected Daniel and others, and even you, but possibly where your father was concerned Yahweh could see things in the future that we can't." Elijah knew that answer didn't begin to satisfy Isaac but there wasn't an answer that could. "You will see your father again, I promise you."

"If Baal isn't a god, what difference would it make anyway if you bow down and kiss his image?" asked the boy angrily.

"The people of Zidon and Israel don't just bow down to his image. They burn their children on his altars. If Baal were just a stone or brass image and we bowed to it, that's praise that belongs to Yahweh, but Baal is not just those things. He's a demon, a lord of the demons, like a captain under Satan." Elijah's voice rose with emotion. "Yahweh has given life to all of us, and everything necessary for a good life, but the people of Israel and Zidon praise Baal for it. They praise him for the rains. That's why Yahweh hasn't given us rain. Does that make sense?"

Isaac thought about what Elijah said for a minute then answered, "I've heard people talk who have seen his priests do great magical things. How do you explain that? My uncle worships Baal, and he saw a priest walk into a fire higher than a man's head and stand there. When he came out his clothes weren't even burned." Isaac looked defiant as though there could be no argument greater than that.

"No one said that they don't have power. You remember the story of Moses?" Isaac slowly nodded his head yes, and Elijah continued. "Every miracle that Moses did, the magicians of Egypt were able to do, until Yahweh turned the dust of the earth into lice. When Moses cast down his staff, it turned into a viper. The magicians cast down two staffs that turned into vipers. Do you know what happened?"

It was obvious that Isaac knew the answer, but he looked down without saying anything.

Elijah added, "I know how to make and shoot a bow." Isaac looked up at Elijah, but still didn't speak. Elijah smiled, "I'm very good with a bow, at least I used to be."

"You could help me to find a good piece of wood, but you haven't convinced me that Elohim is more of a god than Baal."

"I can't prove it to you with just words, so I'll pray that Yahweh proves to you that He alone is God. Will that be good enough?"

Isaac didn't want it to appear that he was softening and just nodded.

"You must be getting hungry?" Elijah asked, but again didn't get an answer. He took the two vessels of water and emptied what remained in one into the other, then placed the attached strap around his neck. He found an untrimmed pole that he had cut and leaned against the tree earlier, catching the trunk in a fork at the top. The uncut branches made a stable ladder that he carefully eased upward on. Isaac was puzzled and a little amazed at Elijah's strange actions. His eyes widened as he watched Elijah slowly put his right hand into the beehive.

Isaac was afraid to move as hundreds of bees swarmed around Elijah, many of them landing on him. Several came near Isaac and one landed on his arm. Isaac's heart pounded as he tried in vain to slow his breathing to hide any movement. It seemed much longer, but the bee was there for only a few seconds. Elijah's hand reached back into the hive again and again, filling the vase with honey-comb and honey. Amidst the buzz of the bees Isaac could hear what sounded like a hum coming from Elijah.

The bees continued to crawl over Elijah as he lowered himself a step at a time by way of the uneven branches. At the bottom he stood still for several minutes, waiting for the bees to go back to their business of making honey. When there were only a few left buzzing around, he moved over to the stone Isaac had been sitting on, took a seat and opened the linen bag that contained their bread. "It's been a long time since I've eaten anything as sweet as honey," he said to tempt Isaac. He broke a piece of a loaf, held the vessel up and waited as the honey oozed onto the bread in front of Isaac's view. "Sit down and eat some honey with your bread."

"We could have been stung to death," Isaac said, even though he didn't really believe it.

"I've done that many times since I was a boy and have never been stung yet," responded Elijah, between bites.

Isaac sat down next to Elijah and began to eat the bread and honey. He couldn't remember anything that tasted so good. They sat in silence, eating, until Isaac was too full to be comfortable, then he asked, "How do you do that?"

"All the animals of the earth were put here for God and man. When we approach them as God's stewards, they respond to us as they would to the Almighty. I've found that when I sing the praises of Yahweh where they can hear, and move slowly, so they know I'm not going to harm them, they don't mind sharing with me the good things God has given to them." Elijah put away what was left, and took a drink of water. "Let's go find some wood for a bow," Elijah said, as he started out from under the shade of the tree. Isaac reluctantly followed and lagged behind for the first half a mile, before he slowly caught up.

It took most of the afternoon to find the perfect piece of wood for Isaac's bow. It was after dark when they came in dragging several fire logs by a rope that Elijah had fashioned into a harness, which they both wore over their shoulders.

The following morning they returned for more wood and, to keep Elijah from being seen, didn't arrive back at Delah's until after dark. They never mentioned to her that a large portion of the day had been spent working on Isaac's bow. The next day Elijah, wearing only breech pants, chopped the tree trunks into pieces small enough to fit into the oven. Isaac sat nearby shaving the most minute strands of wood from between marks that Elijah had made on the bow. Afraid of over trimming it even by a hair's breadth, he would interrupt Elijah to inspect the bow at about half hour intervals. He was amazed at how much it looked like the bows of the archers in the army of King Ethbaal. "This is a real bow," Isaac said, as though he just realized they were creating a weapon.

Elijah's fingers slowly stroked the surface of the bow searching for any irregularity. "Tomorrow we'll have to sift some fine sand for polishing."

Delah stepped from the house into the court. Looking at Isaac she said, "Didn't you ask if you could go see your friends today?"

Isaac looked to Elijah. "Would it be all right? I'll gather up the wood when I get back. I haven't seen them since...." His voice fell off sharply without finishing the sentence.

Elijah answered quickly before Isaac had time to dwell on the thought. "We can finish this tomorrow. Go see your friends."

Isaac stood the bow in the corner of the court. "I won't show them the bow until it's finished."

Delah walked Isaac to the gate, "Remember, don't tell anyone that Elijah is staying with us. We might all die if you do." She bolted the gate behind him and came back to where Elijah was preparing to chop again. "That's the first time he's been outside that gate by himself since Azor was killed." She paused, "He's beginning to like you. He would never leave me alone before, or even alone with you."

Suddenly Elijah realized they were alone and put on the old tunic that he had been using for work. "He said something about all the prophets and worshipers of Elohim being killed because of me. Can you tell me about that?"

"Didn't you know?" she asked, as though it were impossible for anyone not to know.

"No, I told you that I didn't see another person for more than a year and a half. Five hundred and thirty-five days, to be exact."

"Ahab and Jezebel blamed the drought on the prophets of Elohim at first, then on all the worshipers of God. Whoever wouldn't bow to Baal and kiss his image was put to death. Thousands died. Some were burned alive, some on the altars of Baal, but most were killed by the sword. Azor was beheaded right over there." Tears welled in her eyes as she nodded toward the center of the court twenty feet away, between them and the gate. "Jezebel convinced her father, King Ethbaal, that Zidon had to be freed from the heresy of Yahweh worship before Baal would send the rain. The drought has been as devastating here as it has in Israel. Before Jezebel poisoned the king's mind, we were free to worship any god. Now we must worship Baal and bow to him."

"Why didn't they kill you?" A moment later the sorrow on her face made him regret asking the question. "Forgive me," he added.

Her voice cracked with pain. "I bowed to Baal and kissed his image. I would have done anything to save Azor. What hurts the worst is that I betrayed him. He pleaded with me not to do it." Through tears she looked at Elijah, then broke into sobs and rushed into the house.

"Elijah! Elijah!" Delah's voice shattered the stillness just before daylight. The penetrating cry pierced the door, followed an instant later by a sharp rapping. Startled from his sleep, Elijah wrapped himself in a blanket as he fumbled through the dark toward the door. By the panic in her voice he knew something was terribly wrong.

He reached to take hold of the bolt and his hand met hers. She had reached through the hole in the door to open it for herself. The moment they touched she clasped his wrist tightly and he felt the urgency she was feeling. "Delah," he spoke her name softly as she released him so the door could be opened.

"It's Isaac. Hurry down." She turned and started back to the steps. "And bring the power of Yahweh Elohim with you." She was barely visible for an instant in the darkness, then disappeared down the steps.

He quickly slid into Azor's old robe and entered the house less than a minute behind her. She was kneeling by Isaac's bed in the dim light of a single lamp. With a wet cloth she wiped the beads of sweat from the boy's face. He was laboring for each breath and rolled his head slowly from side to side. Next to Isaac lay the unfinished bow. Elijah stood behind Delah, watching, hoping that Yahweh would somehow show him something. There had to be a reason, a cause, but he couldn't determine either. "What has happened to him?" he asked softly.

"When he went to bed last night, he said he wasn't feeling well. I thought he must have played too hard with his friends, his first time out in a year. He called for me in the middle of the night." Delah clasped Isaac's right hand in hers and held it to her cheek. "He can't hear me when I talk to him now. He's gotten much worse in the last few hours." Her voice cracked as she held back the tears. She turned and looked up at Elijah. He dropped to one knee as she began to speak just above a whisper. "I've never seen anyone this sick that lived. Please, intercede with Yahweh for him." She reached and took hold of Elijah's arm with one hand as she continued to hold Isaac's hand in the other. Looking deep into his eyes she pleaded, "Please," as though he held some supernatural power to heal her son.

"The Almighty Yahweh is merciful, he will have compassion on Isaac." Elijah hoped that what he had said was true as he stood and watched a few moments longer. Not knowing what else to do he returned to the roof to pray. He was standing there with his hands raised toward heaven when the dim glow of the sun began to silhouette the mountains to the east. A pleasant breeze wafted in from the ocean, carrying the smell of salt water. It didn't seem right that things could be this serene with a young boy so sick. But that's the way life was. No matter what happened to men, the sun would dawn again and the tides would rise and fall. And, if everyone were to die, the wind would continue to blow in from the sea.

"Great Yahweh, this young boy is sick and needs for you to reach down from your throne and heal him with your touch." As Elijah stood there he pulled from his memory every passage of the scriptures that could help him find grounds to call on God for help. In the wilderness the Israelites were healed of poisonous snakebites. Miriam was healed of leprosy but Yahweh also inflicted her with the disease. He felt helpless. How desperately he needed Yahweh. What could he do to move God?

Elijah returned to Delah and Isaac to find that she hadn't moved from his side in the past two hours. As he watched he felt his own heart ache with hers. Isaac looked to be worse. He seemed to be laboring harder for each breath. "He needs strength so his body can fight this sickness." She turned slowly and looked up at Elijah, the first time she acknowledged him since he had returned.

A mixture of warm water and honey, or honey and wine, were remedies his family had used for many sicknesses. He didn't have wine but he knew where he could find honey. He left the room, placing a black kaffiyeh that had belonged to Azor upon his head. He hurried across the court and out the gate. When he was out of sight of Zarephath, he tucked the bottom of his robe into his belt and began to run. His stride stretched out and he settled into a steady pace as his feet pounded the dry earth.

He returned to Delah's house before midday with a juglet filled with honey from the tree that he and Issac had found earlier. He eased quietly into the house as Delah was pouring water into a cup.

"For Isaac?" he asked, inquiring about the cup in her hand.

"Yes," she answered solemnly.

"With that fever he needs plenty of water. Stir just a little of this honey into it for strength." Elijah forced a half smile as he handed the juglet to her. She took the vessel from him but didn't respond beyond that and didn't allow their eyes to meet.

While Delah was stirring some of the honey into the cup, Elijah looked in on Isaac and touched his forehead to determine the intensity of the fever. Never had he seen anyone this sick. He reached across Isaac and took the unfinished bow from beside him.

He exited the house into the court, built a fire in the bread oven and began to mix meal into dough. Silently he prayed but couldn't grasp an answer for Isaac's illness or take hold of Yahweh for his healing. Nothing came to him and he was becoming desperate. He let the dough set as the oven heated, and began to polish the bow. Leather against wood with sand as fine as dust between the pieces, he sat on a small stool next to the oven working on the bow, slowly polishing away any small imperfections. Every few minutes he would reach over to feel of the hardened clay mound that formed the oven to determine if sufficient heat to bake bread were stored in its walls. He laid aside the bow and slid a half dozen round dough cakes into the oven.

When the bread was done he took it from the oven and let it begin cooling as he polished on the bow a few minutes longer. Delah stepped from the house and stared at Elijah for a moment.

Disdainfully she scolded, "That's the way you seek Elohim in behalf of Isaac, by playing with a child's toy?"

As he stood he answered, "I have prayed as earnestly for Isaac as I could. I know that he will live. Isn't he any better?"

"No, Elijah, he's dying," she answered as she dropped her head and took a deep breath, trying hard to keep from breaking into sobs.

Elijah picked up one of the loaves and stepped over to her. "You should have something to eat. Isaac will live, I know it." Her red eyes told Elijah of the painful tears she had shed over her son.

"I wish I could believe that, but I will not eat anything until Yahweh heals him." She looked into his eyes. "You are the man who stopped the rain. Isn't there something more you could do?" Tears welled up in her eyes as she studied his for some sign of hope. "If Yahweh would take me in his place?" She waited a moment then added, "He wouldn't have me, for I betrayed him."

"Elohim is far more understanding and compassionate than most people know. I don't care what it looks like, Isaac will live." For a moment his words gave her hope, then unbelief stole it away. She laid her head onto his chest and began to cry uncontrollably. There was something comforting about her being that close, but he also felt uncomfortable.

He put his arms around her and held her for a few moments. "You should go back and tend to Isaac." He said as he released his hold on her.

She turned to leave, then looked back. "Please continue to pray." He nodded, then watched her until she disappeared into the house.

He didn't understand. Why was this happening? What was wrong? Why hadn't Elohim answered? He stood there trying to sort through the situation when he heard a heart-wrenching cry that came through the doorway of the house. "Yahweh has taken Isaac. No! Please, no!" Delah's cry pierced his heart with her pain. He started towards the door when Delah stepped through it with Isaac's lifeless body draped over her arms. Nearly hysterical with anguish, she stumbled forward. "Why have you come to me, prophet of El Shaddai? Did you come to make me pay for my sins with the life of my son?"

She began to collapse to the ground with shrieks of pain when Elijah caught her and Isaac. "No, Yahweh, no, please! Take my life and let him live." She screamed and kept screaming, "Take my life and not Isaac."

He lowered her slowly to the ground and took hold of Isaac. "Give him to me." She clung to her son as Elijah tried to lift him out of her arms.

"Please don't take him away from me, please." Each cry was like a knife piercing his heart. He couldn't hold back the tears.

With his vision blurred, he tried to look into her eyes. Holding Isaac with his right arm, he stroked her brow with his free hand. "Let me take him." He tried to remain calm for her sake, but his voice cracked as he tried to hold back his own sobs.

Crushed with unbearable grief, she released her hold on Isaac and slumped to the ground, sobbing and wishing that she too could die.

Elijah carried Isaac across the court and up the steps to his room on the roof. He laid him upon his own bed, then lifted his hands toward heaven. "O Yahweh, Yahweh, please help. I'm not worthy to speak your name but there isn't any God but you, and only you can create life with a word." Elijah called out through sobs and tears of his own. Through the open windows of his room his voice could be heard far out into the city and sent a sharp chill through everyone who heard him. Everywhere people stopped and looked around or towards the heavens. Delah, still lying on the stone court, quivered as the name of Yahweh, called with such a pleading powerful voice, reached deep into her soul.

Elijah's voice softened so that only someone present could have heard what he had to say. "Have you brought more suffering upon this widow who has sheltered me, by taking the life of her son?"

If there were some way to trade his life for Isaac's or to impart the life from his own spirit into Isaac? If the Glory that rested upon Moses rested on me, he thought. "How do I get there? I need to be there now, now, now." Elijah wrestled with himself knowing that he didn't have much time to become what he should have already been. He looked at the palms of his hands and studied them for a few moments. "Help me Yahweh, help me." He turned to the lifeless body of Isaac and stretched the boy's arms out and pressed his palms against Isaac's and held them there for several moments. He lifted his hands heavenward as he prayed, "Yahweh, let my hands be your hands. Let your Spirit come upon me."

He lay down upon Isaac and pressed the palms of his hands upon the boy's hands. "O Yahweh Elohim, let his life return into him." Elijah waited a minute, but nothing happened. He got up and paced around the room. There was power with Yahweh to create life and there was power to restore life, but how could he move Yahweh to meet him? There had to be a way. Elijah was more desperate than ever. He felt that time was running out. Was there some way to transfer life from himself to Isaac? Whatever was going to happen had to happen quickly. Again he stretched his body upon Isaac's, pressing his palms against the boy's. Nothing happened. Then it entered his mind that "Elohim breathed the breath of life into Adam." Elijah blew his breath into Isaac's face. "Yahweh El Shaddai, please send life back into this child. Have mercy on his mother who has suffered so much."

Elijah couldn't give up, he couldn't let the boy go. He searched for the words that would move God. "Great El Shaddai, would you have his mother believe that you are a God that would take her son to punish her? The demon Baal delights in taking the lives of children but you, Yahweh, are the giver of life."

It wasn't like Yahweh to take life except in judgment, and Elijah knew that wasn't the case with this boy. He stood by the bed and reached upward toward heaven again and again tears streamed down his face. "O Yahweh, have mercy upon this widow and her son," he cried. For a few moments he stood there with his arms stretched toward God, then looking down at Isaac, he stroked his head. His body had grown cool and was becoming stiff. Elijah covered him with a blanket then placed a robe over that. "Because he is merciful, Yahweh will answer me," Elijah said out loud.

He laid down upon Isaac's body a third time and pressed his hands firmly against Isaac's. "O Yahweh, my God, let this child's life return to him again!" Elijah rested his left cheek against Isaac's. A couple of long minutes slowly passed.

Then as clearly as if someone had spoken directly into his ear the words came into Elijah's mind, "I have heard and I have answered." Chills ran over Elijah's body.

The next instant Isaac jerked his face away from Elijah's scratchy beard, startling Elijah. He could feel life surging back into Isaac. It was a strange sensation. The boy's heart began to pound hard and his body shuddered beneath Elijah, who raised up to look into Isaac's face. Again his body shuddered and this time his eyes opened but they were rolled back into his head. Elijah could feel warmth emanating from the boy's body. Isaac's eyes closed then opened slowly. Elijah could see that they were trying to focus into his own. The pupils dilated and retracted several times then stared coldly into Elijah's. After a few moments they settled into a natural gaze.

"Elijah, it's you." Isaac spoke softly, then slowly glanced around the room. Turning back to see Elijah again, he said, "There is only one God and he sent me back to comfort my mother and tell her that her sins are forgotten. Your prayers were heard, Elijah."

Elijah wrapped his arms around Isaac and held him tightly as his heart broke. "Thank you my God. Yahweh, thank you." Tears streamed from Elijah, some of them dripping onto Isaac who turned to avoid them. Elijah sensed his discomfort and raised up. "I didn't mean to get you wet," he chuckled through his weeping. "We must get you to your mother. How do you feel?"

Isaac thought for a moment. "Different, something is different."

Elijah stood and helped Isaac to his feet. He couldn't stand without teetering. "I think it may be a little while before you'll be able to walk. I'll have to carry you, do you mind?"

Isaac quickly answered, "No, I must see my mother."

Elijah stooped down and put Isaac over his shoulders like a sack of grain. "This is how you're going this time."

"No! Elijah, this hurts!" Isaac cried in vain.

"You'll live till we get downstairs."

Delah was lying in the court where Elijah had left her. Exhausted from wailing for so long, she still sobbed quietly and didn't hear them descending the stairs. Suddenly she was aware of a presence she instantly knew to be Yahweh El Shaddai. "Yahweh," she said as a peace rushed over her and in that instant she knew that God wasn't holding her sins against her.

She raised her face from the stone floor to see Elijah and Isaac coming toward her. The presence of Yahweh and the joy of seeing Isaac alive overwhelmed her. She began to cry anew but this time they were joyous tears. She stood and ran to meet them as they crossed the court.

"Bless the name of Shaddai Elohim, who has been so merciful to me!" she shouted through her tears as she reached to take Isaac from Elijah's shoulder.

"He hasn't regained his strength yet," Elijah said as he slid Isaac from his shoulder into Delah's arms. "I told you that your son would live."

Elijah was amazed at how easily she carried Isaac as she danced around and around, crying and laughing at the same time. She stopped momentarily and looked back at Elijah who was standing there watching as tears streamed down his face. "Elijah, you are a prophet of Yahweh Elohim and his word lives in you."

His mind flashed back for an instant to the first time he had heard a statement like that coming from a woman. A memory he would never forget. The first time he met Adah. He touched the side of his face remembering the feel of her touch.

Delah began to dance again until she saw the strange look on Elijah's face. "Elijah, what's wrong?" she stopped in her tracks.

"Nothing. This is a great and wondrous day." He smiled back at her and began to dance with them as he sang, "Great is the power of Yahweh Shaddai Elohim and great is his mercy. If all men could know him all men would praise him."

In a few minutes Isaac interrupted Delah, "Mother, put me down, please, I can walk." Elijah stopped to watch as Delah cautiously lowered Isaac to his feet. Isaac took several steps. "See I'm fine. Could I have some of the bread by the oven there?"

"Yes, let's eat," Delah answered then looked at Elijah. "Could we have the honey with bread tonight?"

"Yes, let's have honey and bread," he replied.

They sat on mats in the court and ate as the sun went down. None of them had ever been more thankful to be alive than they were that evening.

In the months that followed Elijah and Isaac were inseparable. Elijah taught Isaac the Law of Moses and to read as well as a scribe. They gathered wood and practiced with the bow.

Every night Elijah would lie on his bed unable to sleep for pondering and reliving the moment Elohim sent Isaac's life back into him, the events that led up to that point and the things that Isaac had to tell when he returned. Sometimes the thoughts would bring tears of gratitude for Yahweh's mercy. There must be a way to consistently receive answers, even answers like that great miracle, he questioned. Sometimes the searching would continue until it was time to rise.

Isaac had become accurate with the bow, to the point that he could hit anything he aimed at from the width of the thirty-two cubit court. He had paced it off, trying to stretch it as much as any twelve year old boy would for the sake of boasting, but even Elijah was impressed. After his studies one afternoon Isaac took out the bow as Elijah started up the stairs to his room to pray. Something was stirring in his spirit. He was beginning to feel that the time for Israel's judgment to end was drawing near. If his count was correct, this was the twelve hundred and fortieth day since he had prophesied to Ahab.

"Elijah," Isaac called to him before he had reached the top of the stairs. "Why don't we go hunting?"

"What would we hunt?" Elijah answered, calling down to Isaac.

"We could hunt deer."

"The deer are wise, they've gone north to the mountains." A moment later Elijah added, "To hunt deer you need iron tips for the arrows, not just a sharp stick." Elijah could remember the kind of desires that filled a boy's heart. He thought for a moment then asked, "Do you know of a place in the ocean where fish can be seen in the water?"

"There is a place where my father and I would catch fish with a net. There is a rock near there where you can look down and see fish. We couldn't cast a net there; it was too rough and deep."

"If we could find some river reeds I can make arrow points for shooting fish. It's not like hunting deer but right now it might be all that we can do."

"My father's net, we still have it," excitedly, Isaac nearly shouted. He laid the bow down and ran into the house. Elijah turned and started back down the steps when Isaac reappeared carrying the net. "It's torn in a couple of places but it can be mended."

Isaac met Elijah as he reached the bottom of the steps. Elijah took it from his hands and spread the round net out upon the ground and began to examine the tears. "It won't take much to mend this," Elijah said as he looked up at Isaac. "Do you want to fish with the net?"

"Sometimes you can't see the fish from the rock. If they're not there we can fish with the net and if they are you can use the net and I'll use the bow." He hesitated then added, "If it's all right with you?" He looked at Elijah for approval.

"I can fix the net but it's been so dry maybe we can't find any reeds."

"I know where there used to be a wadi and there were more reeds than stars."

"It hasn't rained for more than three years. Do you think there will still be reeds there?" Elijah answered so that Isaac wouldn't get his hopes too high.

"We can see and it isn't that far."

"Tomorrow we'll go, we'll leave before daylight."

"We must be away from the city long before light. I don't want them to find you, ever."

The ground was dry where there had once been a pond and marsh. Some of the reeds had not been dead long and were still useable. Along the edge of what had once been the marsh were many small dead trees, straight and cured dry. Perfect for arrow shafts. They returned with enough good reed wood and arrow shafts to make all the arrows they would need. Elijah carved arrow tips from the reeds. They became very hard when they were held over a fire until they were nearly black. Each tip was several inches long and barbed to keep its prey from escaping. By the time the net was mended, three days had passed.

Delah accompanied them on the two-hour walk to the stretch of ocean where Azor used to bring Isaac to fish. They arrived before daylight and built a fire. The rock that Isaac had told Elijah about came straight up out of the ocean about ten cubits. From the shore side the rock broke off in such a way that made it easy to climb, with broken ledges, none more than waist high. Before it was light enough to see beneath the ocean's surface, Isaac was on the top of the rock trying to look into the dark emerald water.

The place was secluded. Cliffs jutted out into the water at both ends of a sandy beach and behind them the cliffs rose vertically from the sand.

Elijah waded into the surf chest deep and began casting the net. In a short while he had caught a dozen fish large enough to roast over the fire but too small for boasting.

"Isaac," Delah called when the fish were done, a couple of hours after daylight. She stood and watched Isaac maneuver down from his craggy perch. Elijah was wading back to shore as Isaac reached his mother who had taken a seat by the fire. "Haven't you seen any fish yet?" she asked Isaac as he dropped to both knees at her side.

"I think I might have seen some earlier but I couldn't be sure," he answered as he reached for one of the fish at the end of a stick over the fire. "May I take this back with me?"

"Don't forget to give thanks."

She had barely gotten the words out of her mouth and Isaac was running back toward the rock. "I won't," he called back.

Isaac had been gone just a few seconds when Elijah came shivering up to the fire. The white britches he wore had belonged to Azor. They were heavy with water and dripped with every step. He pulled his robe around his wet body and sat as close to the fire as he could get.

"Eat some, it will help warm you," Delah said as she pulled the stick with the largest fish out of the sand and handed it to Elijah. "You've been in the water too long."

She stood and took the blanket she was sitting on and wrapped it around his shoulders. As she sat back down Elijah looked over at her. The moment their eyes met she looked out to sea, afraid of revealing what she was feeling for him. In that instant she spotted a ship and was able to change the subject before Elijah had a chance to think about her obvious attempt at keeping their eyes from meeting. "Those are like the ships Azor helped to build."

A moment later, she added with pride, "They are the swiftest ships in the world." When she looked back at him their eyes did meet for an instant. She turned back to the ship. After a long moment she began to examine the fish still roasting, and without looking at Elijah said, "Thank you for allowing me to come here with you and Isaac. I've not been away from Zarephath in more than two years. I know if I were not here you wouldn't be wearing those heavy wet britches."

She looked away from Elijah and grimaced. How could she have said that without realizing how it might have sounded? She wished that she could have taken it back but knew that anything she could say in her defense would just make things worse. "I'm going to take another fish to Isaac," she said as she pulled a stick from the sand. Briskly walking toward Isaac, she sighed, relieved to be out of Elijah's presence.

Elijah knew what she had done, and what she was feeling, and smiled to himself. He had been sensing that his time with them would soon be coming to an end. He knew that his course was set, and no matter what he felt for them, he couldn't let it deter him.

"Elijah," her voice broke into his thoughts. He turned to see her approaching from behind. She hadn't had time to reach Isaac and still held the fish in her hand. "Isaac wants you to look, I think he has spotted something." When Isaac was sure they were both watching he aimed down from the rock into the sea. It was several seconds before he released the arrow then he stared down into the water for a moment. He quickly climbed down from the rock and plunged into the surf. A minute later Isaac was running toward them awkwardly carrying a fish as long as his arm. He slowed to a fast walk as he came near. The smile on his face told them of the great feeling of accomplishment he had inside.

"Can I have the knife?" Isaac asked. Delah handed him the knife, knowing for what reason he was asking. He headed for the encroaching waves and returned a short time later with a fish ready for skewering. The three sat by the fire as Isaac's fish roasted. By early afternoon Isaac was ready to try for another one. He waited atop the craggy monument until it was nearly dark but he never saw another fish. Elijah netted a few more small ones that were cooking as night approached.

There had been only light conversation since Delah embarrassed herself early in the day and for the past half-hour Elijah had been humming a low melody. "What is that song?" Delah asked. "It sends chills up my back."

Elijah stopped to think because he hadn't realized that he had been singing or humming at all. With a querying look on his face he thought for a moment. "It's a song I haven't remembered for years." At that moment Isaac came walking up next to the fire and stood there but didn't speak. He felt something, a presence he remembered from when he left his body. Elijah began to hum again, then said "The Spirit of Elohim sent it to me just for you. It is one of King David's. The words are something like this, 'Judge not your servant: for in your sight shall no man living be justified'."

"Why would that be for me?" Delah sounded fearful as though she thought Yahweh was about to pronounce judgment upon her.

Elijah knew what went through her mind and answered, "No!" shaking his head then added, "David broke many commandments but he found forgiveness when the law said he should die. By the Spirit of El Shaddai he went through time and took hold of an atonement that is yet to come. This is what God wants you to know."

The presence of Elohim could be felt by the three of them and in those minutes everything seemed so very clear and easily grasped. The material things of earth were insignificant as the supernatural things at that moment seemed tangible.

"I will worship and serve you, Oh Yahweh." Elijah couldn't contain the feeling and burst into singing as he stood to his feet and began to dance. Isaac followed him first then Delah, dancing around the fire. Each sang a different song that came to them a line at a time, but it blended so perfectly that they were all amazed.

"El Shaddai is the strength of my life and has become the song that I sing," was the first line of Delah's song.

Isaac sang, "The angels of Elohim surround those who know him. El guides the arrows of the righteous and with the shield of Shaddai defends them."

The time that elapsed would never be known. It seemed like only a few minutes and then, as suddenly as it had begun, Yahweh's presence was gone and the three fell to the sandy ground, exhausted. They lay there laughing until Delah stopped and solemnly sat up. Elijah and Isaac looked at her. "You are going to be leaving." Elijah had been feeling it for some time but didn't know when and didn't answer her.

Delah stood and began to gather the things they had brought with them. It was a quiet walk back to Zarephath. Delah walked ahead of them and hardly spoke, though Isaac asked several times if it were true. "It may be," Elijah answered him the third time. The full moon was two thirds of its path through the heavens by the time they were home.

Elijah fell asleep quickly then was suddenly awake. "Go show yourself to Ahab, and I will send rain upon the earth." It was clear, it was direct, and Elijah had no doubt that it was the voice of God. The previous day was one that Elijah would cherish but knew he would probably never have another like it. He didn't sleep after that and before the sun appeared, slowly he opened the door to his small room for the last time. His things were in a sack that he carried as he quietly eased down the stairs. Before he reached the gate he heard Delah's footsteps behind him. "I was afraid you might leave before I had a chance to give this to you." Delah handed Elijah a skillfully woven mantle that appeared blue in the dim light. "I made it for you. You don't deserve to have to wear clothes that belonged to someone else or that are worn out." She slid the strap of a half-filled goat skin water bag onto his shoulder and put a linen sack with eight loaves of bread into his hand. "You'll need this." With a light embrace she placed her head on his chest. "I'll never forget you; neither will Isaac."

He could feel his heart breaking as silent tears began to stream down his face. "Watch for the rain." The lump in his throat kept him from saying anything more for several seconds. "And I'll never forget you." He was able to get it out without his voice cracking. Delah turned and ran to the house. She stopped in the doorway and watched Elijah pass through the court gate.

Elijah traveled a well-worn trail along the seacoast southward, unable to keep his mind on his purpose. His thoughts kept drifting back over the past two years with Delah and Isaac and wondered if he would ever have a wife and son. He wondered where Adah was and what she might be doing and if she ever thought of him.

Around midday he left the path to rest under the shade of a tree that looked out over the great sea. He sat there for a short time studying the mantle, woven in three shades of blue, and marveled at how expertly it was done, and wondered how she had kept it hidden from him. It was the finest garment he had ever owned. He glanced out at the horizon and the haze on the sea that separated the water from the blue heavens and ran his hand over the mantle as though it was a pet. It was as fine as a king's robe and would be excellent for his meeting with Ahab.

Elijah stayed east of the city of Tyre and avoided all contact with people. On the third day he came to a harbor where a dozen small fishing boats were moored. The fishermen were mending their nets and he passed without being noticed. Crossing a dry riverbed that, before the drought, had fed into the harbor, he followed it southward along a range of mountains on his right. The cliffs and canyons that he passed held a stark silent beauty that Elijah found irresistible. "O, Yahweh, what is it that is drawing me to these mountains?" He prayed as he made his way up one of the narrow canyons, stopping to survey the beauty and listen to his inner being every few minutes.

He slowly worked his way over the rough terrain of large boulders and limestone outcroppings. The face of the cliff on his left looked damp which seemed impossible after three and a half years of drought. He climbed to where he could touch the rock with his hand; it was wet. He moved on up the canyon searching for a way to get up the cliff. There was a natural ledge that turned back and sloped upwards making an easy path that the wild goats had used so long that their hooves had worn into the limestone. Near the top of the cliff water bled from the mountain into a pool about two cubits across and a hand's breadth deep then spilled over onto the small path and on down the face of the cliff. "Is this why I've come to this place?" Elijah said to himself as he knelt and drank then filled the water skin.

He stood there for several minutes and surveyed the terrain. From his vantage point on the cliff he saw what looked like the entrance to a small cave on the opposite wall of the canyon, but maybe it was only a shadow. He climbed down and made his way over to the western wall and found that it was indeed the entrance to a cave. He stooped down and squeezed through the narrow opening into a small passageway. About thirty cubits into the cave it opened up into a large cavern. He couldn't tell how large the room was until he had made a torch and returned. He stood there amazed when the light from the torch wouldn't carry across the room to illuminate the far wall. The floor sloped down then leveled out. "A narrow entrance that could easily be concealed and room enough to hide an army," he thought as he crept along watching the shadows dance to the flicker of the diminishing torch. By the dying flame he found his way out of the cave and camped by its entrance.

The following morning he found that the mountain sloped more gradually toward the summit above the cliffs. He walked along the top of the cliff until he came to an overlook about a hundred and fifty cubits above a broad valley. After admiring the vista before him he continued on to the top then followed the ridge eastward toward Samaria. He came to a pile of twelve large stones, each half the size of an ox. It had been an altar that had been built to Yahweh and probably torn down by the worshipers of Baal.

From there he could look out over the great sea and to the south he saw a brown haze of dust that hung over the land. To the east he saw the mount of Jezreel where the palace of Jezebel stood. He thought about the evil that Omri and Ahab and Jezebel had forced upon the land and the thousands of children that had died on the altars of Baal and became angry. He stretched out his hands toward Jezreel. His voice deepened as he began to call out. "Great El Shaddai." His words echoed between the canyons, "Bind the powers of darkness that enslave this land that you gave to Abraham and his children forever. Bind the demons of Baal and Ashtoreth and Moloch and have no mercy on their priests."

Jezebel was seated next to her daughter, Athaliah, at the moment Elijah prayed. Both were having their faces painted by the eunuchs. Jezebel's eyes widened. She sat very tense for a moment, looking into the face of the eunuch. Her gaze sent a chill of fear through him. He began to back away when she stood and pushed him to the side. "Summon Zohelethbal, the priest," she ordered as she took a step forward, but her strength seemed to melt away as she slowly knelt with weakness and trembling. "O great Baal, renew my strength," she pleaded. Her voice quivered as she spoke.

Athaliah rushed to her mother's side and laid her hand on Jezebel's head. "O, Mother, Baal will help you."

Eunuchs and maids rushed to her aid while others went to summon the physicians and Zohelethbal. A young strong guard pushed those around her aside and helped Jezebel to her feet. With urgency she exclaimed, "It's Elijah, he's near. Help me to my bed and bring Zohelethbal to me."

After several minutes Elijah lowered his hands and continued toward his destiny. Traveling along the ridge southeastward, he came to a grove and altar that sat at the peak of one of the highest summits on the ridge. He stood by the altar for several minutes, wondering if the bloodstains down the sides were animal or the blood of children. It was an altar of Baal. After several minutes he continued on, down toward the plain of Megiddo.

Jezebel ordered a search of the city but found nothing. She felt his nearness and the next day it grew stronger.

The farms along the way lay desolate and barren. Most of the inhabitants had moved to the coast, or near the Jordan River. The river had been kept alive by the rain and melting snows from Mount Hermon but was now only a third its normal size. Many Israelites had gone to Judah or some other country seeking relief from the drought. From what he saw he knew that Ahab had all the more reason to find him. With a bounty of a talent of gold hanging over him, should he dare go to Samaria or anywhere that he might be recognized? If he did get to Samaria, how would he get to Ahab without announcing himself? He began to feel uneasy about walking directly into the king's city and decided to go to Tishbeh to find an ally, someone who would go before him, someone he could trust.

The following day he passed south of the city Jezreel through the valley by the same name. When he came near, Jezebel ordered the city searched a second time and spent most of the day in a tower looking out over her domain, searching as far as her eyes could see in one direction then another, but she never spotted Elijah.

Late in the morning on the sixth day, as Elijah neared the village of Tishbeh, he began to feel something ominous regarding the hamlet he grew up in. Maybe he was just realizing that things there had to have changed greatly. Perhaps they had all fled from Ahab, leaving their homes to be taken over by strangers, or maybe they left because the water had dried up. In that case no one would be there. He wasn't prepared for what he saw as he cleared the last rise from where the entire village should have been seen. Tishbeh was gone.

For several minutes he stood there wondering what could have happened. "How can this be?" He asked himself. "No! Yahweh," he cried out as he dropped the water skin, the bread, and the mantle to the ground.

Elijah had never felt such anger before, so intense that he could have killed with his bare hands. "It is that cursed witch and Baal worshiper, Jezebel, and her puppet king husband!" His eyes teared and he trembled with anger as he picked up his things and walked on. Slowly he wandered through the rubble of what had been the house he built. "Avenge the people of Tishbeh and Israel, El Shaddai." As he ambled through the broken walls and burned timbers of houses on his way to Johanan's, he kept repeating, "Avenge them, avenge them."

He sat on one of the stones by the indentation in the ground, which had been the pool where he and Adah had sat and talked for hours. The trees that once shaded the area had been burned and their charred trunks reached up from the ground three to six cubits. "Elohim, show how mighty you are against this evil. Let Israel see your great power. Bring down the prophets of Baal. Bring them down to the dust of the earth and let none of them go into a grave but let them be as the dung upon the ground." Elijah couldn't have imagined the kind of power he was invoking from God as he prayed.

It was several hours before Elijah could release his anger and motivate himself enough to formulate another plan. He would go to the school of Jehew. Had all the prophets in Israel been killed, as Delah told him they were? If not, he might find where they were. He needed to know what the situation in Israel was truly like.

Elijah pressed on the rest of that day and the following. Night had fallen when he came to the plain beneath the mount where the school stood. He made his way up the hill in the dark. When he reached the plateau he could see just enough to tell that the school had been destroyed and assumed that Jehew and the prophets were dead.

Troubled, Elijah spent most of the night sitting beneath the low-hanging tree on the side of the mountain where he and Jehew had sat and talked many times. A few hours before daybreak he leaned against the trunk of the tree and fell asleep. Just after daylight something, a dream or a sound or a touch, startled him. Pensively he glanced around. There, ten cubits away, was someone stealthily walking away from him. Momentarily he feared that he had been discovered and glanced around to see if the intruder was alone. There didn't seem to be any one else there. "Who are you?" Elijah called.

The man turned and continued to slowly back away as he answered, "I thought you might have been someone I knew." The voice sounded familiar but Elijah couldn't remember from where. He was a young man with a thin reddish-brown beard that didn't cover his face as an older man's might have.

Elijah stood, "I said, who are you?"

"I am of the inhabitants of Judah." The intruder's fear was obvious. Had he recognized Elijah? He kept moving towards a copper colored horse that he had left a short distance away.

If the young man had recognized him, Elijah knew when he reached the horse he would be gone and would tell where he had seen the prophet sought by Ahab. Before the day's end, the hills would be covered with people who coveted the riches of a talent of gold his life would bring them. "I won't harm you," Elijah called to him. He didn't stop and didn't answer but stepped away more quickly. Without considering what he was going to do if he caught him, suddenly Elijah made a dash toward the young stranger.

The sudden bolt caught him off guard. It took a second to turn and dart in the direction of the horse. The man leaped onto the back of the startled, wide-eyed, animal that snorted and shot into a gallop, leaving a broken rein attached to a bush. Before the rider could take a firm hold of the horse's mane, Elijah leaped into the air and slammed into him from the right rear. Both men toppled to the ground and the horse galloped away, leaving behind a cloud of dust. The impact to the ground knocked the horseman unconscious. Elijah turned him onto his back to get a better look at his face. He knew he had seen him before, but where? He put some water on the empty bread bag and gently touched it to the man's brow.

Several minutes later he opened his eyes and looked up at Elijah. "Why did you knock me off of my horse?"

"Why did you run from me?" Elijah answered. "And why didn't you tell me who you are?"

Suddenly a familiar-looking smile began to appear on the young stranger's bearded face. "Elijah! It's me, Zechariah." He raised up and gave Elijah a hardy embrace. "Where have you been these years?"

"Son of my friend Jehew, I am so glad to find you alive." Elijah returned his embrace then helped him to his feet. "Is it true that all the prophets of Yahweh have been put to death?"

"Only those who wouldn't bow to the image of Baal."

"And your father?"

"There are a hundred of the Lord's prophets hidden in a cave somewhere here in Israel. He is among them."

"How did you escape the sword?"

"My father sent me to Tishbeh to warn your brothers, then told me to take my mother and sisters to Judah. This is the first time I've been back in Israel. I've come to find my father. I am an advisor, a prophet to King Jehoshaphat, and he has sent me to bring my father to Judah. Jehoshaphat knew of my father's prophecy to King Baasha and wants him as an advisor. King Jehoshaphat is wise and is surrounding himself with the most faithful of Yahweh's prophets."

Elijah embraced Zechariah again as he said, "Bless Yahweh Elohim who has spared you, my son, and Jehew, the most faithful of his servants." He pushed him back at arm's length. "What a fine man you've grown to be." As Elijah released him he said, "Forgive me for losing your horse. I'll help you find her."

"There isn't anything here in Israel for her to eat and she knows the way back to Judah. She also has the king's mark on her, so I will get her back if she is gone. But, we will make an effort to find her."

For several hours they tracked the horse until it became apparent that she was returning toward home with great speed. They stopped to rest in a wooded area where there were many green trees and even a few hardy palms, which clung to life. As they sat in the shade Zechariah said, "There isn't anywhere that King Ahab hasn't looked for you. Do you know about the talent of gold he has offered to anyone who brings you to him?"

"Yes, I was told about it."

"Come to Judah with me. Jehoshaphat would welcome you. He has sent priests throughout the country to teach the Scriptures to everyone and Judah is prospering."

"Yahweh has sent me to Ahab. He is going to send the rain and prove to Israel that Baal Melkart is not a god."

"How will He prove that?"

"I don't know yet, but it will be shown to me."

"Let me go with you," Zechariah asked. When Elijah hesitated to answer he added, "Let me be your servant. I could learn from you."

"How could I face Jehew if you should get killed because of me?"

"Elijah, I could be killed for just being here in Israel. Jezebel still has anyone put to death that doesn't bow to Baal. She especially enjoys killing El's prophets to appease her demon idol."

Elijah stood. "Come, let's go. The trail of this horse doesn't lead to Samaria."

As Zechariah stood he asked, "What is your plan?"

"To somehow get to King Ahab. Beyond that Yahweh hasn't shown to me what He is going to do, but I know that He is going to require the blood of the children sacrificed on the altars of Baal from Baal's priests."

As they made their way north, Zechariah informed Elijah of all that had happened since Elijah had prophesied this drought to Ahab. Elijah maintained a steady pace and seemed to grow sullen as the day wore on into evening. When they neared the city of Shechem, Zechariah found that Elijah's mind had drifted away and he was talking to only himself. Elijah stopped and stared toward Shechem momentarily. He then left the road on the right down a steep slope. "Elijah!" Zechariah called as he watched him half slide down the embankment. "This isn't the way to Samaria."

Elijah stopped and looked up at Zechariah, about thirty cubits behind. He continued to stare at Zechariah for a long minute, then slowly his eyes changed, coming into focus on his young friend. "Forgive me, Zechariah, I've been in the spirit. Elohim is sending me to the valley of Tirzah. I must be there by early morning."

"It isn't that far. I remember this area. We can be there in two or three hours." Zechariah let that settle then continued; "We haven't eaten today. Are you not hungry?"

"There is no place out here to buy food. Even if there was, I haven't a shekel of iron or brass. Maybe we can find a honey tree when we get to lower ground. I've looked for locusts; there aren't any."

"I have enough silver for both of us. Let me go into Shechem and buy something for us to eat."

Elijah turned and looked east then northeast. "I will meet you just over that ridge," he said as he pointed in the direction he had chosen for them to meet. "Don't be long. I have an appointment with Ahab." Zechariah went on to Shechem as Elijah climbed the next ridge.

Just before dark Zechariah found Elijah sitting next to what had been a small brook at the bottom of a ravine. Facing his direction, Elijah watched him make his way down the steep hillside.

"It's getting ready to happen, I can feel it." Elijah turned his eyes to the streambed as Zechariah came near. "In just a few days this little stream will be overflowing its banks and the prophets can return to their homes. There will be thunder like you've never heard it before." Elijah sprang to his feet. "Glory to Yahweh Elohim! The fire of El Shaddai burns in my soul. I may be consumed by it unless I can release it."

Zechariah could see a fire in his eyes as he shouted with his hands stretched towards heaven. "I said, Glory to El Shaddai!" Elijah's voice echoed through the hills.

Not at the school or among the prophets in Judah had Zechariah seen or felt the fire of the Holy Spirit burn so fervently upon a prophet.

"We can travel for another half hour before it's too dark to see." Elijah, following the streambed, began a rapid walk eastward as Zechariah ran to catch up.

That night they camped and cooked a roast of lamb, ate figs and bread and slept soundly from near exhaustion. But, at first light they were on the move again.

They arrived at an overlook that sloped down toward the valley of Tirzah. Elijah stood as though he was entranced for several minutes, then turned to Zechariah. "Keep out of sight in those rocks down there," he said as he pointed to an outcrop of stone about halfway down the hill. "There is a rider coming that I must meet."

"Who is he?"

"I don't know yet, but he will know me. I thought it would be Ahab, but it's someone else. We must hurry, he's very near."

Zechariah went to the place where he was instructed to hide as Elijah cut straight down the slope. Before he reached the valley floor, a lone dromedary and rider came into view through the distorting waves of shimmering heat, looking more like a mirage than something real. Elijah found a chest high stone, changed into the blue mantle and took a seat atop the boulder facing the approaching rider. When the camel and rider were a few hundred cubits away Elijah stood to his feet on the rock, making himself as tall as the man riding.

The camel came to a halt about twenty cubits away and the rider stared at Elijah as though he was awed by the spectacle before him. Nudging the camel to kneel, the man dismounted, dropped to his knees and bowed with his face to the ground. "Are you not my lord Elijah?"

Elijah recognized the king's steward. "I am. Go tell your master, Elijah is here," He jumped to the ground and stood by the rock.

Obadiah raised up to look at Elijah. "What is my sin, that you would send me to Ahab to be put to death? As surely as Yahweh Elohim lives, there is not a nation or kingdom where my master hasn't sent to look for you. He has made kings to swear by their gods that they didn't know where you were. Now you tell me to go to the king and say, 'Elijah is here.' The Spirit of Yahweh may carry you away when I leave."

When Elijah didn't answer he continued, "If I tell Ahab that you are here and he doesn't find you he will have me put to death. Yet I, your servant, have worshipped Yahweh since I was a boy. Have you not heard, my lord, what I did when Jezebel was killing the prophets of Yahweh? I hid a hundred of Yahweh's prophets in two caves and fed them and gave them water. And now you tell me to go to the king and say, 'Elijah is here.' He will put me to death. Nevertheless, I am at your direction, prophet of our most high God."

"As Yahweh El Shaddai lives, whom I serve, I will present myself to Ahab this day."

Obadiah stood and said, "I left Ahab more than an hour ago. If I hurry I can have him back here before evening."

"Go, bring the king back. If he wants to see me, bring him alone."

Obadiah mounted the kneeling dromedary, and with his rod tapped her into standing. They turned and loped awkwardly back up the valley. Zechariah came down from hiding as Elijah watched Obadiah ride out of sight. "Who was that?" Zechariah asked.

"He's the governor of the house of Ahab. He has gone to bring the king to us."

"Is his name Obadiah?"

The tension in Zechariah's voice caused Elijah to look directly at him. "Yes, that's Obadiah."

"He is the man who hid and fed the prophets. He would know where to find my father." Feeling the weight of the straw bag in his hand, he realized that there was still food. "Perhaps we'll have time to eat before they return." They sat on the ground at the base of the boulder, shaded from the morning sun and ate.

"Zechariah, I am learning that Yahweh is never without a plan. I didn't know how to get to Ahab. I thought you might be my messenger to the king but who could be more perfect than the governor of the king's own house?" Elijah broke a piece of bread he was holding then looked at the young prophet. "Don't let them see your face when they return. Only Elohim knows what will happen this day."

"Do you know yet what you will do?"

"What El Shaddai has shown me makes my heart pound just to think about it, but I won't speak it out loud until I speak it into the ears of the king." Elijah took a bite of bread and chewed it for a minute. "When you hear what He is sending me to do, then you can choose whether to go with me or return to Judah. This requires a great act of faith and if I am wrong, I'll be killed. So will you if you go with me." He took another bite of bread. "I wouldn't, I couldn't, have been ready before now. It has taken these past years to make me willing to do what I am about to do."

When they had eaten, Elijah leaned back and quickly drifted into a light sleep. Zechariah felt responsible to keep watch as Elijah slept for the next several hours. "Elijah," he gently shook him. "I see two riders coming."

Elijah opened his eyes and saw Ahab and Obadiah riding toward them. "Find someplace to keep out of sight," he said as he stood. Zechariah left as Elijah climbed back onto the boulder. Ahab was riding a white camel. He wore white britches and tunic with a purple kaffiyeh over his head held in place with a thin golden ajhal and a matching purple mantle. Elijah thought it strange that his guard didn't accompany him.

The king and Obadiah slowed from a gallop to a walk as they came near. Ahab brought his camel to a halt next to Elijah. They were at eye level, four cubits apart. "Is it really you, you troubler of Israel?" Ahab said with obviously mixed feelings.

Elijah wasn't as confident when he looked into the king's eyes as he had been the night before, when he could feel the power of the Spirit on him. He wasn't going to let the king see anything but a bold defiance, though. "I have not troubled Israel, but you and your father's house. You have forsaken the commandments of Yahweh and have followed Baal." As he spoke the fire began to burn inside him again. "Now summon all the people of Israel to meet me on Mount Carmel and bring the four hundred and fifty prophets of Baal and the four hundred prophets of Ashtoreth who eat at Jezebel's table."

The look in Elijah's eyes unnerved the king for a moment. "For what purpose?" he slowly replied.

"To let Baal prove he is a god or let Yahweh El Shaddai prove that he is the only God. On Carmel there is an altar of Yahweh Elohim that has been broken down by the worshipers of your god. We will meet there. Below the summit there is a valley where the people of Israel can gather."

"Do you know how badly this drought has weakened Israel? We are in search of grass to keep the few remaining horses and mules alive. We have been able to support only a few thousand soldiers and are in jeopardy of being invaded by Syria or Philistia." Ahab's subtle condemnation only provoked anger in Elijah.

Sternly, Elijah replied, "If Israel doesn't turn back to Yahweh Elohim, He will give all this land to the Syrians and Philistines, and you and your children will be destroyed from the earth. Your children will be burned on the altars of Baal and Chemosh and Moloch." Elijah jumped down from the boulder and began up the rocky slope as Ahab watched him leave. Elijah stopped and turned. "Bring two bull oxen to Mount Carmel on the new moon after next, and have all Israel there," he called back, then continued up to where Zechariah was waiting for him.

Ahab turned his camel to face Obadiah. "What do you think of that madman?"

"My Lord King, his robe was not the robe of a madman, it was as bright as if he had, this day, been carried to earth by the Spirit of his God. And didn't he foretell the king of this drought? Forgive your servant Obadiah for saying what I believe." When Obadiah perceived that it was safe to continue he said, "He is not a mere man but a messenger from Yahweh Elohim."

"Obadiah, I have always respected your wisdom and I have always known that you were a follower of the God of Abraham. I saw to it that you were never asked to bow to Baal and whether or not you would have, I don't know, but what you said about Elijah.... I wouldn't let reach the ears of the Queen. She truly rules the worshipers of Baal. For me, one god is the same as another. I have worshipped and sacrificed to some, including Yahweh, and I have cursed them all and not been struck down."

"We will see what kind of proof that madman has to offer to show that Yahweh is a god, or that he even exists. We will see if Yahweh's messenger has any power when he comes face to face with the prophets of Baal."

As they turned their camels to return up the valley, Obadiah rode in silence beside the king, his mind churning. Having witnessed the cruelties of Ahab and Jezebel against the people of Israel, he wondered if Ahab would survive this meeting with Elijah.

"Zechariah!" Elijah called when he reached an area on the hillside where he believed the young prophet to be hiding.

From Elijah's far right among the rocks, Zechariah answered, "I'm here, Elijah."

After hearing Elijah's plan, Zechariah elected to go with him. He knew that if Elijah were wrong it would mean death for both of them.

Zechariah traded silver for a few sheep, which they drove before them to the cave Elijah had discovered at Carmel. There was a little grass in the canyon, enough to sustain the sheep. Elijah was delighted to take turns sitting by a fire under the stars watching the sheep by night like he had done as a boy. It reminded him of a time when life was so much simpler, the time when he had begun to seek Elohim for himself and not as a ritual of habit that was handed to him.

The woman shuddered as she disrobed before the two priests of Baal. She had come here to ask the priests to petition Baal on behalf of her starving family. She hesitated, this was a great price. She cringed as the two naked priests reached out to touch her. She had never been touched before by anyone, except her husband. Maybe death was a better choice, but then she thought of her young children and, with no copper or silver to pay, there was no other sacrifice that she could make to appease Baal.

Nearby, inside the great sanctuary of the temple of Baal, the air was a bluish smoky hue. The sun shot shafts of light through the skylights and it filtered through the smoke that drifted up from the incense altars near the image of Baal. Through a pair of bronze doors in the circular auditorium the high priest was addressing an assembly that Jezebel had called.

"Servants of the great god Baal, the high priestess of Ashtoreth, whom Baal has exalted to be queen over this nation, Queen Jezebel, in her wisdom, has summoned you to this assembly." Zohelethbal stood in the center of the circular inner room of the temple. Seated around him, on the stone benches that climbed steeply away from the center with each rung, were more than four hundred of the highest ranking, honored priests of Baal, and the priests and priestesses of Ashtoreth. This room was also filled with a sweet thick incense smoke.

The high priest continued, "Except for the few camps of the prophets of Yahweh, the old God of Israel, that are scattered through the hills, which we are continuing to search out and destroy, there is no one in Israel who doesn't bow to the great Baal."

Jezebel sat in the most honored seat in front of the speaker and, with her glances, gave approval to what he was saying.

"You have all heard that the prophet Elijah, who pronounced this terrible dearth upon the land by his evil god, has returned and met with King Ahab, and has challenged us to prove that Baal is greater than his God. Elijah has said that he will prove that Yahweh is the only God. His God once ruled this land, but Israel is now under the dominion of Baal, who is worshipped and honored by the people of Israel. We clearly hold a powerful advantage over him. There are over three thousand priests and prophets of Baal and Ashtoreth in Israel. There are groves and high places and temples in every city, and the women that serve in the temples are more than twenty thousand.

"This prophet of Yahweh stands alone. He doesn't have any hope of prevailing against the almighty Baal."

Zohelethbal's powerful voice reverberated through the cavernous room. "We have searched the land and found three hundred sacred children, all male, ten years and younger, all born from the fertility worship, the most pleasing of sacrifices to Baal. On our high day, the next full moon, we will begin a sacred convocation that will last through the second day of the month Abib.

"Each day, for fifteen days, twenty sacrifices will be offered to Baal. We are still searching for virgins to be offered to Ashtoreth. We have two hundred between the ages of twelve and seventeen. On the new moon the four hundred and fifty priests of this great temple, and the four hundred appointed priests of Ashtoreth will confront Elijah at Mount Carmel, and we will put an end to the worship of Yahweh Elohim forever, then Baal will return the rain to our land."

When Zohelethbal had finished speaking, the room came alive with a roar of shouts and praises for Baal. The musicians began to play and the floor became crowded with dancing priests. They began slicing themselves across the chest and legs, offering blood sacrifices to their god.

The giant brass doors swung open to the great hall and the idol of Baal. The temple rapidly filled with priests and temple prostitutes. Though it was ten days to the full moon, the orgy that followed was spontaneous and spread out of the temple into the court of Ashtoreth. It continued for three days.

In the days before the new moon, the valley below the summit of Mount Carmel began to fill with people. There was a spring at the foot of the mountain that had not gone dry, and the local people had been drawing water from it, since most of their wells had gone dry.

It was two days before the confrontation, and Elijah walked along the top of the cliff, on his way to pray at the summit of Mount Carmel. Hundreds of the people camped below suddenly felt something that made them look around, as though eyes were upon them. In the tents, gathering wood, or cooking, each one took a look behind them, looking for the unseen eyes. "It's him!" a woman by a campfire shouted, as she pointed to the top of the cliff a hundred and fifty cubits above. Everyone in the open looked up at Elijah, as he stood there for several minutes, then turned and disappeared into the rocks above him.

A few hours before daylight, Elijah traded watches with Zechariah and returned to the cave to escape the wind that had blown continuously through the canyon that night. He tried to sleep, but sleep wouldn't come this night. Elijah tried to quiet his racing mind, in hopes of just resting for the day that lay ahead. At first light, on the first day of the month Abib, Elijah stepped from the cave. His breath steamed into clouds in the cool morning air. Zechariah was headed toward him from the canyon. "I didn't want to leave the comfort of the fire, but I knew that you would be rising about this time," he said as he walked up to Elijah.

"It was a cool night, but the sun will soon warm us," said Elijah as he surveyed the valley below them. He studied his companion for a moment. "This is a day that will change Israel forever, Zechariah." There was a fire in Elijah's eyes that sent a shiver through his young apprentice.

The distant look on Elijah's face faded as he returned to the world about him. "There are many hungry in Israel. We can't take the sheep with us, and we will not be returning for a while. Among the people that are gathered, find the poorest and distribute the sheep among them." There was a moment of hesitation in Zechariah. He started to speak, but held it and turned back to gather the sheep. Elijah started toward the mountain, then turned back and called, "I will meet you at the top."

Elijah followed the goat path around the ledge to the top of the cliff, then walked up the steep, then gently upward-rolling slope, to the top of the mountain. King Ahab, his guard, and hundreds of the priests of Baal awaited him near the broken altar of God. Thousands were camped on the slopes of Carmel, and the king's tent was pitched five hundred cubits east of the altar.

A dozen of the king's guard sat around a fire talking. Captain Jehu and his first officer, Bidkar, were in their number, roasting small chunks of meat on sticks, as they speculated about what might happen that day. All were in agreement that Elijah was at a great disadvantage against so many priests of Baal. Bidkar spoke up, "The Elohim of Abraham has forsaken this land, perhaps defeated by Baal. For one man to plead for his return, to try to make him god of these mountains again, it cannot happen. It is for the gods to battle."

Captain Jehu said, "Elijah is either a madman, or..." Jehu quickly glanced at each of the men before he continued. "If he fails today I know for certain he will be burned alive on the altar of Baal. Ahab told me that he swore an oath to Queen Jezebel, that when Elijah failed, he would have him burned and his bones ground to powder." He looked into the flames of the warm fire they were gathered around for a moment. "But once Yahweh Elohim was truly a great God over Israel, and remember, Elijah said that it wouldn't rain and it hasn't, and the prophets of Baal have prayed for rain for more than three years without success."

There was a short silence as they thought about what he said, then before anyone spoke, Jehu said, "Hush." He raised his hand to silence the already silent men. It was obvious that he had heard something, as he stood to look around. There in the distance walking toward them was a lone figure. "It's him, he's here!" They stood and looked in the direction of Elijah.

The crowd stepped aside to make a path for the prophet. He walked to where two tethered oxen stood, and stopped and admired their strength and size. He scratched each animal on the neck for a minute, then continued past Jehu and his men.

Elijah stopped and studied the broken altar. Jehu hurried to his chariot that stood near by, took the reins from their keeper, wheeled around and rode up to Elijah.

Jehu said, "I am Captain Jehu, captain over the chariots of Israel. You have come a long way. Would you ride with me to the tent of the king?"

Jehu extended a hand to Elijah to help him up onto his chariot. There was a moment of hesitation, as Elijah looked into Jehu's eyes, then took his hand. "Thank you, Captain Jehu," said the prophet. Jehu maneuvered the chariot skillfully through the gathering crowd as they rode the short distance to Ahab's tent.

"Inform the king that Elijah is here," Jehu said to one of the guards at the entrance of the king's tent, as he stepped from the chariot, followed by Elijah.

"Yes, captain," the guard answered.

Captain Jehu bowed slightly, but Elijah bowed to the ground then stood when the king appeared. "King Ahab, today, Yahweh El Shaddai will prove that he alone is God. East of here, on the next peak, which is higher than this one, there is an altar of Baal and a grove. Let the priests of Baal choose a bull to sacrifice to their god, and I will take the other to sacrifice to Yahweh. The god who answers by fire is God."

The king looked over at a guard. "Bring Zohelethbal here quickly." Then he turned to his aide and said, "Get a chair for Elijah." He re-entered the tent without addressing the prophet.

Ten minutes later Zohelethbal arrived with an entourage of three priests and two servants. The king's aide stepped into the tent to inform Ahab. It was another five minutes before the king stepped out in his full royal armor of gold chain mail. He and Zohelethbal walked out away from everyone to talk in private.

After obviously relating to the priest the terms of Elijah's challenge, and anything else that involved Elijah, they returned.

As they returned, Zohelethbal looked into Elijah's eyes and saw a confidence and a strength that was alarming, but he tried not to let it show as he said, "Baal is the most powerful of the gods. He rules the fire, the sun and the lightning. You foolish prophet, Yahweh is a weak and defeated God."

Ahab raised his hand to silence Baal's high priest, then spoke, "It is agreed, your terms are acceptable," Ahab said to Elijah.

When Ahab had finished, Zohelethbal spoke up, "My Lord, King, let the king decree that if either god should fail to answer, then the false prophets representing the heresy should be put to death."

Before Ahab could answer, Elijah spoke, "Let it be decreed as Zohelethbal has suggested."

Supposing that it would forever settle the controversy in favor of Baal, and eliminate the annoyance of Elijah, Ahab answered, "It is decreed that the god who fails to answer, his servants shall be cut off this day."

Elijah, speaking to Ahab and Zohelethbal, said, "Let me speak to the people." Ahab nodded approval, and Elijah walked down the hill to the cliff, where he could speak to the largest number of people, though there were multitudes camped on every slope.

Standing on the cliff overlooking the valley where thousands were camped now, Elijah shouted, "How long will you, Israel, waver between two opinions?" His voice echoed and caught the attention of the multitude. "If Yahweh be God, then serve him, but if Baal is god then serve him."

There was a minute of total silence, shattered only when he continued. "I am the only one of Yahweh's prophets left in Israel, but Baal has four hundred and fifty. Let them choose a bull to cut into pieces, to offer to Baal. Let them lay the pieces on the wood, but put no fire to it. I will offer the other as a sacrifice to Yahweh, but will not light a fire under it."

Elijah's burning gaze swept the crowd below. "You call upon the name of your gods, and I will call upon the name of Yahweh Elohim, the God of Abraham. The god who answers by fire is God." There was a clamoring which began below the cliff and at Elijah's back and grew into a low roar as the thousands discussed the challenge.

Elijah returned to the top to be met by Zohelethbal, who, with a confident smile, said, "It is a fair challenge, but you will die this day. Yahweh is no god."

Elijah smiled back, "This day eight hundred and fifty of you will pay for the rivers of innocent blood you've shed. Choose one of the bulls and prepare it first, since there are four hundred and fifty of you, and call on your god, but don't put fire under the sacrifice."

Ahab's chariot led the way to the altar of Baal. As they came near the summit, thousands crowded on the slopes around. Soldiers with spears shoved the crowd back away from the altar. The large company of priests made quick work of butchering the ox and laying it on the altar.

Zohelethbal disrobed to a loincloth, exposing his body covered with scars. He stood next to the altar and raised his hands toward the sun. "Oh Great Baal, we honor you this day. Hear the prayers of your servants and bring glory to your name. Prove for all time that you are the god above all gods. Receive this sacrifice and consume it with the fire of the sun." For several minutes he kept his hands stretched upward. Then the priests began, with dozens of instruments, to play their most sacred music. Hundreds of others began to dance around the altar. They called to Baal as they danced themselves into a frenzy. As the morning wore on, their shouts to Baal began to sound more and more like the shrieks of wild or wounded animals. They became drunk with the dance and with a concoction each stopped to drink, as other priests refilled goblet after goblet. Some climbed onto the waist-high altar and lay on top of the sacrifice, offering themselves to be consumed by the fire of Baal.

Thousands of Baal worshipers bowed to the ground on the slopes leading to the summit where the altar stood. The continuous low roar of their combined prayers, along with the shouts and shrieks of the priests and the conversations of those who waited to see the outcome, made it impossible to speak at a normal level and be heard. Many hoped for the death of Elijah and wanted to see and participate in the celebration and orgy that would ensue.

Zohelethbal was standing to the side about midday, when Elijah walked over next to him and shouted into the confusion, "Maybe Baal is sleeping and you're not shouting loud enough to awaken him."

A hush began to sweep out from those nearest to Elijah, when they realized he was speaking. A few moments later, except for the priests, everyone was quiet, waiting to see what Elijah would say next. "Maybe he is visiting Queen Ashtoreth, and doesn't want to be disturbed."

Many of the people were shocked and angered at Elijah's outright blaspheming of Baal. Those who believed in Baal and Yahweh, and the many other gods, were sure that through his contempt of Baal, he had insured his own defeat.

Blood was beginning to cover the ground from the self inflicted wounds of sacrifice the priests offered with honed daggers. "Shout louder. If he is a god, he will hear," taunted Elijah.

The priests of Ashtoreth occupied about a third of the inner circle of people around the area of wailing, dancing servants of Baal. Some of them sneered mockingly back at Elijah. Upon the carrying poles, a nude three cubit idol of Ashtoreth, holding her breasts in her hands, was hoisted into the air, then placed to rest on the shoulders of her priests, above the throng of people for all to see. To honor her, the priests of Baal stripped to nothing when they saw their goddess.

Elijah looked at Zohelethbal, glanced over his scarred body and then stared into his eyes. "You are going to die today," pronounced Elijah. Raw fear ran through Zohelethbal. For a brief moment, it showed on his face. Elijah shouted again at the bloodied priests. "Baal must be on a trip and is too far away to hear. Shout louder," Elijah jeered then turned to Zohelethbal again. "Maybe Baal has gone deaf." Before Elijah could finish what he was about to say, one of the bloodied, wild-eyed priests, spinning as he danced, whirled into Elijah. Elijah caught him by the shoulders to keep them both from falling to the ground. For a moment their eyes met. Something the priest saw in Elijah's eyes frightened him. He staggered backward then turned and ran into the crowd that stood by. They parted, making a path for him to exit without getting his blood on their robes. Zohelethbal looked at Elijah, wondering what the subordinate priest had seen. Elijah looked at the blood he had on his hands from the man's bleeding wounds. "This is unclean, I must wash my hands. But hear me before I go, Zohelethbal. Baal is no god. Yahweh El Shaddai will answer me, and you and all of them will die."

"I have seen the power of Baal, he is a god," Zohelethbal defensively answered.

Angrily Elijah retorted, "You have seen the power of Satan through your blood thirsty demon Baal. They were cast out of the presence of the true God. Maybe it's the women, the wealth and the virgins you've raped to death that have kept you from seeing the truth, you bastard of an Ashtoreth whore!"

"Why don't you tell that to the high priestess, Queen Jezebel?"

"You won't be around to see it when I do," Elijah answered, making sure their eyes met as he spoke before he turned and walked away.

The crowd made a path for Elijah as he went to find water to wash the blood from his hands. "Elijah!" a voice called from somewhere in the crowd. He recognized Zechariah's voice and turned in his direction as the people parted to the right and left. "Elijah! Over here," Zechariah called again.

After a minute Zechariah and Micaiah were standing in Elijah's path. "Look who is here, Micaiah." Zechariah had to shout above the roar of the crowd.

Micaiah looked beaten and defeated. They embraced as Elijah asked, "Where have you been, my friend?"

"I prophesied to Ahab that the wrath of El Shaddai would consume him and his children for killing his prophets. I was beaten and thrown into prison. This was the third time. I think he begins to believe that what I say might be right and he lets me out. This time he released me to see you and the God of Abraham defeated and to watch you burn on the altar of Baal. You will prevail but I fear to speak in the name of Yahweh again. I haven't bowed to Baal, but I don't think I can endure any more pain." Tears welled up in Micaiah's eyes as he felt shame for his weakness. "Do all that is in your heart, for El Shaddai is with you."

"Elohim will avenge your suffering and renew you this day. Come with me. We must restore the altar of Yahweh and then we will destroy the priests of Baal and Ashtoreth."

As the three walked west toward the altar of Yahweh the multitude divided, some staying to watch Baal's priests and some following Elijah, Micaiah and Zechariah. When they were near the altar on higher ground above the people, Elijah turned and called to the multitude, "Have all Israel come here to me."

The three began to work on the altar. Using poles for leverage, they were able to maneuver the first four stones of the altar into place, and were working on the fifth, when they saw Captain Jehu coming toward them in his chariot. He was followed by Bidkar in another chariot, and a dozen footmen.

Jehu pulled his team to a halt next to them. "I have never bowed to Baal. Bidkar has never bowed to any god, and the rest of these men believe in Yahweh Elohim and have never bowed to Baal. Would you allow us to help you?"

Elijah looked at the size of the stones, then at Jehu and his men. "We need a cart of water. Could you provide that for us?"

Jehu motioned toward Bidkar. "Take one of the carts to the spring below. There are a few baths of water left. Bring them here first. Take as many men as you need." As Bidkar reined his chariot team around, Jehu turned to one of the footmen. "Bring some ropes and find some levers."

"Are you and these men seed of Abraham and Israel? No man can touch the stones of this altar unless he is of Israel." Elijah stated the conditions by which they could help.

"These men are Hebrew and I am the grandson of Nimshi of the tribe of Reuben," Jehu stated proudly.

"Help us then. We need wood and the altar must be repaired by the time of the evening sacrifice."

With the help of Jehu's men, the stones of the altar were quickly fitted together. Its tabletop was five cubits from the ground. "Dig a trench around the base of the altar," Elijah ordered. The men looked at Jehu to see if they were to carry out Elijah's command. Though Jehu and his men had never seen an altar with a trench at the base, he nodded for them to do as Elijah had instructed.

Jehu walked with Elijah as he went around the altar inspecting it and the depth of the trench as the men continued to dig. "Prophet of Yahweh, will He really answer you this day?" Jehu cocked his head sideways and glanced upward from the corner of his eye as he asked.

"He will," Elijah answered confidently then turned to Zechariah. "Bring the ox." Looking back at Jehu, he said, "It is time. Send word to King Ahab that we are ready. The prophets of Baal have had most of the day but at the time of the evening sacrifice, Yahweh El Shaddai of Israel will answer by fire."

When the altar was just the way Elijah wanted it, with two large steps on the north side, and the trench the proper depth, he walked up to the soldiers who were standing by waiting for their next order. "Yahweh Elohim will not forget your labor and you will never forget this day. When you pray, pray towards the holy city Jerusalem and Yahweh will give heed to your prayer. When the people gather around keep them away from the altar. Stay seventy cubits back lest you and they be consumed with the sacrifice. This is sacred ground."

When Elijah had finished speaking to them, Jehu ordered to the next in command, "See to it. Bring over the rest of the platoon and keep the people back seventy cubits from the altar."

At that moment Zechariah led the massive red ox to Elijah next to the altar. Elijah stroked the animal's muscled left shoulder then placed his hand on the ox's thick long horn on the same side. He looked at Zechariah, "I've never seen a more beautiful beast. In a famine like this he could only belong to the king." The ox, chewing cud, paid little attention to the two men until Elijah began to scratch his neck, then the great beast leaned into his hand. "You like that," Elijah spoke to the ox. As he continued to scratch the ox's neck he said, "Your life, great ox, will save the lives of thousands of children and will save Israel from the judgment of El Shaddai."

Zechariah handed Elijah a large dagger. "Jehu gave it to us and Obadiah is sending more. He told me where to find my father."

Elijah looked around to find Jehu at the edge of the seventy-cubit perimeter standing by his chariot and nodded a thank you, but didn't see Obadiah. A sea of people was growing on all sides and in the distance coming from the altar of Baal the earth looked as if it were moving as the entire multitude walked toward them in the low area between the two summits. Elijah saw Ahab in his chariot with Zohelethbal riding at the king's side.

Zechariah continued, "Elohim has spoken to my father and the prophets about this day but Obadiah didn't have the time to tell me what He revealed."

A soldier walked up to them carrying several knives, an ax, and a brass pan. "These are from Obadiah," he said as he laid them on the ground.

Elijah placed the pan under the ox's neck, took the dagger and, with a shallow insertion, cut into one of the arteries that pulsated to the animal's head. The ox continued to chew the cud with no indication that he had felt any pain or that he was beginning to bleed to death. The pan quickly filled with blood and as it did the ox began to sway as though he was drunk. Elijah removed the pan of blood moments before the ox collapsed to his knees and as the animal's life bled away, its eyes blinked sleepily then closed. His breathing became slow and shallow then the large beast rolled onto his side and died a few minutes later.

Elijah climbed the two steps and poured the blood onto the altar. The blood ran into the cracks and down the sides. "Yahweh Elohim, let the blood sanctify this altar and let the sacrifice that is about to be offered be pleasing to you." Elijah prayed as though he was offering any other sacrifice to Yahweh and not as though his life depended on God answering by fire. He made several trips up the altar steps to place the wood in order then he began to lay the meat over the wood as Micaiah and Zechariah cut the ox into pieces. Once when he came down he backed into Zohelethbal.

"I have come to see what kind of trickery you've planned to light the fire that Yahweh is supposed to send," Zohelethbal sneered.

Elijah angrily shoved the high priest backward. "This is holy ground! You can't bring your filth here! Get back with the rest of the people!" At that moment the prophet's rage scared Zohelethbal who turned and stumbled to the ground to get away from him. Elijah would have pursued him to the line formed by Jehu's men but one of King Ahab's guard stepped between them with a sword. It took a moment for Elijah to regain control of his emotions.

Between the altar and the clamoring multitude Elijah slowly walked around the sacrifice and altar when everything was in order. He stopped near Captain Jehu. "Sir, would you have your men, Hebrews, bring four of the largest water pots to pour on the sacrifice."

Jehu looked stunned as he slowly answered, "Prophet of Yahweh, are you sure that's what you want?"

"Yes, Captain Jehu."

Jehu turned to Bidkar who stood next to him. "Bring four of the water jars." Bidkar turned and pushed his way through the crowd. Two minutes later four soldiers walked through the cleared area, each with a large earthen water jug on his shoulder. Elijah stood on the second step and called to the first soldier that approached, "Hand it here to me." One at a time, each handed him a jug as he emptied them onto the sacrifice.

When he had emptied the pots Elijah said to Jehu, "Have them do it again." As they went after water the second time Elijah went to where Ahab was seated. Zohelethbal stood at the king's side. "Does that satisfy you that there isn't any trickery?" He stared hard at the high priest as he spoke but turned toward the altar as the men brought the pots of water back. Elijah nodded for them to pour the water on the sacrifice a second time. When the pots were again empty, from across the way, Jehu looked to Elijah to see if the prophet wanted more water. Elijah held up three fingers and nodded.

Several minutes later when the men returned a third time Elijah returned to the altar and Zohelethbal leaned down and whispered into Ahab's ear, "Elijah has gone mad. His God will never answer."

Ahab snapped back, "Baal didn't answer four hundred and fifty of you. Keep quiet and let's see what this man will do. Perhaps you should pray to Yahweh. There is hardly a family in Israel that hasn't given at least one child to Baal and Baal hasn't answered like you assured me he would. What do you think these people will do to you if Yahweh answers Elijah by fire and they feel like they've been deceived? Even I couldn't stop them from killing you, nor would I try. You agreed to the terms and I've given my word."

"Move back away from the altar," Elijah said to Micaiah and Zechariah as he approached and looked to see that the trench around it was filled with water.

Elijah stood about ten cubits away from the altar and stretched his hands toward heaven, much the same as Zohelethbal had earlier when he prayed to Baal. The great audience became quiet. "Yahweh Elohim of Abraham, Isaac, and Israel!" His voice was deep and carried far and the sound of the name of God, Yahweh, sent chills over everyone who heard it. He paused for a moment to think about how to pray.

Zohelethbal quivered at the sound. Ahab noticed it out of the corner of his eye and turned and said, "I think you have much to fear. Elijah is no ordinary man and when he talks to Yahweh Elohim there is power in his voice. I've never heard anything like it before."

Elijah inhaled deeply and continued louder than before. "Let it be known this day that you are Elohim over Israel and I am your servant, and I have done all these things at your command. Hear me, O Yahweh, hear me, that these people may know that you are Yahweh Elohim and that by your great mercy you have turned their hearts back again."

The mild breeze that had blown all day suddenly stopped. The only sounds that could be heard were the teams of chariot horses in the distance, fighting against their keepers and harnesses, as though they sensed danger and wanted to flee. It was the way they would react if they had caught scent of a near-by lion.

Elijah stepped back from the altar, realizing that his prayer was going to be answered with more force than even he could have imagined. Everyone knew in those silent moments that Yahweh El Shaddai was God, and he was about to prove it. The very presence of God could be felt in the still air surrounding Mount Carmel.

Fear gripped the assembled crowd. Even Elijah was backing away from the altar. The seventy-foot perimeter began to grow wider as the closest spectators pushed back into the crowd, trying to put more distance between them and Elijah. Ahab stood as he gazed upward. With drawn swords, his guards opened a path through the people as the king backed slowly away.

For one instant a giant ball of fire could be seen high in the expanse above earth shooting at an angle downward toward them. Elijah fell to his knees. Others who were not pressed into the midst of the tightly packed throng dove to the ground.

Elijah could hear his own heart pounding, as his mind shifted into slow motion. He was keenly aware of the altar, with the wood stacked neatly on top, the blood red pieces of the sacrifice glistening in the afternoon sun, and the blood and water dripping from the stones. His eyes were drawn to the surface of the water in the trench that stood silvery silent, like a mirror reflecting the sky above. As he watched, the tranquil surface changed from silver to a brilliant glowing orange, then a white hot yellow as it rippled to life, reflecting the blinding brilliance of the fireball streaking toward the altar.

The sight was forever etched in Elijah's mind, as the fireball exploded into the altar with the blinding light of a thousand bolts of lightning. The earth jerked, then shook as the thunderous impact deafened the multitude and left them with ears ringing, as it echoed and crescendoed off the rocks and canyons of the surrounding hills. Many of the people had their feet shaken out from under them, as even the distant hills trembled and the earth quaked.

Earth and dust were blown into the air and engulfed them like a brown gray fog, while the more solid chunks rained back upon them for several minutes. All who were left standing dropped to their knees, and bowed with their faces to the ground. Where the altar had stood a moment before, was a smoking crater, directly in front of Elijah. It looked to be the width of seven or eight chariots across. For several minutes there wasn't a movement among the people. Most were praying to the God of Elijah for forgiveness and mercy.

Elijah began to slowly rise to his feet, when Captain Jehu shouted, "Yahweh, he is Elohim! Yahweh, he is Elohim!" The third time he said it, a roar of voices joined him. The fourth time, it spread to the valley below. Everyone joined in, except the priests and prophets of Baal and Ashtoreth. The worship lasted for half an hour, during which time King Ahab's troops, at the command of Jehu, surrounded the eight hundred and fifty servants of the defeated gods.

Elijah raised his hands to silence the people. It was nearly a minute before all were quiet. "Seize the prophets of Baal. Don't let any escape! Seize them and bring them down to the Kishon valley."

When Elijah had finished speaking, Captain Jehu approached him and bowed to his knees before him. "My lord Elijah, servant of the Great Yahweh El Shaddai, from this day on I shall serve the God of Abraham. My sword is the sword of Yahweh. What would you have me to do?"

Elijah answered, "Go with me, down to the Kishon River, to slay the wicked priests of Baal."

"My men have already captured them. I'll have them brought down, if we can keep the people from killing them before we can get them there."

Elijah was accompanied by Jehu, Obadiah, Micaiah and Zechariah, as they followed the masses that went before them. Jehu's men had to fight the people back to keep them from beating and kicking the priests of Baal and Ashtoreth, as they forced them down the slope toward the Kishon River bed.

Ahab intercepted them in his chariot. He wanted to ask Elijah to spare the lives of the Baal priests, but he didn't want to appear weak before Captain Jehu. Instead he said, "Elohim of Abraham answered mightily, but the challenge was only to Baal. Do with those priests as you please, but until the priests of Ashtoreth accept the challenge, they are not to be killed." There was a moment of uncomfortable silence between them, then Ahab looked at Captain Jehu and said, "When everything is settled here, take the troops to Samaria."

Ahab's driver reined his chariot up the hill, and rode eastward, as Jehu turned to Elijah and said, "There was a great victory for Yahweh here today. That is Ahab's way of showing you that he is still king. Because he built the great temple of Baal in Samaria, you made him look bad today. Without even trying, he has promoted the worship of Baal as much as Jezebel."

When Elijah reached the valley, Zohelethbal and his priests were crowded into the dry riverbed, surrounded by a violent, shouting throng of people. One angry man broke through Jehu's guards, and began clubbing as many of the priests as his wild, violent swings could reach. One priest raised his forearm against the blows. With the next strike the arm snapped like a piece of dry kindling. "My children, my children," screamed the attacker. "For the promise of rain, you burned them! For no reason!" he cried, and only at the threat of death by one of the soldiers, did the man back away.

Elijah took a long, hard look at the priests, then turned to Jehu and said, "Don't do anything you or your men might be punished for. Let me have a dozen swords." Jehu studied Elijah for a long moment, then pulled his sword from its sheath and gave it to him. He turned to his guards, and ordered eleven of his men to give up their swords. Elijah added, "After I execute Zohelethbal, I will find twelve angry men from this crowd that are willing to help slay the rest."

The priests gathered around Zohelethbal, seeking protection, as Elijah walked rapidly toward them. "Where is our priestess, Zohelethbal? Where is Queen Jezebel to save us?" shouted one priest angrily. "Do something! We're about to die!" The terrified priests of Baal searched frantically through the crowd, hoping for deliverance. "You fool, Zohelethbal, call upon the king! This was your idea! Don't let us die with you!" screamed one of the men.

The priests parted, leaving Zohelethbal face to face with Elijah. "Now you know it wasn't trickery," Elijah said, as Zohelethbal tried to edge back into the protection of the group. Zohelethbal's glance behind Elijah gave away an assailant at Elijah's back. Elijah turned quickly, to see a priest with a dagger raised to thrust into his back suddenly stopped in midair. Half of an arrow shaft appeared on each side of his neck just below his ears. Elijah jumped to one side to miss the man as he fell forward. He looked at Jehu, who held the bow, and nodded a thank you for the second time that day.

Elijah turned back to face Zohelethbal and shouted, "I told you that you were going to die today!" Elijah lunged forward, as he swung Jehu's sword overhead. The priests next to Zohelethbal dodged to each side, leaving him exposed. The rotating sword stopped with a thud and stuck, half way through Zohelethbal's neck. The high priest fell heavily to the ground. The rest of the priests backed away from Elijah, as the sand beneath Zohelethbal's body turned red with the blood that poured from his neck. Elijah pulled Jehu's sword from the high priest's lifeless body, and turned and walked away.

Jehu and his men forced the priests to kneel in the sand of the riverbed. A group of angry volunteers systematically executed them all, except for a few that had escaped into the crowd after they failed to conjure Baal's favor earlier in the day.

The sandy river bed turned red with the blood of the slain priests. For two hundred cubits their bodies lined the dry stream.

As the crowd was dispersing to the south and east, one man stopped Elijah and shoved a small purse into his hand, then disappeared into the crowd. Elijah looked into it, to find that it was filled with gold, then glanced around to find the man, but he was nowhere to be seen.

Ahab met Elijah and said loudly, above the roar of the people, "The God of Abraham is truly a great God."

"The God of Abraham is the only God. Go up to your tent, eat and drink and prepare to return home, for there is a sound of thunder of a great rain." Elijah stepped past King Ahab to find Zechariah.

Elijah took Zechariah west, along the ridge of Mount Carmel, to where a clump of tall green trees shaded the ground. Four hundred cubits beyond that was the highest point on the mountain chain, west of the altar of Baal. "I will pray here for Yahweh to send the rain. Go up to the top and look out at the ocean and tell me what you see," instructed Elijah. Zechariah solemnly nodded, then began up the slope, feeling joyful and lighthearted, and full of pride from being on the side of Elijah. He had stood with the prophet of God when nearly all of Israel was against him. He felt like shouting praises to the God of Abraham who had prevailed.

Zechariah looked back and saw Elijah bowed to the ground, with his head between his knees. With all of his strength, he sped into a run to the top, and looked out over the beautiful horizon of blue sea.

"God of my fathers, I bless your great name for hearing your servant and sparing this great people that you have chosen to call your people, the seed of your friend Abraham. Send now the rain upon the land which you gave to them." Elijah remained bowed and silent, listening until he heard Zechariah's running steps coming toward him. He raised up just as the young prophet reached him.

"There is nothing there. What am I supposed to look for?" Zechariah panted out.

Elijah smiled, as the scene reminded him of another time years before, when the anxious Zechariah had delivered a message to him on a mountaintop. "Go look again." As Zechariah spun about to return to the summit, Elijah bowed to the ground and poured himself completely into his prayer. "Yahweh El Shaddai, hear now your servant who has brought all of Israel together, and followed your instructions before their eyes, and promised them that the God of their fathers would send the rain." Elijah lost himself in his prayer, and didn't know how much time had passed.

"Elijah," Zechariah called softly. Elijah looked up to see Zechariah standing in front of him, and hoped for some positive news.

"I don't see anything but the ocean. What should I be looking for?"

"I'm not certain," Elijah answered, as he looked up. "The rain comes from the west, and I feel that when Elohim answers, we will know by looking to the sea in the west. Go back. We will be here for as long as it takes."

"Yahweh Elohim, ruler of heaven and earth, Baal is no god. Neither are any of the Baals gods, but you alone. You rule over the sun that rules the day, and you rule the moon that rules the night. You rule the earth and the sea. Send your word to the sea, that the sea would give water to the thirsty land. Let not the people say that you were unable to bring the rain, lest they believe in some other god." For several minutes he was silent, then he looked up to see Zechariah standing at the top looking back at him. When Zechariah saw Elijah raise up, he came running down the slope. It took several minutes.

"There isn't anything there." Zechariah's pounding stride jolted his words, as he spoke before coming to a stop.

"Once before I had to pray several times before Yahweh answered. Go back. He has promised. It isn't possible for Yahweh to break his word. He will answer today. Tell me if you should see any sign."

This was Zechariah's fourth trip to the summit, and he was no longer running to the top. Elijah watched him most of the way up before he began to pray again. "Great El Shaddai, for the sake of your word, remember your promise to send the rain. For their transgressions, your people have suffered greatly. Now have mercy upon them. Their cattle have died, and their fields lie barren, and there is little left to eat. Have mercy upon the seed of Abraham."

"Elijah!" Zechariah's voice interrupted Elijah's prayer and thoughts. Standing over him, the young prophet continued, as Elijah looked up. "There are hundreds of large birds over the valley. Could that be a sign?"

"Those are vultures. They've come to eat the flesh of Baal's priests. It's not a sign from Elohim." Elijah was disappointed in the young prophet because he had grown weary of his duty as lookout. Elijah knew that this son of Jehew looked up to him, but how could he be weary so quickly, after seeing the power of Yahweh? He had great hopes for him, but Zechariah had never really suffered or sacrificed, and didn't have the endurance to accomplish anything great.

"Have faith, Zechariah, have faith. Yahweh will answer when I find the words He is waiting to hear. I feel that I am close. Return to the top, and bring me word of what you see. Maybe by then I will have the answer." For a minute Elijah watched him as he returned to the summit. He had to put him out of his mind and return his soul to seeking God. Elijah quickly repeated everything he had already prayed, but there wasn't any power left in his words.

Zechariah went to the top and straight back. The discouragement on his face was evident when Elijah asked him to return for the sixth time. Elijah again repeated everything he had already prayed, but the words were like a cold campfire, without a spark of life.

He was asking himself the question, 'Why isn't Yahweh answering,' when Zechariah returned. "There is smoke from Ahab's camp and a thousand buzzards to the east but there isn't anything to the west. Do you want me to go back again?"

The negative tone in his voice made Elijah sorry to have to ask him to return to the top a seventh time. "Yes, my son, return to the top."

Wearily, Zechariah began to trudge up the slope as Elijah asked himself, "What is wrong? What is wrong?" Instantly it was clear. He was asking Yahweh Elohim to fulfill a promise he had made; a promise to him and a promise to Abraham and a promise to Solomon. He had said all the right words, but by not going far enough to give Him thanks, he had been prodding God to answer his prayers, when God had already promised this thing. He was asking for something that, in the mind of Yahweh, was already done. Fear gripped Elijah momentarily, as he realized that, without meaning to, he had insulted the word of his God, implying by his unbelieving prayers that Yahweh would not honor his promise.

Relief flooded Elijah's soul, that Yahweh had not exacted vengeance upon him for this transgression, but had given him this revelation. He jumped to his feet and shouted, "Bless the name of the God of Abraham. Let all the earth praise his name. He alone is God, Yahweh Elohim, Yahweh-Jireh, El Shaddai is his name."

He couldn't hold back the tears of joy, for he knew that the God of Abraham was also the God of Elijah, and had heard his prayer. Zechariah heard the shouting coming from Elijah and turned to see the prophet dancing in a circle. Elijah called to him, "Son of Jehew, hurry to the top and tell me what you see now." Zechariah could hear Elijah praising God all the way to the top. "Let the heavens and earth and stars and sun praise your holy name. I exult in my heart, and with my lips I praise you, merciful Yahweh."

Rising out of the sea was a hand. Each finger was distinct, like the reflection of a man's hand in a bronze mirror. Was it the hand of Yahweh, or was it a cloud? It was far out at sea and looked small, but it must have been very large. Zechariah could hardly believe his eyes. He turned and ran back down the hill for the seventh time. "Elijah!" he called, "A cloud, a cloud like a man's hand coming up out of the sea!"

He was breathless when he reached Elijah. "A cloud the shape of a man's hand coming up out of the sea. The hand of Yahweh, it's His sign! The rain is coming."

"Rest a few minutes, then go and tell Ahab to ready his chariot and hurry, or the rain will prevent him from returning to Jezreel. I want to stay and rejoice in my God, but I'll be along shortly."

A short while later, as Elijah walked toward Ahab's tent, he saw the king climbing onto his chariot. With two other chariots, and a runner in front, they headed east. Elijah tucked his mantle into his belt and ran to the king's tent, where he met Zechariah. "Get a horse from Captain Jehu and meet me in Jezreel," instructed Elijah. Before Zechariah could respond, Elijah was running after Ahab's chariot.

Elijah had never felt the power of Yahweh as strongly as he felt it then. To be the fastest of the tribe of Gad was a dream he had realized as a young man, but it was nothing to compare with the speed he felt in his legs and body now. He overtook the chariots that were moving along at a fast walk, and moved into position as a runner before the king's chariot. Ahab understood it for what Elijah, directed by the Spirit of Elohim, intended it to be, an act of respect.

Ahab remembered how fast Elijah ran from his troops three years before. The king knew he had to be twice the age of his own runners, guessing him to be thirty-five to forty years of age. It was not for a man of his years to attempt something like this. Maybe, Ahab thought, it was just his arrogance because of the way the day had turned out for him.

Ahab took the reins from his driver and nudged the four horses into a fast trot. Elijah picked up the pace, and stayed in front of them. Within fifteen miles, the first runner fell to the side, doubled over in pain and gasping for breath. Perturbed that Elijah could maintain that pace, Ahab whipped the team into a gallop. The horses were on Elijah's heels before he realized they had changed gaits. He knew then that the king was going to put him to the test, and moved out in front of them by twenty cubits.

Ahab whipped the horses into a full run but couldn't gain on Elijah. Thunder rolled continuously in the distance as they raced the last three miles to Jezreel.

Elijah felt as though he would burst with the supernatural strength Yahweh had given him if he couldn't praise God, and he did with each stride. The thought raced through his mind, "Yahweh is my strength." He was so excited that he wanted to invent new words to praise God for his greatness.

Thunder rolled again, this time much closer. The horses began to lather, and the chariots behind Ahab's fell farther and farther to the rear. The king's horses weakened from the pace and slowed slightly. Elijah's lead lengthened; thirty cubits, forty cubits, fifty cubits.

Lightning flashed as deafening cracks of thunder ripped the air. A moment later they were deluged by large drops of rain. Elijah knew he had won and leapt into the air as he shouted, "Glory to you, El Shaddai, glory to you!"

Ahab knew that his horses wouldn't last to reach Jezreel at that pace and pulled them back to a slow gallop. As the gates of Jezreel came into view in the distance, the rain came down in torrents. Hindered by the softening ground, the tired team loped along. The heavy wheels of the chariot were miring several inches into the mud by the time they reached the city gate.

Elijah stepped to the side and bowed on one knee. The king pulled the team to a halt next to the prophet, half smiled, and nodded a salutation of respect. Water ran from their faces in small streams as Elijah broke into a joyous grin.

One of Jezebel's eunuchs awaited Ahab's return at a guardroom over the entrance to the palace. When he spotted Ahab approaching the gate, he ran through the palace, down the steps to the lower level to Eber's room and rapped at his door. "My lord Eber," he called. "The king has just arrived."

"Return to your duties," Eber answered as he opened the door. He followed the young eunuch down the hall to Jezebel's private dressing area. "Notify the queen that King Ahab has arrived," he said to one of the queen's handmaids on duty outside Jezebel's wardrobe room. It was several minutes before the queen appeared. She was dressed in a royal purple gown in preparation for Ahab's return. Eber bowed to one knee. "Your Highness, please permit your servant to speak."

"Stand and look me in the eye and say whatever it is you have to say." Jezebel was obviously irritated that he had chosen this moment to ask for an audience.

"Highness, I've had a bad feeling most of this day," Eber said as he rose to his feet. "The king has returned. I adjure you to approach him softly."

Jezebel's anger rose as she said, "This is a great day. Lord Baal has sent the rain. I will celebrate with the king tonight!"

"Have you not felt it in the air since this afternoon?" Eber asked.

Jezebel paused. It wasn't like Eber to feel things from the spirit world. Could it be that she had overlooked something? She thought for a moment then closed her eyes, breathed deeply and prayed in her spirit, "Lord Baal, greatest god in all the earth, speak to me, Queen of Israel." She stood silently for several minutes as Eber watched. She looked somewhat perplexed when she reopened her eyes. "I cannot reach Baal. He is not communicating to me," she said, visibly upset. She then soothed herself as she added, "He is busy with the rain. I have been watching the glorious shafts of light he is casting to earth. That's proof that he is god over Israel. I have never seen so much lightning. Did you see any of it, Eber?"

"No, my queen, I did not."

"Eber, you are imagining things. You don't have the gift that Tamara has." Jezebel caught her mistake and added with a blush of embarrassment, "the gift she had." Angered by her error and knowing that Eber knew the real reason Tamara had died, she ordered curtly, "Return to your duties!"

Jezebel suddenly felt very alone as she walked down the long stone corridor. She stopped and listened to the silence. Eber's footsteps faded into the stillness as he exited the corridor through a side door in the other direction. Jezebel took a few more steps but the sound of her sandals echoing in the dim hallway bothered her. Something was wrong. The world of the gods and the world of men were too quiet. She had felt this kind of loneliness only one other time, after Tamara's execution. She had chosen to leave her attendants behind, but now wished that she hadn't. There was an ominous feeling as she stooped down to remove her sandals. She would carry them until she reached the safety of the presence of other people. Her sandals were tucked to her breast under her right arm when she stood, but she couldn't move forward. Jezebel was terrified as she was gripped by this unseen force.

At that moment Elijah walked down the street near the palace, feeling very much alone in the cold rain. He was looking for an inn to find food and warmth from the cold. A chill reached deep inside him through his soaked clothes. Several times he saw people dancing in the rain. Once eight people filed out of a house in front of him, dancing and singing to the sound of timbrels carried by the women in the group. All of Israel would be celebrating this night, he thought, but why was he feeling so alone, and why was the joy he had known earlier gone?

Jezebel felt Elijah's presence as she stood there in the silence. "Lord Baal, please do not forsake me, but give me strength against this enemy," she pleaded desperately. Suddenly she realized that if he were alive, things must have gone wrong at Mt. Carmel. The power was not as strong as it had been at other times when he was near, but she began to tremble and had to brace herself against the wall. She was able to resist the weakness that had caused her to collapse under this power before. As Elijah moved further away from the palace, she regained strength enough to run. The sound of her bare feet against the marble floor was almost lost in the darkened hallway, adding to her sense of fear and isolation.

Jezebel was relieved to be around other people again, even if it was only the guards standing watch at the end of the long hall. She stopped to put her sandals back on, and to regain her composure before joining Ahab.

The king was seated in the entrance hall with a servant washing his feet and a handmaid drying his hair with a towel. Jezebel entered, approached and bowed to one knee. "My Lord King, is this not a great day for the king and for Israel and for the god of King Ahab, Lord Baal?" She had resolved not to betray the doubt she had just felt.

"No, it is not!" Ahab returned angrily. "The rain does not bring back the thousands of horses we've lost, nor the army we no longer can afford, nor does it fill the treasury. And Baal is no longer the god of Israel. Your Baal wouldn't answer four hundred and fifty priests, but Yahweh answered one prophet in the most dramatic way possible. I would not have believed it if I had not seen it with my own eyes.

"And, my Queen, priestess of Ashtoreth, Yahweh sent the rain according to Elijah's word, just the way Elijah said he would three years ago."

Ahab reached up and took hold of the maid's arm with one hand and the towel with the other. "Stop!" he said sternly as he took the towel from her hand. "All of your priests and prophets are dead. In front of all Israel Zohelethbal accepted Elijah's challenge, and was so bold as to add that the loser be put to death. And now he and the rest are dead."

"Dead? Who is dead? What are you talking about, Ahab? You are not making sense!" shouted Jezebel.

Jezebel listened, dumbfounded, as Ahab recounted the events of the day. She was afraid to try to awaken herself from this bad dream, afraid that she wasn't asleep, and that the terrible tale that Ahab was telling was true.

"For half a day the priests of Baal cried out to your god, but he didn't answer them. Most of Israel laughed at Elijah behind his back as he repaired an old altar that had been torn down. It was about five cubits high, and was made of large stones, unlike the altars of Baal.

"No one believed that his God would answer, but when he prayed they stopped laughing. You could feel a power in the air, unlike anything that I ever experienced. All the people knew it was going to happen before it happened. I cannot explain it. Perhaps it was like being in the presence of a god. I've heard you speak of such things before, but it was the first time I ever felt anything like this.

"Then the fire came from the clear blue sky, not lightning, but a ball of fire that burned the sacrifice." Ahab's voice rose, "But not just the sacrifice. It burned the stones, even the ground in a circle maybe twenty cubits around the altar. Elijah poured three barrels of water on this altar and it was all burned up, gone, and some of the earth still burned afterward." His words, the pitch in his voice and the image she pictured sent a chill of fear and awe through Jezebel.

The handmaid behind Ahab and the servant at his feet were stunned. It was clear to Jezebel that Ahab, who had never known fear, was afraid of Elijah and his God.

"My lord, King of Israel, have you not lost a battle and yet won the war? Battles on earth are won or lost by the gods and there are many gods. Perhaps Yahweh became ally to other gods and was able to overpower Baal for a time. And don't forget which God and which prophet has made us vulnerable to our enemies. Elijah is the enemy of the king, and of Israel. Your father honored many gods, Baal above all others, and Israel became the greatest nation on earth. It has been a hundred years since Yahweh supposedly made this nation great, or that may even be just a legend." Jezebel's voice became even more intense. "Elijah is your enemy! Put him to death before he raises a rebellion against you and takes your throne!"

There was a silence as the king considered the counsel of his queen.

"Would Israel follow Elijah if he were to lead a rebellion against you right now?" she asked.

The events of the day had overshadowed Ahab's political instincts, but now the reality of the danger to his throne loomed in his mind like the rain clouds over Israel that night.

"If you don't stop him he will take your throne." Jezebel drove her point home as forcefully as she dared.

Ahab pondered these things as he paced back and forth. "All Israel would turn against me if I were to raise a hand against Elijah now," he said, almost to himself. "And it's almost certain that Jehu would not go against Elijah and the people of Israel if it came to a battle."

Impatiently, Jezebel interrupted Ahab. "Enough of this! I will kill this hairy dog myself! You can say that I did it without your knowledge, or that he was raising an army against you; and he may well be!"

Jezebel turned to the servants still standing near Ahab, "Get Eber, now! Find Obadiah!"

On the outskirts of Jezreel was a lively inn that was celebrating the rain when Elijah banged on the gate set in the wall surrounding the inn. The gatekeeper looked through a small portal and said, in a raspy voice, "A copper shekel to enter, sir." The hinged gate squeaked ajar and Elijah stepped sideways through the opening. A slightly bent old man moved back under a leaky roof beside the gate. The roof should have been large enough to keep the rain off of him and one more.

"Isn't it marvelous that Lord Baal has been appeased and sent us rain again?" he asked. The light from a torch exaggerated the lines in his face as he shifted to one side to avoid a drip that was leaking through. At that moment lightning lit up the night, and the rumble of thunder rose and ebbed in crescendos across the sky until it was no longer audible. "He is a mighty god, is he not? Even he seems to be celebrating tonight. The thunder is his laughter after each lightning bolt he casts to earth," said the old man.

Elijah studied him as he spoke, and continued to stare when he finished, to the point that the old man felt uncomfortable and added, to escape his gaze, "You must be cold. Your handsome robe is soaked."

"I don't have a shekel of copper for you, but I have gold."

"With gold to spend, you haven't the need for a copper shekel. You are welcome. There are merchants from the east, and women to suit the liking of any man."

Elijah stepped from under the dripping roof into the pouring rain. He walked across the court between camels lying on the ground, chewing cud and paying little attention to large drops of rain pelting their coats.

Upon opening the door of the inn he was greeted by a servant who bowed to him. "Noble sir, food, drink, a place to sleep, or perhaps a beautiful woman with which to worship the great lord Baal?"

It was obvious that word of the day's events hadn't reached Jezreel. Elijah and the king had arrived long before any one else, so the inn's patrons believed that Baal had brought the rain.

In front of him in the large room were three long low tables that were crowded with men sitting on the floor eating and drinking. Others leaned against the walls watching a nude woman at the far end. She gyrated to the sound of a single small drum before a life size image of a seated Baal. A gyration would begin with one foot and climb her body as she slowly turned. The motion reminded Elijah of a slithering viper. The movement was almost hypnotic. She rubbed her body over the clay image, kissing the idol at every opportunity.

There were eight, maybe ten lewdly clad prostitutes standing near the front, waiting to be hired for whatever purpose a man might believe would please lord Baal. The worship of this demon satisfied the lusts of men and fed the hunger of the greedy. A man who believed in no god might profess allegiance to Baal for the pleasures it offered. Elijah had never seen or imagined a spectacle like this before. He now realized how Baal worship had spread so quickly over Israel. The woman was beautiful and very enticing. Once she looked toward Elijah, but he was sure she wasn't seeing anything. Her eyes were distant and glazed.

The servant allowed Elijah to watch uninterrupted for a minute, then asked, "What will your pleasure be, sir?"

With the back of his left hand he slowly pushed the servant to the side without saying a word. There was something about the strength in Elijah's arm that kept him from resisting. It was as though no man could have resisted his power. With each breath Elijah could feel the power growing inside. The Spirit of Yahweh was upon him. It was like being the invincible finger of God.

He found a nearly clear path to the front on the right side of the room, and had to nudge only two men aside. When he reached the front, the woman was wrapped around the idol with her breasts pressed against it. Beads of sweat on her body caught the flickering light.

He took her by the arm just below the shoulder and began to pull her upward. Because the pain of his grip on her was too great, she released her hold of Baal and rose by the strength of his lifting power. He shoved the idol over with his foot, toppling it to the floor. Several men near the front stood to come to her aid. His eyes met hers for one instant, and for the first time he saw her clearly. He froze momentarily with shock, his mind reeling.

A moment later, he was seized by three men. They were shouting at him but he didn't hear them. He released Adah who fell to the floor.

Elijah screamed, "Aaaaaaah!" with such force that it struck fear into the men who had taken hold of him. As though they were leaves in the wind, he tossed one to the side and another in the opposite direction. The third he lifted over his head and threw onto one of the tables, then grabbed the table and turned it over.

A soldier standing nearby drew a sword and came at him. Elijah dodged his thrust, grabbed him by the arm, and slung him around. He wrenched the sword from the soldier's hand, then hammered the butt of the sword into his side. The blow knocked the breath from the soldier's lungs and disabled him for the moment.

"I am Elijah! I am Elijah! Hear that, Baal!" he shouted insanely, then turned and wielded the sword through the air, coming down on the idol's neck, shattering the head from the body. He continued to hack at the image, shattering away little pieces with each blow.

He jerked his wet mantle off and threw it over Adah's naked body as she stared at him in fear. Everyone else in the room was also staring at this mad man who had suddenly appeared in their midst. The soldier got to his feet and feebly came at him. Elijah turned and slapped him across the cheek with the broad side of the sword, drawing blood from the cheekbone below his left eye. Elijah grabbed him by the hair of his head and pulled him forward as he kicked his feet from under him. The soldier fell forward to the floor, but turned to get up, to find the point of the sword at his throat. "Come at me once more and I'll kill you!" Elijah shouted. There was no doubt that he meant what he said. The soldier scooted away to safety.

Elijah turned and shouted, "Yahweh Elohim is now God over Israel! The God of Abraham answered by fire, and sent the rain! We have put to death four hundred fifty priests of Baal!

"Go ahead, worship Baal and bring another drought upon the land!" He lunged forward and turned over a second table onto eight men. With a chopping blow he swung at the toppled table's edge, sending a chip and splinters flying. Someone came at him from behind. He spun around and caught the attacker in the rib cage with the point of the now jagged blade. The assailant stopped before the sword penetrated the ribs. He backed away as blood from the wound colored the hole in his robe.

"There is no god but the God of Abraham." Each person felt the soul-piercing gaze of this wild man as he looked slowly around the room. "Who is the proprietor of this den of whores and Baal worship?" demanded the prophet.

Several people looked in the direction of a plump, round, well-dressed man. Elijah walked over to him and placed the point of the sword under his chin. "If I see a sight like this the next time I come here, I will sever your head just as I did the head of Baal."

"Sever my head, why don't you, servant of Yahweh." Elijah turned to see Adah standing behind him with his mantle on. "I worship Baal and I serve him with my body, so sever my head." She was more mature, but as beautiful as the last time he saw her. But there was hardness that hadn't been there before.

"Johanan is dead, my sister is dead and two of their daughters are temple whores. We hid in the hills but they found us, or some of us. Johanan wouldn't bow to Baal but I bowed and kissed him and now I like kissing him. He is my god!" She stormed angrily at Elijah.

"The queen says that I represent Ashtoreth more completely than any other priestess. She has watched me with more than thirty men at a time. Great men have bowed to Baal for my body.

"I was forced to serve in the temple. The first year I didn't cease to pray for deliverance, but Yahweh wouldn't listen to my prayers. I bore Baal a son who was offered on the altar in the presence of Jezebel. At that moment I began to believe that Yahweh Elohim had forsaken Israel, or had been driven away by the greater Baal. Glory to the great Baal. Then I decided I would serve him and please him with all my might."

"Why didn't you go to Judah like I said?" He struggled for anything to say, his heart feeling as if it would burst.

"Because I thought if I stayed you might come back to me after you had done what your God called you to do."

She opened the mantle to reveal her body to him. "This was yours, Elijah. Zohelethbal the high priest of Baal has enjoyed my favors in the presence of Baal many times."

"It will never happen again!" Elijah spat through clenched teeth. A mixture of anger and pain arose in him, the veins in his neck visibly pulsating.

"Why? Are you, Oh great prophet, going to sever my head?" Though spoken sarcastically, it was still the soft voice he once loved to hear.

"No, because I severed Zohelethbal's head this day!" Elijah grimaced as he raised the sword above his head. There was a silence of shock and disbelief. This was Elijah. She knew that he had spoken the truth and was stunned for a moment.

Elijah looked around the room and spoke to them all as he spoke to her. "You have heard about the challenge I presented to King Ahab and the priests of Baal. Baal failed to answer, but Yahweh did not, and we killed all of the priests of Baal this day. Baal isn't a god but a demon that steals your children, and turns your daughters into whores.

"Most of you don't believe it's possible that only one god exists, but now you will see that it's true. Yahweh Elohim is the only God. It was He that sent the rain! Give him the praise!"

Some of the men had backed toward the door, then ran when they had the chance. Others watched Elijah cautiously as they listened. Could this mad man be telling the truth? They waited to see what might happen next.

Elijah looked back at Adah. "I can not apologize for obeying Yahweh. He would have turned this nation into ashes like he did Sodom and Gomorra if someone hadn't followed him to turn the hearts of the people back."

Elijah turned toward Adah, "And what would have happened to you if you hadn't bowed to Baal?"

Adah thought for a moment. "I would have been killed. But because I was a virgin, I would more likely have been forced into temple prostitution, or offered as a sacrifice."

"You are not called to account for what you have no power to change. If you had died, your reward from Yahweh would have been great. But you live and your son died, and now you will give account for choosing to serve Baal. I have found Yahweh to be very merciful, as King David discovered he was. If you will cry out to Yahweh-Tsidkenu, Yahweh your protector, he will be there. You will find him."

"What about us?" she asked, then quickly added before he could answer, "I know that the great Elijah would never have anything to do with a woman as defiled as I. That's what you think, isn't it? I am unclean, defiled! "

There was a contemptuous defiance in her words. "And who are you, but the son of a Moabite whore. That's right, Oh great Elijah, your mother was a whore." His heart was already breaking but that statement cut him deeply.

"My son is dead!" she screamed at him. Then in surly tones, masking her broken heart, she added, "And where are your sons? I praise the dead, which are already dead, more than the living that are still alive. Better are they than both, which have not been, who have not seen the evil done under the sun."

He recognized the words of Solomon. She looked at him for a moment, wishing for what could never be, then said, "Go back to your God and I'll go back to mine." She took off the mantle and slowly handed it to him. She stood before him naked to make him desire her and feel remorse for the time they never had. It was a kind of revenge, but she wouldn't have seduced him if she could have. She still loved him. She turned to walk away.

The next moment the door swung open and Captain Jehu stepped in with two of his officers and Zechariah. Zechariah rushed over to Elijah. The others stood looking at the chaos for a moment before their eyes settled on Adah as she walked away. She disappeared through an archway followed by the other prostitutes. Unable to speak for a moment, Zechariah stammered with his eyes still on the empty doorway, "Jehu said this was the only inn in Jezreel. We thought we might find you here. Who was that?"

The owner of the inn hurried over to Jehu. "This man nearly killed one of Ahab's men and destroyed my Baal."

Jehu looked into the round face of the innkeeper. "This man is Elijah! You are lucky that he didn't kill you, little man! Now bring some food for me and these men!"

Elijah stood there with his heart in pain as Zechariah and the others, including those who witnessed his outrage, began to set the tables upright.

They all turned to look at Elijah when they heard the clang of the sword, as he tossed it from his hand.

Jehu approached Elijah. "What happened here, Elijah? Are you all right?"

"He came at me with a sword, and I took it from him and destroyed their Baal," said Elijah. "He was foolish to try to protect the demon idol in this place. If Baal were a god, he could defend himself."

"The soldier was one of Jezebel's guard. He will be killed if the king, or Jezebel, should learn that a single unarmed man overtook him. He will likely make you out as a mad man who attacked poor Baal. They will be here soon!"

Interested in knowing Elijah's relationship to the beautiful woman who had just left the room, Jehu asked, "Was that woman someone you know?"

"Before the drought we were to be married, but all of this kept us apart. She said she was forced to be a temple prostitute, and now she is angry with Yahweh and hates me. She was a good woman." The fire was gone from Elijah's eyes when he looked into Jehu's and added, "She had a son who was burned on the altar of Baal."

Jehu answered, "I'm not a prophet but I know people. I've seen many men die and some women. A good person is one who faces death and dies if he has to without renouncing what he believes."

The implication that Adah hadn't been a good woman from the beginning roused anger in Elijah, but it was diverted when the door opened, turning everyone's attention to a young courier who entered. Water was dripping from his short hair and smooth boyish face. He looked around the room, then he eyes settled on Elijah. "Are you the man Elijah?" he asked. When Elijah nodded, he unwrapped a scroll protected in leather and began to read.

"From Queen Jezebel, in whom the spirit of the goddess Ashtoreth dwells. The Queen of the great Baal, to Elijah, prophet of Yahweh Elohim. So let the gods do to me and more, if by this time tomorrow I do not make your life like one of the great men you slew this day."

Jehu strode over to the messenger. "Where is the queen's guard now?"

The young man would have resisted, but he feared the stare of the captain, suspecting that he might be Jehu. "You're Jehu, aren't you?" the young man asked. Jehu didn't answer but his look assured him that he was. "The queen has called the guard to the palace."

"Get out!" Jehu commanded sternly. The courier hurriedly departed and Jehu turned back to face Elijah. "Jezebel's guard is faithful to her. They are all Baal worshipers. They weren't at Mount Carmel, and they will come after you, for they didn't see the power of Yahweh today. And, it doesn't matter what Ahab believes. After today, he will still hold you responsible for the great drought that brought the kingdom to its knees."

Jehu stepped closer to Elijah and placed his hands on his

shoulders. "Leave Jezreel! Perhaps Judah is where you belong for now. I will stall them as long as I can."

Zechariah came over to Elijah and took the mantle from his hand and wrapped it around Elijah's shoulders. "Jezebel's guard could be one step behind the messenger. We must go."

Jehu commanded his two men, "Find them blankets and food." When they didn't move fast enough he shouted, "Now!"

Moments later, when Zechariah had pressured Elijah to the door, Jehu's men met them with food and blankets.

Zechariah and Elijah stepped from the warm room into the pouring rain and the blackness of the night.

Thunder continued to roll across the sky of thick gray clouds on the day after the new moon. Water in the Kishon riverbed was beginning to flow again and its current toward the sea was carrying the bodies of the slain priests. Through the early hours of morning the water rose. Before nightfall all the dead servants of Baal would find their final resting places in the watery depths of the great sea.

The cold rain and moonless night made the flight of Elijah and Zechariah from Jezreel arduous. They stumbled slowly along a rough road leading south, unable to see even an outline of the ground.

Chilled by the cold rain, first light found them sheltering under a limestone overhang in the hills just a few miles from where they began the night before. Wet and shivering, fatigued and discouraged to the point of despair, and unable to find anything to start a fire with, they rested as best they could.

Zechariah lay with his back against Elijah's chest, his face just a few inches from the water that dripped from the overhanging rock. Elijah's back was against the cold stone as he pondered their plight and wished he hadn't allowed the son of his friend and mentor to come with him. Zechariah drifted in and out of a restless sleep, interrupted by bone-chilling tremors. Elijah also trembled from the cold, but was more concerned for the health of Zechariah than for his own comfort. He knew they couldn't survive this continuing cold rain much longer in clothes already soaked.

Elijah left Zechariah and ventured back into the steady heavy drizzle. The hillside was covered with dead trees from which he hacked limbs, using the small gold handled dagger that had so recently seen such different service. He made several trips, dragging back a small bundle each time.

When he was once again under the small shelter of rock, he began to carve away the bark and outer layers of wood. He found the wood under the outer layers dry and easy to ignite, and soon had a small fire going. Elijah shook Zechariah, "Sit up and eat." When Zechariah didn't respond, he pulled him up into a sitting position by the sleeve of his robe. "Zechariah, Zechariah!" Elijah called as he slapped him gently on the side of his face. His cheek felt feverish to Elijah's touch.

"I'm so cold," Zechariah said through trembling blue lips.

"Eat and get warm or you are going to die." Elijah cradled him against his chest. They ate and dried their clothes and slept again. Elijah had to make another wet trip for wood and they spent the following night there in the shallow two-by-six cubits of dry space with just enough clearance to sit up under the ledge.

The second day Elijah gave the last of the food to Zechariah before they continued southward. With the rain still falling and Zechariah weak and feverish, they slowly made their way toward the safety of Judah, avoiding the cities of Beth-Haggan and Dothan. Still many miles from the haven of Jehoshaphat's domain, they entered Tirzah long after dark with Zechariah's arm over Elijah's shoulder. Elijah pulled him along forcing him to take each step. It was near midnight when Elijah banged at the gate of the family of Micaiah.

Several minutes passed before the sliding portal in the gate opened. A white bearded old man held a lantern close to the small opening next to his face, trying to peer through the rain and darkness at the source of the intrusive banging. Elijah could see his eyes better than they could see him.

"I don't know if you will remember me but I was here several years ago with Micaiah. I'm Elijah." He paused for an answer then continued when there wasn't an immediate response. "He was with me a couple of days ago at Mount Carmel. Is he here? We need his help."

The gate slowly opened. "My son, Micaiah, has spoken of you often. Come in. Yes, I remember when you came here with my son years ago. Micaiah stays in Samaria most of the time now, but I am expecting him any day." When the white bearded gentleman saw Zechariah's condition he asked, "What is wrong with your friend?"

"He has gotten a chill from the rain. This is the son of the prophet Jehew."

"Oh yes, I know Jehew, I've met him. It was here in Tirzah that he prophesied the destruction of King Baasha. That's how Micaiah came to know him. He inspired Micaiah to follow in his footsteps; to become a scholar of the law. He was Micaiah's teacher."

The old man's white beard seemed to glow from the light as he held up the lantern to see Zechariah more closely. With his other hand he held a blanket over his head. A time or two the blanket slid to the back of his head as he moved. He was bald on the top of his head, with long hair that grew from the sides to join his facial hair. He studied Zechariah's face for a moment, then said, "Come quickly, we must get his son out of the rain."

They moved swiftly across the small court into the house as Micaiah's father held up the lantern to light the way. Elijah eased Zechariah onto a couch as the old man's wife came into the room. Her hair was as white as his beard and hung down to her waist. "Make some broth and bring blankets. This is Jehew's son and he is sick, and this is Elijah."

She was apprehensive for an instant, then said, "The king's men were in Tirzah today looking for him."

The old man answered back, "I know, I saw them too! Bring the blankets."

When she left the room he turned to Elijah, "The king has accused you of treason. He claims that you are raising an army to take the throne. Is this true?"

"Yahweh has chosen me to be a prophet and judge over Israel. He hasn't called me to be king, or to overthrow Ahab. Yahweh will do that in his own time. When Micaiah comes, ask him what happened at Mount Carmel. He will tell you what my purpose is. I could have called upon the people to stone Ahab, and at that moment they would have done so, but instead I bowed before the king. Why the king would do such a thing as this, after witnessing the power of Yahweh, I can't understand."

The old man answered, "It's not just the king, it's that sorceress Jezebel. She has cast her spell on him." His voice dropped to a low raspy whisper. "I have heard that Zidonian witchcraft is very powerful and it is said that she has a eunuch who practices magic from the east. And that is very powerful too."

The old man's eyes widened as though the mention of witchcraft itself was evil. "She had a slave, a sorceress, Tamara, who angered her by saying something that opposed her belief and the queen had her burned on the altar of Baal. Jezebel's only allegiance is to Baal and, besides myself, the only people I know who believe that Yahweh is the only god are my son, Micaiah, Jehew and you. Even my wife believes that Yahweh is only one of many gods.

"The king has a legion of advisors, prophets who believe in Yahweh and Baal and Moloch and a hundred others. They also believe that Jezebel is the incarnation of Ashtoreth, which gives her great influence over them. The king is afraid of Micaiah, my son, because his prophecies do not agree with those of the king's prophets. Ahab has had him beaten and thrown into prison several times."

"I know, Micaiah told me." Elijah answered.

"There is once again a reward of a talent of gold for you." The white bearded old man hesitated for a moment, then finished what he had begun to say. "Or for your head carried to the king." He turned and knelt by Zechariah. "We must get these wet clothes off of him." He looked over his shoulder at Elijah as he began to remove the wet robe from Zechariah. "You can stay as long as you need to, but you are not safe anywhere in Israel."

Elijah moved closer to help remove Zechariah's robe. "Forgive me, sir, I don't remember your name. It's been many years since we met."

"My name is Imla, son of Ezbon, and my wife's name is Zillah."

Zechariah grew worse over the next couple of days. Then on the sixth day from the time the rains began, the sun rose bright into a partially blue sky and Elijah's young helper began to recover. Elijah insisted that he stay in bed until his brow was no longer warm to the touch.

On the tenth day after their arrival they prepared to leave and were waiting for the sun to go down when Micaiah knocked at the gate. Elijah and Zechariah stepped from the court into the house as Imla, fearful that his visitors had been reported to the king, checked to see who was there.

"Micaiah!" he shouted as he opened the gate and embraced his son. Zillah came running from the house when she heard his name.

She threw her arms around him as tears streamed from her eyes. "My heart aches with fear for you. Please never go back to Samaria." She clung to him as she pleaded, "Stay here where you are safe."

He returned her embrace then spotted Elijah and Zechariah as they stepped from the house. "Mama, I am doing well," he said as he gently pulled her arms from around his neck.

"You lie to your mother!" she scolded, "I know what the king has done to you."

Micaiah gave his father a quick embrace. "Papa, are you doing well?"

"Yes, yes, we are doing well. We have visitors, friends of yours."

"I see," he said as he stepped past his father and mother in Elijah's direction. "Are you headed to Judah?" he asked as he gave Elijah then Zechariah a hug.

"Where else would we be safe from Ahab?"

"Not in Judah, not now. Ahab is there now to secure a treaty that allows the worshipers of Yahweh in Israel to worship at the temple in Jerusalem. Ahab believes that Yahweh Elohim is a great god who can strengthen him, and he is there to do sacrifice. It makes him look good to Jehoshaphat, and to the people of Israel. He doesn't believe that Yahweh is the only god, but wants to appease all gods after he saw such power at Carmel. This gives him the excuse that he's been looking for to approach Jehoshaphat. An alliance with Judah would strengthen Israel against Syria and Moab and Philistia.

"He has spread the word that you are raising a rebellion against him. You are a fugitive. Jehoshaphat has wanted to reunite the kingdom through some kind of peace agreement. If he were to give you asylum now, that would be an act of war. He believes the report. Everyone as far away as Egypt knows about the ongoing war between you and Jezebel, so it's not a hard thing to believe that you would raise an army against Ahab. By the power of Yahweh, you should raise an army against him. Right now most of Israel would follow you."

Zillah cried out, "My son, you shouldn't say such things! If anyone should hear you the king would have you whipped to death." She came closer. "Please promise me that you won't say such things."

"The man is the most vile king Israel has ever known!" Micaiah tersely replied. "He will destroy this nation. Yahweh will forsake us and our enemies will enslave all that they don't kill. Mama, Baal is not a god, but a demon! He couldn't answer the prayers of four hundred and fifty of his priests but Yahweh answered the prayer of Elijah and sent fire that burned up even the rocks and ground."

She took hold of his robe as she pleaded through teary eyes, "Micaiah! Please don't say such things about Baal. He can hear you, as he hears everything."

Micaiah took her by the wrists and looked into her eyes as she clung to his robe. Softly he said, "There is only one God, mother, Yahweh Elohim." Glancing over her head he said to Elijah, "You are not safe in Israel or Judah. Go to Egypt until Yahweh brings judgment upon Ahab and Jezebel; and he will."

Elijah said, "We've put your family in jeopardy by being here. I don't know where we will go, but when it gets dark we will continue south. Perhaps we'll receive direction. I've prayed these last ten days and I still don't know where I'm to go or what to do."

"Have one last meal here so that I may break bread with you." Micaiah's invitation was one that would have been rude to refuse.

Night had settled over the land when they continued their flight from the reaches of Ahab and Jezebel. In two days they were in the Judean controlled territory of Ephraim. They made camp a short distance from Bethel, then Zechariah went into the city for supplies, and to find out what conditions existed for Elijah to find refuge in Judah.

Elijah was sitting by the fire mending his sandals when his companion returned. Elijah watched Zechariah approach. He could tell by the look on his face that the news wasn't good. "It's worse than we thought," Zechariah said when he came within speaking distance.

He seated himself across from Elijah as he added, "King Jehoshaphat is allowing Ahab's troops into Judah in small bands to search for you, and the people of Judah have been warned not to harbor you. There is a reward of a talent of gold to anyone who turns you over to Ahab." Zechariah could see the despair on Elijah's face as Elijah dropped his gaze toward the small fire without responding.

For several long minutes the only sound that was heard was the crackle from the flames. Then, trying to sound uplifting, Zechariah said, "I've given it some thought and I think we would be safe in Beersheba. It's so far south I don't think they will go there in search of you. It's like it's not even a part of Judah. Mostly desert people live there. And, if we needed to go on to Egypt, it would be only a day's journey out of the way."

Elijah raised his eyes to meet Zechariah's. "They're not looking for you, so there's no need for you to go any further. Your home is in Jerusalem now, and that's where you should be. Find your father and take him to King Jehoshaphat. Advise the king against the wickedness of Ahab."

"My father may already be in Jerusalem. I sent word to him by Obadiah when we were at Carmel. I'm going with you."

Elijah, trying to brighten up the conversation, said, "I hear it gets really hot in Beersheba."

The following morning they began the three-day trek to Beersheba. When they reached the city where they hoped to find safety, they found a large walled inn that could accommodate large caravans of many camels. They stayed there while Zechariah kept his ears open, trying to find out if word of Elijah and the reward for his head had gotten this far south.

Elijah stayed out of sight as much as possible and daily went into the desert crying out to Yahweh, but the heavens were silent. News of the fire of Yahweh at Mount Carmel had reached the city but had been dismissed as an exaggeration by the teachers and prophets at Beersheba. News that Elijah was a fugitive hadn't reached that far and perhaps wouldn't since the other wasn't believed.

Beersheba was a large oasis on a major trade route that had grown into a hub of commerce, with goods coming from the east, west and north. On the south side of the city was a large fortress under construction. It was being built to keep the route open and free from robbers. The city bustled with caravans, traders, troops and chariots.

With the inn being a caravan station, Elijah began to feel that he should travel to Egypt with the next caravan going in that direction. The innkeeper told him that it could be a few days to a month before a caravan on the way to Egypt might come through.

Since the news of a reward on his head hadn't reached this far south, Elijah began to venture into the market place. He and Zechariah attended the day long teaching of scriptures that took place each Sabbath. From one of the eight towers on the wall of the fortress a wooden platform was extended, where the priest would stand and read, occasionally stopping to expound on what was being read. Elijah and Zechariah fashioned a canopy from a blanket to sit under, the same as most of the listeners had. Around noon there was a two-hour rest period for eating, talking, and relaxing.

"We have received word from Jerusalem." The voice of the priest carried through the camp and turned everyone's attention back to the platform on the tower earlier than expected.

"It is known that we are now at peace with Israel, there is an alliance between Israel and Judah." The priest's words were clear and deliberate. "King Ahab has brought back the worship of Yahweh to Israel and the people of Israel will sacrifice in Jerusalem as the law commands.

"More than a week ago we received word that Yahweh Elohim of Abraham answered a prophet named Elijah by fire in northern Israel. The teachers of the temple at Jerusalem believe that he did this by sorcery. People of Judah, be not deceived. It is known by all the teachers of the law, that since Solomon built the glorious temple, Yahweh does not work through such signs any longer.

"The great signs of Yahweh in the past were to bring us to this land and the building of the temple where our Yahweh dwells. False prophets like Elijah will deceive people who look for signs. Today men have come from Samaria in search of Elijah. He attempted to raise an army to overthrow King Ahab. If Yahweh had answered Elijah and not some demon, would he need an army to take Ahab's throne or would he flee from mere men? Did Moses flee from Pharaoh after he had stood in the presence of El Shaddai?

"With the men of Samaria is a man who can identify him and there is a reward of a talent of gold for anyone who knows where he is, or who brings his head to King Ahab. He is a hairy man of average height, he is a Gadite from the land of Gilead." As the people began to whisper the priest raised hands to silence them so he could continue. "King Jehoshaphat has promised King Ahab full cooperation in their search for him." The priest turned and walked back into the fortress tower.

Elijah and Zechariah glanced around to see if any of Ahab's men were close by. In a whisper, Elijah said to his companion, "Why can't I find peace somewhere in this world?" He was glad that he had worn a kaffiyeh on his head, it hid most of the hair that would have betrayed him otherwise. "We must find a way out of here without arousing suspicion."

"There are so many people moving around right now that no one would notice if you were to walk away," Zechariah said as he continued to search for someone who looked familiar that might recognize them. "There were so many people at Mount Carmel that would know us but we wouldn't recognize them."

Elijah weighed the situation for a moment then said, "This is the Sabbath. They won't begin a search today, and I don't think they will be looking for me here. There was no mention of you." He thought for another moment then said, "Zechariah, you must find out if your father is with King Jehoshaphat and the two of you must keep the wicked influences of Jezebel and Ahab out of Judah. The last few days as I've prayed, I realized that the prince of darkness and the spirit of Baal are still fighting for control over the minds of the people of Israel. If they kill me, then they would undo what was accomplished at Mount Carmel. It's so clear now, because of his defeat at Carmel, the evil one has launched an attack on Judah. You and your father must see that their evil does not spread here. If you can, prevent any kind of an alliance.

"Zechariah!" The change in Elijah's voice caused Zechariah to look directly at him as he said more sternly now, "The wicked one knows that from these people will come the Messiah, and he's trying to prevent it."

Elijah stood. His stare remained locked on Zechariah. "You must succeed! If you don't, it may mean the end of the royal line." Elijah took the bag of gold from his belt and tossed it to his young helper. "Return Jehoshaphat's gold. You've been a good friend. I cannot repay you for your help, but thank you. One thing you lack as a prophet is the kind of patience that your father has. Give my regards to him." Zechariah started to get up. "No," Elijah said softly. "Stay seated. Don't do anything to attract attention."

"Where will you go?" Zechariah asked regretfully, knowing that Elijah was about to leave him.

"Only Yahweh knows." Elijah turned and walked away. Zechariah watched him as he worked his way through the crowd and disappeared.

The wind began to blow dust across the barren landscape as night crept from the east, and the western sky faded from yellow to orange, then pink and purple. Elijah wandered southward as he considered where he might go, away from the reach of Ahab and Jezebel. It didn't seem to matter anymore, and the rising moon in its last quarter reminded him of how quickly things had changed. When the new moon announced the beginning of the month, his name was spoken along with the great servants of Yahweh: Moses, Gideon, Samuel, and David. But now he was a fugitive and his name a curse word.

The memory of Adah as he first knew her, and what she had become, tore at his heart. Perhaps he was wrong in leaving her, but at the time he had no way of knowing what fate awaited him when he went to face Ahab. The loss of his lifelong friend, Johanan, and the fate of his family would have enraged the prophet at any other time. Now it brought tears that accompanied his aching heart. He wept for several hours as he walked, remembering those that had meant so much to him. The longer he dwelt on them, the deeper the despair rooted itself.

Sometime in the middle of the night, Elijah found a little shelter from the wind, under a broom tree at the end of a small clump of the low, bushy shrubs. He sat and leaned against the small tree trunk, pulled the mantle around his head, and tucked his face between his knees.

In the hours before first light, the only good thing he could find about being alive was the fragrance of desert flowers, carried on the air that diminished to a breeze in the early hours.

When a small band of light stretched across the eastern horizon, he raised his head and stared into the dawning day. "I have endured enough, Yahweh Elohim," he spoke softly. He thought for a minute then said it a second time, "I have endured enough." He raised his voice as he choked back the tears and prayed. "Take my life, please, Yahweh, take my life! I am no better than my fathers, and I don't want to go on living." He wept until his insides ached.

It was mid morning when Elijah laid down and pulled the mantle around his head, and wished that he could go to sleep and never wake up. He quickly fell asleep from exhaustion.

Something touched Elijah on the shoulder and woke him. In the same instant he heard the words, "Get up and eat." Startled, he wrenched himself into a sitting position, but there wasn't anyone there. The sun was nearly overhead. He glanced around and saw a jug of water, a small fire, and a cake of bread still cooking on a hot stone surrounded by glowing coals.

"Who is there?" He jumped to his feet and looked in every direction. There was no one in the small clump of trees, and he could see for miles across the broad vistas. He drew his gold handled dagger as he shouted, "Is someone there?"

Perplexed, he gripped the dagger tightly as he cautiously stepped from the shade of the broom tree into the bright sun, and walked a short distance out into the desert. There was no place for anyone to hide, and there were no tracks in the sand. He walked back to the tree and stood there for several minutes, watching the flames of the fire and the bread cooking on the rock.

He remained poised, as he knelt to one knee and took the pitcher of water. He sloshed it around, smelled of it, then gulped down a long, cold drink.

"This could only be Yahweh," Elijah said aloud then asked, "but what does it mean?" The bread was turning a light brown. It had cooked long enough and he didn't want it to burn. He cautiously removed the large cake of bread and broke it, but it was too hot to hold. He dropped the steaming bread onto the hem of his robe where he let it cool for several minutes before he picked it up again.

He continued to look around every several seconds, as he began to eat. He had never tasted bread as good. It was slightly sweet, and unlike anything he had ever eaten.

When he finished eating, he took another drink and wished that there were more, as he tried to analyze what it all meant. Though he no longer wanted to live, he was still alive. He sat quietly for an hour, thinking about the strange meal he had just eaten, and questioned his own sanity. Perhaps he had gone mad, but no, he now knew that nothing was beyond the ability of Yahweh. His eyes began to feel heavy. He fought it for a while then lay down and yielded to sleep. The last thought that crossed his mind was that the meal of bread had been a very real dream.

"Rise up and eat." It was the voice he had heard before. Something nudged him in the ribs. Just a tint of color was left in the evening sky as Elijah opened his eyes. This time he slowly turned his head toward the light of a fire. A gray haired soldier sat across the fire from him, stirring the coals with a stick. Elijah sat up and studied the man who wore a kilt, a light blue tunic, and a solid gold breastplate. The lacing of his sandals crisscrossed around the calves of his legs and the sheath of his sword stretched out behind him on the ground. "Eat, for the journey is too great for you." The man's friendly countenance made Elijah feel at ease as he smiled and nodded for Elijah to take some of the bread that was again baking on the stone.

Elijah broke the bread and took a bite. "Where am I going?" The soldier didn't answer and his gaze suddenly made Elijah feel uncomfortable. Elijah extended half the cake of bread toward the messenger and asked. "Would you like some?" Suddenly he was gone, not like he had disappeared but as though he had never been there. Elijah was sure that he had seen a vision, but he had bread in both hands. "What does this mean? Where am I going?"

Elijah shivered with a chill as he glanced around to see if he were really alone. His mind reeled with questions as he tried to enjoy the bread as before. He was glad for the fire, a sort of friendly companion that he kept alive through the night. Could he have built the fire and not remembered it? No, he was sure that he had not, and his belly was full, very full in fact. The soldier had been a messenger from Yahweh.

As he sat under the broom tree and watched the sun rise the second morning, he prayed for direction and strained to hear the voice of Yahweh, but the only sound came from the songs of the birds as they flew in and out of the tree. He stood and looked north, east, south and west, then turned back south and began to walk. "Why south?" he tried to analyze it but couldn't give himself any reason but that it felt right. And if he were wrong? Well, an angel had met him before. For some reason Yahweh wanted him to live. But there wasn't anything to the south.

Elijah almost talked himself out of going that direction. He stopped and looked back at the broom tree and the shrubs that grew around it. Things were really no different today. Ahab still wanted to take his life. He would go south away from Israel. If Yahweh kept him alive, he would live and if Yahweh allowed him to die, he would die.

That day he traveled south, deeper into the desert as he thought and rethought the events of the past month, and the words of the angel. Day after day he looked to Yahweh for direction, but found nothing but an uncertain unction to move southward. The meaning of the angel's words became apparent when he found nothing to eat, and yet didn't grow hungry. But why wasn't there a clear direction?

The days were hot, but at night he built and slept by a fire, for the company of the flames as much as for their warmth. And each night he kept track of time by the phases of the moon. The month Elul passed, and the moon was waxing brighter since its new birth at the beginning of Tishri. Summer was gone; it wouldn't be long to the solstice at the end of Kislev.

For several days he ambled along, covering only a few miles each day. The urge to go south had left him, and all that remained was a desire to leave this world. In the evening he sat by the fire, watching the moon climb into the night sky, and calculated that he had been in the desert thirty-nine days. He had been sustained miraculously, without food and very little water. For what? To die here? That didn't make sense. He determined to go no further, but would die here unless Yahweh spoke to him.

Like any shepherd would, he had camped with his back to a mountain, and as the day dawned he decided to climb the stone sentinel that had guarded his back through the night. From there he could look out and find a direction or there he would die.

As he made his way up the lower slope of the mountain, covered with brush and loose stone that sometimes caused his feet to slide from under him, a strange feeling rose up inside. There was a sense of the nearness of Yahweh. He was sure, yes, Yahweh was close. Suddenly he realized that he had been traveling toward Mount Horeb. Where he was now walking, Moses had walked hundreds of years before. As clearly as if someone had just told him, he knew that he was on the mountain of Shaddai Elohim. Elijah rushed toward the top. Skirting around cliffs, he pulled himself up by branches and small crevices in the rock. Numerous times he slipped and fell, until his shins were scuffed and bleeding. When he reached the summit he could see for miles in all directions. He was inspired because he was sure that Yahweh had met Moses there.

"Yahweh Elohim," he shouted but there was no response. He found a place to sit and waited. Sure that Yahweh was going to appear in some form, he began to sing. "Yahweh is good, his mercy is everlasting. The foundation of the world is his word. He directs the paths of the stars and each he calls by name. Yahweh Elohim is good, his mercy everlasting." He sang and prayed but there was no answer.

There remained about two hours of daylight when Elijah became discouraged and thought it best to move down from the summit to find a place to spend the night. Maybe this isn't Horeb, he thought.

Choosing a path on the far side that looked less difficult than the one he came up, he began the descent. In a short time he slid onto a plateau at the top of a cliff. He turned to cross the leveled area and found a cave hidden in the rocks, visible from nowhere but where he stood. He broke branches from nearby shrubs and built a fire, and from the fire made a torch. At the entrance of the cave he stretched the torch into the darkness and stepped in behind the light. The entrance was high enough for him to stand upright and walk through, but slanted downward some ten cubits to his left. Inside it opened up into a large room with a small tunnel to one side leading into the mountain. Elijah moved the fire into the cave where black coals of a previous fire told of other visitors long before. This is where he would stay until Yahweh showed him what he should do, or until he died.

Some of the first rays of the morning sun found their way into the mouth of the cave and sent swords of light that cut holes in the darkness. Elijah turned his head away and closed his eyes again. "What are you doing here, Elijah?" It was the voice he had longed to hear.

He jumped to his feet. "I have been zealous for you, Yahweh Elohim Shaddai. Israel has rejected your covenant, broken down your altars, and killed your prophets with the sword. I am the only one left and they want to kill me also."

"Go and stand on the mountain and I will pass by." The voice of God echoed in his mind and in his ears, unlike any other time Yahweh had spoken to him.

As Elijah reached the outside, a dark cloud moved across the face of the sun. A strong wind began to blow across the rocky slopes of Mount Horeb, rapidly increasing in intensity. Small sticks and bits of stone stung his face as he was pushed back into the cave by the howling, raging wind. Elijah could see the wind twisting together like fingers wrapping around the mountain. Boulders began to fly in the wind like stones hurled from a boy's sling. There has never been a wind like this before, thought Elijah. It was terrifying, an awesome thing to behold.

As Elijah knelt to the ground just inside the cave entrance and prayed, the wind ripped a wide path through the mountain adjacent to him, throwing the pieces high into the sky.

Fear gripped Elijah. "Have mercy on me, Yahweh," he prayed. Within his chest and through the veins of his neck, his heart pounded as he watched the incredible sight. The dust from the mountainside darkened the sun, as the wind swept it aloft. Large stones crashed down upon the ledge where he had been standing. For several minutes it continued. Then, the wind began to subside, and as quickly as it came, it was gone.

Elijah tried to stand but found himself too weak. As his strength returned, he, slowly and with great difficulty, rose to his feet and crept out onto the plateau. At first he couldn't tell if the ground was trembling, or if it was his own body. He looked at his hands and they were shaking. Suddenly the earth beneath him lurched hard and he fell to the ground. The mountain began to shake violently under Elijah as he tried in vain to reach the cave. The shaking carried him close to the cliff's edge. He was on the verge of going over and falling a couple of hundred cubits straight down when the quaking stopped. He held his breath as he slowly stood to his feet.

"What does this mean, Yahweh?" asked Elijah as he peered out. There were large cracks in the earth where smoke and steam were rising, and some of the brush on the mountainside was ablaze.

Large boulders began crashing down the slope from above. Elijah turned and looked up the mountain as a boulder shot overhead past him. A brightly glowing river of molten rock was flowing toward him, dislodging the rocks. There wasn't any place to take refuge but in the cave. Without another choice, Elijah stepped back into the cave entrance. He looked out, hoping to find a way of escape, when the glowing stream of rock began to pour down over the mouth of the cave from above.

Before it came close, Elijah could feel the intense heat on his face and moved back deeper into the cave. Pressed against the back wall, he watched as the lava poured over the low side of the entrance. He knew that if it moved a few cubits to the other side, he would be sealed within forever. Maybe this was where Yahweh would end his life.

The lava began to slow, then stopped, but the glowing rock made the inside of the cave feel like the inside of a bread oven.

"What are you doing here, Elijah?" This time the voice of Yahweh was like a breeze outside whispering through the rocks. Elijah heard it clearly, but as he thought about it, he was sure that anyone else would have heard only the wind.

He stepped close to the cave entrance. With his mantle shielding his face from the intense heat of the glowing rock, he lunged past it to the cooler air outside.

"What are you doing here, Elijah?" This time the voice came from within.

With great fear he spoke very softly. "I have been very zealous for you, Yahweh Elohim Shaddai. Israel has forsaken your covenant, broken down your altars, and put your prophets to death with the sword. I am the only one left, and they want to take my life also."

"Return the way you came, then go to the wilderness of Damascus. Anoint Hazael to be king over Syria, and Jehu, the son of Nimshi, you shall anoint to be king over Israel.

"Find Elisha, the son of Shaphat from Abel Meholah, and anoint him to be prophet in your stead. Jehu will slay all who escape the sword of Hazael, and Elisha will slay all that escape the sword of Jehu.

"Yet have I reserved seven thousand in Israel, all whose knees have not bowed down to Baal, nor have they kissed his image." Elijah felt engulfed in the presence of Yahweh as he spoke but when he had finished speaking the presence was gone. He had been instructed clearly and had many things to think about.

Yahweh had said it, then repeated it, "What are you doing here, Elijah?" Had he been completely out of the will of Elohim by fleeing from Ahab and coming here? Elohim had sustained him miraculously.

Elijah made his way down the mountain between the burning bushes and open fissures. An hour later as he walked away from the base of Mount Horeb, he turned back and watched the smoke from the smoldering mountain ascend toward heaven.

He knew Captain Jehu, and he had heard of Hazael of Syria, governor under King Ben-Hadad. Shaphat of Abel Meholah was a respected man in Israel, from one of the great families and a military hero, but he had never heard of Elisha, the son of Shaphat. He could remember no teacher or prophet by that name.

Elijah had a raging hunger that was curbed only slightly by eating locust on his eighteen-day return trip. Thirst wasn't a problem. The desert streams overflowed throughout the region because of the unusually heavy rains. Elijah welcomed the cool drenching that took place for short periods each day and cooled him from the desert heat.

The words of Yahweh frightened him for Israel. He had resented the nation, but now that the destruction of Israel was imminent, he prayed for them. Most were good people who had been deceived by their leaders and false prophets. The swords of Hazael, Jehu, and Elisha had already been prepared by Elohim.

Day and night he prayed, "Yahweh Elohim, have mercy on Israel, your people. Remember your covenant with Abraham. Bring judgment upon those who have taught them lies and deceived them, but for the rest, teach them the truth."

Elijah was beginning to believe that the course was unchangeable and Yahweh's will couldn't be altered. He sat by a fire the last night before he reached the border of Judah.

"I will delay my judgment on Israel for now. Find Elisha and turn the people away from following idols, for in the day I anoint Jehu to be king, all who haven't repented from following Baal will die by the sword. And Hazael will put to death all that haven't returned to me. I brought them out of bondage in Egypt, and have been a father to them. Their children belong to me, but they offer them to Baal and Ashtoreth and Moloch."

Elijah wept when he heard those words, for he knew there was still hope. "Oh, merciful, Yahweh, thank you, thank you. You are kind and your mercy everlasting." With his tears he worshipped Elohim until morning.

By the time he reached Beersheba, Elijah had figured out what Yahweh had done. It was a lesson hard to articulate into words, but it was something he would somehow have to convey to this Elisha, if he was to follow in his footsteps as prophet and judge of Israel.

El Shaddai never forsakes his servants. Elijah was trying to put what he had learned into concise thoughts. He ran in fear of Jezebel's edict, then prayed to die in the desert. Elijah chuckled to himself as he thought about it. What difference does it make which way one dies? To die of thirst and starvation seemed far worse than being beheaded by Ahab, yet he had been willing to accept that as an alternative. Now that he knew of the great power of El Shaddai to protect him, he would never be afraid of man again. He realized, after witnessing this awesome display, that it hadn't been necessary for him to run from Jezebel, or to go to Mount Horeb. The power of Elohim had been with him all the time, but he hadn't known it.

Elijah was hardly noticed as he strode through the city of Beersheba and traveled the main roads north toward Israel, Samaria, and the small town of Abel-Meholah, the meadow of dancing.

Because the treasury of Israel was empty, Ahab exacted a levy of one third of all possessions from every citizen returning to reclaim houses and land. Having learned beforehand of the taxation, Shaphat and his sons left most of their wealth in Ephraim, in the care of his brother, before returning to Israel. To reestablish the farm, they brought oxen, camels, and flocks of sheep and goats. Ahab's men took the best third of all they brought with them.

The showers that came several times a week since the first day of the month Ehul, when Yahweh answered Elijah, had softened the ground. Shaphat's sons and servants began plowing the large tract of fertile Jordan valley that had belonged to the family since the days of Joshua.

As the family settled in and repaired the old home and tilled the ground, Elisha began to feel restless. The tales and rumors of Elijah

varied greatly. Some claimed he was a sorcerer, others said that he was
a false prophet, and others thought he was a rebel, set on overthrowing
the throne of Ahab. A few, like Elisha, knew that he was a messenger
sent from Yahweh.

Shortly after returning to Abel-Meholah, Elisha harnessed one of
the camels and rode a half-day's journey to Tishbeh. The news that
Tishbeh had been destroyed wasn't exaggerated; the highest wall left
standing was less than waist high.

What sort of man is this Tishbite, he asked himself, as he walked
through the rubble of the town. What sort of man was he, that the
powers of darkness would go to such lengths to strike back at one
man? And why was he so fascinated with Elijah? Was it because Elijah
was used more mightily than any prophet since Moses, Gideon or
Samson? And, like them, he didn't come through the ranks, with the
approval of the priests and esteemed teachers of the day.

Elisha camped by the pool where Elijah and Adah had sat and
talked for hours on end. The beautiful trees were gone but the pool and
stream had returned since the rains.

How Elisha wanted to be used by Yahweh. He spent the night
praying to that end. "Oh great Yahweh Elohim, I know that I'm not
handsome to look upon but I am the son of a wealthy man and my
inheritance is great. All of that will I give to you, and will surrender
my rights to this world, if only you, in your mercy will use me to
bring glory to your name. Though I am a son of Abraham, I am
empty without you."

Before daylight his prayers were accompanied with tears of anguish, or desperation. He felt that his life was passing, and, unless
Yahweh answered him now, his chance of fulfillment would be gone
forever. When morning arrived, he didn't feel as though his prayers
had prevailed. He harnessed the camel and returned to Abel-Meholah
and the plowing.

In the days that followed, Elisha plead with Yahweh in silent
prayer, as he guided the plow across the long stretches of ground
in the Jordan valley. He saw his life without any significance unless
Yahweh answered him, but why would the God of Elijah take the
time to listen to him?

It was five days since his trip to Tishbeh when, in the early
morning light, as he organized the servants and plowmen for the
day's work, his mind was suddenly distracted, like someone calling
from a distance, but there was no call. His mind would just drift
away in the middle of a thought. "Elijah, the son of Hilkaih, is
coming for you today."

The fleeting thought jumped into his mind, but he forced it aside and said to himself, concentrate on what you are doing. Perhaps he hadn't rested well but it had been days since he had slept without being interrupted by dreams or troubling thoughts. He was troubled, but he couldn't put his finger on the problem. He pushed everything aside, hitched the oxen, and led the eleven servants and teams into the field for the day's work.

It was around mid-morning when Elijah topped the rise overlooking the valley where Elisha and the servants tilled the ground of what looked like an endless field. A third of a mile away, Elijah could smell the freshly turned soil, and the roots of wild herbs brought to the surface. Still a couple of miles from Abel-Meholah, he was unaware that Elisha was one of the men in the valley below.

Elisha was caught off guard when a whispering breeze sent a chill over his body, making him quiver. He stopped and attempted to shake it off, but the chills continued to run through him. He scanned the hills to the west, but saw nothing, then prodded the oxen forward and brought them to a halt a minute later. Could it be the sickness returning after so many years? There had been chills with the fever, but they weren't like these, and he felt strong and whole. His actions caught Elijah's attention. Suddenly Elijah knew that the man he was watching was Elisha, the son of Shaphat, the one that Yahweh had called to be prophet and judge of Israel.

Elisha continued plowing, and Elijah zigzagged down the steep slope until he reached the edge of the field at the bottom. Reaching the end of the row, Elisha turned the oxen around and spotted the prophet coming toward him over the plowed ground. His heart began to pound as Elijah approached. Still a great distance away, he looked more like a mirage than a man. Unaware of the identity of the approaching figure, he instinctively knew that he was a messenger from Elohim, and the chill ran through his body again. He trembled for a moment, then trembled again.

Elisha stood motionless, watching the man approach. Suddenly he remembered being told Elijah wore a blue cloak. "It's Elijah," he said softly to himself. Then he remembered the thought that had jumped into his mind earlier that morning. "Elijah is coming for you."

There wasn't a sound in the air when their eyes met. Elijah walked up to Elisha, who wasn't sure what to expect, removed his cloak and placed it on the shoulders of Elisha, then continued towards the Jordan River. Elisha looked at the cloak that draped down from his shoulders, then touched it with his hand. Joy welled up inside of him. This was the greatest thing that could have happened. The oxen were startled when Elisha bolted after Elijah. "My lord Elijah, let me embrace my father and mother and kiss them good-bye, then I will follow you."

Without a beard, Elisha looked younger than Elijah had expected him to be, but this servant of Yahweh was what Elisha had envisioned from the description he had heard of the prophet.

"Go, return," Elijah answered him, then looked him in the eyes and asked, "What have I done to you?" The light that beamed from Elisha's face told Elijah that he understood completely.

Elisha handed the mantle back to Elijah. "You may need this."

"Do what you must do, I'll be by the Jordan," said Elijah. He watched as Elisha took the oxen and led them away. Elijah started towards the river when he heard Elisha call the servants. He looked back to see the other teams of oxen, and the drivers, heading in the same direction as Elisha.

Elijah was sitting on the bank of the river, staring at the dark blue water and the reflection of the campfire dancing on the ripples, when Elisha found him. "My lord Elijah." Elisha's voice brought Elijah's thoughts back to the present. He turned to see Elisha and his uncovered bald head, as the young man took a seat beside him. "I will never cease to be thankful that you have chosen me to teach the ways of Yahweh," said Elisha, suddenly aware that he had forgotten to cover his head before coming into the presence of Elijah. "It looks terrible, doesn't it? I look like one of the Ashtoreth priests."

Elijah smiled at Elisha as he said, "And I look like an ape. Together we make a good team."

Expecting the prophet to be more solemn, he was caught off guard by Elijah's sense of humor, and broke into uncontrollable laughter that lasted for several minutes. He was embarrassed that he couldn't hold the laughter back, and, the more he tried to suppress it, the more the laughter burst from his diaphragm. Before he regained control Elijah was laughing at Elisha.

Elijah's mood changed to a more somber note. He studied Elisha for several moments, then spoke, "Yahweh has seven thousand in Israel who haven't bowed to Baal, but he saw something in you that caused him to choose you to be judge over his people. The time is short. I pleaded with Yahweh Elohim to have mercy on Israel, and he has delayed judgment for a short time. The sword of Syria has been honed for judgment against this land. We have to expel the belief that there is more than one God. As long as the people are taught and believe such heresy, the door is open for any demon, like Melkart or Ashtoreth or Moloch, to gain power over them."

Elisha interrupted Elijah, "What about Jezebel? You know that she will have you killed, and there are thousands in Israel that would be glad to remove your head and take it to her for a talent of gold."

"I don't think I want to give her my head," Elijah answered, then picked up a pebble from the ground beside him. "See this pebble? With a sling it could crush a man's skull but it's only a small piece of the mountain."

There was silence for a couple of minutes as Elisha thought about the meaning of his statement. "I almost forgot, I brought you something," Elisha said, as he reached into a cloth bag and pulled out a chunk of cooked meat wrapped in a napkin. He handed it to Elijah, then reached in again and brought out a cake of bread. Elijah took his knife and sliced off a bite of the roast.

"I'm not ungrateful for Yahweh's plentiful supply of locusts, but I give him praise for giving me real meat to eat, and I thank you for being his vessel that brought it." Elijah took a bite then asked, "Is this what took you so long to get here?"

"Yes, I killed the team of oxen I was plowing with and gave the meat to my family and the servants." He looked at Elijah with resolve as he added, "I'm not going back, this is my life now."

"What does your father think?"

"He has always known that the only way for me to find contentment was to follow Yahweh Elohim. He's glad for me." He hesitated to ask, but he had to know, "What did you mean about the mountain?"

Elijah thought for a long minute then answered, "I've seen wind rip through a mountain and throw rocks as large as houses into the air. It doesn't seem possible but I saw it. El Shaddai was demonstrating to me the awesome power that is within him.

"And, right here with us now, in the invisible world, is a multitude of warriors. Just one of them could destroy all of Ahab's forces.

"I will never flee from mere man again. Yahweh is the only one I will ever fear." For the next several minutes the only sound that could be heard was the river swirling by. "You, Elisha, will deliver the truth to the prophets of Israel, and all who won't listen, Yahweh will destroy. You will prophesy to kings."

"My father is wealthy, he will give us anything we need. What should I ask for?" asked Elisha absently, as he thought about the remarkable things Elijah had just told him.

"Only the books of the law and of Moses and a few sheep," answered Elijah. "I have a place at Mount Carmel. It's only a cave, but that's where we will stay until you are ready, and Yahweh sends me on to a greater ministry."

Seated in the splendid column lined throne room that had been built by King Solomon a hundred years earlier, King Jehoshaphat of Judah considered his options as he listened to the ambassador from Egypt present a plan for an alliance against the expanding aggression of Shalmaneser the third. The plan called for twenty thousand Egyptian troops to be stationed in the east of Judah, with other types of assistance, supplies and twenty talents of gold each year that the threat persisted. Other troops would be kept in readiness and could be marched to Judah within ten days, should it be necessary.

The barrel chested Jehoshaphat listened to the details as he pondered the proposal. He had already entered into an alliance with Ahab of Israel and King Ethbaal of Phoenicia for the purpose of defending their lands against the Assyrians. It was true that Shalmaneser was a persistent threat, and the alliance's forces were still no match for the might of Assyria, but neither did he trust the Egyptians.

"We will talk of this matter again tomorrow." Jehoshaphat stood. "The steward will see that you have everything to make your stay comfortable."

As the ambassador was leaving and Jehoshaphat was preparing to exit through a door behind the throne, one of the king's aids caught up to him. "Jehew the scribe desires to speak to Your Highness. He seems to think it is urgent."

"If Jehew believes it's urgent, then it must be. Send him in." The king reseated himself on the throne to receive the scribe.

Bowing to the floor before Jehoshaphat, Jehew said, "My Lord the King, live forever."

"Rise up, Jehew, and tell me what message you have brought to me," Jehoshaphat said, as he rose up from the throne and stepped down the three steps to Jehew's level. The prophet stood. The king could tell by the serious look on Jehew's face that he felt his message was of great importance. "We will speak in private," the king said as he led the way to a room at the right rear of the throne.

The room was fifteen by fifteen cubits. One wall was filled with half-cubit-square compartments an arm length deep, and most contained scrolls. There was a table with twelve chairs, lighted lamps, and a large window, through which came most of the light for the room. "Sit down, Jehew," said the king. Jehew hesitated to sit while the king continued to stand, but obeyed and took a seat at the side of the table. Jehoshaphat slowly strolled around the table and sat across from him. "What has Yahweh shown you?"

"My Lord, you brought me here from Israel to advise you, yet you didn't consult me, or allow me to seek the will of Yahweh, before entering into a treaty with Israel." Jehoshaphat's stern gaze made Jehew uncomfortable and he hesitated for a moment, waiting for an acknowledgment.

"Say on," the king said softly, sensing Jehew's discomfort.

"Israel is at the doorway of judgment, but Yahweh has stayed his wrath from Ahab one last time. It is your protection of their southern border that will allow them to exist, and that is the will of El Shaddai. But to allow Athaliah to wed your son, Joram, to form an alliance with Israel, is not the will of Yahweh. Joram is heir to the throne, and the same wicked spirit that controls Jezebel and rules Israel abides in her daughter Athaliah. In that, you should have sought the will of Yahweh. If he is allowed to marry her, he cannot inherit the throne."

King Jehoshaphat interrupted. "How can I go back on my word?"

Jehew answered, "The evil one, the prince of darkness, desires to destroy your children from the earth. It has been known for a hundred years that the eternal king, the eternal Melchizedek, will be born of the seed of David. Satan put it in the heart of Pharaoh to kill the sons of Abraham to prevent the holy one from being born.

"You have fallen into his plan to import the evil from Israel to infiltrate the royal seed of Judah. If this wedding takes place, Baal will rule the country from the throne of the Kings from which the great ruler is to come. You must prevent Joram from taking the throne, or stop the wedding. Let another of your sons rule Judah!"

"It has been promised to him," the king answered, then added a moment later, "I'm strong, I'll live for many years, but I will consider what you've said."

Jehew bowed his head in regret, took a deep breath, then looked into the king's eyes. "It would be better for Judah, and the royal family, if you were to kill Joram this day and go to war with Israel, rather than to have an alliance that the wicked one will use to thwart the purpose of

Yahweh." Jehew relied on the king's kind nature to keep him from being executed when he continued, "Don't be deceived!"

The king pushed his chair back, stood to his feet and shouted, "That's enough, Jehew!" He gave Jehew a hard look then added, "Joram is my son. He is young, but he has a good heart."

"And the devils will harden his heart the way they have Ahab's," Jehew replied and stood to his feet. Pressing his luck further, he added, "Do not aid Ahab in his search or persecution of Elijah, or you will bring judgment upon yourself."

"Leave me alone, Jehew!" the king ordered sharply, dismissing the prophet. As Jehew bowed from his presence, Jehoshaphat wondered if all that Jehew had predicted was true as he watched the prophet leave the room.

In the palace of Israel in Samaria, in the king's bedchamber, Jezebel pressed her naked body against Ahab's. He breathed out a contented sigh and partially opened one eye to the daylight and her smiling face. "My lord," she said softly, "I thought you were going to sleep the day away."

"Have you been here all night?" he asked in a half whisper.

"Yes, I missed you. You were gone to Judah for so long. I just wanted to be near you. You must have been well pleased with me last night. You fell immediately to sleep and hardly moved until just now." He smiled and completely opened his eyes.

She pressed against him more firmly and asked, "Tell me about the trip. Was Jehoshaphat receptive to a marriage between Athaliah and his son, Joram, as an alliance covenant?"

"Yes, and Jehoshaphat is a man who will stand by his word," Ahab said as he sat up, his eyes traveling her uncovered body.

To keep him from being distracted, she snuggled closer and placed her head on his chest where he couldn't see her. "In the king's absence, I have received word that Elijah has returned to Israel and is rebuilding the old school of Jehew the seer. I sent my guard out to find him, but he is as elusive as the wind. I didn't order the school destroyed because I was sure that you would when you returned."

Ahab's answer was slow and deliberate. "No, I cannot destroy the school again. Jehew is among the advisors of Jehoshaphat, and I know he is already against me. I made a good impression in Judah, so I will not do anything to destroy what I have accomplished."

Surprised by his answer, she raised up, "And what of Elijah!"

"I don't know about Elijah. He's close to Jehew. I told the king that he was stirring a rebellion against me, but I don't think he believed me because of Jehew's influence. While I was in Judah, Zechariah, Jehew's son, arrived. He was at Mount Carmel with Elijah and I know he told Jehoshaphat a different story.

"Jehoshaphat believes in only one God, Yahweh. He doesn't believe that Ashtoreth is the bride of Yahweh, or that she is even a goddess. What we've heard about the Law of Moses being taught throughout Judah isn't the half. The followers of Yahweh have been bringing their teachings into Israel. Some feel that in order to be true to Yahweh, it is their duty to keep all the tribes true to the God they believe brought them out of Egypt. The great following behind Elijah is in part the result of Jehoshaphat's dedication to Yahweh. They say he is the only God."

Jezebel raised up to face Ahab. "What a foolish notion. A god cannot exist alone just as man cannot exist alone. I have stood in the presence of Baal and talked with him. I have seen his might and glory. Yahweh may be a god, but he isn't the only god." She spoke sharply in defense of her belief. There was a moment of silence before she added, "My Lord, Elijah is the enemy of the throne. One day he will destroy us if you don't have him put to death. He stays at a cave at Mount Carmel. You have enough men that he couldn't escape."

Sternly he answered, "It isn't a good time to lift my sword against Elijah. Besides, you weren't at Mount Carmel. You didn't see what I saw. What Elijah's God did was the most convincing display of power that I have ever seen from any god. Sometimes I still see it in my sleep. Maybe if you had been there you would think differently about Yahweh." His voice rose sharply, "There isn't any way I could kill that troublesome prophet without Jehoshaphat finding out." Ahab thought for a moment then slowly added, "Perhaps I could throw him into prison and let him rot there."

She replied, "And if you had been with me in the presence of Baal, you would also think differently about Yahweh. And that hairy false prophet could still raise an army. He even has you afraid of his God."

Ahab interrupted her, "I have never been afraid of men or gods until that day at Mount Carmel." Ahab's gaze fixed as though he were seeing it again. Slowly he said, "That day I knew what real fear was."

Jezebel wanted to leave the subject of Elijah's God. Prison wasn't what she wanted for Elijah, but if he were in prison she might be able to convince Ahab to put him to death. After a minute of silence she said, "The temple of Ashtoreth in the valley of Jezreel is complete. Not one shekel came from the treasury of Israel. It was built by the worshipers of the great goddess, and I have chosen a woman to be high priestess over this temple. I would like for you to see her, and see if you approve of my choice."

Ahab answered, "I am not a judge of such matters. You see to it."

"She is here now, and it would only take a little of the king's time." When he was slow to answer she continued, "My Lord, this is a very important matter." Again when he was slow to answer she clapped her hands. Musicians began to play in an adjoining room and Adah came dancing in through the curtain that separated the rooms. She was wearing one of the queen's own gowns, and a headband woven from golden threads, with small gold chains which hung below the ears on each side. Sensuously, she moved to the rhythm and began to remove the gown. Jezebel stood, picked up a robe lying near, and wrapped it around herself. "I will leave you to determine if she is worthy to be called a high priestess."

As Jezebel left the room, Ahab's gaze traced the lines of Adah's body. He had never seen a woman as beautiful as the one standing before him. Jezebel was still beautiful, but not nearly as beautiful as she had been in the early years of their marriage, and this woman had a softness about her that Jezebel never had.

Jezebel was joined by her small entourage of two handmaids and a eunuch that had waited outside through the night. "Summon Eber," she commanded the boy eunuch. "Bring him to the bath."

Jezebel was bathing in her square, chest deep pool, when Eber entered, knelt on both knees, and bowed. "Your highness, I live to serve the great Queen of Israel. Here is your servant Eber."

"Eber," she said, as their eyes met. The black pupils of her eyes seemed to be eternally deep, deeper than he had ever seen them. Her continuous gaze frightened him, but he knew better than to show that fear. Truly there is a goddess dwelling in her, he thought. "What do you think of the old God that was supposed to have brought the Hebrews out of Egypt?"

He thought for a moment, trying to come up with an answer that would satisfy her. "I know little about that God. I worship only Baal and Ashtoreth, the gods of my queen."

Testing him, she said, "I know that you have heard what the God of Elijah did at Mount Carmel, have you not?"

"Your Highness, there isn't anyone in the world who hasn't heard of that." He hesitated a moment, then added, trying to appease her, "That has probably been exaggerated though. Things have a way of growing larger, the more they are told."

Her eyes continued to burn through him. "I think not. Ahab has never had much respect for any god, and he is not one to exaggerate; he has a real fear of the God of Elijah." To Eber's relief, she turned her gaze to the water, as she rippled the surface with her hands.

"When he tells what he beheld at Carmel, it is reasonable that he should fear a god of such power. Baal, who rides the chariot of the sun, has never answered me with such power and I have offered him many thousands of sacrifices, not just one ox, like Elijah offered to Yahweh. I am going to entreat Yahweh, the God of Elijah. With such power I will rule Israel, and Judah, and maybe the world. Most of the worshipers of Yahweh in Israel already believe that Ashtoreth is the queen of Yahweh, and the fullness of Ashtoreth dwells in me.

"Get ten of the finest oxen that can be found and find out as much about Yahweh as you can. Have my carriage readied." As Eber was waiting for her to dismiss him she added, "I hate Samaria where all the king's wives dwell. From now on we shall stay at my palace in Jezreel." She looked back at Eber. "Carry out my instructions and bring the ointment. Yahweh may enjoy my dancing before him." Eber turned to leave when she called out one last command, "Send two of my guard to escort Adah to me when she leaves the king's chambers."

By the following morning, when Adah hadn't reappeared from the king's chambers, Jezebel was not pleased. Ahab had many wives, and it wasn't unusual for another woman to be with him, but she did not allow such relationships to threaten her position. She particularly did not allow slave women to become competitive with her. Jezebel had chosen Adah to accompany her to Jezreel, where she had intended to install her as priestess of Ashtoreth in the temple there. She had now changed her mind, and left for Jezreel without her. Adah would live to regret her loss of loyalty to the queen, she vowed, and sent a scribe to help Eber learn as much about her background as he could.

Ahab kept Adah with him for five days. He had never known a woman as gentle and warm with lips as soft against his own. Of his forty-two wives and the queen, he preferred the tender caresses of this priestess of Ashtoreth above them all. He vowed to send for her later, when the affairs of state were not calling him away.

Adah was beginning to understand the nature of Jezebel, and feared that she had been too pleasing to the king. When she left Ahab's chamber, one of Jezebel's eunuchs was waiting to take her to Jezreel to appear before the queen. All of the horror stories that she had heard about Jezebel ran through her mind. She did not want to face this woman, but she had no choice.

Eber, escorted by six of the queen's guard, caught up with Jezebel in Jezreel a week later. He bowed before the queen as she sat upon her throne. "Your Highness, I have followed your instructions."

"Tell me what you have learned about the God Yahweh, and about Adah," Jezebel commanded.

"The oxen and all provisions have been sent ahead to Mount Carmel, but I have learned that the ancient law of Yahweh forbids the offer of sacrifice to Him, except by a member of the Hebrew tribe of Levi."

Jezebel answered with confidence, "I am the embodiment of the queen of heaven. He will accept a sacrifice from me. I know for certain that Elijah is not a Levite and his God accepts sacrifices from him." Jezebel stood. "What of Adah?"

Eber knew she would like what he had found out about her. "She was once betrothed to Elijah," he answered. Shocked, Jezebel stared at Eber for a moment, then she smiled. When he saw her smile, he felt a little smug and continued, "She will arrive within a few hours. She was with the king until he had to leave yesterday. You will also be glad to know that King Ahab has sent men to Mount Carmel, and to Dothan to capture Elijah."

Surprised, she repeated, "Dothan?"

"Yes, your Highness, he is in Dothan. They are building a school there."

Jezebel voice betrayed her disbelief that he would be so fearless and bold. "Does he not fear the king? Dothan, between here and Samaria?"

"He is calling the king's prophets, and the schools which teach that Ashtoreth is a goddess and bride of Yahweh, false prophets and worshipers of demons. He has a large following of people who believe in only one God, Yahweh. He has a follower, Elisha, who is an eloquent and convincing speaker, and they plan to convert all Israel to their belief.

"The people fear Elijah more than they fear the king. And, there is a third school of this kind in Tirzah. The louder he speaks out against Baal and Ashtoreth, the louder those who follow him speak out against them, and against you and the king."

Stunned, Jezebel sat down on her throne and pondered for a few moments. "I want Adah brought to me the moment she arrives," she said as she stood and walked from the room.

Jezebel was standing at a window that looked out over the Jezreel valley, and the temple of Ashtoreth below, when Adah was announced. She came in and knelt at the feet of the queen. "Your Highness, glorious Queen of Israel."

Jezebel continued to look out the window as she spoke. "Was the king pleased with you?"

Adah answered timidly, not knowing what Jezebel wanted to hear. "Yes, Your Highness, but not as pleased as he is with the queen."

"Well chosen words," Jezebel said as she turned to face Adah. "Stand up!" she commanded and Adah slowly rose to her feet. "What kept you so long with the king?"

"I told the king that I had to attend to the temple, but he wouldn't give me leave," Adah answered, knowing that there wasn't an answer that would satisfy Jezebel.

Jezebel felt a rage building inside and changed the subject, so that she wouldn't betray her true feelings. "I've just learned that you were once betrothed to Elijah. Is this true?"

Adah's heart sank within her. She knew how Jezebel hated Elijah, and now the queen had another reason to vent this anger upon her, but she could not deny what Jezebel already knew. "Yes, your highness," she answered quietly, "I was to be married to Elijah. He turned to me when his God wouldn't answer him."

Jezebel's softer voice made Adah feel as though the danger of angering the queen had passed. "The king has sent men to capture him, but it's not likely that they will bring him in. They haven't been able to capture him in nearly four years," said Jezebel. She turned and looked directly into Adah's eyes as she continued, "Go to him. Convince him to marry you, with the king's blessings. Convince him to stop teaching against Ashtoreth! Most of Israel believes that she is the queen of heaven and the wife of Yahweh."

Adah had many reasons for not wanting to go to Elijah, but she knew better than to voice them to Jezebel. "Yes, my queen." She was hesitant as she continued, "But I doubt that he will listen to me. Elijah is not like other men. The pleasures of life do not interest him."

The pent up anger in Jezebel exploded into a rage. "Do you believe that a woman could seduce the greatest king Israel has ever known for a week, and not be able seduce this pitiful ape of a prophet?" she stormed.

Again, Jezebel lowered her voice and spoke softly, hiding her anger. "You may leave." Adah stood, relieved to be leaving the presence of the queen. As she approached the doorway, her heart sank when Jezebel called to her softly, "Adah."

When she turned to face Jezebel, there was a look on the queen's face that frightened her. Adah's voice quivered slightly. She struggled to hold back the tears as she answered, "Yes, your Highness."

"Before you leave, I will instruct you what to say." Jezebel knew that Adah realized that to fail in this mission would result in severe punishment, and it pleased her to wield this power over one who had so recently betrayed her.

Adah, unable to answer at that moment, nodded then left the room, holding back the tears until she was far enough away to let them out without fear of Jezebel hearing. She knew that Ahab had fallen in love with her. If only he was near, he would deliver her from Jezebel.

She spent the night trying to find a way out of this situation. Could she escape to Samaria before her absence was noticed, or could she persuade Elijah to marry her, or at the very least, convince him to cease from speaking against the queen of heaven? She knew that he would never stop preaching his convictions. If she made it to Ahab, would Jezebel somehow get her away from him and punish her? She wept through the night.

Within sight of the walled city of Dothan, Elijah was using an ax to square a beam when he looked up to see ten horsemen riding toward them. Thirty men were working with him at different tasks to complete the roof on the building that was to be the school of Yahweh at Dothan.

"Riders approaching," someone called.

Elisha trotted to Elijah's side. "You should leave."

"They can do nothing to me that Yahweh doesn't allow. Besides, they can't take me to Samaria." The workmen stopped and watched as the horsemen rode straight to Elijah and Elisha, suspecting which one might be Elijah from a description of him. They pulled their horses to a halt and the captain looked down at Elijah and asked, "Are you Elijah?"

Boldly Elijah spoke up, "I am Elijah, servant of the Most High God."

"Take him!" the captain shouted. Six of the men jumped to the ground and took hold of Elijah, shoving Elisha to the side.

Elijah looked up at the captain and said, "In the name of the God of Abraham, El Shaddai, Yahweh, you cannot take me to Samaria."

Arrogantly the captain asked, "And why can't I?"

"After you rode out of Samaria this morning, King Ben-Hadad and the army of Syria besieged the city, and your king, Ahab." Elijah paused a moment, then continued, "You should return and fight for your king."

Taken aback by Eilijah's words, the soldiers suddenly realized that they were surrounded by the workmen. They looked around at the men, armed with adz and clubs, and slings and axes. There was no mistaking, by their angry stares, that they would attack at the slightest provocation.

The captain knew that he and his men wouldn't stand a chance if they tried to take Elijah now. "You are as crazy as the king's prophets say you are." He leaned from his mount toward Elijah, "Hear me, prophet. You may be safe for now, but we'll be back with enough men to trample all of you into the ground."

Elijah's face hardened and he raised his voice so that all of Ahab's men could hear. "If you come back, you'll not return again to Samaria," he thundered. The look in his eyes burned into the men's souls as he said, "You have a mission from Yahweh, the most high God. I sent a messenger to the king yesterday. If you should get through to Ahab, tell him to follow the boy's instructions to call upon Yahweh, and he will defeat Ben-Hadad." Then Elijah ordered, "Now leave this place!"

The captain nodded to his men and they remounted. "How do I know that what you say is true?" he asked Elijah.

"The God of Abraham is going to give Ahab one last chance to prove himself. Go see for yourself that Samaria is surrounded."

"How can Israel defend herself, since there is hardly an army left?" the captain asked.

Elijah half smiled. "If Israel had an army, Yahweh would let them be defeated by Ben-Hadad. But now Ahab will see the mighty hand of El Shaddai, the God of Israel. Now go back to the king, and tell him to follow the instructions of the young man that I sent to him." The captain reined his horse around and heeled it hard in the flanks as he bolted toward Samaria, followed by the other riders.

The following day, around mid-afternoon, from the roof where Elijah was working, one of the men working near him called, "There is a small company coming. I believe its Jezebel's guard and the queen herself."

Elijah and all the other men stood to behold the rare sighting of the queen. The queen's carriage, borne on the shoulders of twenty men, and the troops that accompanied them, bypassed the gate of the city of Dothan and headed in their direction. Elijah surmised that the queen, in her arrogance, was coming to deliver some sort of ultimatum to him. He climbed down a ladder to meet her. The carriage stopped twenty cubits in front of him and was lowered. Elijah bowed his head slightly.

Adah felt the power of the presence of Yahweh as she stepped from the carriage, something she hadn't felt since the day they parted on the roof of their house back in Tishbeh. "Elijah, it's only me," Adah called, as she uncovered her face.

Surprised by her familiar soft voice, Elijah looked into her face and said "Adah!" He swiftly walked to greet her. "Why have you come here?"

She didn't answer him immediately, and was afraid to look into his eyes, but she said, "I knew you would be back to defy the queen's edict." She took him by the arm and began to walk away from the workmen and soldiers, out toward a clump of large trees.

After walking for a minute, Elijah asked again, "Why have you come here?"

Adah knew that she couldn't be completely truthful, but also knew that she had to be as truthful as she could, for he would discern instantly a full lie. She thought out each line before she spoke. "The queen learned recently that we were once to be married. She sends her apology for what she has done to you and to us."

They strolled quietly for a minute until they were hidden from the sun under the canopy of trees. She stopped and looked him in the eyes for the first time since she arrived. When Adah saw how alive his eyes were, she fumbled for the words that were on the tip of her tongue a moment earlier. "What....what do those trees remind you of?"

"The olive trees at Johanan's." Elijah leaned back against a large rock amidst the grove and smiled. She returned a smile that warmed his heart and reminded him of the relationship they once knew. She looked radiant in the white robe that she wore. "The last time I saw you, I thought you hated me," he said, as the scene from the inn rushed through his mind, bringing a twinge of pain with it.

"No, I could never hate you, Elijah. You were the love of my life." They strolled to where the ground was broken off into a gully, then she asked, "Could we sit here for a few minutes?"

"What about your robe?" he asked.

"It belongs to the queen, she won't mind if I get it dirty." She stepped to the lower ground and sat down. "Remember the pool under the olive trees? That first day, you tossed stones into it every time you spoke because you were nervous. Today that's how I feel."

He stood for a moment longer, then sat down beside her. "Why have you come to see me?"

She took his hand in hers and studied his fingers as she spoke. "Elijah, we still have a chance." He pulled back slightly, but she refused to let him pull away from her. "No, wait, listen." She looked back into his face. "Please." There was a moment of silence before she spoke again. "Jezebel has given me to you, if you will have me to wife. And, the queen will give you a home in any city in Israel. I will be yours, and only yours. Please, Elijah."

His mind reeled as she moved very close. He felt her breath on his face, then he felt her soft lips against his. Suddenly an arousing image of her naked body, the way she appeared the night in the inn, filled his mind.

He pulled away and stood to his feet. "Only Yahweh knows how badly I want this." He raised his head heavenward, closed his eyes, and said, "Yahweh, help me, what am I to do?"

He looked down at her. "This is all too easy for you." Not out of anger, but out of pain, his voice rose. "How many men have you known? And would I be any different to you than they were?"

She stood and took his face in her hands and looked into his eyes. With tears beginning to flow down her cheeks, she pleaded, "I would be different to you."

Whatever she had been and done meant little to Elijah at that moment. Could it be that Yahweh in his mercy, knowing how Elijah had longed for a family, was sending this to him? There were several moments when Elijah, wishing that this were the will of God, accepted it as such.

He suddenly realized how one question would answer everything. "Adah, who is your God?" When she hesitated, he took her by the shoulders. "Who was the last God you gave homage to?"

She had been so close to winning him. If only she could give an answer he would accept. The silence before she answered was long enough that they both knew there wasn't a right answer. "Elijah, your God will be my God."

Elijah hung his head and refused to look at her. She was all that a man could want, but would Yahweh allow him to have her? Again he raised his head toward heaven. "Oh, Yahweh, why have you tested me like this?"

A painful image filled his head and tears welled in his own eyes. He could hardly speak when he looked at her again. "So badly do I want you." He closed his eyes and related the scene he was seeing. "At eventide, only ten days ago on the king's bed, of your own free will, you told Ahab that you had fallen in love with him. And full of witchcraft, Jezebel sent you to keep me from speaking against her and her gods. Jezebel is defeated and she knows it."

There was a moment of embarrassed silence between them. Adah began to weep uncontrollably as she sat down. "I didn't know that I would ever see you again."

Through tears of his own, Elijah said softly, "The last time I saw you, it was the image of Baal that you loved."

"Elijah, please, I'll be different. I'll be like Sarah of old if you'll have me." In a whisper that he could hardly hear, she added, "The queen will have you killed."

"The queen and her demons have been defeated. There isn't anything they can do against me. Yahweh El Shaddai is my shield. I will go to Samaria and preach against Ashtoreth, and Yahweh will smite the hand that touches me."

He stopped for a moment, knowing that her eyes would rise to meet his again. When they did, he asked, "Do you still believe that she is the queen of heaven?"

Her eyes answered before her lips, "Yes, I do. I've felt her power."

"You chose the easy road. Now it's become the most difficult.

Your Ashtoreth is only another demon, one of some rank, but still a demon."

"Elijah, the queen will punish me if you won't have me," she cried.

"I told you that she is defeated. She can have no power over you unless you give her the power. Don't return to her. I have friends who will take care of you, but you must give up the worship of Ashtoreth."

"I can't deny what I have seen."

"And I can't deny what I have seen," he responded. "How many children have you seen slaughtered on the altar of Ashtoreth and Baal?"

She screamed back, "I saw my own son burned in the fire of Baal and I pray that he is in a better world than this one!"

"Adah, remember the teachings of Moses and return to the God you once knew."

In anger she answered, "I believe that Yahweh is a great God. I believe that he did a mighty thing on Mount Carmel, but there are other gods, Elijah... powerful gods.

"I'll return to Jezebel, and bow low and accept her displeasure with me until I can reach King Ahab. He will take care of me. He loves me above all of his wives, even Jezebel," Adah sobbed, as she stood and ran towards the carriage.

Elijah's heart ached as he watched her being hoisted into the air in the queen's carriage. With the queen's banner flying at the front, the brightly uniformed guard, and the carriage carrying Adah, turned back towards Jezreel.

Shortly after Adah was out of sight, Elijah left Elisha to oversee the building work, and withdrew into the hills where he remained for days.

By the time Adah's carriage and escort reached the city of Ibleam, the highway was inundated by people fleeing north, away from the region around Samaria. Adah called down from her carriage to a man in a half run carrying a bundle on his head, "Sir, you sir." The man looked up at her and slowed to the pace of the slaves with her weight on their shoulders. "What is happening?" Adah called to him.

"Ben-Hadad has besieged Samaria. His army fills the hills. More men than I have ever seen." The man panted out several breaths before he could continue. "Everywhere they go, they slaughter people for sport and rape the women and girls." Without waiting for a response, the man continued past them.

The captain of the queen's guard got the information at the same time and shouted out, "Double pace!" The carriage began to move like a ship through the sea of people, as they made a path rather than be trampled.

When Adah arrived at the palace in Jezreel, she was ushered immediately into Jezebel's chambers and onto the terrace where the queen was waiting for her. Adah bowed before Jezebel's couch where the queen had reclined. "Great benevolent Queen of Israel, have mercy on your servant for I have failed to persuade Elijah to marry me."

Sounding somewhat subdued, Jezebel replied, "At the moment we have greater concerns. No doubt you know by now that Ben-Hadad has surrounded Samaria with an army twenty times greater than Israel can muster right now. And when they've leveled Samaria, they'll be here next." There was a moment of tense silence before she continued, "Captain Jehu, the fiercest of all men, is with the king, but there can be only five to ten thousand men with them. All the army of Israel number no more than twenty thousand, thanks to your Elijah. Syria came against us knowing it would be an easy victory." She thought for a minute then continued, "I should have pushed the marriage of Athaliah before now, then we could call on Judah for help." Jezebel sat up and put her feet on the floor. "Adah, sit here by me."

Adah eased onto the couch with Jezebel, knowing that it was unlike the queen to allow anyone to be that close to her. When Adah was comfortable Jezebel said, "It would have been better for Israel, and for me if Elijah had wanted you."

"I said what you told me to say, but he won't have me because of my involvement in the worship of Baal and Ashtoreth," Adah answered in her defense.

Jezebel breathed deeply then said, "I suppose it doesn't matter now. It looks as though Ben-Hadad will be the next king of Israel. It might interest you to know that Elijah told the men who were sent to capture him that Ahab will defeat the Syrians, but the king has nothing to fight with. No more than a few chariots."

Adah spoke up, "My Queen, forgive me, but if Elijah said that Ahab will defeat Syria, it will be so."

Jezebel tilted her head slightly as she looked at Adah. "You must know much about Elijah's God."

"Yahweh was the only God I knew. In my home it was forbidden to mention the name of any other god."

Jezebel asked, "And now what do you believe?"

Adah thought for a moment then answered, "I do not know how many god's there are, but I have danced with Baal in the sacred ceremony. I've seen glorious beings that people of this plane would never believe, and Ashtoreth has carried me to distant places. But, at this time it seems that Yahweh has gotten the victory in Israel."

She pondered her next statement momentarily before continuing. "There aren't many who worship Baal openly any longer, but there are still many worshipers of Ashtoreth, though no one has offered a child to her since Mount Carmel. That is except the few sacred children born to the priestesses from her worship."

Again Jezebel sighed, then answered, "I am ready to concede that perhaps you are right. I have planned a sacrifice to Yahweh of ten fine oxen. Everything is waiting at Mount Carmel, but because of this matter my trip has been delayed. Do you think Yahweh will accept a sacrifice from me?"

"I don't know, but according to the law it is forbidden for a woman to perform the duty of a priest, and there are many laws surrounding the service to Yahweh." Adah began to relax somewhat, and knew that it was unusual for Jezebel to talk to anyone as though they were on the same level with her.

Attempting to prove to Adah that she was worthy to offer sacrifices to Yahweh she answered, "I am also having a temple built to Yahweh here in Jezreel. It isn't a large temple but there aren't many worshipers of Yahweh here and I have very qualified priests to oversee the worship."

Without thinking that she was asking a question that might provoke an angry response Adah asked, "Are they Levites?"

"Levites!" Jezebel half shouted, then asked, "Is Elijah a Levite? And Yahweh sent fire when he offered a sacrifice. My priests have made many sacrifices to the gods. They are as qualified as Elijah, and they are all Hebrews. Like you, I have also been in the presence of the gods. I know what delights the gods. I am qualified to perform this sacrifice."

She sighed then added, "It doesn't matter now. I could only gather five hundred men to defend Jezreel, and I've been considering returning to Zidon until this is over, but you believe Ahab will be victorious because of what Elijah said."

With strong conviction Adah answered, "Yes, I do. I cannot accept Elijah's God as the only god, but I know that he has great power from Yahweh, his god, just like you have great power from Ashtoreth, my queen."

There were several moments of silence before Jezebel said, "The soldiers that were sent to capture Elijah couldn't get through to Samaria, so they came here. They were in Dothan the day before you arrived there. Samaria was surrounded by Ben-Hadad after they left the city. They didn't know it, but Elijah knew.

"You will accompany me to do homage to Yahweh, but for now I will await word from Samaria. You will go to the temple and entreat the favor of Ashtoreth, but you must first pass a test."

Jezebel clapped her hands and a young man entered, wearing the robe of the highest-ranking priest of Baal. He bowed before Jezebel. "This is Mattan. He is only about your age but the gods have blessed him with great gifts. He is advisor to Athaliah, and will go to Judah with her." Jezebel looked at him. "Rise, Mattan, servant of Baal. Tell me what the gods show you about this woman."

Mattan took Adah by the hand and pulled her to her feet. "She is from the east of Jordan," he said, as he looked her over. "She was once a worshiper of the old God of Israel. She bore a son that was offered to Baal, though she did not offer him willingly and turned against the god she was taught to believe in." Adah froze in shock as he spoke in disquieting monotones, revealing more than she wanted the queen to know.

"She has given her body for the glory of Baal and the queen of heaven. She has found great favor with the king." Adah turned to look at Jezebel, whose eyes widened. "She is now confused about the gods, and no longer wants to give her body for the glory of Ashtoreth." Adah's heart began to pound. "She fears the queen's wrath and her heart is pounding with fear right now. She wants to give herself only to the king and hopes that he will send for her as he has promised."

Angrily Jezebel interrupted, "Ahab was going to send for you, was he? You must have been very pleasing to him!"

Mattan paused and looked her in the face before continuing. "He would have sent for you if the Syrians had not invaded."

Jezebel stood and spoke to Adah in a soft voice. "Did you forget to tell me these things? Adah, my dear, you should never lie to the queen." Jezebels' venomous voice was under tight control. "I thought Mattan might tell me more than you would." Speaking to Mattan as she looked at Adah, she questioned, "Does the king love her?"

"Yes, he loves me!" Adah shouted before Mattan could answer. "And Elijah was able to tell me what I said in the king's bed chamber." She turned angrily to the priest. "Can you do that, Mattan?"

Mattan nodded, "Yes, he loves her."

Addressing Adah, Jezebel said, "I don't care that the king loves you. He loves many women, but I think he loves you too much. And why not, you're very beautiful. But I can't let anyone have more sway over the king than I, now can I?" She glanced at Mattan then back at Adah. "Mattan, do you think that she can still bring glory to the queen of heaven?"

He stepped closer to Adah and began to remove her robe. "Yes, I'm sure she can." Adah, not knowing what to do, yielded as he removed her robe then stared at her body. "I can see why the king desires you so much."

"Do with her as Baal directs you," Jezebel ordered. "She is yours until you leave for Judah, then I believe Baal would have her for a sacrifice. Take her with you to the temple. My guard will escort you there."

At his nudging, Adah walked silently before Mattan to the door. "Great Queen of Israel," Adah called out, as she turned back to see Jezebel for the last time. "Please allow your servant to dance for the great Baal one last time."

Mattan was about to protest when Jezebel answered, "I think that would be fitting for a high priestess who is about to depart from this world to the world of the gods." Adah bowed slightly to Jezebel before they passed from the room and were joined by four guards. She was given only a blanket to cover with until they reached the temple, where she was locked into a cell.

Adah had seen many children die on the altars of Baal and Ashtoreth. Some of them died easy deaths, depending on the frenzied state of the priests, but she had never seen a virgin or a slave that didn't suffer hours before the final blow to the head, or dagger to the throat or chest. Some had lasted for days, being brutally raped over and over. She knew that the goddess, Ashtoreth and the green ointment would carry her far away from her body and she would be aware of nothing that took place.

The following morning the women of the temple bathed her. This time there wouldn't be any preliminary preparation through fasting. She was anointed with the green ointment, and given the sacred wine to drink.

Orgiastic worship and sacrificing took place in the temple from the middle of the night until the setting of the sun the next day, when Adah was brought out from her waiting chamber. Her heavy eyelids half covered her dilated eyes, and she was supported from each side by a priestess. Her dulled mind was able to take in part of the scene of the drunken, naked worshipers, all waiting for her to dance. The music began to fill her head and her green covered body began to move to its rhythm. A blue smoky haze filled the room as smoke from the burning pit drifted away from the column, rising through the smoke hole in the roof. The smell of burning flesh mixed with the sweet incense to give the familiar smell of Ashtoreth worship.

What she was doing was a sacred honor, given to only the highest ranking in the service of Ashtoreth and Baal. She had been in this state before, but not at this new temple of Ashtoreth, the temple that she had been chosen by Jezebel to preside over. This would be her last dance for Ashtoreth, and as the minutes passed, she began to feel honored to die for the queen of heaven.

Her spirit slipped away from time to time, but her body continued to move. Her bare feet became stained with fresh blood when she danced near the altar and image of the large breasted Ashtoreth that towered over the room. On either side of the image was a stone column, taller than her height, in the shape of the male organ.

She began to lose control over her body movements and knew that she didn't have long. With her last bit of strength she climbed onto the altar. Her soul escaped into another plane, and left her body to be used and mutilated and burned. At the very end Adah, only vaguely aware that her body still lived, was thrown into the sacrificial fire.

Jezebel had not been in attendance. There was something about Adah that reminded her of Tamara, and she didn't want to relive that experience. She decided that it would appear more stately to be waiting for word from Samaria.

****

The Syrian troops saw Ahab's position as hopeless against such overwhelming odds and expected an easy victory. They didn't anticipate an aggressive move from Israel but Ahab, with no other choice, was considering trusting the prophecy that had been delivered to him by Elijah's messenger. In his mind, it came down to only two choices, either take a chance that Yahweh would do what the prophet said and deliver the Syrian army into his hands, or face certain death, or worse, at the hand of Ben-Hadad when the city eventually fell.

Ahab, according to the instructions of the prophet, gathered the young officers of the provincial commanders and took the offensive with seven thousand men. Instead of surrendering the besieged city, the gate of Samaria opened and the small army rode out in full battle armor.

The men of Israel clung to the word of the prophet, and as they came near the defensive position of King Ben-Hadad, they somehow knew that victory was theirs. Most had never known the presence of Yahweh before that day and none would ever forget it. The air was charged as they anxiously awaited the signal to attack.

Ahab ordered the attack flag waved and the men of Israel charged the Syrian army. As the men rushed toward the battle line they shouted as one voice, "Yahweh has given us victory." The Syrians had never heard anything like in it battle and it struck fear into them. The Israeli's were invincible, and it seemed as though they moved with lightning speed. They charged through the Syrian line and it broke upon contact. More than a hundred thousand of the enemy died by the weapons of Israel that day. When he saw that his troops were defeated, Ben-Hadad escaped on horseback with the mounted soldiers.

Three days later, as they returned from pursuing the Syrians, the troops worshipped Yahweh every mile of the journey. They sang, "Praise Yahweh, who gives victory to the children of Abraham. El Shaddai defends them with the shield of His arm." The hills rang with the sound of their song. That day Ahab vowed never to give homage to Baal again, but he clung to the belief of Ashtoreth as the queen of heaven.

The people of Samaria were dancing in the streets when Ahab and his men entered the city. His chariot was being pulled by four matching white horses taken from the Syrian camp. The city roared with celebration, and those closest to the parade bowed to the ground as the king rode past. Never had Ahab been greeted like this, but never before had a victory meant so much to the people of Samaria.

Upon entering the palace, Ahab summoned the steward. "Send for Obadiah!" he shouted, as his attendants began ministering to him. Two men removed his armor, as a woman bearing a pitcher offered him wine. When he was seated another woman removed his sandals and began to wash his feet. He took a long sip of wine and wearily leaned back in his chair and closed his eyes.

"My Lord Ahab." Obadiah's voice interrupted his rest. He looked to see his steward bowing in front of him.

"Obadiah, it was a great victory," the king said as he stood. "Walk with me to the council chamber." Obadiah stood and walked at the king's side as Ahab continued exuberantly. "Today is a great day for Israel. We took great spoil from our enemy." He paused and smiled, reflecting on the events. "I divided it with the men. Tomorrow you will inventory what will be the beginning of the new treasury of the nation."

The king placed his hand on Obadiah's shoulder. Unaccustomed to such familiarity from the king, Obadiah was momentarily startled and gave Ahab a quizzical glance. The king caught the expressive look and slapped Obadiah on the back. "It is a very good day, my faithful friend. We have recovered from the Syrians in one day what we lost in the years of the great drought and the famine. And, it was the word of Yahweh that gave us victory. The men sang praises all the way back to Samaria. It made the hair stand up on the back of my neck."

As they approached the council chamber, a guard opened the door for them. When it was closed behind them, Ahab said, "Sit there," and indicated a chair at the table with a nod of his head. "Tomorrow wagons of silver and gold will be brought here, and weapons. Those who escaped took the horses. The ones they left behind weren't worth keeping, except for a couple of chariots and teams taken in battle, like the team of whites I brought back. Ben-Hadad had all the governors of Syria with him. We came upon them in the woods where their chariots were useless. With seven thousand men we killed more than a hundred thousand, and it was because of a prophecy from Yahweh.

"I want you to find some of Yahweh's prophets. I want four hundred to replace the prophets of Baal that Elijah killed. I will never go to battle again without their consultation. Who do you know that can bring that many good prophets together?"

Obadiah didn't have to think about it but for an instant. "Elijah."

Ahab thought for a moment. "It can't be Elijah or Micaiah. They don't like me, and Elijah could raise an army against me."

"There were many more prophets in the land before you purged Israel." That comment drew a sharp look from Ahab. Obadiah continued, "I have heard of a man by the name of Zedekiah in the city of Arubboth, son of Chenaanah, who was a prophet before anyone knew of Elijah. He was a great prophet before the drought, but he bowed to Baal to live."

"There isn't anything wrong with a man wanting to live, and Baal worship is only practiced by a few these days. Find Zedekiah and bring him here."

Obadiah took a chance because of Ahab's good humor and said, "My Lord King, Baal is hardly worshipped, but the same orgies and sacrifices take place in the temple of Ashtoreth."

"I do not know about the goddess Ashtoreth, but I will concern myself with only Yahweh. Send for Zedekiah. The prophets will make intercession continually to Yahweh for me." Ahab pulled at the whiskers of his beard as he thought for a moment. "Obadiah, send for a priestess of Ashtoreth at the temple in Jezreel. Her name is Adah. I want to bring her here to Samaria. I want her here to enjoy this great victory with me. I am going to take her for a mistress."

There was a minute of silence before Obadiah asked, "Is that all, Sire?"

"Yes, Obadiah, see to those things immediately."

Zedekiah was at the palace in Samaria when Jezebel arrived, accompanying Athaliah that far on her journey to Jerusalem and her wedding to Joram, son of Jehoshaphat. When Ahab learned that Jezebel had arrived, he left his chamber and was seated upon the throne before he allowed the queen to be brought before him. She bowed to the floor. "My Lord, great King of Israel, live forever. Here is your servant Jezebel."

Ahab turned to one of the scribes and ordered, "Have the queen's throne brought in."

"That's not necessary, unless you require my presence here in Samaria," Jezebel said as she rose to her feet. "Your daughter, the next Queen of Judah, is prepared and adorned for your inspection and awaits you in the court." Ahab stood and was descending the throne steps when Jezebel spoke again. "My Lord, I have some disappointing news for you. The priestess Adah, whom you sent for, is in the land of the gods. She felt that the queen of heaven had called for her personal attendance." Ahab stopped and his change of expression revealed the grief he felt at the news of Adah. Jezebel added, hoping to distract him for a moment, "I am going to sacrifice to Yahweh on behalf of you and Israel."

There was a long silence before Ahab answered, "There is a prophet here now, an advisor and servant of Yahweh. I will send him with you. His name is Zedekiah."

Jezebel wasn't interested in having any prophet of Yahweh along, but it wasn't the time to turn down an offer from the king. "Thank you, my gracious Lord."

The following day Ahab and a treasure wagon of gifts for Jehoshaphat, followed by a large pompous parade, escorted Athaliah to Judah. Jezebel, with Eber, her guard, a large body of attendants and Zedekiah and two priests, left for Mount Carmel.

Each evening when they camped, Jezebel invited Zedekiah to dine with her and questioned him extensively about Yahweh and his law. She found him to be an unattractive man with an austere personality, and very dedicated to his belief. He, unlike Elijah, allowed everyone the freedom to believe the way they pleased, and, though he served Yahweh, he didn't discount the existence of other gods. He was a stout man with light skin, indicating that he didn't work or spend time in the sun. His black beard was unkempt, and his clothes were drab in appearance, which Jezebel perceived to be for the appearance of piety, rather than for the genuine attribute.

It is just such drab, hypocritical people that make this god so difficult to admire, Jezebel thought.

On the third day they arrived at Mount Carmel. Jezebel, in her carriage, was transported up the slope to her camp that had been prepared three weeks earlier. After a quick inspection of the tent and facilities, she got back onto her carriage and ordered, "Take me to the site where Yahweh consumed the sacrifice of Elijah."

The sun was low in the sky when the carriage, resting on the shoulders of the slaves, approached the site where the altar of Yahweh once stood. Her mounted guard and the footmen stopped and stood at attention, as the queen's carriage was lowered to the ground, and Jezebel stepped down and walked to the edge of the crater where Yahweh had answered Elijah. There was complete silence as everyone in the group stood in awe, viewing the sunken scorched earth.

From where Jezebel stood she could see where the altar had once been. An electrifying chill ran up her back, then she suddenly had the feeling that she was being watched from another plane. She glanced around, then commanded sharply, "Move back away from this place!" She was overwhelmed by the awesome power it must have taken to burn the stones and the ground, as she remembered Ahab's description of the event, an event that had made a believer of a powerful man who had very little regard for the gods.

"Zedekiah, Yahweh is your God. Walk out there." She ordered the prophet, as she stepped back away from the circle. Zedekiah, afraid to refuse and afraid to go forward, chose to obey the queen and haltingly placed one foot into the crater. He nervously laughed then took another step. In a minute he was standing in the center of the circle, but Jezebel refused to venture into the area. "I don't like this place," she said and turned back to her carriage.

The next morning an altar was constructed and Zedekiah prepared the first sacrifice. Jezebel watched from the seat of her carriage a short distance away. Zedekiah prayed with outstretched arms as the ox burned. His voice rang out; "Elohim of Abraham, the Queen of Israel honors you with these sacrifices. Hear the petitions of the queen over your people."

The second day he prayed again, and again there was no answer. Jezebel came near the altar and stretched her hands toward heaven the same as Zedekiah. She stood there in silence for more than an hour as the smoke rose upward. On the third day she had her guard, handmaids and attendants bow before the altar and remain that way throughout the day, as the sacrifice burned. This she did for eight days, but there was no answer.

At daylight on the tenth day, Jezebel summoned Zedekiah to her tent. She was sitting cross-legged on a carpet when he was brought in and bowed before her. "Your Highness."

Her cold stare gave away her displeasure with him before she spoke. "Why is it that Elijah has greater favor with your God than you do?" He was about to give an answer when she cut him off. "Return to Samaria. I have no further need of your services." Again he tried to give an explanation when she said, "Leave immediately!" He stood and left without attempting to answer. When he had cleared the tent door, Eber was ushered in.

He bowed to the floor. "Great wise Queen, your servant Eber is humbled in the presence of your glory."

"You are filled with lies, Eber. The only thing you're concerned with is keeping your head attached to your neck.

"I am going to dance before Yahweh. You will oversee the burning of the sacrifice today. Bring me the sacred ointment, and while I'm being anointed, prepare the sacrifice."

Eber stood and nodded as he replied, "Yes, Your Highness." When he had returned to his tent, he pried at the lid on the jar of ointment. The seal of resin cracked and the handled top came loose from the clay jar. Immediately, from the stench, Eber knew that something was wrong with the costly mixture. It had never been prepared this far in advance. He carried it to the tent door where he could tilt it into the morning sun. He was horrified. The ointment was alive with worms, green from the concoction itself.

Eber knew that it would mean his life if Jezebel were to discover what had happened. He quickly mixed very powerful herbs and spices into some wine. As it sat for a few minutes, letting the substances mingle, he mixed up incense as strong as Tamara once inhaled.

Jezebel was being bathed when Eber brought the wine and incense to her. He bowed to the ground. "Your Highness, this is special wine I've prepared for the occasion." Still on his knees, he reached the juglet of wine toward one of the maids who took it from his hand, then looked at the queen for direction. With a nod from Jezebel, she poured the queen a goblet of wine and gave it to her.

Jezebel sipped slowly. "This is excellent, Eber. Where is the ceremonial ointment?"

"I have further preparation to make on the ointment, but take the incense and begin preparing yourself for the ointment. Allow me to return to my task." She waved her hand, dismissing him to continue.

Eber returned to his tent and the spoiled green slime. He spooned the ointment from one pot into another separating out the worms. Several times he nearly vomited from the stench. When that task was finished he added enough perfume to partially cloak the rotting smell. After passing along orders to slaughter the ox, he returned to the queen's tent to find Jezebel in the state of delirium that he had hoped the wine would produce. The queen's attendants were drunk on the incense and didn't notice the smell of the ointment as they applied it to Jezebel's naked body.

With the sacrifice burning, Jezebel was carried to the altar, but was unable to stand for more than a few moments without falling. Her body was soon covered with dirt and grass that clung to the green paste. Had it been anyone but the queen, those few allowed to be present would have laughed. But, for fear that someone might report to the queen later, all held their peace. Jezebel soon slipped into unconsciousness and was carried to her tent. It was three days before she opened her eyes, but was months recovering in Jezreel. She had no memory of being transported by Yahweh, or any other god, to the realm of the gods, and attributed the months of headaches and fatigue that followed to the wrath of Baal brought on by her worship of the god of Elijah.

During the time she was recovering, she determined to build a temple for Yahweh in Jezreel to regain some of the influence she had lost when Elijah defeated the priests of Baal and Ashtoreth. She wouldn't participate in the worship, but the priests would have to be approved by her.

From her personal wealth she built a modest temple on the east of Jezreel, and controlled what was taught there to a large degree. The priests of Yahweh had to be worshipers of the queen of heaven and could say nothing against Baal or the king. From the beginning, the temple was too small to accommodate the many worshipers of Yahweh who now felt the freedom to worship the God of Abraham.

lijah withdrew to the cave at Mount Carmel, where he remained until the word of Yahweh came to him. Eleven months had passed since God had defeated Ben-Hadad before the army of Israel. At the end of this time, Elijah called a gathering of the prophets from all Israel. They came immediately, and arrived at the cave in small groups, over a period of three days.

A week lacking a day passed after their arrival, and still Elijah said nothing about the reason he had called them together. The prophets were used to the sometimes eccentric behavior of their revered leader, and they waited patiently until he was ready to disclose his purpose for calling them here.

One evening as they were gathered around the fire to sing, Elijah stood and a hush swept over them.

It was rumored among them that the Spirit of Yahweh was going to move in an exceptional way when he wore the blue striped robe of Delah. This evening, Elijah was wearing the beautiful robe.

For several moments before he spoke, the only sound that could be heard was the crackle of the fire. "It is expedient for Israel that we have come here," he began. "Ben-Hadad is even now approaching this land that El Shaddai gave to Abraham and his descendants forever. The Syrians claim that Yahweh is God only of the hills, but not of the plains. They claim that their gods are the gods of plains. They have said that they can defeat Israel on the plains.

"Yahweh has heard their words and knows their thoughts. It is the will of Yahweh to destroy the Syrians forever. But Ahab, who now sacrifices to Yahweh, has begun to believe that because of some noble quality in himself, Yahweh honors him.

"Jezebel, that evil sorceress of Ashtoreth, is continually planting thoughts of vain pride in Ahab's ears. He has begun to believe that it was because of him that Yahweh gave them victory over Ben-Hadad and his army last year. It is not I who has called you here, but Yahweh. It is he that has brought you to this place, at this time.

"I do not know the plan of Yahweh, but I do know that He alone is God, and that the army of Israel cannot be defeated if He fights for them. We are here to intercede for our nation against the Syrians. Until they are defeated, we will remain in prayer.

"Seven of you young men who are willing to go to the battle field will be the eyes for the rest of us. The Spirit of Yahweh will be upon you to deliver God's word to Ahab.

"El Shaddai will show again to Israel that he has chosen them to be called His children. Yahweh will defeat Ben-Hadad, but it will be for His Glory, not for the glory of Ahab." When Elijah had finished speaking he sat down. Everything remained quiet for several moments, as the prophets considered his words. Then Elijah rose to his feet and shouted, "Let us sing and dance and worship our God with all of our being, so our hearts will be prepared to pray."

Israel had nearly a year to prepare for the return of Ben-Hadad, though they still lacked the resources to match the Syrian army. During that year Ahab gathered four hundred counselors, all claiming to be prophets of Yahweh, all hired under Zedekiah, false prophet of Israel. All maintained the prevailing belief of Israel, one that Zedekiah didn't oppose, that Ashtoreth was the queen of heaven.

For a brief period of time, Ahab was encouraged with his new prophets, as they were quick to tell him what he wanted to hear. Soon, however, he came to realize that the only accurate predictions these supposed prophets ever made was when they followed the words of the occasional visitors from the prophet schools created by his long time enemy, Elijah. Then, his prophets would affirm the prediction of Elijah's students.

This lack of direct prophetic direction bothered Ahab, but not as much as the reports by his spies that large numbers of troops were gathering outside Israel's borders.

At the end of the battle in Samaria the year before, the prophet of Yahweh had prophesied to Ahab that Ben-Hadad would return in the spring. Now Ben-Hadad was amassing an army greater than the one he had lost the year before, and was about to bring them together at Aphek, east of the Sea of Chinneroth, in Ramoth-Gilead. Aphek was an easily defensible city with high, heavily fortified walls. It was one of the cities that was taken from Israel by Ben-Hadad's father. Aphek was a seemingly unbreachable fortress, within easy striking distance of any target in Israel.

As Ben-Hadad's army began their march against Israel, they crossed the Jordan onto Israeli soil several miles below the sea, and headed west to the plain of Jezreel, where they camped. They knew that Ahab would be drawn away from the gods of the hills, where Israel had defeated them before. Because Megiddo, the major trade center of Israel, and Jezreel, the palace of the queen, were at risk, King Ahab would have to engage them on the battlefield of their choosing, where they believed they would prevail by the strength of their gods.

When word reached Ahab, he hurried to meet the invasion, and called another two thousand men from the city of Megiddo, at the west end of the valley. He divided his troops and planted the first between Jezreel and the Syrians. The second he placed between the Syrians and Megiddo, where they could retreat and withstand a powerful onslaught if need be. In two separate camps, they waited for Ben-Hadad to make the first move. The Syrian camp filled the lower part of the Jezreel valley.

Advised by the astrologers to wait, Ben-Hadad delayed seven days, during which time one of the seven prophets sent by Elijah to observe, was moved upon by the Spirit of Yahweh, and walked into the camp of Ahab. To the side of Ahab's tent, the king's own prophets were discussing what they believed the will of Elohim was for the army of Israel. The young prophet caught their attention when he approached the king's tent and was intercepted by one of the guards who blocked his path. Sternly the guard asked, "What is your business with the king?"

"Tell the king that I am from the school of the prophets at Dothan and I am here at the word of Yahweh," responded the young man. The guard took a hard look into his face, then turned and entered the king's tent. A moment later, Ahab appeared in the doorway. The young prophet bowed slightly and began to speak immediately, "Thus says Yahweh: because the Syrians have said, Yahweh is God of the hills, but he is not God of the valleys and plains, I will give you victory over them, and you will know that I am Yahweh Elohim Shaddai." Without being dismissed from the king's presence, the young prophet turned and began to walk away.

"Young man!" the king called. The prophet stopped and turned half way around. Ahab hurried over to him. "Wait a moment. Come sit and talk with me. Have some bread and wine for your journey back."

"Yahweh told me to deliver that message, but for me not to remain in this camp. I cannot stay." The young prophet turned and continued away from Ahab.

The following morning at daybreak, Ahab was awakened by one of the servants sent to notify him of movement in the Syrian camp. At the doorway, a sentry told the king that it looked like Ben-Hadad was planning an attack. Within half an hour Israel's small army was standing ready to take the offensive, while Syria was still maneuvering her troops into position.

The sun was just above the horizon, with Israel's troops lined up, when one soldier shouted, "By the word of the prophet, we defeated Ben-Hadad a year ago. Give the glory to Yahweh!" Then he shouted even louder, "The victory belongs to Yahweh!" The second time he shouted it, he was joined by hundreds more, and the third time the camp to the west joined the shout. When it had been repeated several more times, all twenty-four thousand men of Israel were shouting. The earth seemed to tremble with the roar of the shout, and it sent fear into the Syrians.

Ahab gave the order to attack. The Hebrews were fearless, they charged forward at full speed across the valley. The Syrians were unnerved by the ferocity of Israel and broke rank to run before the front lines collided. The slaughter that ensued was quicker, and more complete, than the first battle the year before.

When there wasn't any doubt that he had been defeated, Ben-Hadad fled with twenty-seven thousand men, toward Syria.

Ahab pursued the Syrians across the Jordan northward, but the chase ended at Aphek, where Ben-Hadad and the remnant of his army took refuge from Israel behind the city's high walls.

Two of the seven prophets sent by Elijah to follow the battle ran west toward Mount Carmel, to inform Elijah and the intercessors of what had just happened. The others stayed to observe Ahab and to see the prophecy fulfilled.

The two runners found the prophets at the foot of Mount Carmel gathered in small groups, praying or talking outside Elijah's cave. All were fasting for Israel. The runners found Elijah seated among a dozen of the older prophets. Elijah stood as the young men approached, laboring for breath with each step. They collapsed to the ground in front of him as the other men gathered around. "Rest a minute, the message will keep," Elijah said as he stooped beside them. Others handed them water that they gulped down like thirsty young colts.

After a few moments one of them coughed out as he panted, "Ben-Hadad has taken..." He took a couple of quick breaths then continued, "...refuge in the city of Aphek. He still has more men than Ahab. High walls. Ahab is unable to take them."

Elijah turned and looked around, then stood. Everyone was watching him, wondering what sort of response he would have to this turn of events. Would this keep Yahweh from delivering Israel from the threat of the Syrians?

Elijah laughed loudly. It was a joy he couldn't contain, and he shouted as he laughed. "Now, El Shaddai will manifest his glory. This is his handiwork." Elijah extended a hand to help one of the young prophets to his feet, as some of the crowd helped the other messenger up. Elijah embraced him as he continued to laugh, and then he lifted his hands toward heaven. "Great is your wisdom, Oh Yahweh." He looked back at the prophets waiting for him to disclose what he knew. "Tomorrow before the sun has risen above the hills, Yahweh El Shaddai will defeat the Syrians without the help of the sword of man or Ahab. Let every man here give the God of our fathers the praise due His name."

That evening, the worship in song and dance was exuberant, and the air was alive with the presence of El Shaddai.

As the sun was setting, the five prophets who had continued their vigil over the army of Israel were camped a short distance from King Ahab and his men, and could see the many fires from their encampment. Far beyond them could be seen the walls of Aphek.

Within the high thick walls, Ben-Hadad felt secure. His forces outnumbered Ahab's, and the city could withstand a long siege. Along the wall, sentries were spaced about twenty cubits apart, and the rest of the army was camped near the wall, or on the roofs of buildings that joined the wall, so that they could move into a defensive position at the first sign of an attack.

Ahab knew that he couldn't attack the city without losing most of his small army, and he didn't have the provisions to maintain a long siege.

At daybreak there was a rumbling sound that woke every man in both camps. The rumbling lasted for half a minute, then stopped. Several minutes later it returned and brought Ahab to the doorway of his tent. Every man stood to his feet. The five young prophets stood around their fire, looking towards Ahab's camp and to the city beyond.

"Look!" shouted one of Ahab's guards as he pointed toward the gate of Aphek. At that moment, half of the forty cubit towers on each side of the gate dropped into the ground, and what remained above ground toppled back into the city. From that point, the wall fell inward, as the rumbling continued and the earth began to tremble under their feet.

While the earth was still quaking, Ahab shouted, "Every man gird on his sword!" The order was repeated throughout the camp, but it was only when the ground stopped trembling that the order could be carried out.

With sword or spear in hand, they ran toward Aphek and vaulted over the pile of stone that had been the wall. Ahab was one of the first over the wall, sliding down the backside on loose stone and mortar. At the bottom was a man trapped and crushed from the waist down by a huge stone.

A skull-crushing blow from the king's sword silenced his screams of pain. The dust that hung in the air made it difficult to breathe, and cries from the trapped and dying filled the city. The injured that weren't buried in the rubble were quickly silenced. Segments of the wall that remained stood no higher than ten cubits. Several arrows were fired from what was left of the Syrian army, but they were quickly overpowered by overwhelming numbers of Israeli troops.

There were only a few hundred of Ben-Hadad's men left, and they were quickly finished off. The rest were buried under mounds of large stones and rubble. The Israelis took captive the young women, and slaughtered the rest.

The five young prophets came running into the city behind the army, praising God. "Praise Yahweh, his mercy endures forever."

Ben-Hadad took refuge in a house in the inner part of the city, but he knew it would be only a matter of time before they found him, so he sent a message to King Ahab. "Noble King Ahab, have mercy, I pray, and let me live."

Three days passed before the young prophets returned to Mount Carmel, with news of the miraculous victory Yahweh had given to Israel. The good news was tempered with the news that Ahab had spared King Ben-Hadad, a man that Elohim had appointed to die. For the promise of the return of the cities lost earlier, Ahab had spared the man whose life would be traded for his own.

One of the young prophets stood in the midst of the congregation and told how the Spirit of Yahweh had moved him to prophesy to the king, and how he had boldly prophesied Ahab's destruction for disobeying Yahweh's command to kill Ben-Hadad.

When he had taken a seat again, Elijah came to sit beside him and spoke softly, so only he could hear. "Every man is important to Yahweh until they begin to feel their own importance, then they are cut off like Ben-Hadad was supposed to be, and will be." Elijah placed his hand on his shoulder. "Yahweh has used a donkey to speak, and could use even a stone. Every prophet who has ever prophesied has felt what you are feeling. Only give thanks that he found you worthy to be used."

"I don't mean to be so arrogant," the young man, convicted, answered Elijah.

Elijah smiled at him and wiped away a tear that was moving down his face. "All of us that are older men have felt the pride you feel. Most of us were a long time putting it under control, and didn't know why Yahweh wasn't using us. Give him the glory, and the next time will be very soon." Elijah remained at his side as they sang the praises of El Shaddai that evening.

After the battle at Aphek, Ahab rested at Jezreel, and that pleased Jezebel, for the king had spent little time with her the past two years. The palace was on the north side of the city of Jezreel, overlooking the beautiful Jezreel valley to the north.

Ahab would sit with his sons and look out for hours at a time over the beautiful terraced vineyards of Naboth, who owned the hillside next to the palace. He drank Jezebel's fine wine, and replayed again and again the two great victories he had gotten over Syria, remembering every detail that he could recall, and marveling at the odds, and the outcome.

He had heard of the walls of Jericho falling before the armies of Israel hundreds of years before, but had dispelled it as a myth. What he had witnessed at Aphek, and the prophecies foretelling his victories, caused him to rethink the Jericho story.

Jezebel often joined Ahab on the roof, under a canopy, where he enjoyed the view and the breeze that came from the northwest. His thoughts seemed to stay on other things, and he failed to give her the attention she sought from him.

One evening before the sun set, he was partly reclined on his couch, tasting the wine in his cup every few minutes, when the queen came into his presence and bowed to the ground with sensual things on her mind. Her eyes painted, her cheeks and lips pomegranate red, the sheer cloth wrapped around her revealed every facet and curve and the color of her skin beneath. "My Lord, Ahab, is there any service I could render to the king?"

Ahab's eyes, made watery by the wine, toured her body, then he said, "Sit here by me." He sat up to make room for her, but stopped her in front of him, before she could be seated. He pulled at the loose fitting garment and Jezebel allowed it to fall to the floor. The two servants turned away. A moment later Ahab ordered, "Leave us," and pulled her onto the couch. He began to caress her body with his hands, but her delight turned to disappointment when she first saw the distraction in his eyes.

The next words from his tongue, made thick by the wine, confirmed what she knew he was thinking. "The towers dropped into the ground ten, fifteen cubits and the gates were ripped from the walls." He spoke more slowly, trying hard to make his words crisp. "Then the wall fell into the city and killed an entire army. Have you ever heard of the like?"

Jezebel's disappointment turned to hatred. She would never again have his full attention. She both hated and feared the God of Elijah, and the prophet that had resurrected the belief in the old God of the Hebrews.

Wearing animal furs as he returned from a hunt, Ahab looked more like a desert tribesman than a king. The stout bay beneath him labored up Jezreel's north slope, as he led the party of twenty guards, Prince Ahaziah, four friends, and a dozen mules loaded with supplies and game, deer and sheep taken in the hunt. Shadows of white clouds passing overhead ran across the ground as the horses found footing along the rain washed road. With the palace looming ahead, Ahab pulled his lathered horse to a halt along the terraced vineyard of Naboth on their left. "What would be a fair price to offer Naboth for this vineyard?" asked Ahab as he turned to his son, Ahaziah.

Ahaziah, now twenty, and just beginning to sport a thin reddish-black beard, looked back at the many rows of grapevines and servants of Naboth that were working in the rows. Then he answered, "They've been here for as long as I can remember, and they have never produced large, quality grapes. As a vineyard, I wouldn't think it would be worth much, but the view is as grand as the view from the palace." Ahab watched him as he spoke and saw such a likeness to his mother.

"I'm going to buy it from him." Ahab spoke confidently, sure that Naboth wouldn't refuse him. "I don't like those vines so close to the palace. When they're green, an enemy could reach the wall without being spotted, and I would like to have a garden of my own, something low that couldn't hide an enemy, a garden of vegetables perhaps.

"Wait here," he said as he turned his horse and rode down the row between the grapevines where a servant was working. The servant stopped working and watched as the king rode toward him and fearfully bowed when he came near. Looking down from his horse, Ahab asked, "Is Naboth here today?"

"No, my Lord," the man answered with his head down, afraid to look at King Ahab.

"Tell Naboth that the king would like to talk with him. Have him meet me at the palace tomorrow." Without waiting for a reply, Ahab backed his horse out of the narrow path between the vines. At the end of the row, he backed into the side of Ahaziah's horse before turning up the hill. With his son at his side the rest followed them on to the palace. Early the next day, when Naboth's presence was announced, Ahab met him in the entryway to the palace.

Naboth bowed on one knee. "My Lord Ahab, your highness."

"Rise, Naboth." As the silver-haired Naboth rose the king added, "It's been many years since I've seen you face to face." Ahab turned to one of the servants present and ordered mildly, "Bring wine for Naboth." A minute later two more servants appeared, one with two ornately decorated silver goblets, the other with a jug of wine. Ahab was served first but he handed his goblet to Naboth and took the second. "Come with me," he said to Naboth, as he led the way into the court followed by the servants bearing the wine. They climbed the long stairs to the roof, then to the wall, then into a tower and finally to the highest overlook of the palace, atop a tower.

Naboth, still unsure of why he was here, and for what reason the king had sent for him, said to make conversation, "It is beautiful, the most beautiful valley I have ever seen."

Ahab pointed across the Jezreel valley. "That's where I defeated Ben-Hadad." There was a minute of silence as they surveyed the landscape. "You own the land from here to the valley?" he asked as he looked back at Naboth.

"Yes, my Lord."

Ahab chose his words carefully. "Your vineyard has never done that well here. I would like to give you a better vineyard, with richer soil and a better water supply in exchange for this one." When Naboth didn't answer immediately Ahab added, "I'll give you twice the land."

"My Lord, it is a generous offer, but this land has been in my family since the days of Joshua. It was our inheritance in this land. My fathers fought the Canaanites and the Philistines, and it was commanded that the land should remain for their children's children forever."

Ahab, with a look of stunned disbelief that anyone would refuse such a generous offer from the king, said, "I will give you its worth in gold. Please allow me to have this land for a garden."

Though he feared the king, Naboth spoke boldly. "Yahweh forbid that I should sell the inheritance of my fathers to anyone."

Naboth had bowed to the image of Baal to save his own life, but had experienced terrible shame and humiliation at doing so, and despised both Ahab and Jezebel for the purging. He could see how much the king wanted the land and took a certain vengeful pride in withholding it from him. And, though he felt responsible to keep the land for his sons and their sons, the offer of more and better land was enticing, but he wouldn't have given it to Ahab at any price. "My Lord, forgive me, but I cannot."

Ahab's heart pounded as he struggled to control the anger within him. The thought of ordering Naboth slain crossed his mind, but he was constrained by the fear of losing the credibility he had worked so hard to gain with the worshipers of Yahweh. "I will give twice the value in gold."

"As king of Israel, you know the law of Yahweh and why I cannot sell the land of my fathers," Naboth answered to his last offer.

The muscles in Ahab's jaw flexed as he stared at Naboth. "He will show you out," Ahab said as he handed his cup to the attending servant, turned and rapidly descended the stairs. Upon entering his quarters he shouted, "Bring wine!" He sat in his bed drinking, until the reflection of the sun coming through the windows began to fade from the ivory tile on the opposite wall.

How could Naboth have refused to sell the land to him? After all, he was king and the one who had prevented Syria from enslaving all of Israel, those that they didn't kill. And they were notorious for torturing their enemies, sometimes for days. Didn't Naboth and all of Israel owe him a debt of gratitude? As he drank and thought, his self-righteous anger grew. When his eyes could no longer focus and the wine reeled his mind with each movement of his head, he threw the cup across the room and shouted, "I am the king! Bring me a gold cup! I will not drink from a silver cup!"

When Jezebel heard of the king's condition, she came to his bedroom the way he knew and anticipated that she would. She sat on the edge of his bed and displayed a very sympathetic attitude. "My lord, why are you troubled?" she asked as she stroked the side of his head.

"It's the people of Israel. They don't appreciate me for saving them from being driven from their land. They would have all become slaves to the Syrians if it wasn't for me," slurred Ahab. Taking a deep breath he continued, "How many times have I risked my life in battle for them? Naboth refused to sell his worthless vineyard to me for double what a good vineyard is worth. I offered him gold and he said," Ahab took another deep breath before he could continue. "Yahweh forbid that he should give the inheritance of his fathers to me for money."

Jezebel interrupted, "He is a worshiper of Yahweh?"

"He must be," Ahab replied.

Jezebel quickly realized that she was in a position, with her connection to the temple, to eliminate Naboth and regain lost favor with Ahab. "Great King, do you not rule over the kingdom of Israel? Let your heart be merry, don't be troubled over this matter. It is but a small thing." She leaned forward pressing her breast against his chest and laying her head on his shoulder. She whispered into his ear, "Come and dine. I have had your favorite foods prepared."

Ahab asked, "What do you mean, it is but a small thing?"

"My Lord, lend to me your signet ring and I will give you the vineyard of Naboth the fool." She raised up to meet his eyes with hers. He looked into her face for a moment, then extended his hand for her to remove the ring. She helped him to his feet and steadied him with her arm around his waist as they went in to dine.

After sending to inquire of the chief priest of the temple of Yahweh in Jezreel, and learning that Naboth was an elder, she began to formulate a plan.

She sent letters to the nobles and elders in the name of the king, ordering a fast in honor of Yahweh.

She chose two priests from the now secret society of Baal worship, the only Baal worship that still offered human sacrifices of children, and which she controlled from a distance. The priests of Baal, posing as priests of Yahweh coming from Judah, would be honored and seated next to Naboth, when he was seated among the nobles. The three-day fast would end with a feast, as was customary.

It was an unusual request, but one that couldn't be refused since the letter arrived with the king's seal. The priests and elders didn't know for what reason the king had ordered this, except to worship Yahweh and honor Naboth, and Jezebel felt sure that no one would ever know the truth. She would afterward see that the two false priests disappeared. She had ways of doing that, then only she would know.

On the day of the feast, when the fast had ended, the false priests obeyed Jezebel's orders and befriended Naboth, hoping to find something in his conversation they could twist to use against him. The news that Naboth had refused to sell his vineyard to the king was common knowledge, so it seemed a normal question when one of them asked him why he refused to sell it to Ahab.

Naboth responded by saying, "You cannot kill the prophets of Yahweh one day and pretend to worship Yahweh the next." Feeling that he was in safe company, he added, "Ahab built a glorious temple to Baal in Samaria and look at this small temple of Yahweh here in Jezreel. Baal is clearly Ahab's god. And, the vineyard was the inheritance of my fathers."

They had struck a sensitive cord, one that brought Naboth's emotions to the surface, and put him in danger of breaking the law by speaking against the king.

The man who had begun the conversation with Naboth looked at his co-conspirator, who took the signal and continued by asking, "Why would he allow a temple for Yahweh to be built here in Jezreel at all if he were not a worshiper?"

Naboth answered sternly, "Since Elijah met the priests of Baal at Mount Carmel and defeated them and killed them, there are not so many that worship openly anymore. Several of the Baal priests have been stoned to death since the fire at Mount Carmel. What choice does Ahab have? It is not popular with the people to be a Baal worshiper, but Ahab protects Jezebel's temple to the queen of heaven in the valley below here.

"In Megiddo they still offer children to Baal. Sometimes at night you can hear the screams and see the light from the fires burning in the high places. If Ahab is a true worshiper of Yahweh, why doesn't he stop such things?" Carried away by his indignation, Naboth continued, "I pray that Yahweh will soon deliver us from the wicked reign of Ahab and his queen who believes that she is some goddess. She, Jezebel, is Ahab's god! It is she that he worships."

They knew that this would be the most that they would get from Naboth to use against him and made eye contact, the signal to accuse him.

"This man has blasphemed Yahweh!" the one shouted as he jumped to his feet.

The other stood and said, "Yes, I heard it myself with my own ears. He blasphemed Yahweh and cursed the king, saying that he was evil." This they twisted from Naboth's statements, then fell back on rehearsed accusations. "He said that because of the evil Yahweh has sent upon Israel, He isn't worthy of our worship."

The high priest of the temple stood, as he suddenly realized that this whole situation had been planned to have Naboth killed, but there wasn't anything he could do against the word of two witnesses. Suddenly everyone was standing, and Naboth was being shoved toward the door. The priests from Judah were well educated and informed men, perfect, too perfect to be real. The high priest was the only one who didn't follow the crowd to stone Naboth.

Led by the two false priests, Naboth was struck repeatedly and called blasphemer, and never allowed to speak, as he was dragged outside the city gate and stoned to death.

When Jezebel received the news that Naboth had been killed she had a scribe, knowledgeable in the worship of Yahweh, draw up a decree that Ahab would issue and send throughout the land.

"Be it known that Naboth, the Jezreelite, has been stoned to death by the elders of Jezreel, according to the Law of Moses for blaspheming the God of Abraham. All lands owned by Naboth shall not pass on to his heirs, but are henceforth the property of the realm. The heirs shall die for the blasphemy of the fathers, that the iniquity be cut off from Israel. So shall it be to anyone who speaks against the King of Israel, or blasphemes Yahweh El Shaddai."

With the deception complete, Jezebel knew that, for the most part, Israel would support the next order she would give in the name of Ahab. She ordered her guard to slay the three sons of Naboth, a directive that was carried out before Ahab arrived at the palace in the late afternoon.

Jezebel greeted him, bowing on both knees with her head to the floor, the most submissive posture she could take. "My Lord, Ahab."

"The queen shouldn't bow as low as a servant," Ahab said as he reached to pull her to her feet.

When she was standing she bowed again with her head. "Great ruler of Israel, Naboth is dead. He blasphemed the God of Elijah, and was stoned by the nobles and elders of Jezreel. The vineyard of Naboth is yours."

"And what of his sons?" Ahab asked.

"My Lord, I have taken care of them and I have asked one of the scribes to draw up a decree that will resolve that issue and will add greater punishment to all who speak against the king, and against Yahweh. Come, you must see if it meets your approval." Jezebel escorted Ahab to the room of the scribes where all scrolls documenting victories, the laws, and decrees were kept.

Upon reading the proclamation, Ahab ordered it sent to all tribes and regions in the land, then hurried out to look over his newly acquired property. He didn't know how Jezebel had accomplished it, but there were times when she seemed to do the impossible, and this was one of them.

Ahab, on horseback, escorted by two guards and Captain Jehu, was riding along surveying the vineyard and adjoining land which had belonged to Naboth, when he spotted a solitary figure approaching from the valley below. He pulled his horse to a halt and studied the man as he came toward them. From the angle of the sun and the distance, he couldn't distinguish the color of the man's robe. He hoped it wasn't Elijah, but deep down in his soul, he knew that it was.

Two days ago Yahweh had told Elijah to come to Jezreel and meet Ahab in the vineyard of Naboth. Without stopping to rest, Elijah continued toward them until the blue stripes of his robe were clearly visible.

The king sat his horse in silence until Captain Jehu spoke. "Isn't that Elijah?"

Ahab sullenly replied, "Yes, it is."

Jezebel had been agitated throughout the day, but didn't realize the cause of the agitation until Elijah began his ascent in her direction. She was looking through her gowns to choose something appropriately enticing to meet Ahab when he returned. She felt the presence and began to tremble. As the paralyzing fear clutched her from her innermost being, she took a seat on the couch. Despite her face paint, she turned pale. "Your highness, are you all right?" one of the handmaids asked as she knelt next to the queen.

"He's here," Jezebel whispered, "Call the guard." The handmaid scurried from the room and returned a moment later with a guard. Jezebel motioned for one of the eunuchs in attendance to take her arm. "Take me to the roof," she ordered, clutching the guard's arm, as he helped her to her feet. With the guard at one side and the eunuch at her other, she ascended the flights of stairs that led to the roof. There she looked out and saw the prophet as he approached the king.

Elijah stopped lower on the hill, about fifteen cubits in front of Ahab. "Thus says Yahweh," Elijah spoke loudly in a baritone voice that hardly seemed his own. "You have murdered, and now you've come to steal. In the place where dogs licked the blood of Naboth, dogs shall lick your blood."

There was a hard look between them. Ahab was amazed at how little Elijah had changed since the first time they met, and his eyes seemed to sparkle as they burned through the king, provoking a response from him. "Have you found me, Oh my enemy?"

Elijah shifted his weight and leaned against the staff, which he moved up the hill in front of him and braced on the ground. "Yes, I have found you, you who have sold yourself to do wickedly in the eyes of Yahweh." Elijah began to tremble as the Spirit of God built inside him. His voice rose to a bemoaning wail that sent chills through the four men. "Behold, I will bring destruction on you and upon your seed, and will cut off every son of Ahab in Israel, both slave and free. I will make your house like the house of Jeroboam, the son of Nebat, and Baasha, the son of Ahijah, because you have provoked me to anger, and made my people Israel to sin against me.

"And concerning Jezebel, thus says Yahweh, the dogs shall eat her flesh by the wall of Jezreel. The dogs shall eat the flesh of all who have issued forth from Ahab who die in the city, and the fowls of the air shall eat the flesh of the seed of Ahab who die in the fields.

"You have done great abominations in following idols like the Amorites did. They were overthrown, and their lands and houses given to Israel. You and your father have made Israel to commit the same abominations and have stirred the wrath of El Shaddai."

Elijah closed his eyes and bowed his head as he leaned more heavily on the staff, recovering from the physical drain of having the power that destroys or creates stars flow through a mortal being. An unearthly silence engulfed them, until he looked up and locked gazes with Jehu for a moment, as though he were going to say something, then turned away.

Jehu could see the anger on the king's face as Elijah turned and began to descend the mount. Ahab muttered, "This is what the queen has brought upon me."

Afraid that he had missed something spoken to him, Captain Jehu asked, "Sire, did you speak to me?"

Ahab turned to Jehu and answered curtly, "No, I did not!"

Jezebel watched Elijah as he made his way slowly down the slope away from Ahab. She knew that this visit from the prophet would precipitate another disaster, and she knew that he had come because of the plot and stoning of Naboth.

The last time she had watched him leave after delivering a decree from Yahweh, he was fleeing for his life. This time he didn't bow to the king, and he defiantly walked away without showing any fear. The mixture of terror and anger in her was on the verge of becoming rage. She spit out a prophecy of her own, "Let his prophecies fall to the ground. Let Yahweh refuse to hear his prayer and may the gods damn his soul."

As she turned to face the sun, she lifted her hands and prayed, "Great Baal, torment him the way he has tormented me, your servant." Her body was trembling when she looked back toward the prophet, now a little more than two hundred cubits away. He stopped, turned around, and looked directly at her. He was too far away to see the features of his face, but she could feel his gaze. Ahab and Jehu turned to see why the prophet had stopped and was looking at the palace. His stare intimidated Jezebel even more and he called out to her, "I have no fear of you!" A minute passed before Elijah turned away. The queen seemed frozen in place, as she watched Ahab angrily turn and kick his horse into a gallop toward the palace gate.

Fear gripped Jezebel as she turned and slowly made her way into the palace. Breathing with great difficulty, her mind spinning, she would have collapsed but for the guard on her left who supported her.

Ahab returned to the palace long enough to have his chariot hitched, then proceeded on to Samaria where he would fast for a month, from the new moon to the following new moon, praying for forgiveness to the God of Elijah, Yahweh. From his previous experiences with the prophet, he knew he had something to fear, so he had all the prophets in the court fast with him.

Jezebel had defeated herself. By the time she recovered from the attack of fear, Ahab was gone. Rather than receiving the recognition she sought, she had caused Ahab to seek Yahweh, and it would be the better part of a year before she would see him again.

232

From one of the narrow tower windows in the gray light before dawn, Jezebel looked out over the Jezreel valley and the vineyard that had been Naboth's. Ahab had left without telling her what judgment Elijah had pronounced against them. She knew that the king was afraid, he had never reacted like this to anything. This was the second week of his seclusion in Samaria, and even she couldn't reach him. As she stood there weighing the matter, she decided to send for Captain Jehu.

A week later Jehu arrived at Jezreel early in the morning. His presence was announced to Jezebel, who wasn't prepared to see him. She kept him waiting for more than an hour, while she dressed in her most royal apparel and had the eunuchs paint her face to perfection. After all, he was a very attractive man and carried great influence with the people of Israel, an influence she wanted on her side.

When Jehu was brought before her in the throne room, he bowed to the floor. He hated her, but he recognized her power to destroy people in devious ways that would never cross Ahab's mind. After plots like the one against Naboth, he now suspected she was behind the whole thing. Rumors had surfaced about the two so-called priests of Yahweh who had witnessed against the innocent man. They had disappeared, and the talk was that they had been sacrificed on the altar of Baal.

How beautifully radiant she was, he thought, recognizing that she was as sinister as she was beautiful. He bowed low as he addressed her, "Your Highness, your servant Jehu, captain of the chariots of Israel, has come at your request."

Jezebel spoke softly but firmly, sensing his discomfort at bowing to her. "Arise, Captain." Jehu stood at her command. She continued, "I've not seen the king since he went into seclusion, or since the day he encountered the prophet Elijah. Perhaps you can tell me what message Elijah claims to have been given from his God."

Jehu hesitated before answering, as he considered what he might say without angering Ahab or offending her. "My Queen, the great King Ahab may want to tell you himself."

Jehu's answer was what she expected. "A wise reply, Captain Jehu. I want to help in any way that I can. Understand this, I have a great deal of influence with the king. I can destroy men, or I can see that they are promoted. Your refusal to answer might give me reason to turn the king against you. And, I can do that."

Jehu knew Ahab well and knew that he would be easier to deal with than Jezebel. He answered slowly, choosing his words carefully, "I didn't understand all of what he said, but you may not want the entire court to hear the message Elijah brought from Yahweh." Jezebel looked in the direction of one then another of those in attendance, and, with a slight motion of her hand, dismissed them, including the guards, until there were eight people left. Jehu quickly glanced around the room. Besides himself and the queen, two priests of Baal, an astrologer, two priests of Ashtoreth, and a eunuch scribe remained.

"Proceed, captain," she ordered softly.

"Your Highness, the prophet said that Yahweh was angry with the king, and that all of his descendants would be destroyed. He said that the birds would eat the flesh of those who die in the fields and the dogs would eat the flesh of those who die in the cities."

Jezebel angled her gaze upward as she absorbed what Jehu was saying, then she asked, "And what did he say about me?"

After a long moment of tense silence that grew more tense with each second, he slowly uttered, "He said that the dogs would eat your flesh."

She tried to remain calm, but her hands began to tremble as they rested on the arms of the throne. She pulled them to her lap when she saw that the shaking had become obvious to Jehu, who glanced at her left hand, but was trying to pretend that he hadn't noticed. Jezebel's voice cracked when she ordered, "You may leave now, captain." Jehu bowed to one knee then stood and walked from the room.

Jehu was barely out of sight when Jezebel's face flushed, it became difficult for her to breathe and, as she struggled for air, the trembling grew worse. The physicians were quickly brought in and she was carried to her bed. The physical symptoms of her anguish disappeared before the day was over, but she lay for days in a depression and refused any attempt to be comforted by her attendants. Eber came to see the queen several times, but was denied an audience with her. On the tenth day she summoned Eber.

She was half lying, half sitting on her couch, wrapped in a blanket, her left breast exposed and she was without any face paint. Her hair wasn't immaculately dressed as he had always seen it before, but had been quickly braided into a long thick strand that hung down her back for the purpose of meeting him. Eber came in and bowed. He remained on his knees as he spoke. "Your Highness, thank you for allowing me to see you. I have been concerned about you and have been to see you several times but was never allowed to come in."

Eber's concern seemed genuine and moved her. "I haven't wanted to see anyone." She paused a moment before proceeding to give what she thought would be her last command to the short man from the east. "I do not wish to live any longer, Eber. I want you to prepare something that will allow me to cross easily into the realm of the gods, where I can find happiness again."

Eber's voice denoted his sorrow at her request. "Great queen, goddess among the gods, you are needed here. You are loved by so many, and I love you above all others. Please don't choose to leave us to sorrow over you. I know that whatever troubles you can be resolved."

Jezebel closed her eyes and rubbed her left temple as though her head ached. Several moments passed before she spoke. "Elijah has decreed that his God will bring great evil against the royal family, against Ahab, all his children and me.

"Baal hasn't protected Israel or Ahab from the curse of Yahweh, and the priests of Baal haven't been effective against Elijah. I have sacrificed and danced before Yahweh and he has refused to be entreated by me. We sacrifice to Baal in the high places in secret, but he hasn't raised up any priests or prophets with powers like the ones Elijah killed.

"I have no where to turn for protection against his god and I can't bear to see the seed of a great king like Ahab destroyed from the earth, nor do I wish to be eaten by dogs." There was a plea in her voice unlike anything he had ever known from her. She asked for his services the second time. "Please, Eber, help me. Give me something to let me cross over."

Eber thought for a moment then answered, "When you built the glorious temple of Baal, people of Ekron came and worshipped Baal with great sacrifices. Then they later built a great temple to Baal, or Baal-Zebub as they refer to him; a temple much like the one in Samaria, and I hear that they have great and powerful priests, and there they sacrifice openly. Among the people of Ekron you are known as a goddess. You are a goddess. Send sacrifices to Ekron, and have them petition Baal to drive out this Hebrew God and restore the worship of Baal in the land like it once was."

Jezebel's face brightened, "If they could do that, then the people would again give to Ashtoreth, the goddess that dwells in me, the worship she deserves." Jezebel sat up. "I will go to Ekron myself, and offer great sacrifices to Baal and the people there will give me honor and praise, and I will dance for Baal like before."

Jezebel stood, holding the blanket loosely around her. "I will have new gowns made and new bright banners for my guard." Eber stood as Jezebel made plans. "Eber, find the captain of my guard and tell him to ready the men. Send in the handmaids." As Eber left the room, Jezebel dropped the blanket in a heap on the floor and began to spin and dance in anticipation of dancing before hundreds of Baal worshipers again.

With gifts of camels and horses, silver and gold for the Philistine kings and a company of more than three hundred, her fifty man guard, her carriage bearers, priests that accompanied an idol of Baal, her attendants and numerous sacrifices, animal and human, Jezebel began her pilgrimage to Ekron.

In great splendor the caravan of wagons and camels entered Ekron. She found that her reputation had preceded her, and that her powers multiplied many times over through the telling of great battles fought and won by Israel with the power of the gods and her spells. Among the Philistines Jezebel found the praise and admiration she sought and craved. They hailed her as a goddess and her worshipers brought her gifts of silver and gold.

In the temple of Baal, a throne was built for Ashtoreth next to the giant bronze idol, and Jezebel was enthroned there with the status of a goddess. She presided over the worship of her mate Baal. Daily prayers and incantations were made against Yahweh, entreating Baal to conquer the god of the Hebrews, and to restore his worship and glory in Israel.

After many days of sacrifice and worship the priests assured Jezebel that she no longer had anything to fear from the Hebrew God. They told her that he had been conquered by Baal, and was now powerless over her and King Ahab. She couldn't forget how her own priests had been powerless against Elijah but she didn't allow that to stop her from relishing the admiration that was being given to her.

It had been years since Jezebel had received that type of esteem, even worship, and she gloried in it. As a goddess, she could assign partners for the orgiastic fertility worship on the three days of the full moon each month, and could even designate the individuals that she believed Baal selected to die upon the altar. Her regal composure and appearance added to the image of her as a goddess, and the people obeyed willingly, eager to die for the pleasure of Baal with the promise of a better life in the realm of the gods.

The total wild abandonment to the worship of Baal in the orgies, and the constant stream of blood that flowed from the altar satisfied Jezebel's sadistic nature more than anything she had ever experienced. A three cubit platform rose from the floor where the priests performed sexual acts with young virgins, some no more than ten or twelve years old, in full view of an audience of more than a thousand.

To the rear of the stage was a higher level another three cubits above the first where the idol of Baal stood. Her throne sat next to the bronze idol that was heated until it glowed red. Infants belonging to the worshipers were placed in the searing arms of the god. Their screams lasted only for a couple of seconds. When the priests finished with the virgins on the platform, the young girls were passed to the audience. Many did not live through the ordeal. Their bodies were then burned as sacrifices to Baal.

In drunken frenzies, men and women would sometimes sacrifice themselves to the gods, believing that they would receive great riches in the next world. Many women climbed onto the platform for the sacred honor of having intercourse with the priests, and the blessing and prosperity they believed it would bring them.

She was there three months when Ahab sent word for her to come to Samaria. Rumor had first reached Israel more than a year before that Shalmaneser III, King of Assyria, with the mightiest military force on the earth, had plans to conquer the world and was pushing in their direction. Both Ahab and Jezebel feared that the invading Assyrians would fulfill the prophecy of Elijah.

Ahab had spared King Ben-Hadad after defeating Syria, but Ben-Hadad hadn't kept his vow to return the cities to Israel in exchange for his life. Ahab was growing impatient with his delays but, in the face of certain defeat, and with the words of Elijah looming over them, Ahab joined Syria and Phoenicia against Assyria, and marched north to meet the threat before the enemy reached their borders. Lacking men, Ahab left a contingent to defend the borders of Israel while he took only ten thousand men and two thousand chariots to the campaign. Ishbaal, Jezebel's half brother, the Phoenician king of Zidon, led an army of one hundred twenty thousand men, the largest of the forces, and Ben-Hadad a hundred thousand.

Ahab was away for more than two years during which time Prince Ahaziah recruited and trained another forty thousand troops. And, though the final battle wasn't decisive, and each side was left with heavy losses, the Assyrians were stopped at the battle of Qarqar.

The two years of war with Assyria was the most trying time in Jezebel's life. Every day she expected to hear that Israel and her allies had been defeated. She knew if that happened, the fulfillment of Elijah's prophecy wouldn't be far behind.

She remained in Samaria during the war because it was better fortified than Jezreel, and because it was the seat of power. She would help to guide Ahaziah, should he be crowned king if Ahab didn't return.

When word reached Jezebel that Ahab was returning unconquered, she was sure that the priests of Ekron had been right, and the God of Elijah was now powerless over them.

Ahab rode an exceedingly worn-looking, tired, dark bay as he led his troops home from the war. Only four thousand eight hundred ninety men of the ten thousand man army he had taken into battle survived, and fewer than six hundred of the two thousand chariots returned with them.

They brought three hundred thirty-one Assyrian captives bound in chains. Twenty prisoners hadn't survived the trip. Ahab had allowed the Israelite army to vent their anger for their losses on some by hacking them to death. He saw that as a way of deterring the rest from rebelling. They knew that the slightest infraction would bring the same instant reprisal and so they were quick to obey.

When the mount of Samaria, crowned with its city and palace, loomed ahead, the hearts of the men soared and the pace quickened involuntarily. Ahab nudged the weakened animal beneath him into a slightly faster walk.

A third of a mile ahead of them stood a man in the road. Ahab pulled his horse to a halt. Though he couldn't make out any feature of the person to distinguish them from any other, he knew it was Micaiah and dreaded to face the prophet. More slowly than before, he walked the tired horse toward the lone figure. The anxious men behind him crowded forward, wishing that he would move faster but knowing better than to break rank.

Ahab again pulled his horse to a halt when Micaiah was only a few cubits in front of him. For a moment there was a cold gaze between them. Ahab motioned to his first officer who rode behind him to take the men on to Samaria. As the troops began moving around them, armor and swords clattering and footsteps beating out a rhythm, Ahab spoke sharply to Micaiah, "I told you to keep your distance from me by staying in Tirzah! Why do I see your face in front of me this day?"

Over the sound of the men passing, Micaiah spoke loudly, "You are alive when many others are dead. Does that not tell you how merciful

the God of Abraham is? As long as there is life, there is hope. Destroy
the temple of Baal you built and the high places, and take away the
golden calves in Bethel and turn to Yahweh with all of your heart.
Yahweh might repent of the judgment that is intended for you and
your sons and your daughters. He has spared you this long."

The king wasn't in the mood to discuss this with Micaiah, but he did
reluctantly answer, "I sacrifice to Yahweh, but you know that I cannot
destroy the temple that I built."

"If you destroy not the temple, El Shaddai will destroy you."

Ahab turned, looked back, selected a couple of men and ordered,
"Seize him! Chain him with the Assyrians and treat him no differently
than the rest!"

Micaiah offered no resistance when they took him and was thrown
into prison with the Assyrians when they reached Samaria.

For days Ahab thought about the words of Micaiah and Elijah,
and even considered destroying the temple, but it was the most
beautiful structure in the land and a great achievement, and he had
survived the bloodiest war of his life. If Yahweh were going to
destroy him, wouldn't that have been the time? Yet he lived. At the
end of the month he sent and had Micaiah released with orders
never to set foot in Samaria again.

As Ahab settled back into life in Samaria, he sent a message asking
Ben-Hadad to return the Syrian occupied lands of Israel in Gilead.
Ben-Hadad answered by saying that he needed those lands to compen-
sate for the great losses he had sustained against Assyria. Ben-Hadad
resented Ahab and felt disgraced by the two victories lost to Israel with
overwhelming numbers in his favor, and felt that returning captured
lands to Ahab would be more humiliating.

Ahab began making plans to go to war against Syria to recover the
cities. This time he vowed to kill the king he once spared. Ahab's anger
against Ben-Hadad grew into a consuming hatred as he thought about
the Syrian king's promise and betrayal. This time he would fulfill the will
of Yahweh, but the two years of fighting with Assyria had again depleted
Israel's resources and ability to initiate another war.

Ahab summoned Obadiah into the counsel chamber alone. Ahab was
seated at a table, engrossed in a map of the land of Gilead, when Obadiah
entered and bowed from the waist, but went unnoticed. "My Lord Ahab."

Ahab glanced up momentarily. "Sit down, Obadiah."

Obadiah took a seat across from Ahab and sat silently for several
minutes until Ahab looked up again. "Ben-Hadad controls much of
the northern territory of Gilead and the great city of Ramoth, a
strategic location. This is an area that Ben-Hadad vowed to return

in exchange for his life. The prophets of Yahweh were right, he should have been killed.

"I am going to invite King Jehoshaphat to Samaria. We'll have a feast and games in his honor, an event he will never forget. We'll make sport of the Assyrian prisoners, since Shalmaneser has refused to pay a ransom for their release. Then I will ask him to join me against Syria." Obadiah sat up and listened intently as Ahab continued. "You make preparations, whatever the expense. My son, Ahaziah, will be sent as envoy to bring an invitation to Jehoshaphat. We will invite him to race his fastest chariots against ours and pit his archers and javelin throwers against us.

"I will ask him to bring his son and our mutual grandsons, whom I've never seen. It'll be a joyous time for all of us. Israel could use something to renew the spirit of the people after all that has happened." Ahab's voice deepened with regret, as though he blamed himself for Israel's failures. "We lost a lot of fine men to Assyria and Ben-Hadad controls the most important cities of Gilead." His countenance brightened some, as he remembered his previous victories against Syria. "Remember the joy that came over the country when we defeated that whimpering dog before? We will have a month of celebrating then with the help of Judah we will drive Syria out of our land. What do you feel about it, Obadiah?"

"It is a good plan," Obadiah answered quickly, then added more slowly, "Maybe we should seek Elijah's advice before we proceed."

Ahab pondered a few moments before he said anything. "You know that Elijah hates me. I also hate him. I hope that I never lay eyes on him again. He has brought me nothing but trouble. I have four hundred prophets who will give me the counsel of Yahweh."

Obadiah knew that the king's prophets were more interested in status and wealth, rather than the will of Yahweh, but he wouldn't say it to the king. "I will begin making preparations immediately," he answered instead.

"I know I can entrust this matter to you." Ahab gave Obadiah a half-smile of approval. "See to it, Obadiah." Obadiah left the room with Ahab still pondering over the map.

It took six months of preparation for the visit of Judah's King Jehoshaphat, who arrived in splendor, accompanied by more than a thousand of his most valiant men. They camped several miles south of Samaria, then at dawn the next morning, marched into the city. The road was lined with the citizens of Israel. Jehoshaphat led the parade in a golden chariot with wide iron wheels. The men marched five abreast, fifty to each unit. In front of each unit were four of the finest chariots in the world, and in each were a driver and a spearman. At the rear of each unit was a wagon carrying a large drum that sounded the timing for each precise step.

The sight was impressive, unlike anything Israel had ever seen. The whole procession moved along like a giant caterpillar. The army Ahab inherited from his father Omri had been the most powerful and valiant in the world. Ahab had once been willing to pit them against Judah, but now that seemed foolish.

"Because they look good doesn't mean they can fight," Ahab said to Obadiah. They watched from a bulwark above the palace gate as the procession entered the city and approached the palace.

Within the palace walls, Jehoshaphat received a royal welcome. Ahab's elite guard, standing at attention to welcome the visiting king, reminded Jehoshaphat of the fierce fighting men he had encountered with his father Asa, when they fought against Israel during the reign of King Omri.

As desperately as Ahab had tried to conceal his lack of military strength, Jehoshaphat knew exactly what his numbers were. He surmised that per man they might be formidable, but against his professional army of three hundred thousand and a trained militia of a thousand thousand that could be mustered in two days time, Israel's army could offer little resistance.

Though they were now allied through the marriage of Athaliah to his son, Jehoshaphat felt it was important to know the strength of his one-time enemy and to stay prepared. Ahab was, after all, regarded as the best military leader in the region, regardless of his current resources.

The following week was filled with celebration and feasting. Jehoshaphat found Jezebel to be the most charming woman he had ever met, and her gentle way dispelled most of the terrible things he had heard about her. Rulers are most often defamed and their faults exaggerated, he thought, and concluded that most of what he had heard was untrue.

At the end of a week, the two kings rode out to the fortified cities of Israel. Ahab was especially proud of the great walled fortress of Megiddo, which guarded the trade route to Egypt, and the countries of the east. There in the valley of Megiddo, Ahab had assembled four thousand of the new chariots that had been under construction since the great losses against Shalmaneser. They raced from the west, eastward below the castle as the kings watched from the wall. It was an impressive sight. The dust that followed rose to darken the horizon to the south. As the cloud drifted eastward, the chariots returned to fill the valley. All turned to face up the hill of Megiddo and the two kings who stood upon the wall of the city.

The bowman from each chariot stepped to the ground and bowed to his knee to honor King Jehoshaphat. Ahab ordered one of the guards, "Signal for Captain Jehu to come up." They watched as Jehu's chariot, pulled by four spirited steeds, two dark chestnuts, a bay and a black, rolled up the narrow road to the city.

As Jehu came through the gate, Jehoshaphat turned to Ahab and said, "Those are some of the finest horses I've ever seen."

"That's what I want to show you. They are his own horses, the fastest in Israel, and he is the most skilled charioteer I've ever seen." There was a moment of silence then Ahab continued. "He will most likely beat your teams and my teams in the races. Come, I will introduce you." They began around the walkway toward the steps as Ahab said, "His grandfather, Nimshi, first brought that blood line from Egypt."

Jehu, standing by his chariot, bowed to one knee when Ahab and Jehoshaphat approached. "Stand up, Captain," Ahab ordered firmly. "This is the captain of the chariots of Israel."

Jehoshaphat wrapped his arm around the muzzle of the chestnut next to them and began to stroke her face. "They have large jaws for mares," he said as he turned back to face Jehu. He noticed a crack in the hoof of the same animal and bent down to lift the foot but the horse pawed at him. He jumped back and straightened to face Jehu again. "As fine as I have ever seen. Your king says that you will probably beat my team in the race. Do you think that's true, Captain?"

With confidence he answered, "Sire, with all due respect, I intend to win." The look in his eyes said to Jehoshaphat that he believed it.

The king of Judah asked, calling Jehu's attention to the horse's infirmity, "What about her foot?"

"This isn't the team I'm going to race. The sister to her is faster. I wouldn't have risked my best team today." Jehu stepped to the horse's side, lifted her foot and brushed away the dirt with his fingers. After studying the hoof for a minute, he said, "She cracked it racing up the valley just now, but it will heal."

Jehoshaphat looked at one of the middle horse on the left side of the chariot tongue, patting her on the shoulder, then moved to the last one and began to scratch her neck. She leaned into his hand to increase the pressure of his touch. "These are some of the finest horses I've ever seen. Are they from the same stallion?"

"No, Your Highness, but they are from the same blood line," Jehu answered as he moved around the team and stood next to Jehoshaphat.

"I would pay you well for the stallion that sired this one." Jehoshaphat stepped back to the first mare with the cracked hoof.

"He died last year, but my family wouldn't have sold him at any price. I have one of his sons, a full brother to her and he is as good as the sire that fathered them. If you would accept it, I would like very much to make him a gift to you."

Jehoshaphat looked at Ahab then at Jehu. "How could I repay such a gift?"

"If you were to repay the gift, it wouldn't be a gift. It will be a few days before I can have him in Samaria."

Jehoshaphat smiled and said, "I should say I cannot accept such a gift, but the truth is that I would like to have a stallion from her blood lines too much to be pretentious. Captain, with much gratitude, I accept your gift."

"I will have him in Samaria within a week." As Jehu spoke, he glanced at Ahab, and because he knew him well, he detected displeasure that only a few could have seen. Though he was trying to aid in winning Jehoshaphat's confidence, he had agitated King Ahab. He hadn't realized that in giving Jehoshaphat one of the finest stallions in the country, he had made Ahab jealous of his respect for the king of Judah.

"Perhaps your king would allow you to ride back to Samaria with us," Jehoshaphat said as he looked to Ahab for his approval.

Jehu spoke up before Ahab could answer. "My place is here with the chariots of Israel." Turning to Ahab, he said, "My Lord, if you will allow me to return to my men."

Ahab nodded. Jehu took hold of a lead attached to the center mare and led the horses and chariot away. Jehoshaphat watched Jehu until he was out of sight then turned to Ahab and said, "A fine officer."

"The finest in Israel," Ahab answered.

The day dawned hot and was becoming humid as Jezebel readied herself for the festive day ahead. A eunuch knelt on one knee beside the queen's chair as he gently blended rose color to her cheeks and a deep purple above her eyes. Another eunuch stood at her side slowly waving a large fan to stir the air and cool the queen as a young maid stood behind her, braiding her hair. The eunuch leaned in close to her face to paint her eyes. Jezebel said, "You are very handsome."

Caught off guard he stammered for a moment, then got out the words, "Thank..., thank you, Your Highness."

Jezebel ran her hand over his arm teasingly. "It's too bad you are a eunuch. You would make a very attractive priest." She could see that her comment was met with unexpressed resentment and changed the subject, "I'll wager you that the Assyrian is beaten today."

"And what would you wager?" The eunuch moved back a little so he could see her face better.

"I'll wager your freedom," she said arrogantly, then asked, "How many has he beaten now? I wasn't there yesterday."

"I heard that he killed three men yesterday. I think that makes thirteen in all. But I have nothing to wager. Even the clothes I wear belong to you." He paused for a response, and when she didn't answer he added, "If anyone can beat the Assyrian, Jotham can. Until he became a commander, he had never been beaten in the arena."

Jezebel frowned, and spoke as though she were talking to herself, "He is making Israel look bad in front of King Jehoshaphat. Ahab has promised the Assyrians their freedom if he beats Jotham today, but I think that is a mistake. Jotham was the best there has ever been, but he hasn't been in the arena in five years." The eunuch was used to these one sided conversations. He knew that this was the queen's way of mulling over her thoughts, and that she wasn't really interested in his opinion.

Jezebel smiled and asked "Would you fight the Assyrian for your freedom?"

"Noooo! No, I've heard that he is a giant and he has defeated everyone that has gone against him." He stood and looked to see that his work was perfect, then fear gripped him, as he suddenly suspected that she had plans to make sport of him in the arena. "Your Highness, please, I've never held a sword in my hand."

"You've had enough of your parts cut off. We'll make sure you don't lose anymore. Today you will go with me, armed with a fan."

Jezebel arrived deliberately late to avoid having to sit through the boring battles leading to the contest everyone was waiting for. She wasn't late enough and had to sit through three matches before the Assyrian and Jotham entered through the two opposing gates in the arena. She sat in the king's pavilion behind Ahab and Jehoshaphat. Prince Ahaziah, being next in line to the throne, sat next to Ahab. There were about thirty guests and attendants beneath the royal canopy.

Captain Jehu's heart pounded as he watched the two men enter the arena, facing each other for the first time. He was on the level of the arena pit, and watched through spaces in the timber wall. Only one would be alive when it was over and it could very well be the Assyrian.

Jotham was one of Jehu's most valiant officers and a close friend. He was strong and large, but not as large as the Assyrian, and he was now forty, maybe ten years older than the man he had to fight. The Assyrian was fighting for his life, but Jotham and the thirteen men who had lost their lives to him in previous battles did it for glory and gold.

Surely there wasn't anyone more self-assured or arrogant than an Israelite warrior who felt invincible and wanted to be a legend in his own time, like the great men that King David had recorded for history. "Damn your pride, Jotham, damn your pride. It's going to kill you," Jehu said to himself in an angry whisper. There were too many real wars and battles to fight to waste good men for the pleasure of the royalty and the wealthiest of Israel; and for the king's guest, King Jehoshaphat.

The men of Israel had been victors two-to-one against these captives, but they had been in prison for most of a year and were not in fighting condition. But this Assyrian, who stood a head taller than the others and was thick chested, seemed unbeatable. And now Ahab had raised the stakes. If the Assyrian won, he and the hundred or so captives left could go free. And, to the challenger Jotham, a thousand shekels of gold if he won, more than he could earn in a lifetime. Ahab felt that Jotham, who had never been beaten, was Israel's best hope for defeating the Assyrian, and had offered him this large sum to enter the arena one last time.

Jotham had chosen a large sword to battle the Assyrian who used his own more primitive scimitar. From the two-handed handle of the scimitar the blade extended half a cubit then curved into a bow shape another two and a half cubits and could only be wielded by a man of his stature. The overall length was as long as the height of an average man.

Separated by as much distance as the circular arena would allow, the two men faced each other as they moved slowly around the ring, each sizing the other, looking for weaknesses, planning a strategy. Suddenly with great speed the Assyrian bolted toward Jotham. He swung the scimitar at Jotham like he was chopping a tree. From the momentum of the swing he brought the blade up and crossed the path of his first stroke. Several times their blades clashed, but Jotham was staying out of his way, waiting for an opening. Twice Jotham was backed into the sharp wooden spike poles that encircled them row upon row but dropped to the ground and rolled to safety. There were thirty cubits across the circle in which to maneuver, and he needed the entire space to avoid the sharp blade. There were four platforms at equal distance around the circle above the spiked poles, where archers were stationed to kill combatants who tried to escape the arena.

The long black curls that hung down from the Assyrian's head dripped with sweat. He had a thick bronze shield attached to his chest, supported by wide leather belts over his shoulders that crossed in the back, a short leather kilt that hung from the waist, and thick leather shin guards.

At that moment the Assyrian swung at Jotham and struck one of the pickets. The blade stuck in the pole momentarily. Jotham tumbled into the clear and came around with his straight-bladed sword, striking the thick-legged Assyrian in the shin. The edge glanced from the leather guard on the front of the leg to open a deep gash in his bulging calf. The Assyrian nearly toppled, but caught himself and fell only to his knees. The crowd came alive. The roar was deafening.

Jotham scrambled to his feet as his sword, still in motion, sailed horizontally toward the enemy's face. As instinct takes over in the instant that determines life or death, the Assyrian threw himself backward dodging the sword, but the polished steel caught him above the forehead and peeled back a piece of his scalp. His fate and the fate of a hundred countrymen would be determined in the next one half second. With all of his might he swung his sword as the ground rushed up at him. His mind reeled from the blow he had sustained but he was sure that the blade connected. Unable to focus, he rolled to escape the range of Jotham's sword. In the process he heard the clash of Jotham's bronze scale armor as the Hebrew fell to the ground. A moment later, as blood blinded his right eye, he saw with the left that Jotham was down and his leg bent back and nearly severed below the knee. He climbed to his feet using his sword as a crutch and limped over to his downed adversary. "Hebrew, you are a dead dog."

The arena was between two steep hills and the roar reverberated back and forth, as the onlookers that had been seated stood to their feet, shouting for Jotham to get up.

In his anger Jehu pushed his way through the crowd to one of the platforms where the ready archers stood. He started up the ladder with the intention of killing the Assyrian before he killed Jotham, but was stopped when a strong arm reached up and grabbed him by the shoulder. Jezebel caught sight of the man in the hooded robe as he reached up to take hold of Jehu. She had been feeling the strange sensation she had learned to associate with the presence of Elijah since she had arrived at the arena. Now, as she watched, it intensified and she felt the trembling begin. She was sure it must be Elijah.

Jehu turned to see who it was that had a hold of him. Beneath the hood he looked into the smooth stern face of Elisha.

"Elijah sent me." He waited a moment, then added when Jehu didn't step down. "Jotham is dead and there was nothing you could have done."

Jehu stepped back to the ground and turned back to the arena as Elisha continued, "Yahweh has a purpose for you, but if you had killed the Assyrian, Ahab would have killed you."

The Assyrian took a broad stance as Jotham struggled to sit up. Feebly, Jotham attempted to swing his sword but was met with the Assyrian's scimitar that severed his hand and drove his forearm into the ground. The Assyrian rested the sword on his shoulder and with a vengeful angry sneer looked up at the two kings sitting on their thrones beneath their cool canopy, surrounded by attendants and their queens or wives. With a piece of his scalp peeled back and blood streaming from the wound, he was hideous to look at.

Jezebel called the eunuch she had brought with her. "Quickly get the captain of my guard."

As he turned and left, Ahab turned and whispered to Jezebel, "Is something wrong?"

"Elijah is here." Ahab dreaded another confrontation with the prophet but couldn't imagine any other reason for him to be there.

"What should we do?" he asked.

"I'm sending my guard to bring him to me. I'll have him thrown in prison. Later we will determine his fate."

"Don't do anything to attract attention," whispered Ahab. "See to it, but do it quietly."

Jezebel stood and moved to the outside, out of sight of Jehoshaphat, to a place where she could see the entire crowd and keep watch on the man with Captain Jehu.

A moment later the scimitar sliced through the air with a swish. Thud. Jotham's head toppled from his half-sitting torso propped on one arm. The brass scales clattered as his body slumped to the ground. Jehu looked angrily at Ahab but wasn't seen by him, but Jezebel caught his glance.

The crowd jeered as the Assyrian triumphantly raised his sword skyward. After a full minute Ahab stood and the roar died into complete silence. "Countrymen, let it be known to all the world that the King of Israel is merciful. This great Assyrian warrior has fought valiantly and won the freedom of his countrymen and himself. Set these men free to return to their home and country."

As the small gate was opened and the Assyrian limped to freedom, Captain Jehu and Elisha were suddenly surrounded by ten of Jezebel's guard. Two of them took hold of Elisha. Jehu pulled out a dagger and pushed them back. They backed away, as he demanded of their commander, "What is this about?"

"The queen has ordered that this man be arrested, and you are interfering. Do you know what the punishment is for interfering with an officer of the realm?"

Jehu was about to answer when he heard the familiar voice of Bidkar, his first officer, behind him. "Captain, is there any trouble here?" Jehu turned to make eye contact with Bidkar. They knew each other well enough to understand eye signals. Moving his eyes only, he glanced to the left and Bidkar disappeared back into the throng of people.

Jehu turned back to the captain of the queen's guard and leaned to whisper to him. "I swear that you will regret this."

He knew that Jehu wasn't one to make empty threats. "Jehu, I am only following orders." Suddenly out of the crowd appeared two of Jehu's men for every one of the queen's guard.

When Jehu saw that he was now in control, he whispered to Elisha, "Give my regards to Elijah. Now go!" And Elisha melted into the multitude.

A second later the captain of Jezebel's guard said, "The queen will hear about this."

Jehu answered, then dropped to one knee, "You can tell her now. Here she comes." They turned to see the crowd parting and bowing to the ground as the queen, surrounded by an escort, made her way towards them.

"Where is Elijah?" she demanded as she approached.

Jehu answered. "Your Highness, Elijah was never here."

"Who was the man that was with you?"

Jehu was impressed to look up at Jezebel as he spoke again. "That was only a friend," he said as their eyes met.

Then something strange happened. A look of fear came over Jezebel as her eyes met Jehu's. Her voice quivered as she spoke. "It was you, it was you! I feel that presence now." She stared at Jehu in confusion, then turned to her escort and demanded, "Get me away from here!"

Jezebel's attendants helped her away, and, when she was far enough away, the captain of her guard said to Jehu as he stood up, "What happened to the queen?"

Jehu knew better than to say what he thought so he answered, "I don't know." But, deep down, Jehu realized that Yahweh had intervened in his behalf for protecting his messenger.

****

Ahaziah had left the crowd behind and was riding back to Samaria with two other princes of Israel, half brothers, sons of Ahab, when they heard a galloping horse approaching. They turned to see one of Jezebel's guards racing toward them. The rider pulled his horse to a stop next to Ahaziah. "The queen wants to see you. She awaits you at the arena."

"What is this about?"

"The queen will tell you herself." The rider turned and galloped away in the direction he came.

The three men sat there for a moment, then Ahaziah asked, "Will you ride back with me?" They agreed and rode back with the queen's son.

He seldom had contact with her, and Ahaziah wondered for what reason his mother had asked him to meet her at the arena. As they neared the arena, they passed Jezebel's carriage and the carriage men that awaited the queen. One of her guards pointed to the arena. Ahaziah said to his two companions, "Wait here."

Jezebel was strolling around the arena when Ahaziah found her. "You are a very handsome man," she said as he approached. They faced each other. He was tall, and she had to tilt her head back to look into his face.

"Why have you sent for me?"

"Your father has made a mistake in setting the Assyrians free. He didn't think it would come to that, and he would change it if he could, but for his word's sake he can't with Jehoshaphat here. He sent Jehu to guard them safely away from Samaria and the thousands that would like to see them killed. It angers me to see them go free; and not only me, but also everyone in Israel.

"Take my guard, they are all mounted, waiting for you. After Jehu leaves them, kill them all. Jehu is a threat to your throne. He is popular with the people and he has the support of Elijah, and if he should turn on Ahab, I feel that he would have enough support to succeed. Elijah has already renounced Ahab, and Ahab fears him.

"You know what punishment follows disobeying a command from the king. Ahab will hold Jehu accountable for the death of the Assyrians, and then your throne will be secure."

"And what of my father's word?"

"What he did wasn't popular with the people. He would ride out after them himself if he could. When you become king and the people find out, they will praise you, but for now you mustn't tell anyone. My guard can be trusted. They know if they breathe a word I will have their tongues cut out, that is before I have them slowly roasted alive."

When Ahaziah hesitated, Jezebel's voice sharpened. "You must hurry! They will try to reach their own country as quickly as they can." He turned to leave, then stopped. He glanced down to see that they were standing on ground stained with Jotham's blood. "They have a two hour head start." Her voice distracted him from the red ground. "The guard waits over the ridge there." She pointed in the direction of a not too distant ridge. As he walked away, he glanced back at her for an instant. The power behind the throne, he thought.

Rocks from the crowd pelted the Assyrians as they walked the dusty road leading from Samaria. Jehu in his chariot led the way. His men kept the crowd pushed to the side of the road, as the ragged captives made their way homeward. After several were injured, Jehu turned around and rode into the middle of the band. He glanced around at some of them nursing wounds inflicted by the hurled rocks, and then he raised his hands for the people to be silent. They weren't quiet immediately, but because he continued to keep his arms high they began to quiet until it spread through the thousands that had come for revenge for the many Israelites who had died in the war with Assyria.

"Countrymen, countrymen!" he shouted, "Assyria lost thousands of men in the war also. These men have fought for their freedom and have earned it on the king's word. The next one to throw a stone I will have the archers shoot. Now return to Samaria!" The archers readied their bows and the people began to disperse.

Several miles outside of Samaria, Jehu sent the Assyrians, unarmed, on their way, and detailed a chariot with driver, a spearman and a mounted rider to follow them out of the country while he returned.

The following morning Jehu was working with one of his chariot teams preparing for the race. The racecourse was around the base of a hill a short distance from Samaria. The course was mostly level, except at the north side of the hill, where the grade rose slowly then dropped as it turned southwest. Dozens of people stood in small groups watching as Jehu drove his team violently around the course. It took four minutes for a good team in full gallop to circle the hill. In a race like the one he faced in two days, young horses had been known to die in six laps around. The race would be eight laps and would require seasoned horses with stamina to win. Jehu prided himself in knowing horses and attributed his many wins to not only the blood of the stock, but in knowing the mood of his team and the nature of each horse.

Where the grade rose and dropped at the north end of the hill the chariot had a tendency to slide. The weight of the chariot threw his team off balance on his first trip around. They almost didn't recover, but when they did, he cracked the whip over their heads. The horses pushed into the wind and Jehu felt the exhilaration of being one with the chariot and horses.

For the next few minutes he was lost in the sound of the pounding hooves, the swishing of the air past his face, and the speed with which he passed over the ground. He knew that the horses felt it also by the way they raced each other and arrogantly lifted their tails to be carried in the air behind them. It felt right. He knew they were ready and he knew they were the right team to win.

During his third trip around he spotted two of the chariots under his command, Bidkar, and a half dozen of his men waiting to see him. He was moving too fast to pull the team to a stop, but began to pull back on the reins. Well beyond them, he was able to turn the chariot and came back. The panting, lathered horses pulled his chariot to a halt next to the other two waiting.

"Captain Jehu," Bidkar began. "The Assyrians have been killed, butchered."

"What are you talking about?"

"One of the men you sent to follow them out of Israel came to me this morning before daylight. He died a few minutes later with an arrow in his back."

Jehu interrupted, "Who did this thing?"

"Ahaziah and the queen's guard. And when the men tried to stop them, they were also killed. The man who escaped was shot in the back as he tried to outrun them back to Samaria. They were mounted and ran the Assyrians down and cut them to pieces."

"For what reason would Ahaziah do such a thing?" Jehu wondered.

"The only thing that has come to mind is that Ahaziah or the queen wants to blame us, but particularly you."

"But what would they have to gain by that? Ahab knows that I wouldn't do such a thing."

"The queen knows that we've turned back to Yahweh, all of your men, since Elijah met her Baal prophets on Mount Carmel, and she knows that you would back Elijah against her. What else could be the motive?"

Jehu thought for a moment. "Take as many men as you need. Swear them to secrecy, then ride out and find the bodies of the Assyrians and dispose of them where they will never be found." He hesitated a moment as an idea came to mind. "Wait! Don't bury them. Take them to the high places and burn them on the altars of Baal, and be quick, before word reaches the ears of the king. Make a trail that crosses the Jordan so it looks as if they made it to Syria. We know that the Syrians would kill them. Ahab will believe that."

Jehu waved the men off. "Go now! It is important to hurry." Bidkar and the men with him turned and rode quickly away.

By late afternoon Bidkar returned and found Jehu at the stables of Ahab, where he was keeping his horses. Jehu was leading one of his horses down the long corridor away from him, between the stalls on each side. "Captain!" Bidkar shouted. Jehu turned to see, then waited for his first officer who hurried to meet him. Bidkar looked around to make sure no one was in hearing distance. "It is taken care of. There isn't a sign that anyone died out there, but it was bloody. They were hacked into pieces.

"It is fortunate that they didn't follow the road. Most likely they didn't want to encounter another Israelite, so they left the road and stayed to the high ground, where the queen's guard ran them down and butchered them. The bodies will never be found and the men are continuing a trail on the other side of Jordan."

"Good work, Bidkar. I've been thinking. There isn't any way to place the blame where it belongs. I can't accuse the king's son to the king, and he wouldn't punish him if he knew, but I hope that he never believes that I did it. By now they have accused me to Ahab. The first thing he will do is send out a reconnaissance patrol."

Bidkar interrupted, "We spotted a patrol on the way here but they didn't see us. Someone's already reported it to Ahab." He thought for a moment then added, "It wasn't Jezebel's guard that we saw, it was the king's own soldiers."

Jehu looked worried. "We must keep this quiet. This is a very dangerous situation. Was Ahaziah with the patrol?"

"I'm sorry, Captain, I was too far away to tell. Captain, you know that your men are loyal to you. They would die to the last man defending you. You've never asked a man to risk his life in battle that you weren't at the front in the greatest danger. The hand of Yahweh is on you. They will all be standing ready." Bidkar bowed as though he were in the presence of the king then he turned and left, leaving Jehu wondering at the significance of his action.

Jehu's home, located near the palace, was quite large, with a court and garden pool. The day's sunset found him sitting at the edge of the pool making ripples with his fingers, distorting his reflection in the water as he considered what he would do next. He controlled a third of Israel's forces and most of the chariots. He would stand a chance of overthrowing Ahab unless he was thrown into prison first.

"My lord, can I get you anything?" Jehu, startled by one of the household servants, turned to see the Philistine woman taken captive and brought to Samaria as a teen-ager.

"I prefer to be left alone for now."

Suddenly a loud knock at the gate disturbed Jehu's reverie. It was not the knock of a social caller, but that of a soldier with the authority of someone powerful behind him. Jehu sprang to his feet. He was sure that he had waited too long to initiate the first move. Again the knock rang out across the courtyard. He would face Ahab, present his side. He hurried to the gate. They were banging on the gate louder than before as an elderly servant fumbled to open the latch. The double doors in the wall surrounding the home swung open, revealing the captain of Jezebel's guard, the one who had been at the arena, and perhaps two dozen soldiers. Behind the soldiers who stood at the entrance was Jezebel in the midst of ten of her personal guards.

The soldier facing Jehu moved aside. Jezebel stepped forward and looked into Jehu's face. She studied him for a long minute before she ventured further. She was relieved when she didn't feel what she had earlier in his presence. "We must talk, Captain." She waited for him to invite her in, but he just looked at her. The servants were lighting the court lamps at that moment and drew her attention to the court inside. "What a lovely pool," she said as she stepped past Jehu and walked to the water's edge.

There were three servants in the court. None of them recognized her immediately then one said fearfully, "It's the queen," and they bowed to the ground.

She turned to face Jehu who was still at the gate. "Aren't you going to bow to your queen, Jehu?"

He slammed the gate in the face of her escorts. "I don't believe I will," then turned to the servants and ordered, "Leave us!"

"Captain, do you know what the punishment is for disobeying a command from the king or being insubordinate to the king or queen? You've not bowed to me since I've been here. Don't you want to beg my forgiveness and bow before me?"

If it meant that he would die he wasn't going to give her the satisfaction of abasing himself to her ever again. That was obviously what she came for. Jehu bent his knee slightly, and said sarcastically, "Forgive me, great Queen of Baal."

She shrugged at his insolence and said, "The king charged you with seeing that the Assyrians made it out of Israel safely. It has been brought to my attention that they didn't survive. Is that true, Captain?"

"They were taken to the border of Syria. What happened to them beyond that, I couldn't say."

"I saw the way you looked at the Assyrian. You wanted them dead the same as the rest of us."

Jehu could see that she was searching for a way of controlling him, but he hoped that what he was about to say would turn the situation in his favor. "Maybe Ahaziah might know more about the fate of the Assyrians than I. You should ask him."

By the flickering light of the lamps he could see the dismay on her face. She recovered quickly and said, "I'm glad they are dead. After all they were Assyrians. I am surprised at how quickly you covered your tracks."

Jehu walked over and stood next to her by the pool. "What do you want from me?"

"What I really want is your support, Jehu. You are behind Elijah, but if you lent me your support instead, I could revive the worship of Baal like it once was."

"What you really mean is that you want to regain control over the souls of the people. Once they bowed to you as a goddess; now most of them believe you are a demon. How many children have you watched burn alive?"

"The sacrifice of children is for the good of all Israel. It brings the blessings of Baal and Ashtoreth."

Jehu interrupted, "If Yahweh is the only true God, then they were sacrificed for nothing. And let me ask, which God did you encounter earlier today?"

She became defensive when she was reminded of what she had felt at the arena. "Baal is a god. I have communed with him in the land of the gods." She then shouted, "Never, never, speak lowly of my gods again!"

"When you communed with the gods, was it not when you had eaten or drunk or been covered with a paste made from the desert herbs, the ones that drive the wild ass mad when he eats them?"

She tried to conceal her anger as she spoke more softly, "The man who brought the king word of your murdering the Assyrians was thrown into prison after the king's patrol could find no evidence that they were killed. Open the gate and let my guard in. This evening you'll be thrown into prison with him."

Jehu walked over and began to unlatch the gate. "Maybe the man who slew the Assyrians was Ahaziah with the queen's guard. And not only the Assyrians, but also two of the king's men." He paused to let his words sink in. "The third escaped to tell who did it. Ahab may not think those qualities suitable ones to pass the crown to, and he may wonder how the queen's guard happened to be a part of that, since the queen is the only one from whom they take orders." Jehu swung the gate open. "Oh, and one more thing. Do you think that Ahab will approve of the Assyrian's bodies being burned on the altars of Baal today?"

Jezebel stood speechless. Jehu was a more formidable opponent than she had given him credit for. Now she was in the situation that she had wanted to put him in. She was trapped, knowing that Jehu could reveal these things to Ahab at any time.

Her guard stood at the entrance awaiting her command. She shot a vengeful glare in Jehu's direction. In the past, any one who had displeased her to such a degree had been killed, except for her failed attempts to kill Elijah. This time her tongue was tethered by the things Jehu knew, things, that for her sake, must remain a secret.

She forced a smile. "We will talk again, Captain," she said as she strode past him through the open gate. "Tell me one thing. Was that Elijah with you yesterday? Because the presence I felt there, I do not feel here."

Jehu answered, "I haven't seen Elijah in years."

Without saying anything more, she walked away. Jehu watched Jezebel step onto her carriage and be lifted into the air by the carriage slaves, then slowly closed the gate as he wondered how dangerous she would be to him now.

In bed next to his wife, Jehu was awakened early the next morning by one of the household servants. "My lord Jehu," the maid called through the door as she knocked.

Jehu got to the door and opened it enough to see the maid, as the flame from the lamp she held caused the shadows to dance over her robe and face, and more dimly against the walls of the room. She could see only the reflection of the light in the one eye that peered at her through the slight opening. "My Lord, one of your men awaits you in the court outside. He said to tell you that Bidkar sent him."

"Offer him bread and wine. He's probably been on guard all night. I'll be there in a moment."

When Jehu entered the courtyard a few minutes later, the soldier saluted with his right fist and arm across his chest.

"Why has Bidkar sent you to me this time of the night?"

"Bidkar placed me on guard at the king's stables last evening to watch over your horses."

Jehu interrupted. "Yes, I told him to put one of my own men on guard there."

"Just after midnight one of Jezebel's royal guards came into the stable where your horses are kept. I saw him first and stepped into the shadows. I watched as he emptied a vial into some grain and mixed it. Then he began to put the grain into the trough of one of your chariot racers. I stepped up behind him with my sword and told him to eat the grain. He refused until I struck him with the sword several times across his hip. He ate the grain and he died choking and pleading for me to thrust my sword through him. He suffered terribly but I didn't end it for him. I sent for Bidkar and he sent me to you. He is there now."

The young soldier was afraid, and it showed in the way he talked. Jehu answered, "You did well. I would have done the same thing." In a fast walk, they hurried to the king's stable.

The sky was glowing orange with the dawning of the day when they reached the stable. Inside it was still dark. Without saying a word, Bidkar, with a lantern held in front of him, proceeded ahead as they approached. He led them to the stall where the soldier lay in a fetal position, stiffened where he died in pain. Bidkar brushed away the dried grass that covered him.

Jehu spoke softly, "He has the uniform of Jezebel's guard." He stooped down next to Bidkar and moved the light into a position where he could see the man's face more clearly. "I saw him with the queen last evening." As they stood Jehu said, "Quickly, before it gets light, carry him around to Ahaziah's stalls. Put him where he will be found when they come for the prince's horses.

"The queen wants Ahaziah to win the race and she wants

revenge against me. The race is today. We won't keep the horses here any longer."

Bidkar turned to the soldier. "Take two men. Quickly, see that it is done."

As the dead man was carried away, Jehu opened the stalls and led out each of the sleek stallions. There was nothing more that could be done about Jezebel's dead guard. He would have to confront any consequences when they arose but for now, he had to prepare for a race.

Jehu would race four stallions, something that not every charioteer could accomplish. It had taken years of careful breeding to develop the right temperaments, along with the other attributes necessary to make a racer. The process had begun with his grandfather and more than eighteen generations of horses. Stallions required twice the work of a mare, when you could find one that could be trained to work with other stallions. This was only his second all stallion racing team. He had a black and three chestnuts.

As he cared for the horses that morning, he observed that one of the chestnuts, one he had been working in the middle of the team, was nervous and high spirited. Jehu moved him to the outside. He knew that move could cost him the race, but on the end the biting aggressive stallion could only distract one instead of two other horses. The team wasn't what he had hoped they would be on this, the day of the race, but even the best stallions were sometimes temperamental and unpredictable. This was his advantage, and maybe a disadvantage, but they were the best and hopefully would settle down after he warmed them up.

Jehu's horses had settled down considerably by the time they were lining up for the race, agitated only by the other teams, which was normal. Ahaziah, two positions to Jehu's left, had a well-built team of matching whites. All matching teams, except his, pulled the fourteen chariots. On his right King Jehoshaphat had a beautiful team of blacks driven by his son. There were three Phoenician chariots. The one on his immediate left was pulled by a team of bay stallions that concerned Jehu. They were sleek and powerful and he could tell that they were well trained. As he watched the driver he knew that he was intuitively attuned to his animals. It was obvious in the way he held the reins and talked to each horse as they were easing into the line.

All of the high-spirited horses were hard to control when brought close together in a line. Whinnying and snorting, pawing the ground and pulling against the harnesses that held them, the sleek animals were filled with anticipation. As the teams got close, the horses would bite and kick at rivals.

When the fourteen chariots were most evenly aligned, the white banner was raised. For the several moments before the red banner went up, the men held the reins tightly, almost holding their breath. On the end of a long pole the red banner flew in an arch upward as the pole was raised. Instantly the air was filled with the thunderous sound of hooves pounding the ground.

The race began southward, on the west side of the hill around which they would race. That would give the chariots a chance to thin before they came around the north end of the hill, through a pass wide enough for only six chariots. A large boulder about eight cubits high, and about the same width, narrowed the pass on the right side.

Years before, King Omri had chosen this site for the chariot races because of the interesting features, and the challenges and danger it posed. It was Omri's grandson, Ahaziah, who took the lead, but it didn't concern Jehu. Ahaziah had a good team, but he was inexperienced and hadn't worked with them enough, having left his team's training to someone else. They wouldn't hold up for long at the pace he had set, and most of the other drivers were pursuing at the same exhausting speed.

Jehu dropped back to the middle of the pack and allowed the chariots to thin enough to maneuver to the inside of the track. The Phoenician chariot pulled by the bays stayed back with Jehu and ran at his right side. The powerful legs and stone-like hooves of his team threw bits of dirt into his face as they rhythmically pounded the ground. The stallions were filled with fire and pulled against the bits to pass the others but it wasn't time to let them go.

He watched Ahaziah to see how he would take the north curve. It was risky taking the inside at that speed. The chariot wouldn't hold the turn and would have to be brought back toward the center, often times into the path of another chariot. Ahaziah crowded a chariot at his side, forcing it over as he made the turn.

The Phoenician at Jehu's right moved out away from him. He knew that he was planning to take the inside when Jehu did the same as Ahaziah had done. It was too late to change strategies. He entered the curve on the inside and moved to the center as he came out of the turn. The Phoenician moved to the inside behind him. Jehu admired his skill as he observed the way he handled his team. They were good. Jehu knew this would be the one to beat.

The Phoenician moved away from the inside and crowded Jehu, leaving him little space to maneuver. He glanced at Jehu. They smiled at one another, each knowing that the race would be won or lost between just them.

Jehu chose to wait. His opponent would have to make a move soon, then it would be a real race. Ahead, Ahaziah was trying to keep the inside, and so far no one had challenged him, but his horses were rapidly tiring. Ahaziah had four chariots that were beginning to press in around him, one very close on his right.

Jehu knew that they could wait no longer and slackened the reins slightly. It was what the stallions had been waiting for and they pulled nearly a full length ahead of the Phoenician, with seemingly renewed strength. The Phoenician cracked his whip over the heads of the bays. With nostrils flared, the proud animals held their tails out behind them as they stretched their powerful legs to pit their speed against Jehu's stallions.

Another chariot had taken the inside next to the Phoenician, but was no match for the powerful bays. The Phoenician was able to pull ahead, then in front of the team that had tried to crowd him out. Jehu maintained a good lead over the Phoenician as they both weaved through the other chariots toward the front, Jehu's whip now cracking over the backs of his team.

Ahead of Jehu there was a narrow opening between two chariots. He drove the team hard into the gap before it could close. On his left he heard his chariot wheel grinding against the chariot beside him and glanced down to see sparks flying. A moment later sparks were flying from both sides as the three fought for an advantage. Jehu's ears rang from the rush of adrenaline to his brain, combined with the pounding hooves and thundering wheels.

For Jehu it was moments like this that made life worth living, the heat of the battle or the seconds just before. It wasn't the gold or the glory, but the fight, the competition, and the racing of chariots was the greatest of all. The powerful stallions pushed forward and the gap behind him closed, blocking the Phoenician from following.

From the king's pavilion, over the narrow pass, Jezebel seethed with anger as she watched Ahaziah drop from first to second, then third position as Jehu moved rapidly closer to the lead.

Some distance ahead Ahaziah was driving his team hard, but continued to fall further from the lead. In fourth position and three chariot widths from the inside, Ahaziah raised welts and blood on the hindquarters of his team as his whip popped. He was crowding the chariot on his left. In the already dangerous north turn, Ahaziah pulled the team hard to the left to take one position closer to the inside. Jehu had closed the gap between them and was close behind Ahaziah. The Phoenician had gotten through but was too far behind to be a threat. In the middle of the turn the outside horse in Ahaziah's team stumbled and fell. The harness and hitch snapped as the chariot hit the animal full force. The chariot flipped forward and onto its side. Ahaziah was thrown to the outside of the track just a few cubits from the great boulder.

There was no place for Jehu to go. He was blocked on the right and left and had only an instant to pull back hard on the reins. His stallions were in full gallop. His effort did nothing to slow them. The horse on the left side of the team hit the downed mare and flipped forward. In the same instant the horse on the right jumped to try to clear the chariot on its side, the upper wheel still spinning. With the weight of the other horse he couldn't get high enough. The stallion's front legs snapped on impact.

As Jehu's chariot struck Ahaziah's, Jehu leaped into the air aided by the impact and was thrown clear. He tumbled toward the outside of the course away from the thundering chariots that were hugging the inside to avoid another collision. Things turned into slow motion the way they do in the heat of battle, when you know your life might end the next instant. Ahaziah lay unconscious a few cubits behind him. The pounding hooves pulling another chariot would trample him in the next moments. Jehu scrambled in his direction, as Jezebel jumped to her feet and screamed "My son!" Jehu reached Ahaziah, grabbed his foot and pulled with all his might, falling backward to the ground. The hoof that would have crushed Ahaziah's skull was already in the air plunging downward. Jezebel and all who saw it weren't sure that her son hadn't been trampled, or that he had survived the first fall.

Ahab and Jezebel rushed down from the pavilion, with King Jehoshaphat and the physicians hurrying to keep up. They were at Ahaziah's side when he became conscious several minutes later. The physicians, feeling to see if any bones were broken, were pushed aside by Ahaziah as he, still dazed, struggled to his feet with the help of Ahab. He turned to see Jehu standing nearby.

At that minute four teams of four horses each with drivers pulled up to the horses and chariots scattered like debris blocking half of the race course and proceeded to attach ropes to move them. The chariots were being dragged away when one of the drivers looped a rope around one of Jehu's dying horses. Jehu rushed over, pulled the rope from his hand and shoved him back. The man looked to the king for direction and was signaled with a nod that it was all right to proceed without moving the two stallions.

Jehu knelt by one of the stallions, took a knife and cut the large artery in the horses thick neck, so that he could die quickly and with little pain. In a few moments the horse's eyes turned glassy and set. The other stallion lying next to the first began to struggle to get to his feet but was unable with broken legs. Jehu pushed the horse to the ground, knelt and cut the artery in his neck the same as he had the first. He stayed there as the life bled away.

Jehu was joined by Ahaziah, King Ahab and King Jehoshaphat. Jezebel stood back and watched but wouldn't come close. Her eyes were riveted on Captain Jehu as she tried to get a glimpse of his eyes. Once again, she felt the presence that seemed to threaten her existence. Jehu felt her stare and turned to see her cold eyes on him, but there wasn't anything in his eyes to intimidate her. She suddenly realized that the air was thick with the presence and rushed away, back to the pavilion.

Ahab took Jehu by the arm and lifted him to his feet, then escorted him to the side as the noise of approaching chariots grew loud. The wet, lathered, depleted teams, with whips cracking, were nearing the north turn for the last time of the race. When they had thundered past, hooves shaking the ground, and dirt flying in a great cloud, King Ahab made a signal that Jehu didn't see. The king's own elaborately decorated gold chariot, pulled by four matching white horses, came to a halt in front of them. "Captain Jehu," Ahab spoke firmly, as to a warrior. "For being the valiant man that you are, this is my gift to you." Ahab pointed to his chariot. Jehu had no choice but to act delighted. It was a fine gift.

"My King, you are generous but I didn't do anything to deserve such a gift. In battle, I or any of my men would have done no less."

Ahab held his hand to silence Jehu, "You have saved the life of my son, the next king of Israel. This night you will eat at the king's table."

When Ahaziah learned how close he came to death, he never forgot that it was Jehu who saved him.

icaiah's stride was deliberate and confident as he was brought into the court before King Ahab and King Jehoshaphat. Ahab thought that he looked more radiant than he had ever seen him before. Something had changed about him in the months since Ahab had released him from prison and banished him from Samaria.

Micaiah stood tall, the sheen of his wavy silver hair reflected the light of the morning sun and matched his well-groomed beard in color. There was a disarming light in his eyes when they met Ahab's, as he bowed slightly before him. The two kings sat on a waist high platform above the cobblestone court, just inside the city gate. The distinguished Micaiah looked more like an oracle of Yahweh than anyone Ahab had ever seen, as he defiantly turned toward Jehoshaphat and bowed lower before the king of Judah than he did before Ahab.

As Micaiah raised from his knee, Ahab spoke. "I hope that you rested well in the palace last night."

"Yes your Highness, it was better than the dungeon," replied Micaiah. His response drew a sharp look from Ahab that Micaiah ignored. He knew that Ahab had only sent for him from Tirzah at the request of Jehoshaphat. He had been told by his escort why he was being brought to Samaria, and was told that, for his own sake, his prophecy should be the same as the prophecies of the king's advisors, led by the king's puppet prophet Zedekiah. They had prophesied that Ahab and Jehoshaphat would have a great victory if they went against Ben-Hadad to reclaim Ramoth Gilead.

Ahab, unwilling to be provoked in Jehoshaphat's presence, didn't react to Micaiah's remark, but calmly said, "Micaiah, by now you know why I summoned you to Samaria. Zedekiah has said that Yahweh has spoken to him that we will reclaim Ramoth in Gilead with a great victory. What do you say? Should we go against Ben-Hadad to take Ramoth Gilead or not?"

Micaiah knew that he couldn't say what Yahweh had revealed to him during prayer the previous night. It seemed that what God revealed to him never agreed with what the king's prophets prophesied.

Zedekiah and fifty of the king's prophets were standing to one side of the court, waiting to refute whatever he said, and hoping that he would make a fool out of himself so that he would be discredited in the future.

Micaiah raised his voice as he spoke in an uncharacteristically mournful tone, the way that the king's prophets did. "Oh Great King, go and take Ramoth Gilead, and be victorious, for Yahweh will deliver it into your hand."

Ahab recognized Micaiah's sarcasm and abruptly stood and shouted, "How many times have I warned you to tell me nothing but the truth in the name of Yahweh? Now tell me what Yahweh has shown to you."

Micaiah sternly looked at Ahab and said, "You've never wanted to hear the truth unless it supports what you want. If I tell the truth, and it isn't what your prophets have told you, what will you do with me?"

At that moment Ahab regretted having sent for him and didn't want to look badly in front of Jehoshaphat. Without responding to his question Ahab softened the tone in his voice and asked, "I adjure you in the name of Yahweh that you tell me the truth."

For several moments everything was still as Micaiah looked at Jehoshaphat, then back to Ahab, then closed his eyes as though he were reviewing a scene in his head. "I saw all of Israel scattered through the hills, as sheep that have lost their shepherd. Then the word of the Lord came to me and said, 'They have no master. I will send every man to his home in peace'."

Ahab, still standing, turned to Jehoshaphat, who looked very troubled because of the words of prophecy. "I told you that he would not prophesy anything but evil against me." Ahab would have continued, but was interrupted by Micaiah who had not yet opened his eyes.

"Hear the word of Yahweh. I saw Yahweh El Shaddai sitting upon His throne, and ten thousand thousand of the host of heaven standing before him. And Yahweh asked, 'Who can go and persuade Ahab to go to war against Ramoth Gilead, that he will die at the hand of Ben-Hadad, the king that I appointed him to slay; yet he spared him? Ahab's life shall be taken for his disobedience, and I will judge Ben-Hadad.'

"Great and mighty ones approached the throne with plans to bring you, O King, to battle Ben-Hadad, but their plans were not suitable for the task. Then a spirit came and stood before the Lord and said, 'I can persuade Ahab to go to Ramoth Gilead.' And the Lord asked, 'What is your plan?' The spirit answered and said, 'I will go and be a lying spirit in the mouth of all his prophets.'

"'You will go, and persuade him, and prevail. Do as you have said,' answered the Lord.

"Yahweh has put a lying spirit in the mouth of all these, your prophets, and the Lord has planned to rid Israel of your evil."

Zedekiah bolted in Micaiah's direction, but a guard stepped in his path. The guard looked at Ahab for direction. With a slight nod of his head the king sent the guard back to the side and Zedekiah angrily rushed toward Micaiah with a clenched fist and struck the prophet in the side of the face. He shouted, "When did the Spirit of Yahweh depart from me to speak to you?"

Zedekiah attempted to strike him a second time, but Micaiah caught his arm in the air and held him there for several moments as he said, "Zedekiah, when you desire strongly enough to hear the real word of the Lord, and enter into a room alone to pray, then you will know the truth."

Zedekiah was convicted by the stern gaze of Micaiah. He knew that his own motive hadn't been pure and realized that what Micaiah had said was true. At another time and place they could have been allies as Zedekiah knew that Micaiah was an unbending faithful prophet of God and would never have compromised the truth for any reason. He envied Micaiah as he realized at what a high cost he had prophesied the truth.

Two guards pushed between them and seized Micaiah as Ahab ordered, "Take him to prison and tell my son Joash to feed him with death rations only until I return in victory."

As Micaiah was being pulled away by the guards, he shouted back at Ahab and the court, prophets and soldiers, "Hear the word of God! If you, Oh Ahab, return in victory, or if you return at all, know that Yahweh has not spoken by me."

****

Jehu's chariot rested on a ridge overlooking the Jordan River. The Captain watched the joint armies of Judah and Israel crossing into the land of Gilead. It would take all day to get the hundred thousand men, three thousand chariots and the great flocks and herds that provisioned the armies across. With the Jordan swollen, this was the only place the heavy wagons and chariots could cross.

Of all the wars and battles Jehu had fought, this one felt the most ominous. For several reasons, he had a sense of foreboding. They had recently been allied with Syria against Shalmaneser III, and now they were going to war against them.

The thing that gave him the greatest concern was the prophecy of Micaiah against this war. Jehu was afraid that Ahab had insured their defeat by throwing Micaiah into prison and turning Yahweh against them. He had admired Micaiah's boldness in the face of Ahab's four hundred prophets who prophesied a great victory over the Syrians. Jehu knew that Ahab's prophets were hired counselors, and not true servants of Yahweh like Micaiah. If Micaiah were right, they would be defeated and Ahab would die; maybe all of them would die. Either way, Jehu carried a sense of guilt for being a part of this campaign.

There was a strange westward wind blowing in from the desert brushing against his face. He stepped down from his chariot and walked to the brink of the hill, where he could see men by the hundreds entering the river from the west bank and coming out on the east bank, into the land of Gilead.

There was also the unfulfilled prophecy of Elijah still hanging over the king. Jehu couldn't understand what made Ahab think that he could avert the prophecy of Yahweh. He knew that it was only the support that the godly King Jehoshaphat lent to Ahab that gave him the confidence to fight against Ben-Hadad. To make matters worse, the men of both armies knew that Ahab had used the alliance to pressure Jehoshaphat into war with Ben-Hadad.

"Great Yahweh, God of Elijah, protect these your people, the seed of Abraham," Jehu prayed out loud. He remained at the overlook through most of the day, watching and thinking, until it was time to meet with the kings and captains.

By nightfall, when none of the three advance patrols returned, they concluded that the men had been captured, and that Ben-Hadad now knew of their presence. Because of their vulnerability, they worked through the night moving the men and supplies to high ground.

As Captain Jehu oversaw and worked with the troops, it became obvious to him that King Jehoshaphat's fifty thousand men didn't want to be a part of this campaign against Syria. Ahab's mostly ill-trained militia couldn't compare with Judah's highly trained regular army, and they were afraid that Yahweh wouldn't be with them because of the Baal worship that still existed in Israel.

By morning they had set up camp just four miles from Ramoth-Gilead, and had stationed seven five-hundred-man garrisons on the seven highest elevations of the perimeter of the main force. As they were fortifying their positions the alarm trumpet sounded from the most easterly garrison. They prepared for an attack. Half an hour passed. Ben-Hadad knew when they had crossed the Jordan, and that they had gone without rest since the night before. The troops knew that they were vulnerable, and that Ben-Hadad needed this victory to save face with his own nation.

When the anticipated second signal trumpet didn't sound, Jehu led a detachment of five hundred chariots, each with a mounted escort and three thousand footmen, eastward toward the garrison that had first sounded the alarm. Jehu halted within a thousand cubits of the hill where the garrison had been stationed. There wasn't a sign of anyone there except the stones the men had been piling to fortify the position. Jehu stepped down from his chariot and took the horse of his escort.

When Jehu was mounted, he rode along the line of chariots and chose a dozen more riders to accompany him. In a swift gallop they raced up the hill, jumped the low unfinished wall and pulled their horses to a halt when they saw no one alive. The heads of the five hundred men were mounted on spears that reached skyward. It was a gruesome sight, but they had seen the like many times before.

It was obvious that the garrison had been overrun in only a few moments, but there was no sign of an enemy. Jehu surveyed each side of the hill. The enemy had remained hidden by the heavy brush and trees that reached nearly to the top of the hill on the north and east, until they were almost upon the unsuspecting garrison. "They must have taken them completely by surprise," thought Jehu. He remounted and rode back to the tent of Ahab.

Jehoshaphat and Ahab were seated, looking over a map of the area when Jehu was announced and ushered in.

"What news is there from Jotham's camp?" Ahab asked.

Jehu flinched mentally at the mention of his fallen comrade's name, but he answered as though it was a report of the weather, "Jotham was killed at the hand of the Assyrian, in the arena at Samaria." He paused momentarily. "Your captain and his men are dead, their heads on top of their own spears. They were overrun." Ahab and Jehoshaphat looked at each another. Jehu waited for them to look back toward him before continuing. "This may not have been part of their main force. It could have been an advance guard, sent to test our defenses. In any case, we don't have time to finish setting camp. The Syrians know we are tired, and if their main force is in the area, they will attack this afternoon. I would."

Ahab nodded, "I also believe they will attack soon. If we are to gain any advantage, we must attack first. Captain, King Jehoshaphat and I have developed a plan to divert the main force of Ben-Hadad. We have received information that Ben-Hadad has given his captains orders to look for, and attack, only my chariot. Therefore, I will not be wearing my armor, but the armor of a captain like you, and I will ride a war chariot."

Ahab paused for a moment, then continued reflectively, "Ben-Hadad wants my life because I shamed him before his own people." He slowly shook his head in regret. "It would have been far better if I had killed him when I had the chance. That was a terrible mistake." Ahab looked again at Jehoshaphat, then back at Jehu, "Captain, make sure that all troops are ready. We will attack Ramoth-Gilead immediately."

Within the hour they were on the move. Jehoshaphat and his troops swung to the west and north, while Ahab took his men east, with a plan to encircle the city. Ben-Hadad was somewhere ahead of them, and it bothered Jehu that they didn't know the size or location of his main force. None of their scouts had yet spotted the enemy, and the strain, coupled with fatigue from the night before, was beginning to tell on the men. They knew they were being watched; the men could feel it and looked over their shoulders often.

Jehoshaphat was in the front company that led the column, winding along like a snake and spread out over several miles. They began up a long slow slope, when one of the chariot captains riding ahead of the king raised his arm, signaling a halt as he pulled his own chariot to a stop. The column halted as they watched one of the forward scouts gallop down the slope toward them.

Before he reached their position, behind him, at the top of the rise a half-mile ahead, appeared Ben-Hadad's army. The ridge where the enemy now appeared had been too rocky for the chariots, so they had chosen the lower ground and were positioned badly for a stand.

Hundreds of rock-laden wagons were suddenly rolling toward them. The enemy had anticipated their route and had prepared well. There was nothing in their power that could stop the weight of the wagons, designed for such an ambush. In moments they would be crashing into them.

Seconds counted as Jehoshaphat's captain hurriedly pulled his chariot around to the king's. "Sire, we must retreat to the east and save as many men as we can."

Jehoshaphat, half-shouting, ordered, "Give the order, Captain!"

"Take hold of a chariot. Retreat! Retreat to the east!" In an instant there was a chaotic mad rush away from the heavy wagons that were rumbling down the hill and gaining on them. Many of the men that could took hold of a speeding chariot, to be pulled to safety. If they could make it down a short slope into the level fields below, they would be out of the wagons' deadly path. Many of the rock-laden wagons crashed on the rough terrain, releasing the round boulders that continued even faster than the wagons. Hurtling down the steep mountainside, the boulders bounced into the air over the rough terrain, gaining even greater speed as they crashed down the mountain.

One wagon crashed into a chariot that was lagging behind because of the rough terrain. There was a sound like crackling thunder as the timbers of the wagon and chariot came together, cracking and splintering. The boulders were thrown free and crushed the driver of the chariot and the horses, then continued downward.

The remaining wagons followed the huge boulders into the retreating men, crushing them as the whole mountainside now seemed to be moving toward the plain below.

Safely out into the grassy field below, Jehoshaphat had his driver pull to a halt and looked back at the men that had been behind him. Hundreds were dead or dying, and the rest were in disarray, as the stones rolled to a stop at the foot of the mountain. A large segment of the army had made it through, but Jehoshaphat was now cut off from the main body.

Following the slide down the mountain were thousands of mounted Syrians. The captain ordered a wall of shields around the king as the archers and spearmen prepared for the attack. Jehoshaphat stepped down from the chariot and was met by his captain who spoke hurriedly. "We've been cut off. My Lord, we cannot defend you here. The Syrian archers have taken cover in a ravine just over there," the captain pointed as he spoke. "The men haven't had any rest. They will bring all of us down in a few hours. My Lord, you must retreat back to the main body, back behind the fighting."

As the captain was speaking, a thunder of arrows rained down on them, hitting the shields of the troops, and horses and men. From another ridge came a hoard of yelling screaming men, numbering between fifteen and twenty thousand. Jehoshaphat and his captain both looked around to see what strength there was to defend. There were only a few thousand men left with the king. "Sire, make a run for it."

"Toward Ramoth!" Jehoshaphat shouted above the confusion, as he stepped back onto his chariot. The horses of his chariot and the fifty other chariots with him stretched out as they pushed against the harness. Eight hundred thundering hooves filled the air with a heavy cloud of dust behind them. As King Jehoshaphat raced away, the men he left behind were overrun and slaughtered by the Syrians. Several hundred Syrian chariots topped the ridge to the north and drove hard down the slope in pursuit of Jehoshaphat.

Ahead of the chariots of Judah's king was a ravine, with a creek and trees too thick to allow the chariots to cross, even if they could get down the bank. They pulled to a near stop and turned south. The water-worn trenches that cut into the earth where the rain had rushed to meet the stream made travel slow. They would gallop several hundred yards across the rough ground, then rein the horses in and come nearly to a stop, while they eased the chariot wheels across one or more of the erosion trenches. The Syrians were gaining on them.

The captain of the Judean chariots shouted to Jehoshaphat, "Go ahead, my Lord, we will hold them back!" Judah's king hesitated for a moment, knowing that the men would surely die defending him. "Please, my Lord, go!" he shouted a second time. As the king's driver whipped the exhausted team out of a steep wash, the fifty chariots behind them spread out and turned to fight. A hail of arrows rained into the Syrian horses and drivers, stopping ten or more of the rushing chariots. Then they took javelins and spears and brought down several more before they were overrun and pierced with arrow or spear, or cut down with swords. In two minutes the battle was over. Judah's king had time to regain a lead, but he and his driver knew the horses couldn't outrun the fresher Syrian teams.

"Great Yahweh, deliver me! Spare me from the hand of the Syrians that I may live to sing your praises," Jehoshaphat prayed as he looked back, watching the slaughter. "My God Yahweh, I am not worthy that such valiant men should die for me. Have mercy on them and receive them into your kingdom," he spoke out loud with tears streaming down his face. The Syrians stopped. They were no longer following Jehoshaphat's chariot.

King Ben-Hadad, leading the attack, rode his chariot through the carnage then shouted, "These are Judeans, not Israelites! These are Jehoshaphat's men!" His voice cracked as he screamed, "I want Ahab!"

He divided his forces, leaving a quarter of his men to keep Judah occupied while he took the rest around the north side of the city of Ramoth-Gilead to join the troops hidden above the valley to the east.

Ahab, expecting an ambush, moved cautiously along the east side of Ramoth-Gilead, with advance patrols reporting back continuously. Much of the area was wooded, with low growing junipers mixed with broom bushes creating a heavy underbrush.

As they came in view of the city, a hail of arrows rained down on the advance guard from Syrian archers hidden in the thick vegetation. Ahab ordered fire put to the underbrush, as Jehu directed his ground troops in behind the wall of fire and smoke. They burned as they went, routing thousands of Syrian troops. Many died in the flames. Some fleeing into clearings were cut down by Israel's archers.

About halfway around Ramoth-Gilead, Ahab turned inward and secured a defensive position at the highest point near the city. From the woods they cut poles, sharpened one end, and buried the base in the ground with them pointing outward. Within an hour they had a circular, hundred-cubit-across, defensive perimeter and as the work of mounding dirt and stone continued, Ahab and his guard and captains moved into the fortress.

They brought up a hundred battering rams and moved them into position along the wall of Ramoth-Gilead. From within, Syrian soldiers hurled a constant barrage of stones and arrows, and, as the battering rams began pounding, they poured vats of burning oil over the side. Though the large wheeled rams had been left to soak in the Jordan River as long as possible while the army crossed into Gilead, they were beginning to dry, and several were burning as they continued to batter the wall. Smoke filled the sky, and war cries and the shrieks of burned and dying men filled the air.

Through the burning forest to Ahab's back came an organized attack that engaged a large force of Israel's men. Where the undergrowth had been burned away and the singed and smoking trees were still standing, the fighting was hand to hand. The heavy, smoke-filled air was hard to breathe. In some places the heat was unbearable, but still the clash of swords and battle-axes carried through the burned forest. The Syrians continued to look for Ahab instead of pursuing a large-scale engagement of the army of Israel. As one contingent occupied a pocket of men, another skirted around, continuing to look for the elusive king, when together they could have defeated the resistance.

A messenger came riding into the fortification and was ushered over to Ahab, who was standing looking out over the battle that was raging between his position and the city, two thirds of a mile away. Ahab was discussing strategies with two of his captains when the messenger appeared behind them. Ahab turned to face him. "Speak!" he said curtly.

The messenger bowed, then spoke. "Sire, there is a large force attacking from the north, too many to hold back with the men in Jehu's command. Captain Jehu told me to tell you that he believes it is the main body of Ben-Hadad's army. He asks if you can pull the men around from the south flank to reinforce him."

Ahab turned to look northward, but had difficulty seeing what was taking place for the smoke, and dust, as well as the difficult terrain. "I must see for myself," he told his captains. As he jumped onto his chariot, the barricade was moved for the chariots of Ahab and his two captains to pass through. Once outside the fortification another twenty chariots of his guard joined the king. They drove north, staying to the higher ground for several minutes, until they were on the fringe of the most intense fighting. Swords clashed as the men fought hand to hand. They pulled their chariots to a halt and watched the fighting for a few moments. Ahab called to one of the captains with him, "Bring the south flank around. Hurry!" As the chariot pulled away he called to another captain, "Go to King Jehoshaphat. Tell him that we need help! Send reinforcements!"

A young Syrian archer followed a band of his countrymen through a hole they had opened up in Israel's line, but encountered a second line of Jehu's men moving up to reinforce the first. They were badly outnumbered and were quickly overcome. The young bowman fled in the confusion and hid in a clump of young cedars, just below King Ahab's position. Lying on the ground he peered out from under the heavy green branches. His heart pounded and his hands trembled from fear of being discovered at any moment.

The order from Ben-Hadad, to every man at his command, had been to find King Ahab. If this wasn't the king he saw, he must be a high-ranking officer, to be ordering the Israeli captains around with such an air of authority. The Syrian archer raised to one knee and leaned into the trunk of the cedar where there were no branches. He needed the support to steady his shaking hands.

It was perhaps a hundred cubits to where this high-ranking man stood directing the battle from his chariot. He was clad with helmet, breastplate and scale armor. Not the armor he expected on a king, but still difficult to penetrate. The arrow would have to hit him in the throat. He pulled the arrow back. He was shaking too badly. He released the tension for a moment, took a deep breath and pulled back a second time. Again he was shaking too much to take clear aim. He released the arrow. If it missed its mark, he would try again.

"Where is Captain Jehu?" Thud.... The weight of the blow staggered Ahab. He felt a strange sensation in his side below his left arm. He looked down to see the arrow.

The driver felt the sudden shift of the king's weight and turned to see the king bracing against the side of the chariot, with the arrow strangely angled under the breastplate.

Ahab hoped that it wasn't a barbed arrow point when he said to his driver, "Pull it out; it isn't deep."

The driver took hold of the arrow with both hands and pulled. The pain was severe, but Ahab didn't flinch. The arrow had hit the first scale of the scale armor that joined the breastplate. That was what knocked him off balance. The glancing blow sent the arrow under the breastplate. The wound didn't feel severe, but Ahab could feel the warm blood running down his side inside the armor.

"Take me out of here!" Ahab ordered his driver. The driver turned the chariot and raced back toward the fortified command post, where Ahab had the scale armor cut away from the breastplate on his wounded side. Bandaged to slow the bleeding, Ahab remounted his chariot and had himself positioned on a mound where he could be seen by the fighting troops on three sides.

The battering rams were spread out along the eastern wall of the city to divide the resistance in as many points. Ahab watched and hoped for a signal that the wall had been breached. It would mean a quick victory and he needed it. He could feel himself growing weaker. As sunset approached, he felt faint and had to brace himself against the side of the chariot, holding onto the spears holstered beside him. Surely he couldn't die from a wound as slight as this, he thought, but he knew by the way he was feeling that he would have to retire from the battle soon. If only the wall would break. He closed his eyes as he wished for victory. He found himself with no will to reopen them, and was drifting peacefully away.

He fell to his knees. "Your Highness," the chariot driver called as he turned to the king. Several soldiers and aides rushed to the aid of Ahab. Ahab was suddenly in the vineyard of Naboth, looking out over the Jezreel valley. Behind him was the sound of a woman crying. He turned to see the widow of Naboth, dressed in rags.

The young woman approached Ahab, fell at his feet, and took hold of his skirt. "My Lord King, have mercy on me and my sons. Let my husband live, let him live."

"How many sons did Naboth have?" Ahab muttered.

"My Lord, Naboth had three sons. Jezebel had them murdered in your name." Tears streamed downed her face.

Ahab heard a voice from above as he turned and looked up. "I have seen the blood of Naboth, and the blood of his sons."

The king's tent was quickly erected. Ahab was laid onto his mat inside his tent. He never regained consciousness and, just after nightfall, he died.

Israel had inflicted heavy losses on Ben-Hadad's men. Without knowing of the death of Ahab, he withdrew his troops as the sun was going down.

Word spread quickly through the weary troops. They were far from being defeated, but didn't have the heart to continue. When Captain Jehu learned that men were slipping away into the night, he conferred with the other officers, then with King Jehoshaphat. They agreed to discontinue the fight. Jehoshaphat would pull out during the night, and the men of Israel were ordered to withdraw ahead of him.

Once Judah was across the Jordan, Jehoshaphat prepared to make a stand to keep Ben-Hadad from following and taking Israel's territory west of the Jordan. When the Syrian king learned of Ahab's death, he deferred to continue the war, convinced that Israel would never again attempt to retake the cities of Gilead. He also knew that Jehoshaphat still had a formidable army back in Judah, in addition to this contingent of Judah's forces, and he didn't want to risk a full war with him.

Elijah was sitting on one of the knee-high rocks that broke the surface of the grassy field between two ridges at the foot of Mount Carmel. Around him in the grass, or on other white limestone rocks, sat young prophets, listening intently as he expounded the Scriptures.

He rolled up the parchment and said, "When the Spirit of Yahweh comes upon you, He doesn't take away your mind, He incorporates you into himself, so that you can hear and understand his word. There isn't anyone on earth that Yahweh will speak through quite like he will through you. That's why every person is special to Yahweh. Created in the image of Yahweh it is written that man was made, yet every man is different. How can that be? Each man is different yet all are created in His image.

"That is how He reveals different parts of His nature, through the differences of each man. We will know Him more completely, because we will see Him more completely, as each of us reflect slightly different parts of His nature. As many as the stars of heaven are the facets of Yahweh." Elijah's voice tapered off, as his thoughts seemed to drift away. Except for the distant call of a quail, everything became unnaturally still.

The prophets slowly glanced around, as though they expected something to happen. "Ahab has been wounded in battle," Elijah said softly. His words could only be heard by those closest to him. "The king has been wounded. Ahab will die this day."

Elijah glanced over the gathering, then said, "I need to send two runners to Samaria." All but the oldest stood. They knew they weren't fit to be runners. "Who are the two youngest among you?" After a short discussion, one stepped forward, followed a moment later by another.

"Teacher, we are the youngest," one spoke out. They looked to be between eighteen and twenty.

"Are you both fit?" he asked. They both nodded. "Don't let it be known that you are among the prophets. Find Obadiah, the king's steward, and find out what is to become of Micaiah, the only prophet in Samaria with the boldness to speak the prophecy of Yahweh. Without Ahab to protect him, I fear that Jezebel will have him killed. Take provision and hurry. When Ahaziah takes the throne, Jezebel will have more power than she has ever had."

"Elijah!" one of the older men called. Elijah turned to see one of the seasoned prophets in the group wanting to speak. When their eyes met, he asked, "What of the judgment of Jezebel that has been prophesied by you? Will not Yahweh prevent her from harming Micaiah?"

"This is not Jezebel's time. When the seed of Ahab is destroyed, then she will be killed and her flesh eaten by the dogs. It cannot happen until Yahweh calls another king to the throne."

"Who might that king be?"

"I cannot say, lest I jeopardize the life of the man Yahweh has chosen to rule." Again Elijah looked over the group and quickly added the number of men, thirty-eight. "Brothers, if you can remain here, I believe you will be safe, but I know many have duties which must be attended. If you must leave, be careful. Never forget the days when Jezebel killed the prophets. After the days of mourning she will wield more power than ever, and because of me she hates you more than ever. She will blame the death of the king on us.

"Be wise, stay alert, be ready to flee, be ready to fight, and have your ears tuned to Yahweh. Know this. Ahaziah has the same spirit in him that is in his mother. He is not like Ahab, who believed in part.

"Endure for a short time, for Ahaziah will not long be king." Elijah turned to walk away, up a slope that led to a pinnacle where he often retreated to commune with Yahweh.

A week later, the young prophets returned and met Elisha at the mouth of the canyon. He was carrying a wineskin and a basket of grain. "Elisha!" they called from a distance. He turned and watched them trot toward him.

"Micaiah is... still in prison," one breathed out in short bursts. Catching his breath, he added, "And Obadiah doesn't know what will become of Micaiah or himself." Catching another breath he continued. "He said that Ahaziah doesn't like him and he knows that Jezebel will remove him from being governor over the house of Ahab if Ahaziah allows her to do so. He hasn't any influence to help Micaiah."

"Come with me to inform Elijah. We have wine and bread and meat. You will eat before we allow you to return home." One of the young men helped Elisha by carrying the basket of grain.

After the days of mourning for Ahab had passed, Ahaziah officially took the throne, with much pomp and a parade through Samaria in the chariot that had been his father's. Jezebel remained queen and co-regent with her son, and had a throne next to his in the throne room.

Their first order of business was to appoint officials whom they knew and trusted.

They immediately summoned Obadiah before them. His heart pounded with fear as he came in and bowed to one knee before them. "Great King of Israel, live forever. Your servant and governor of the house of Ahab to serve you, my Lord."

"Arise, Obadiah." As the steward stood, Ahaziah said, "I will not have need of your services. I have found someone more qualified than you for the job."

"As you wish, Your Highness." It wasn't any less than Obadiah had expected. He waited to be dismissed, but the time grew into a cold tense minute. He could feel the eyes of all the court upon him.

"I have never liked you, Obadiah," Jezebel broke the silence. "And now Ahab isn't here to protect you." Jezebel gave a nod to the guards. They stepped to Obadiah's side with drawn swords. "I learned some time ago how you disobeyed my edict and protected the prophets of Yahweh, hiding them from me and feeding them from the king's table."

Her face flushed and her voice hardened. "No one in this kingdom can disobey me in matters pertaining to the gods." She stood and looked down the steps leading from the throne. "You will be thrown into prison." Her black eyes penetrated his. "You should pray that I don't have you burned alive. Take him away!"

Ahaziah had never seen that side of his mother before, and was surprised at the authority with which she spoke. He would come to realize just how powerful his mother had become.

Together, they began to revive the worship of Baal. There was little objection to sacrificing those already condemned. Jezebel began to participate in the orgy worship with the highest-ranking priests, beneath the idol of Baal where all the followers could see. Sometimes she would engage in orgies with as many as ten priests, one after another.

Ahaziah never participated in the temple worship, but he kept several of the temple prostitutes at the palace. Some days he remained in the pavilion Ahab had constructed on the roof, with the prostitutes and the ceremonial wine from the temple.

Jezebel was becoming concerned with the effect that this pretense of Baal worship was having on Ahaziah. He would spend days, sometimes weeks in drunken orgies with the prostitutes. He had become so unreliable that Jehoram, his brother, took over the responsibility of judging Israel in the gate of the palace.

Before dawn one morning lightning cracked just outside, startling Jezebel from her nightmarish sleep. The lightning flashed and the thunder rumbled away as she sat up, fearing the next strike. She flinched as another lightning bolt exploded closer.

Boom! Crack! The palace vibrated, as the rumbling traveled into the distance. Before the thunder faded, another exploded, then another. Each time, the night became as light as day for an instant. "Lord Baal, have mercy on the servant of your will," Jezebel prayed.

Every time she slept since the death of Ahab, she experienced the predictions of Elijah and Micaiah in her dreams. "Ahab died in battle. It had nothing to do with the curse of the prophets of Yahweh," she told herself, but it didn't stop the dreams. "I see your great might, Oh Lord Baal. You are greater than the god of Elijah."

As much as she tried to push away the fear of Yahweh and Elijah's prophecy, she could not. She sat there until the storm abated and the day began to dawn. Afraid to sleep, afraid the dreams would return. She was tormented more than ever, afraid of the god she hated, and afraid of offending the god she served.

Suddenly she remembered hearing months before something about Ahab having thrown Micaiah into prison because he had prophesied that Ahab would be killed if he went to war against Syria. Very early, she had Micaiah brought to the throne room.

The months in prison had weighed heavily on him. He was thin and pale, his hair and beard matted, and his robe had worn ragged. Forced before the throne by two soldiers, he refused to bow to Jezebel. One of the guards began to force him to his knees when Jezebel said, "It is enough!" The soldier backed away and bowed, but stood ready to serve the queen's next command.

"Prophet of Yahweh," she addressed him scornfully. "You cast a spell upon the king and he died, and you have spoken against the great god Baal and against me. You are guilty of treason and worthy of death. What do you have to say about these things?" Micaiah stood silent, his eyes locked with hers. He refused to even blink, and had no fear of her reaction. During the months in prison he had prepared himself to die, trusting in the strength of his God.

Jezebel was amazed at the strength in his eyes, for a man so weakened in every other way. A chill ran through her. It was the same presence she felt when she was near Elijah. She looked away. Their eyes had met for only a moment, but it had left her with a trembling that she sought to cover with an angry command. "Take this filthy man out of my sight and clean him! Bring him back this afternoon! He will bow before Ahaziah!"

Jezebel went to Ahaziah's chambers. The guard stationed outside the door bowed and spoke quietly, "Your Highness, the king doesn't want to be disturbed."

"I am his mother, and I am the queen. I will disturb him. Now get out of my way!" The guard bowed again and moved aside. She found Ahaziah lying naked, asleep with four temple prostitutes amidst an array of pillows. Two of the prostitutes were covered with the green ointment that was so familiar to her. She knelt next to her son. "Ahaziah," she called, as she shook him awake.

He opened his glassy eyes and focused on her for a minute, then asked, "What are you doing here?"

"You're the king. You can't keep ignoring your responsibilities. Jehoram judges the people in the gate and the throne stays empty."

Sarcastically he answered, "It is more important for me to give homage to Baal." He looked around to see where the women were.

"You could have any virgin in the land. You could have a hundred virgins. Why do you keep these common temple whores here in the palace?" Jezebel looked around at the women lying unconscious.

"No virgin can do for me what these temple whores do. You should know, you're the same as a temple whore."

She slapped him hard. "I am high priestess of Ashtoreth and worship with only the highest ranking priests!"

Ahaziah grabbed Jezebel's hand and twisted her arm violently. "Mother, you slap me again and I will have you fed to the dogs myself to make sure Elijah's prophecy comes to pass."

For the first time Jezebel realized that she was not dealing with just her son, but the king, and that he had the power to carry out such a threat.

Sounding somewhat apologetic, Ahaziah released Jezebel's arm and said after a moment of silence, "I have restored the worship of Baal and made it a law that anyone who speaks against Baal shall be put to death. I did that for you."

"Forgive me?" Jezebel asked. It was a term he knew she never used, and it showed that she did have some respect for him, or at least for his power. "Micaiah, the prophet that your father threw into prison, will come to stand before you this afternoon. He refuses to bow to me. Have him remove the curse of Yahweh from the house of Ahab and his seed, that your throne may be established forever. Make him bless you and your descendants."

After thinking about it for a moment, he answered, "Yes, I will have him bless me." As though he were suddenly aware of his nakedness, Ahaziah rolled over to hide himself from his mother. "Send in the servants with my robes. I must bathe before I see this prophet." Jezebel rose and left the room.

In the afternoon, when Jezebel and Ahaziah were seated on their thrones, Micaiah was brought before them. Unyielding, he looked first at the king then at Jezebel, who avoided making eye contact.

When it was clear that he wasn't going to bow, Ahaziah spoke, "Prophet of Yahweh, or as you refer to Him, El Shaddai, El Elyon, or Adonai. It makes no difference. The concept of one god is unthinkable to me, but I want the blessing of your god the same as I want the blessing of all gods. I want you to remove the curse of your god from the house of Ahab. Can you do that, prophet?"

"I cannot," Micaiah responded, "but Yahweh might remove his judgment from the house of Ahab if you were to repent, destroy the image of Baal and the pillars of Ashtoreth, burn their temples and forbid the worship of any god but Yahweh, for all other gods are demons. Some are only stone or metal, and have no more power than a tree in the forest."

Arrogantly, Ahaziah answered, "If your God is so great, and the only god, then why are you in my prison? And why am I given the power to have your head removed? I could have you sacrificed to the great god Baal, who would appreciate the sacrifice of the servant of a rival god."

Micaiah looked at Jezebel. "Baal is a demon, cast down from the presence of Yahweh. Queen Jezebel, you remember how the priests of Baal once had power, how they once prophesied, and now they are powerless." He could see in her face that she was aware of what he was saying. "Elijah, by the power of Yahweh, has bound the power of your devil. In Israel he is powerless. That should be proof that he is no god. Unless you renounce him and call on Yahweh to have mercy, you will be cast into eternal torment with Baal and the once great prince, Lucifer."

Jezebel jumped to her feet. "Silence, silence!" she shouted then ordered, "Bring Obadiah up from the dungeon." She reseated herself on her throne and said, "I have heard that Yahweh can send fire down upon sacrifices from a clear sky. Let us see what kind of power your god has."

"Do not mock Yahweh or you will pay," said Micaiah.

"Obadiah committed treason and defied the law by hiding the prophets of Yahweh. He must be a very great man in the sight of your God."

Fire burned in Jezebel's eyes as she sat there in silence, waiting for Obadiah. Ahaziah had wine brought in, and was sipping from the goblet when Obadiah was shoved into their presence beside Micaiah. Obadiah didn't bow. Jezebel stood again. "Steward, don't you bow in the presence of your king?"

"It has been shown to me that I will die this day, but I will die with dignity. I will not bow to either of you corrupters of Israel, you that worship the penis. Oh you fools who bow to stones and wood!" Obadiah broke out laughing.

Infuriated, Jezebel shouted, "Bow before your king!" When Obadiah continued to laugh, she looked at one of the guards, who struck Obadiah behind the knee with a spear shaft, causing his legs to buckle. He fell to his knees.

Ahaziah, amused by all of this, erupted into loud laughter. Astonished, Jezebel turned toward him. He answered her look, "Didn't you think it was funny, what he said?" He knew that his flagrant attitude would only increase her anger, but he didn't care. He was king, and he would take any attitude that he pleased, and she could like it or not.

Ahaziah stood and motioned to one of the court counselors, who then approached the king. Ahaziah whispered into his ear. They conversed in whispers for a minute, then the counselor left the room. "Take our traitor and the prophet into the courtyard!"

"Mother, would you join me in the courtyard? I think you will enjoy the afternoon entertainment." The king's court and attendants filed out behind Ahaziah and Jezebel. Obadiah and Micaiah were taken out through the commoner's hall.

By the time the king had reached the court, beams were being dropped into two of the dozens of holes the exact diameter carved in the stone. The stone pavement around the holes was charred, some nearly black.

As the prisoners were being bound to the poles, King Ahaziah stepped in front of the crowd. "Micaiah here is a friend of Elijah, and a part of those strange prophets that believe there is only one god. One that has always been. If there were such a God I would feel sorry for him or her. To be forever alone! One would have to pity such a god. Who conceived and bore him? No one, he has always been."

Ahaziah turned and looked at Micaiah for a moment. "Even the prophets of my father that sacrifice to Yahweh believe he has a wife, Ashtoreth, and children and brothers. The gods are like us, only ten-thousand times greater, but they are not eternal."

For the first time, Ahaziah experienced fear when he looked

into Micaiah's eyes. He quickly turned away and was momentarily without words. It was a feeling he would never forget. He tried to shake it off, but even as he looked into the faces of the people of his court that he knew so well, he could still see the prophet's eyes.

Hoping that Micaiah would prove him wrong, he challenged the prophet. "Micaiah! Call on your God to give us a sign, and I will release you and Obadiah." He glanced at Jezebel to get her reaction. He could see by the frown on her face that she didn't like the idea. He continued, "It doesn't have to be anything like calling fire from heaven, but you can do that if you like. We want to see a sign from your God."

"Ahaziah!" Micaiah called. "Israel will be given a sign. You and all the seed that issued from Ahab will be cut off and the dogs will eat the flesh of your mother. Both you and she will be cast into the bowels of the earth. Then you and she will know that there is only one God!"

Jezebel hurried to the front. "Burn them! Burn them now!" She was headed in Micaiah's direction, but Ahaziah stepped into her path.

"Let us first see if his God answers him like He answered Elijah." The wild look in her eyes faded into the cold strong composure that was hers.

She slowly sidestepped her son and walked up to Micaiah. "Where is your God, Micaiah? Ask him to send fire from heaven, or for any sign." She turned and looked around.

In a distant empty area of the courtyard were several small birds pecking at the ground. Jezebel walked toward them, away from the gathering. She stopped before she frightened them away and watched for a few seconds. One of the birds flew. She pointed at the bird and followed it through the air. Suddenly the bird tumbled and fell dead to the ground. The crowd gasped. Arrogantly, she strode back to face Micaiah. "That is the power of Baal. Where is the power of your God?"

"Oh foolish woman, Yahweh gives life, Satan and Baal take it. I know that all Israel has heard how Yahweh restored life to a Phoenician boy because Elijah prayed to Yahweh the God of Abraham. How many lives have you sacrificed to your demon? But he has never given one back. Elijah told you that Yahweh would stop the rain and your priests couldn't bring it back. Those signs you didn't believe. How many signs would it take to make you believe?" Micaiah shouted, "Here is a sign for you, King Ahaziah! Next year at this time your brother will be sitting on that throne!"

Ahaziah stepped forward and slapped Micaiah across the mouth, then motioned for the guards to ignite the fires. 'Prophesy again, dead man!" yelled Ahaziah. "Your god won't have to send fire down today, prophet. All he will have to do is put them out for you."

The flames slowly began to burn. First the flames ignited the brush and wood that had been piled chest high around the men, then it began to burn their flesh.

Jezebel waited to hear their screams, but there were none. On the faces of both Micaiah and Obadiah, there was a quiet peaceful strength. Only for a moment did she allow her eyes to meet Micaiah's. The light in his eyes sent a trembling through her body. She turned and ran into the palace.

For a while the group was silent as they watched. It wasn't as entertaining as most deaths by fire, for neither screamed in agony.

The western sky was turning purple as the nude temple priestess danced around the idol of Baal. She was one of King Ahaziah's favorites. He lay back beneath the canopy with several of his friends and as many prostitutes. The women knew that they could be handsomely rewarded or put to death if they failed to please the king.

King Ahaziah had made his brother, Jehoram, captain over the army of Israel, and Jehu captain over half the chariots. His first year as king, they fortified the defense cities and built up the army, in preparation to fight Ben-Hadad again and reclaim Ramoth Gilead. Haunted by the last words of Micaiah, Ahaziah refused to leave the palace of Samaria. In quiet moments he heard the prophet's last prophetic words in his mind and became a prisoner to them.

He had a four cubit stone image of Baal placed next to the pavilion on top of the palace. There he spent most of his time with his friends and the temple prostitutes, consuming wine in a pretense of Baal worship. Drunken orgies there often lasted through the night.

A heavy wooden lattice covered a rectangular roof window, four by six cubits, over a dining hall below. The window allowed light in by day and the smoke from the fires out at night. Ahaziah would sit on the lattice and call to the servants below. Sometimes when he was bored he called down to the servants or the guards to come up and perform sex acts with the prostitutes while he and his friends watched.

When a woman failed to please him, or even on a whim, he would have her tied and beaten. He and his friends would think of sadistic ways to inflict pain then have a soldier carry out their wishes as they drank and laughed while they watched. Ahaziah would often drink most of the day and through the night. On those occasions he would remain in bed the following day raising up only to vomit and scream out orders and curses to anyone that came near. The day after that he would remain in a somber state, taking some interest in the affairs of state.

"Your Highness, Queen Jezebel would like an audience with my Lord the King." One of the soldiers bowed to Ahaziah as he announced the presence of the queen. Ahaziah sat up and looked around at his company of friends then answered, "Send the queen in. The great priestess of Ashtoreth may want to worship her lord, Baal, with us."

Jezebel came in and bowed to the ground before Ahaziah.

Ahaziah sighed then said, "Mother, you know that's not necessary." Then asked sharply, "What do you want?"

"My son, there are affairs of state that need answers. Answers that only you have. Decisions that can only be made by the king of Israel." When he didn't answer immediately, she added, "There is a banquet to honor the priests of Ashtoreth in just a little while. Will you be there? Please, for me. They are already gathering below."

"Mother, you have always wanted to rule Israel. Rule it in my absence." Then sarcastically he added, "I will be down to worship the goddess of Israel with the great high priestess, but while you are here, why don't you worship Baal with my friends?"

Jezebel looked shocked at his suggestion and glanced around to see the reaction of his companions.

"Mother, I have seen your nakedness with the priests in the temple and I was aroused by my own mother. Why would this be different?"

Half-angered she answered, her voice a pitch higher, "The spirit of Ashtoreth dwells in me! I can worship with only the highest priests!"

"Mother, you are interfering with the worship of my god. If you don't want to worship with us, then leave." He knew she wouldn't like his next command, but he was king and he would have whatever he wanted. "Prepare places for my friends. They would like to come to the banquet."

Jezebel, concealing her anger, afraid to say more, bowed again and left. As she made her way down the long stairway, the fear came over her that she had lost all control of Ahaziah, and that he would never change. What would happen to Israel under such poor leadership? She had been closer to him than to Jehoram but now wished that Jehoram were on the throne. Jehoram, only twenty-two, took his responsibility seriously and had earned in one year the respect of the men under his command. Yes, he would make a better king, but he wasn't a Baal worshiper. If he were king, where would that leave her? She pondered the possibilities, then dismissed them all when she realized that Jehoram would never raise his sword against his brother.

Within an hour, smoke from the light fires mixed with the sweet smell of incense began to float up through the lattice of the skylight. Ahaziah got to his feet. "I think it's time to go to the banquet," he said as he walked over to the opening covered by the thick wooden lattice.

He stooped down and leaned forward to take a seat on one of the cross sections as he had many times before, but this time he lost his balance and fell forward. He reached forward to catch himself and break his fall. His hands hit one of the cross sections and slid over the edge, stripping the skin from the inside of his wrists. The old weather worn cross member cracked loudly as his chest slammed against it. Ahaziah's fall was slowed momentarily. His companions turned in the direction of the cracking timbers as they broke beneath the king's weight. The lattice folded and he disappeared through the sky light.

Below was a round fire lamp bowl a cubit across, on a pedestal a cubit and a half high. Ahaziah hit the bowl on his right side, sending the lamp across the floor and leaving a path of oil that quickly began to blaze.

The assembly of priests stood to their feet and the guards rushed in to extinguish the flames. Ahaziah grabbed for his side as the pain shot through his body. He rolled away from the oil and fire. The next instant his robe burst into flames where it had come into contact with the oil. "Aaaaah!" he screamed.

Jezebel ran to her son. She pulled at the burning robe as one of the guards with a lance began to cut away the portion of the garment that was blazing. Before they could remove the burning material another guard dashed the robe with a pitcher of water. With the flame extinguished they removed the seared robe.

He was burned only slightly but beneath him blood was pooling. "Call the physicians!" Jezebel ordered frantically as she raised what remained of the clothing covering his hip and pelvis. She gasped. A large bone protruded from his upper thigh and a gash in his side caused by one of the timbers that he had fallen upon exposed his entrails. "Take him to his bed!"

Ahaziah fainted from the pain as they moved him onto a stretcher. The servants carried the king to his chamber, and lowered him carefully onto the carpets covering the white marble floor.

There was little the physicians could do but give him drugs that kept his mind in a haze. Jezebel sat with him through the night. At daylight she sent a messenger to the high priest of Baal saying, "Inquire of the great Lord Baal in behalf of Ahaziah, if he will live or die."

Throughout that day the priests offered sacrifices to Baal but received no answer from the idol. The high priest knew that if he made a prediction and was wrong it would cost him his life. At the end of the day he returned a message saying, "This day we have not ceased to offer sacrifices for King Ahaziah, but the Great Lord Baal has not spoken."

On the second day the physicians gave no drugs to the king. They knew if he was going to live he would have to eat to keep his strength. As the drug wore off, Ahaziah cried with pain.

Sweat ran from his brow and mingled with the tears that poured from his eyes. Jezebel urged, "You must eat if you are to survive. Please eat."

"I can't, I can't. Give me the wine," he pleaded. "It hurts. Give me the wine. Mix it with the strong potion that Eber mixes." He rested a moment, gathering strength to continue. "I have restored the worship of Baal and offered many sacrifices. Entreat Lord Baal for my healing."

Jezebel, hiding the failure of her priests, wasn't about to mention that she had already had the priests in Samaria pray without answer. She had witnessed greater power in Ekron, so she said, "We will send to Ekron. There is great power there."

Ahaziah was weeping out loud as he spoke through the sobs. "I will give a hundred talents of gold, a thousand virgin sacrifices, a hundred thousand sheep. Please help me."

Jezebel held a cup of broth near his mouth for him to drink. "Drink just a little broth, then I'll give you the wine."

"Give me the wine now!" he screamed, then knocked the cup from her hand. "Be damned, I'm the king! Give me the wine!"

Angrily, she got up from his side as she said to the physicians, "Give him the opiate wine." She turned to one of the guards, "Bring me two of the swiftest riders and send to me the chief scribe." She left the king's bedchamber and went to the scroll room. When the chief scribe came in, she ordered, "Send this message to the high priest of the temple of Baal-Zebub at Ekron of the Philistines.

"From the King of Israel and Jezebel, the high priestess of Ashtoreth and Queen of Israel: My son, Ahaziah the King, was seriously injured in a tragic fall. Inquire of the great god, lord and protector of the Philistines, Lord Baal-Zebub, if he shall live or if he shall die in his bed."

She reasoned for a minute that they would put forth just as much effort for fifty talents as they would for a hundred and continued. "If the Glorious Lord Baal-Zebub will grant King Ahaziah a great miracle of restoration, immediately, King Ahaziah will offer fifty talents of gold and a thousand slaves to the glory of the god of Ekron."

Within minutes the two messengers were racing through the gates of the palace on their way to Ekron. They were only a few miles southwest of Samaria where the road narrowed, with a steep bank sloping away from the road on the right and a cliff on the left, when ahead a pile of brush blocked their path. Pulling their horses to a halt, they surveyed the surroundings, waiting for an ambush. From a cleft in the rock, Elijah jumped down in front of the horses.

Startled, one of the horses reared on its hind legs. The rider clung hard with his legs and took hold of the animal's mane to avoid being thrown. The instant the horse's front hooves touched the ground the rider had his sword drawn. The second rider also drew his sword as the first jumped to the ground.

With the point of the blade touching the wide leather belt around Elijah's waist, he said, "You must be a highwayman." Both men looked again to see if there were others ready to cut them down. "You'll be the first to die," he threatened.

"A highwayman I am not, but a prophet of Yahweh," Elijah answered.

"Did you put this brush in our path?" He pushed against Elijah's belt with the point of the sword as he spoke but felt very uncomfortable when their eyes met. Elijah's thick hair and beard hadn't been trimmed in some time, giving him the appearance of a wild man. But the king's messenger sensed immediately that there was more to him than his appearance revealed. And his speech was that of an educated man.

There was a moment of silence as the man with the sword analyzed what he saw and the strange sensation he felt. Elijah spoke, "Is there not a God in Israel that you go to inquire of Baal-Zebub, the god of Ekron of the Philistines? Return to Ahaziah and tell him that he shall not come down from his bed but shall die because he sought not Yahweh, the God of Israel."

The messenger lowered his sword. "If we return to the king, who should we say sent us back with this word?"

"Tell him and his mother what you have seen. The king will know who sent you." The messengers mounted up, then turned their horses and galloped away as Elijah began to clear the brush from the road.

Jezebel was again by Ahaziah's side, comforting him and attempting to ration the drug in small amounts, just enough to keep the pain at bay and him coherent. One of the counselors stepped quietly into the room and spoke softly for Jezebel to hear, "The messengers you sent to Ekron have returned."

Jezebel studied for a moment then answered in a sharp tone, "They couldn't possibly have reached Ekron and returned this quickly! I'll speak with them outside."

Ahaziah caught the message and interrupted, "No! Send them in. I will hear from them." Jezebel nodded to the counselor to send them in.

The two messengers entered the room. One bowed and remained near the entrance while the other came near Ahaziah's bed and bowed to one knee. "Your Majesty."

The king, his voice reflecting the strain of the injury and his concentration to remain alert under the influence of the drugs, asked, "Why have you returned so quickly?"

"We met a man who claimed he was a prophet. He told us to return and tell you that you will surely die because you didn't turn to Yahweh, but to the god of Ekron."

Ahaziah strained to ask, "What did this man look like?"

"He was a wild-looking man, very hairy, clothed in camel skin and gird about with a wide leather belt. His eyes were blue and unlike any eyes I've ever seen."

"It was Elijah!" Jezebel blurted out. "What about his eyes, did his eyes make you fearful?"

"Not exactly fearful, but I knew he was no ordinary man."

Ahaziah's voice rose with as much anger as he could muster at the moment and weakly he ordered, "Send a fifty man platoon out to bring him to me. He is going to pay with his life!"

That pleased Jezebel but made her tremble with fear at the same time. Elijah was truly no ordinary man. She wondered about the outcome, for Ahab had been unable to capture Elijah in three and a half years, even with thousands of men searching.

Elijah began the walk back to Mount Carmel, but had gone only a few hundred cubits north when he was compelled to turn around. "Again Israel will see my power and you will face the king this day." Elijah's body trembled for a moment and he could feel the hair on his arms and legs rise in ripples as if a cool wind were blowing over him. The voice was from somewhere inside but it was very clear.

Listening for further instructions, Elijah walked slowly in the direction he felt he was being led. He had waited years for Yahweh to speak so clearly again. The first word to meet the king's messengers to Philistia came the day before Ahaziah had fallen. It took that long for him to get here. Now he was going to speak to the king face to face and Yahweh was going to show his power.

A third of a mile south, the road dropped to the level of the fields on the west and on the east a vertical cliff rose sixty cubits above the road. Elijah took a narrow trail up the steep terrain and found that it led to a pinnacle overlooking the road where he could see a great distance in each direction.

Within an hour one of the first messengers led a platoon, forty-eight footmen and three horsemen including the captain, to where they first encountered the prophet. From his vantage point Elijah saw them stop where he had blocked the road with limbs and brush. He was also visible to them and was spotted by the second-in-command. "Captain, look! There on that rock," he said. As he pulled the reins firmly, his horse became nervous, stepping in place as though it smelled danger.

"You've done your job. You've led us to him. Rest your mount a few minutes, then go and tell King Ahaziah we have found the prophet and will be returning with him shortly," the captain said arrogantly to the messenger who had led them this far.

The messenger pulled his mount to the side as the troops continued. He dismounted. This prophet was no ordinary man. After looking into Elijah's eyes, he couldn't picture him coming peacefully. He would stay and watch.

The soldiers came to a halt beneath Elijah atop the cliff. Elijah stepped back from the edge so that the archers couldn't target him. The captain got down from his mount and left his horse with one of the men. "Have the bowmen take positions and target the prophet," he ordered the second in command. The three horses being held by one man were afraid and pulled hard against the reins. The captain walked around the company of men looking up to try to spot Elijah as the archers knelt to one knee and aimed toward the pinnacle where he had been standing.

"Man of Elohim!" the captain shouted, but there was no answer. "Man of Elohim!" he shouted a second time. "The king orders you to come down."

Elijah's arms were stretched toward heaven as he stepped to the edge of the cliff where he was seen by all of them. The archers waited for the order but the captain watched to see what this strange man would do. All of them knew the stories and the legends that had grown from Elijah's reputation. It was hard to know what was true and what was myth.

"If I be a man of Elohim then let fire come from heaven and consume you and your men." Elijah's voice carried clearly. The archers lowered their bows. Everyone looked around. Wild with fear, the horses bolted and pulled free from the man who had been assigned to hold their reins. As they galloped away, the captain turned a sharp look toward the soldier but was quickly distracted. He glanced upward into a blinding light. The earth trembled from a sound a hundred times greater than thunder, and a ball of fire larger than the radius of the ground the platoon occupied shot past Elijah and exploded onto the ground. The impact sent fire in every direction, igniting the trees and grass of the field.

The horse of the messenger watching from a distance went berserk. He grabbed hold of the animal, clinging to its side, scrambling frantically to mount up as they raced away. "Yahweh, you are God!" he cried out as he slid his leg over the galloping animal's back, hoping to appease the God of Elijah.

He reached the palace, trembling uncontrollably as he clung to the back of his horse. Almost delirious, he babbled, "Yahweh will rain fire on us all!" They helped him from his horse and one of the king's counselors tried to question him but what he said didn't make sense. "Yahweh is going to rain fire on us all." He repeated it again and again.

"Where are the men who were sent to capture Elijah?"

"The God of Elijah destroyed them. He sent fire from heaven, burned them up, all are gone. I saw it and He is going to destroy us all."

The counselor ordered two of the guards, "Bring him inside and send for the queen. Tell her I think she needs to see this for herself, but say nothing in the hearing of the king."

In the counsel chamber, the man was seated and somewhat calmer when Jezebel entered the room. Inquisitively, she looked at the king's counselor, knowing that something was out of the ordinary for him to have summoned her.

"Your Highness, I didn't want to trouble the king at this time, so I sent for you. This is the messenger who led the platoon to Elijah. It seems he is beside himself. He claims that Yahweh threw fire from heaven and destroyed the entire platoon."

That same feeling of fear that she had first experienced as a seventeen-year-old bride gripped Jezebel. Several moments passed before she could speak. "It's the prophecy of Elijah!" she gasped.

"There is more. He says that Yahweh is going to rain fire on all of us." He paused a moment then added, partly to ease his own apprehension, "He is out of his head. How could he possibly know that?"

Jezebel turned to the messenger. "What is your name?" The man didn't answer and kept staring blankly at the floor. Jezebel shouted, "Answer me! What is your name?"

The counselor snatched away the messenger's leather cap and grasping his hair, raised his head to face Jezebel. The man seemed not to notice or care.

"His name is Simeon, Your Highness. I inquired of one of the guards that know him."

Jezebel moved close to Simeon and looked into his eyes then slapped him. "Answer me, Simeon!" His eyes began to focus on the queen then she slapped him again. "What did you see? What happened to the soldiers?"

Slowly he began to speak. "Fire, a ball of fire, I saw it falling from the sky. It burned the men and the earth and the trees. It was so bright that it blinded me." Jezebel remembered walking to the edge of the crater where the God of Elijah burned up the sacrifice on Mount Carmel. There was a long moment of silence then Simeon spoke again, "The God of Elijah is the greatest of all the gods."

Jezebel ridiculed, "What does someone like you know about the gods!" She left the room and was met by one of the handmaids.

"Your Highness, Jehoram has just arrived from Jericho."

"Have him meet me in the king's quarters."

Jezebel had returned to Ahaziah's side when Jehoram's presence was announced. He came and bowed and knelt by the king's bed. "I came as soon as I heard. What is your condition?" Ahaziah didn't speak but shook his head slightly, indicating that he wasn't doing very well.

Jehoram could see the pain in his brother's face and looked at their mother for a full explanation. Ahaziah's eyes were closed for the moment, as Jezebel also shook her head no. She added, "We sent men to Ekron to inquire of Baal-Zebub about his recovery, but the messengers were intercepted by Elijah."

King Ahaziah reached out and laid his hand on Jehoram's shoulder. "Brother, I can trust you. Take a platoon and bring that menace to Israel to me. He will prophesy good concerning me if he is faced with death. Please hurry! I don't think I have much longer."

"I'll bring him to you. You are going to live!" Jehoram declared as he stood to his feet.

Jezebel caught up to Jehoram before he reached the entryway and escorted him out and down the long corridor. "My son, listen to me! Send a platoon, but don't go with them. It was reported that Elijah called fire from heaven on an entire platoon." He knew the story about the fire of Carmel and for a moment wondered if Elijah could have destroyed a platoon so easily. Jezebel read his eyes. "Promise you will not go."

He hesitated, not knowing what to answer then said, "I'll watch from a distance to see if such a thing is possible."

Jehoram, with two of his captains in two other chariots, followed the platoon south. From the gates of the city they could see smoke rising. As they came near the area where the first platoon disappeared, some of the nearby trees were still burning. The platoon captain, knowing that the king's brother and commander of the army of Israel was watching, made the pretense of being unmoved by what they had heard, and by the nearby trees still ablaze. There was a circular indentation in the ground where the earth itself was scorched.

Jehoram pulled his chariot to a halt near where the first messenger had watched. A few travelers had also stopped there and refused to continue. Others had made a wide circle into the scorched field.

The captain of the platoon rode to the edge of the crater, but his horse refused to go farther. He dismounted and boldly walked alone into the center looking up along the top of the cliff. "Scatter out," he ordered, figuring that if what they suspected were true it couldn't happen a second time if they weren't together, but scattered. On the edge of the circle that was possibly eighty cubits across was a bronze shield, cut in half, one side disintegrated. The edge was lined with metal beads where liquid bronze had solidified as it cooled. No one spoke as the men passed. Each looked around to see the reaction of the others.

The second-in-command followed the captain into the crater. "He's up there. I can feel it."

The captain was noticeably hesitant to confront the prophet, but didn't have a choice. He cleared the lump from his throat and called, "Prophet of Elohim, are you there?"

Elijah was sitting, leaned back against the cool rock under a ledge. Again the captain called, "Are you there?"

Elijah stood and walked to the edge. The arrows of thirty or forty bowmen were trained on him. From that distance he was a very unimpressive figure and the captain became bolder. He spoke with more authority. "Man of Elohim, come down now!"

Elijah looked directly at the captain. It was obvious that this strange prophet had no fear of them.

Without taking his eyes off the captain, Elijah called out, "If I be a prophet of Elohim, let fire come down from heaven and consume you and your platoon."

For one instant they all knew they were doomed. Then there was a blinding light as fire streaked from heaven. If it was one fireball or many no one could tell, but fire exploded with a deafening roar, blowing balls of flames in every direction. This time the three horses ridden by the officers disintegrated with the men.

The flash momentarily blinded Jehoram, his men, and the handful of travelers standing nearby. The earth under them shook so violently that all but one of the men stumbled, staggered and fell to the ground. Two of the three chariot teams broke free from their handlers and ran wildly. As the third driver fought hard to hold his team and was nearly dragged away by the wild horses, fire from the explosion flew across the expanse and hit him in the front. His clothes and flesh burst into flames. He screamed as he fought the fire with one hand and held the horses with the other. Two of the others got to their feet and ran to his aid. He screamed again, delirious with pain, as they fought the blaze with their own garments. They were able to smother the fire, but his flesh was smoldering when they laid him down and poured water over the burns.

The trees and brush near them were burning. Such an intense heat filled the air that it was difficult to breathe. Each breath inhaled was dry and hot and seemed to be without oxygen. Thunder rumbled across the sky.

Jehoram slowly got to his feet, dismayed. Several minutes of unnatural silence ensued as others got to their feet, brushed off the dust and went to see what could be done for their companions. Jehoram could see the outline of Elijah against the blue sky, still standing on the edge of the cliff. As he watched, Elijah slowly lowered his arms and stepped back out of sight.

Jehoram looked around to see the driver of the remaining chariot lying on the ground, burned and trembling violently. With great difficulty he made his way over to the burned driver. The charred chest of the soldier stopped heaving. He was dead, and the platoon was gone.

Grateful for relief, those remaining began to breathe deeply as the air returned. Jehoram said in awe, "I've never seen or heard of anything like this. Elijah's God is more of a god than any I've ever known." He walked to the remaining chariot and stroked one of the horses, trying to settle them down. "I'm going to take this chariot back to Samaria." Pointing to two of the men he said, "Move up onto the hill there and keep a watch on the prophet." And to the remaining two he ordered, "Circle around the hill above him. I want to know exactly where he is when I return." He stepped up into the chariot and took hold of the reins. "Hah!" he shouted at the team as he cracked the whip over their backs.

Jehoram spent most of an hour describing to his brother and mother what he had witnessed. They knew he wasn't one to exaggerate, and he had never been so awed or perplexed by anything. The scene he described frightened Jezebel, and Ahaziah was suffering so that he could hardly concentrate on what he was hearing.

Ahaziah didn't want to hear more. He wanted only relief and interrupted Jehoram. Taking shallow breaths, because to breathe any deeper was too painful, he said in a loud, painful whisper, "Brother, bring Elijah to me. Take the whole army if necessary, but bring him to me."

The task seemed impossible, but it was evident that Ahaziah was dying and Elijah was either his only hope, or would be the cause of his death. Jehoram didn't know which. "How can I fight against a god?" he asked.

Jezebel spoke up, "You have captains under your command who worship Yahweh, don't you? I know that you do. Send one of them."

"Yes!" How brilliant, he thought. "There is a platoon of men here in Samaria, most of them are worshipers of Yahweh. I have allowed them to keep their Sabbath because they have a reputation for being fearless in battle. How could the God of Elijah destroy his own?" He thought for a moment, then stood to his feet. "Yahweh might cast fire on them because they are in the king's service." He paused again for a moment, then said, "We will see what happens. I will get the men ready and dispatch them at first light in the morning. I will follow them and observe."

"No, there is still enough light to bring him here today. Do it now." There was such sharpness in Jezebel's voice that he knew not to challenge her.

"I'll have the men assemble immediately. We'll be back by night fall."

As Jehoram was leaving the room, Jezebel commanded him, "You are to only watch from a distance. Do not go near this destroyer of Israel."

Elijah sat by a small fire and ate dry bread that he had brought, knowing that anyone approaching from below or above would find the terrain difficult and could be heard from a distance.

He sang just above a whisper, stopping every few minutes to listen. "El Shaddai, clothed in light, rides on the chariot of the clouds and walks on the wings of the wind. His messengers are spirits, his ministers are flames of fire. He looks at the earth and it trembles. He touches the hills and they smoke.

"I will sing to Yahweh as long as I live. I will give praise to El Shaddai forever. I rejoice in the goodness of the El of Abraham. At the voice of his thunder, the wicked tremble."

Elijah's voice died into silence as he realized this would be his last confrontation with the family of Ahab. He remembered the night he had spent praying for Israel on his way from Mount Sinai and realized that it was time for Elisha to continue the work. "Elisha is wise and knows the Scriptures, his mind is sharp and he can recall every line far better than I," Elijah thought. Elisha had become the greatest teacher Elijah had ever known, but there was some ingredient he lacked that Elijah couldn't quite define.

Truly Yahweh knew the heart of every man, for there wasn't another man in Israel so at one with the Scriptures as Elisha. Elijah debated within himself the readiness of Elisha, and wondered if this meant it was time for him to lay down his life.

Elijah's thoughts were interrupted by the sound of approaching men and horses. He stood, moved slowly to the edge and looked down to see the platoon standing at attention a hundred cubits up the road. The captain stood directly below him on the charred ground but hadn't seen him yet. Elijah stepped back out of sight.

"Prophet of El Shaddai, are you there?" the captain called, using a name used most often by those who revered the God of Abraham. His voice wasn't demanding. Elijah stepped into full sight. The captain dropped to his knees when he saw him. "Man of Elohim, please find some value in my life and the life of these fifty servants of yours. Fire from Yahweh burned up two fifty-man platoons. Let my life have some small value in your eyes."

Elijah wasn't able to call upon El Shaddai to send fire on a man who had humbled himself and was pleading for his life and the lives of the men under his command. "Go with him. Go with him, no harm will come to you." The word came to Elijah as he stood there.

Elijah stepped back from the ledge. There was a terrible silence as the captain waited. His heart pounded so loud that he could hear it. Elijah slid on the loose stone, stopped and slid again, choosing his steps carefully until he came into sight. As he got closer his eyes met the eyes of the captain. The captain bowed his head to greet him then stood. He walked to meet Elijah, dropped to his knees, and bowed to the ground.

"My Lord Elijah, my life is yours. Go to King Ahaziah with me and ride in my chariot."

Elijah reached down and pulled the captain to his feet. "I am only a man. It is a sacrilege to bow to me. There is only one God, Yahweh. I will return with you to your king."

Elijah rode in the captain's chariot with the driver while the captain led the way on horseback, leaving the platoon behind as a show of trust.

Jehoram, who had watched Elijah's amazing surrender, drove his chariot hard back to Samaria to advise Ahaziah not to harm the prophet. He had witnessed a power that he never knew existed, and thought that perhaps Elijah would use any excuse to call fire down on the entire city of Samaria.

Jezebel was waiting for Elijah in the courtyard. If he didn't remove the curse from the house of Ahab, she intended to have him burned alive.

As the chariot rolled through the gate, Elijah looked around at the ivory palace he had never been able to see before. He didn't see Jezebel until her voice called to him from behind. He stepped from the chariot and turned in her direction.

"You wicked man, you who brought so much trouble to Israel! You will remove the curse of your God from King Ahaziah and the house of Ahab or you will wish you had!" She boldly threatened him as she approached, but when their eyes met her heart melted with fear. She began to back away, unable at first to unlock her gaze from his. The distance between them widened, then she turned and ran.

The captain walked up and stood next to Elijah for a moment, until Jezebel disappeared inside the palace. "I've never heard of her backing down from anyone," he said. Before this day, he would have been amazed by this unexpected action. But after the events of this day, he understood.

Escorted by two guards and the captain, Elijah was quickly ushered into the king's bedchamber. Jehoram stood by the King.

Ahaziah, barely able to speak, asked, "Prophet, can you make me whole again?"

"Yahweh could have restored you, but you turned instead to the god of the Philistines, Baal-Zebub, a demon, and I alone can do nothing to help you."

Ahaziah's voice rose in anger as he strained to say, "You put this curse on the house of my father! You will remove it!"

"You're wrong. I only declared what Yahweh had already done. There is only one God and he is a jealous God. It is he who has put this curse upon you and your house. I am a mere man, like you."

Calmly and in great pain, the king asked, "Am I going to die?"

"You will never leave this bed." Elijah paused, then added, "Yes, you will die."

"Get out!" Ahaziah's voice cracked, then he broke into a painful cough as the guards nudged Elijah respectfully towards the door.

For several minutes the king coughed. After Elijah left, Jezebel entered the room again and took Ahaziah's hand. He was pale and beads of sweat ran from his forehead. "Mother, help me," he pleaded in a whisper. "Please help me." He repeated his request, then began to cough again. When the coughing stopped, he could hardly breathe. "Please help me. Stop Elijah, bring him back, tell him I'll give him a hundred talents of gold if he will help me."

He gasped for air, wheezing as he inhaled. With great pain his body arched, struggling for one more breath. He squeezed Jezebel's hand so tightly that it brought tears to her eyes. "Mother, help me," he breathed out. His body began to tremble as he struggled for one more breath but his lungs couldn't pull in even the smallest breath. He shook for a half a minute, then became still with his fingers locked around Jezebel's hand.

"No, Ahaziah!" she cried out loud. "No, Ahaziah, my son!" She stood there and wept for more than an hour. No one had ever seen Jezebel weep before.

The mid-morning sun beat down on Elijah and Elisha as they walked along without saying anything, each deep in his own thoughts. Elijah pondered the events of the last few weeks. It is almost over, he thought. With Ahaziah's death, the prophecies of Yahweh concerning Ahab's family were being fulfilled, and now he could sense that his time on earth was coming to a close. The last of the family of Ahab would soon be gone. Jezebel's death had already been pronounced by Yahweh and her power was limited now, since Jehoram was king and much of Israel had renounced Baal. She would be judged and Yahweh would end the dynasty of Omri by making Jehu king. The winds of political change were blowing across the land of the Hebrews.

The tinkling of harness bells brought Elijah's attention back to the dusty road that was leading him and Elisha from Jericho toward the river Jordan. The bells grew louder as two camels and riders lumbered toward them in the opposite direction. The tinkling sound that Elijah would have hardly noticed any other time seemed like music as they passed on the road. The sights and sounds surrounding them seemed especially vivid this day.

They passed a woman with a load of sticks on her back and two young children at her heels, a boy and a girl, each with a few twigs in their little arms, believing they were assisting their mother.

Elijah's eyes and heart welled up. He prayed a silent prayer, "Oh Yahweh, thank you for giving such a wonderful land to your people." They passed an old man leading a donkey laden with possessions and Elijah wondered why he hadn't noticed all these marvelous things in life every day. A half step ahead of him, he watched his companion for a minute. He listened to the shifting of sand and earth beneath the soles of their sandals as they walked.

Back in Jezreel, Jezebel closed her eyes and turned her face to meet the breath of the breeze that blew across the mount. It reminded her of the constant wind that blew in from the great sea in Zidon, where she grew up, carrying the sweet smell of saltwater with it. She sat under an arbor overlooking the Jezreel valley where Naboth's vineyard once grew. Below her on the mount was now an outer defensive wall manned by watchmen. Two of her personal guards were on the palace wall behind her.

The leaves of the young arbor vines fluttered like birds on the wing, creating a soothing, rustling sound. She often resorted here with several of her handmaids to reflect and enjoy the view, but this day she had wanted to be alone as she thought out the preparations for the sacrifice and feast of the full moon. As easy as it should have been to concentrate, thoughts of Elijah kept coming to mind. At first she pushed them aside, but the image of Elijah began imposing itself over all her other thoughts. The strength of his visage grew until she became aware that something of great magnitude was taking place in the ethereal realm, and it had to do with that prophet of Yahweh who had caused her so much trouble.

Jezebel stood to her feet. Suddenly she saw a vision of Tamara on the altar, exactly the way she was the night she was sacrificed. She could see again the look on Tamara's face, the look that had terrified her that night. Jezebel heard the words again, as though she were hearing them for the first time. "He is no ordinary man. The earth would open up and swallow the person who would harm him." Tamara's face had shown a look of horror as she continued, "I am afraid, for his God is God!" Once again, Tamara's eyes pierced Jezebel's soul, as she leveled her gaze at the queen and calmly pronounced, "Jezebel, queen of the devils, the generation of your children will be cut off and this great temple of Baal will be made level with the ground."

Jezebel began to plead to Baal, "Lord Baal, please deliver me, your servant and Queen, from the words of the prophets of Yahweh. Exalt me above them." She felt no safety or comfort from her prayer and collapsed back onto the stone bench in the arbor. This feeling was different, far greater than the confrontations with Elijah that she had experienced in the past. She sensed an overpowering presence gathering in the spirit world, one that was set to overwhelm her like a giant desert sandstorm. She knew that she had to prevail with the gods, but the most powerful people she had known were gone, Tamara and Zohelethbal. There wasn't anyone she could turn to for help.

Back on the dusty road, Elijah broke the silence as he said to Elisha, "You are persistent." Elisha turned to look at his mentor but didn't answer. After another couple of minutes Elijah asked, "Why didn't you stay in Jericho?"

"As Yahweh lives and as you live, for as long as you are here, I will not leave you," Elisha answered, then added, "You know they are following us, don't you? They've come from all over to see what will happen today."

Elijah glanced back over his shoulder, but didn't see anyone but a few travelers. As he looked further back up toward the crest of the ridge that overlooked the Jordan River valley, he saw a group of perhaps fifty men walking along, keeping a respectful distance behind him and Elisha. "Yes, I know. They don't really understand the ways of Yahweh. You must teach them."

"They listen to you but they won't listen to me," said Elisha.

"They will after today." Elijah was confident of that. "This afternoon you will be the judge of Israel."

Elisha had hesitated to ask this question before, but he knew the time was growing short. "Isn't there any hope for Jehoram? He did remove the pillar of Baal from Samaria."

"Did he outlaw the worship of Baal Melkart or destroy the temple? Yahweh is finished with the family of Ahab. They're a weak and lawless people. The time to anoint Jehu king will be revealed to you, but never tell a soul what you know until he's on the throne. Then stand behind him."

In the weeks since the death of King Ahaziah, Elijah had been more withdrawn than ever, leaving most of the ministry to Elisha, but in the past few days there had been a transformation in him. Elisha saw a marked difference in Elijah when they came down to Gilgal to encourage the prophets there.

It was at Gilgal that the prophets first revealed to Elisha what Yahweh had shown them concerning Elijah, and what was about to happen. At first it seemed impossible, but as Elisha dwelt on what they said, he began to feel it in his spirit. Elijah's work here was finished, and Yahweh was going to take him.

They had been at Gilgal only a short time when Elijah wanted to press on to Bethel. It was there that Elijah donned the beautiful robe that Delah had made for him, and had his hair and beard cut shorter than Elisha had ever seen it.

From Bethel they had traveled on to Jericho, where they had spent the previous night. In each city Elijah had asked Elisha to remain, but the pupil had refused to leave his teacher.

Elisha hardly recognized the prophet as he turned to look at him, knowing that they were nearing the end of their journey on earth together. He looked years younger with his hair and beard cut so short. Wearing a nearly white robe, with the blue cloak Delah had made draped over his shoulder, instead of the camel skins and wide belt that people associated with the prophet, Elijah looked very civilized.

Elisha smiled to himself. Elijah had removed the uniform that he had worn for so many years. He was a soldier about to lay down his weapons and return home.

They came to the banks of the swollen Jordan River. To the right of the road a camel caravan was encamped, waiting for the rain swollen river to go down. Hobbled camels grazed along the riverbank, and several men sat in the shade of the tall trees near the river, watching the two prophets walk to the edge of the water.

Elijah ambled up and down the bank of the churning river without apparent purpose for a few minutes, with Elisha following. He stooped down, gathered up a handful of small stones, and thoughtfully tossed them into the muddy waters of the Jordan, one at a time. "How different," he thought, remembering when he had almost drowned in this river many years ago. "How little I understood the ways of Yahweh then." Elijah pondered the changes in his life since that day. "How sweet life can be when Yahweh is in it," he said aloud. Then he stood and walked decisively back to where the road and river met.

Elisha spotted the prophets who had been following them. "The sons of the prophets from Bethel and Jericho have decided to show themselves," he said. Elijah looked back towards Jericho and saw a large group of men walking in their direction.

"The lesson that they learn today will mean more than a lifetime of study. Maybe today they will be encouraged to strive with all their being."

Elijah turned and placed his hand on Elisha's shoulder. "Today, you become their shepherd, with all the responsibility that goes with it. Many men have made themselves shepherds that Yahweh didn't call. They don't have the heart of a shepherd, but I have never known a man with more of a shepherd's heart than you. But, you are too lenient. Remember that you're also the judge of Israel. They will kill you unless they fear the wrath of Yahweh." Elijah looked into the eyes of Elisha for a long moment to drive the point home, then said, "Stay right here, don't move."

He walked back to the water's edge and stood there in silence for several moments. The young prophets that had followed them from Jericho were approaching when Elijah took the cloak from his shoulder, folded it together and slapped the surface of the Jordan. There was a rumbling sound like distant thunder. The men who had been watching from the camp beside the river stood to get a better look. The water above the point where he struck the river began to rise higher onto the bank. It took a minute before it was clear to those watching what was happening.

The group of young prophets had reached the river, and were standing a short distance behind Elijah. Some came down to the water's edge as the river began to back up. Elisha moved down next to Elijah and watched in amazement as the water flowed downstream leaving the gravel streambed exposed. Upstream, the water continued to rise, backing up as if behind an unseen dam.

Elisha took several steps out, then turned to get approval from Elijah, who then walked in behind him. On the far side, the two climbed up out of the streambed and stood there looking back. The standing water then surged violently downstream, churning as it passed over the footprints the two prophets had made only moments before.

Elisha waved to the prophets on the opposite bank, most of whom he knew and had taught, then turned to catch up with Elijah, who had already started across the plain leading to the hills.

By the time Elijah and Elisha had crossed the Jordan River, Jezebel had retreated into the palace throne room and was awaiting the arrival of the high priest she had summoned. If she could only know what was happening with Elijah she might know how to combat the power of the prophet and his God. The only thing she could discern for sure was that he was becoming even more powerful than he was when he called fire down upon the soldiers of Israel.

As the two prophets continued on, Elisha began to feel that their time together was now very short and, not knowing how Yahweh was going to take his master, he asked, "What is going to happen?"

"I don't know, but I trust Yahweh. He brought the seed of Abraham out of Egypt to this land, and he has allowed me to see into the future. This isn't the end, but more like the beginning. The ministry that Yahweh has given me will go on with even greater power."

"Wait!" Elisha said, as he came to a halt. He stood very still for a minute, as Elijah waited to know what he was listening for. "Since we crossed the Jordan, I keep hearing the sound of horses hooves. When I stop to listen I can't hear them. Have you heard anything?"

Elijah paused to listen. "I don't hear anything, but what can I do for you before I am taken away?" he asked.

Elisha dropped his gaze to the ground as he thought. "Please," he hesitated for a moment. "Let me inherit a double portion of your spirit."

Elijah waited a long moment before answering. "You have asked a difficult thing." He paused again and looked away, then back at Elisha. "If it is possible, when I am taken from you, if you see me, then know that what you have asked is yours. If you don't see me, then it wasn't possible." Elijah looked away again, as though someone called his name.

He turned in that direction and began to walk. At that moment Elisha heard an almost indiscernible sound, like the roar of some distant animal or the howl of the wind. He stopped. "Did you hear that?" he asked, but Elijah kept walking without answering.

Something in the distance caught Elisha's attention. Through the waves of heat that shimmered like distant pools of water above the brown earth, he could see what appeared to be a four-horse chariot, driving hard towards them. For an instant it was clearly visible, then it faded into the waves of heat, making him uncertain of what he saw.

It appeared a second time, but much closer. The horses, and chariot and driver, were hard to distinguish from the waves of watery light, except the color was that of blue hot flames. He closed his eyes, then opened them again, thinking it was a mirage, but he could hear the sound of the thundering hooves clearly now.

In only a few moments it had traveled a vast distance and was nearly upon him. The fiery chariot and the horses were real but not of this worldly plane, and they raced directly toward Elisha. Elisha yelled, "Elijah!" as he took several steps backward, then dove to the ground in the face of the fiery apparition. At the last moment, the chariot veered to Elisha's side, throwing dirt onto him as the wheels skidded sideways. He lay there a moment, watching as it roared away, then turned in the direction Elijah had continued without looking back.

Elijah was now standing about fifty yards away. His arms and hands were stretched heavenward as dust began swirling all around him. Coming from the sky was a whirlwind that seemed to be luminous at the center. It slowly dropped down and engulfed the prophet, stirring the dust into a blinding cloud. Elisha covered his face from the stinging sand. Squinting as the dust and sand peppered his skin, he pulled the cloak around his face and peered over the edge at Elijah and the whirlwind. Then for a long minute he couldn't see anything. As the dust began to clear, he could see the whirlwind withdrawing upward.

"My father! My father! The chariots and horsemen of Israel," he called. He got to his feet before the cloud had settled, and stumbled in the direction where he had last seen Elijah. Lying on the ground was the blue mantle that Delah had made for Elijah years before.

Elisha looked up through the dust to the blue sky above. Elijah was gone. "Aaaah!" he cried out, as he grasped the hem of his robe and tore it from the bottom to the top. Elijah was gone.

Tears filled his eyes as he dropped to his knees. Picking up the mantle he buried his face in it and wept.

As Jezebel impatiently awaited the arrival of the high priest the most ominous feeling she had ever known gripped her. She was terrified as she tried in vain to raise the power of Baal to combat this enemy. "O Baal, giver of light and ruler of the darkness, hear now your servant and appear in your power and glory to defend your realm and defeat this wicked God." Jezebel dropped to her knees as she chanted her prayer.

Over and over she chanted. She began to feel that she was winning, and that a sign from Baal had appeared as a glowing orange pillar of light, extending from the floor to the high ceiling. Her court fell to their knees. Jezebel was sure that she had conjured up the power she had been seeking, then she felt herself weakening, as the trembling that had always accompanied the presence of Elijah began to grow from her insides and move outward to her hands and feet. The orange light began to grow, then rapidly flashed into a blinding pillar of white light, engulfing everything in the palace. At that moment Elijah was being engulfed with the whirlwind and into a greater presence of El Shaddai than he had ever known.

As Jezebel trembled from within, the palace itself began to shake and pieces of the ceiling fell. The blinding light flashed from the windows like lightning gone mad. Those who tried to stand and flee were thrown back to the floor. Then, as quickly as it had begun, it was over, and an eerie silence filled the palace. The thick dust suspended in the air, lit by the shafts of afternoon sunlight, created a surreal look inside the palace. Slowly, dazed servants got to their feet.

Jezebel lay gasping for breath, partly under the overturned couch she had been lying upon. Her hair was white on one side with plaster dust, and small drops of blood fell from her arm, where a piece of the ceiling had fallen upon her. The blood in the small crescent shaped cut was stark against her white skin. She reached out and clutched one of the terrified servants near her, and whispered between clenched teeth, "Find Eber! Tell him to come now!"

After Elijah disappeared from sight, half an hour passed before Elisha stood and began the trip back. He reached the river and stopped there a minute. The prophets on the other side were standing in awe, wondering what the student of Elijah might do now.

His vision still blurred with tears, he took the blue mantle, folded it the way Elijah had and struck the river. "Where is the El of Elijah?" he shouted. His voice echoed, and the water began to part in the same manner it had when Elijah struck the river. He crossed the Jordan River on solid ground and the young prophets whispered among themselves, "The spirit of Elijah is on him."

Two weeks later, a still shaken Jezebel was sitting under her arbor, pondering the rumors about Elijah that were being spread by his followers. Her thoughts were interrupted by the sound of footsteps as a handmaid approached.

"Your Highness," the handmaid addressed the queen as she bowed. "Benbaal, the high priest of Ashtoreth at Jericho has arrived with a message for the Queen."

"Bring him to me, but not alone. Bring the two guards at the gate with you." Jezebel had made many enemies and was on constant guard now against being assassinated.

Several minutes later the priest, two guards and the handmaid reappeared at the arbor. Benbaal bowed to the ground. "Great Queen and Priestess of the gods, live forever."

More relaxed, now that she saw he wasn't a threat, she answered, "You may rise." As he stood, she asked, "You have a message for me?"

At first, she was incensed by the fact that he would presume to appear before her in robes dusty from the journey, but then he pleaded, "Forgive me for not having washed before coming into your presence, but I felt the urgency of the message more important." He waited for a response.

Jezebel nodded for him to continue.

"You may already know that Elijah, the prophet of Yahweh, was taken into heaven in a whirlwind, and that it was witnessed by many of Yahweh's prophets at Jericho and many others who were waiting to cross the Jordan River there."

Jezebel sat up straight, waiting for him to go on.

The priest continued, "The Jordan opened up! The water parted for Elijah and his apprentice to cross over to the east side. They walked across the river on dry ground!"

The queen interrupted, "He was taken up in a whirlwind? You're sure of this information?"

"Yes, your Highness. I have talked to men who saw this for themselves, but that may not be the worst of it," the priest went on somberly. "His apprentice, a man named Elisha is said to have been given a double portion of Elijah's spiritual power, both his and Elijah's I suppose. Either way, it is not good. The people are starting to give him credit for great miracles. Many at Jericho believe that it was he and his God Yahweh that cured the waters at Jericho. As you know, they were poisioned since the drought, but now they are as sweet as the spring rain."

The priest's countenance took on a look of despair, as he recounted these things to Jezebel. "The people in Jericho no longer come to worship Baal. They say that Yahweh took Elijah up to defeat Baal, and now Elisha is come to defeat us," said the priest despondently.

"The people are fools!" Jezebel burst out. "They know nothing of the kingdom of the gods. Baal is the greatest of all gods." But she couldn't muster her old enthusiasm when she said these things. She knew that something had gone terribly wrong, but she tried not to show it to her follower. "What of this Elisha? What has he done that anyone has actually seen?" she asked.

Benbaal took a deep breath, "My Queen, he also parted the Jordan when he came back alone from where Elijah was taken up. He took Elijah's magic coat and parted the Jordan again." He looked pleadingly at Jezebel. "You understand that this is the rainy season. No one had crossed the Jordan for a week before Elijah and Elisha!"

"Sorcerer's tricks," retorted Jezebel lamely. "I have seen the Egyptian magicians do such things many times." Jezebel was visibly shaken by these reports, but she now felt she must defend Baal at all costs. She could not let this priest think that she had no answers.

"Your Highness, I too thought this man was only a man, until three days ago. This Elisha is as lacking in hair as his master, Elijah was hairy. He is bald as a pomegranate.

"Elisha was on his way from Jericho, going to Bethel I think, when he was surrounded by a group of rowdy young men. Lawless young brigands mostly. There were sixty or so of them, and they made sport of him, calling him Old Baldhead, and telling him to go up like Elijah, if he was such a man.

"He ignored them at first, then a rock-hard dirt clod struck him on the side of the face and knocked him to the ground, nearly unconscious, I understand.

"The boys taunted him some more, hitting him with sticks and calling him more names. He pleaded with them to leave him alone, but they wouldn't. You know how foolish young men can be.

"Finally, when they would not leave him alone, he stood and stared at them, then lifted his hands to the sky, and called upon Yahweh to judge these young men according to their hearts."

"And what did the great Yahweh do?" asked Jezebel sarcastically.

The priest paused for a moment, afraid now that this had not been a good idea, coming to see Jezebel. He went on, "It got very quiet. The boys were looking at each other, not making sport of him anymore. Then from the woods came a great crashing of limbs and underbrush. The boys looked in that direction and backed away from Elisha.

"Suddenly two bears broke into view through the brush and came charging at them. With one swipe of a claw, the bear almost cut the head off one boy. Blood went everywhere. The bears attacked one after another, chasing the boys down then pouncing on them. Once a bear caught one it only took a second to snuff out his life with a slap of a paw or a crushing bite. The bears brought down and killed forty-two of the sixty-four young men who had taunted Elisha.

"No one mocks the prophet now, and his fame is growing faster than his deeds. The people believe that miracles follow wherever he goes. His fame is even spreading beyond the borders of Israel. Judah, Moab and Syria are already hearing the name Elisha.

"If we don't do something, all Israel will be following Elisha and his God," Benbaal concluded. He had come looking for answers from the High Priestess, but now he was beginning to see through her facade. He realized that Jezebel had no more answers than he, just the same old empty rethoric.

Jezebel's second son, Jehoram, was crowned king of Israel after
the death of his brother, Ahaziah. Jehoram's nephew, who was
also named Ahaziah after his uncle, was now King of Judah. He was
the son of Athaliah, Jezebel's daughter.

In the twelfth year of the reign of King Jehoram of Israel, he took
his nephew, King Ahaziah of Judah, with him and went to battle Syria.
Jehoram's purpose was to retake the city of Ramoth-Gilead, the city
that his father, King Ahab, had died trying to capture.

In the years since Ahab fought Ben-Hadad, the Syrian king had fallen
ill. While on his sick bed, he was murdered by his servant, Hazael, who
took the throne.

In a siege that lasted only a week, Jehoram took Ramoth-Gilead.
Hazael organized a counterattack from Damascus that was repelled by
Israel for twenty-three days, when Hazael retreated with heavy losses.
Jehoram, in the last days of the battle, was knocked from the wall of the
city by a stone hurled from a catapult. He broke several ribs in the fall, and
was in bed for six days before he felt well enough to travel to Jezreel to
finish recuperating. He left Captain Jehu in charge of the defenses of
Ramoth-Gilead.

Elisha had waited eleven years for this day. This morning, in the
darkness before dawn, the word of Yahweh came to him. "Send one of the
young prophets to anoint Captain Jehu to be king over my people Israel."
Here in Dothan, Elisha had found some of the most promising students,
and had moved to the city to teach them. Elnathan was the brightest of
the students in the school of the prophets, and the one Elisha would send.

Elisha sent for him immediately, and shortly after daybreak
he was knocking on Elisha's door. Elisha opened the door.
"Elnathan, come in."

"Master, you have sent for me very early. Is anything wrong?"

"I sent for you because I know your dedication to Yahweh, and I know that you will follow instructions to the last detail. Your life will depend on that, if you are willing to go."

"I am willing to die for the glory of Yahweh. What would you have me do?"

Elisha stepped over to a table and returned with a flask of oil. "Go to Ramoth-Gilead. Find Captain Jehu, the grandson of Nimshi. Take him into a room alone. No one else can be there." Elisha looked at the young prophet for a long moment to make sure that he understood the seriousness of the task he was about to entrust to him. "Take this flask of oil and pour it on his head and say, 'Thus says Yahweh, I have anointed you king over Israel.' Then flee as quickly as you can."

Elisha looked him sternly in the face. "You must not remain there."

Elnathan was awed by the weight of the first charge given him by his master, but he took the mission as a great honor from Yahweh and hurried away to prepare for the journey. He left within the hour, half-running as he started toward Ramoth-Gilead.

Two days later, the young prophet found Captain Jehu just inside the gates of Ramoth Gilead, sitting with the commanders of the army. "Captain Jehu, grandson of Nimshi?"

"I'm Captain Jehu."

"I have a message for you."

"Well, speak up."

"I can only give it to you in private."

Jehu sized him up. The young man without a weapon could hardly be a threat. "Come inside."

Elnathan followed Jehu through a nearby door. He looked around, making sure they were alone. He found a chair and moved it into the middle of the room. "Elisha sent me, Captain, please sit down," he said, as he pulled the flask from his robe.

Jehu gave him a long look, then extended his hand to receive the flask.

Realizing Jehu's concern, Elnathan said, "It's only oil," as he handed it to the captain.

Jehu sniffed the contents, then handed the flask back. "Please be seated, Captain Jehu."

Jehu slowly sat down, and Elnathan began to pour the oil over his head. It was a symbol of honor bestowed upon kings and priests, and sometimes the wealthy. Jehu wondered what this poorly dressed young man could have to do with a ritual reserved for the wealthy and powerful.

"Thus says Yahweh Elohim of Israel: I have anointed you king over the people of Yahweh, over Israel." The words sent an electrifying chill through the young prophet as he spoke them. Then he felt an urge to continue as the Spirit of Yahweh came over him. "You will strike down the house of Ahab. I will avenge the blood of my prophets and all the blood of my servants at the hand of Jezebel. The house of Ahab will perish from the earth. I will cut off from Ahab every male, both bond and free, and will make the house of Ahab like the house of Jeroboam, the son of Nebat, and the house of Baasha, the son of Ahijah.

"The dogs shall eat the flesh of Jezebel by the palace in Jezreel. She shall not find rest in a grave." The young prophet stood silent for a moment, then bolted for the door and past Jehu's comrades outside. They turned to look at the house to see if Jehu would emerge. A moment later, he stepped through the door looking perplexed. Oil dripped from his head and beard.

"Is everything all right?" one of the men called to him as he walked toward them. "What business did a mad man have with you?"

"Did any of you know who he was?" Jehu asked.

"He looked like one of the young prophets." Expecting that the message had been negative, and wanting to reassure Jehu, the officer added, "Whatever he said isn't true. What did he have to say?"

Jehu paused for a moment before he spoke, "He said that Yahweh has anointed me to be king over Israel."

The six men sitting there looked at one another. One spoke up, "I can believe that Yahweh would choose you to be king." The man looked at the other officers sitting there and said, "Who is better qualified to rule Israel than Captain Jehu?"

Each of the men after having served under the captain was glad to have Jehu rule over them as king and bowed before him, one at a time and pledged their lives. "My sword is at your service, my king, and I will follow your command even to the death."

The commanders quickly assembled their soldiers. The trumpets sounded and the army of Israel shouted, "Jehu is King!" From the wall of the city, Jehu motioned for them to be silent. When the roar had grown quiet, Jehu shouted, "If your heart is with me, seal this city that no man escape to tell Jehoram. Prepare to march within the hour. We will take Jezreel. We will fulfill the prophecy of Elijah. We will serve Yahweh, the God of Elijah and the God of Abraham!"

The troops began to shout again, "Jehu is king!"

The horses and camels were quickly harnessed, and the chariots hitched. Jehu had as many of the footmen ride in carts as there was room for, so they could conserve strength for fighting. They crossed the Jordan and camped that evening. They broke camp early the next day, and by mid-morning, were in sight of the palace at Jezreel.

"Troops approaching!" rang through the palace courtyard. A tower lookout spotted Jehu's men while they were still a great distance away in the Jezreel valley.

Within minutes Jehoram had been notified. He dispatched a rider to find out who they were and what were their intentions.

The rider slowed from a gallop as he drew near Jehu's chariot. Jehu came to a halt and the rider began speaking, "King Jehoram wants to know, do you come in peace?"

"What do you have to do with peace? Fall in behind me." The rider knew he didn't have a chance to retreat without being killed, so he fell in behind Jehu.

When the watchmen told Jehoram that the rider had joined the ranks of the advancing army, the king sent a second rider. When the second rider wasn't far away, Jehu halted and waited for him. The rider smiled when he saw that it was Jehu. "King Jehoram wants to know, do you come in peace?"

"What do you have to do with peace? Fall in behind me."

Jehu was afraid that he'd been recognized and didn't want the kings to have time to prepare. He motioned for the chariots and men to follow him, then whipped his team of horses into a hard gallop.

Suspecting it was Captain Jehu, Jehoram and King Ahaziah rode out from Jezreel with all the troops at their command. Two hundred chariots, four hundred horsemen, a hundred camels and riders, and four hundred footmen. They could offer little resistance to the thousands that followed Jehu, though Jehu's chariots and horsemen were half an hour in front of the rest.

Jehu came to a halt and had his men form a line. They were about equally matched, but for every moment he could stall them, the odds grew in his favor.

Jehoram and Ahaziah had their men form a line opposite that of Jehu's, then Jehoram, driving his own chariot, rode out alone to within a hundred and fifty cubits of the captain.

Jehoram called out, "I thought it was you, Jehu. They said the man leading this army drove his chariot like a mad man. What does all this mean? Have you come in peace, Jehu?"

Jehu answered, "How can there be peace in Israel when the idolatry and sorcery and witchcraft of your mother abound?"

Jehoram had never known anything but the utmost respect from Jehu. From the statement Jehu made, he knew he meant to fight. Jehoram turned his chariot and began to run for the safety of his line. Jehu handed the reins to his driver, Bidkar, indicating that he follow Jehoram, as he took his bow and stretched it the full length.

"Ahaziah!..... Treachery!" Jehoram got part of the second warning out, "Treach... ," when Jehu's arrow hit him in the back and came out through his heart in the front. With the reins wrapped tightly in his grip, he fell to the floor of the chariot. The team slowed from the pressure of the bits in their mouths and made a half circle before coming to a stop.

When his troops saw that Jehoram was dead, they fled and Ahaziah turned his chariot and ran.

Jehu pulled to a stop next to Jehoram's chariot, but motioned for his men to follow Ahaziah. He turned to Bidkar. "Take his chariot and dump his body on the field that belonged to Naboth, the Jezreelite. Remember when we rode with his father Ahab, and the prophecy of Elijah."

Jehu looked away for a moment as though he was picturing the event in his mind. "I will never forget those words. 'I, Yahweh, have seen the blood of Naboth and the blood of his sons. In the vineyard of Naboth I will require his blood at the hand of your sons.' Dump his body there that the word of Yahweh be fulfilled."

Bidkar got into Jehoram's chariot and Jehu continued on after Ahaziah. It took a minute for Bidkar to pry the reins from Jehoram's frozen grip, then he turned to carry out Jehu's command.

Judah's King Ahaziah, with about fifty chariots defending his retreat, fled toward Beth Haggan. Jehu had over a hundred chariots in pursuit, but was unable to overtake them. One of Jehu's captains saw where Ahaziah was heading, and took ten of the chariots on a short cut through the rough fields toward a distant ridge. If they could make it over the ridge before he could get around they would be able to intercept him.

Jehu's men pushed their lathered horses over the ridge and raced down the far side, as the Judean chariots came barreling through the valley. Like a wedge, Jehu's men drove into the thundering chariots behind Judah's king. Chariots on both sides toppled as wheel collided against wheel. Archers fired at close range as they downed each other, and swords clashed as the chariots rode abreast. In a number of chariots, both drivers and spearmen were killed, leaving the teams dragging broken chariots wildly down the valley.

One of Jehu's chariots got alongside of King Ahaziah, and, as the two chariots thundered over the ground, the archer was able to get off several arrows at close range. Two found their mark, one in the hip and the other in the king's side under his arm. He was close enough to use a javelin, but as he pulled the javelin from its sheath, the driver was hit in the back with an arrow and slumped forward, falling over the tongue of the chariot then onto the ground under the left wheel. The archer took the reins and pulled the chariot out of the battle. Fleeing toward the safety of Megiddo, he was quickly overtaken by the men of Judah and killed.

All of the men in the ten chariots of Israel died, and Ahaziah's men turned to make a stand. They drove into Jehu's advancing chariots. Chariots collided into chariots. Horses were shot down to stop chariots, and the men thrown to the ground took swords or axes, javelin or bow, and continued the fight on the ground. Men yelled out war cries as they knowingly charged to their death. The men of Judah held off Jehu and his men long enough for Ahaziah to escape.

Jehu later received word that Ahaziah had reached Megiddo and died there from his wounds.

The following morning Jehu and his men, tired and hungry, rode toward Jezreel. There was no resistance from Jezebel's guard, or the troops there. They surrendered without a fight and he quickly secured the city, then rode to find Jezebel.

She knew that he would soon be coming through the palace gates and called her handmaids and eunuchs to assist in preparing her to receive Captain Jehu. She had Eber mix oil, freshly scented with myrrh and labdanum, to rub into her hair as the eunuchs painted her face. She had the cooks prepare the finest meal the palace had to offer, lamb and pheasant with date and raisin cakes. When she was ready she sat by an upper window, in a tower overlooking the front gate, where she could see anyone who entered the palace. She had the gate opened as a sign of submission and welcome to Captain Jehu. A eunuch stood by with a large fan stirring the air to cool her as she pensively waited.

Jezebel knew that life or death for her might be determined by the impression she made on Jehu, and her best chance for survival would be if she could attract and seduce him.

"Jehu approaches!" a watchman called. The message was echoed twice more throughout the palace. Jezebel stood to her feet to watch him ride through the gate. As he passed under the arch, his eyes were drawn up to the window where she stood thirty cubits above the ground. Their eyes met for a moment, then she called down to him, "Have you come in peace, Jehu? Remember Zimri who murdered his master and found no peace."

Everyone in Israel remembered, or had heard, what happened to Zimri. He knew that what she had said was a veiled threat. Jehu could see, through the window beyond Jezebel, that others were in the room with her, and he called, "Who up there is on my side?" Eber and another eunuch looked out from a window on the side of the tower.

"Get away from that window!" Jezebel turned and scolded when Jehu's glance gave them away. Intimidated by her, they started to back away when they heard Jehu again.

"If you are on my side, throw her down." Still very afraid of Jezebel, they stepped away from the window, as her angry stare backed them down.

Jehu called again, "I said, if you are on my side, throw the sorceress out of the window."

More than willing to avenge themselves of her tyranny, tantrums and intimidating threats, two young men recently made eunuchs by Jezebel took hold of the queen and picked her up as she fought back.

"I have treated you like family, and not like slaves!" she shouted. "Take your hands off of me! I'm the queen! Eber, control these fools! I swear by the gods, I'll have you burned on the altar!" screamed Jezebel, as they forced her up into the window, then threw her kicking and screaming down onto the cobblestones three stories below. "Lord Baal!" she screamed, as she plunged to earth.

Only partially conscious, Jezebel's mind raced, trying to make sense of what her body was feeling. She attempted to get up and found herself unable to move her legs or her body. One arm was completely limp and without feeling. She tried to move her mangled, stinging fingers, but could only feel the warm, sticky blood flowing across her hand onto the stones. As her eyes focused, she saw chariot wheels and the legs of rearing horses pawing up and down next to her, then the face of Jehu came into focus. She stretched her other arm toward him in a pleading manner.

Jehu urged his team forward to trample Jezebel, but as horses do, the animals refused to step on her until he took his whip to them. Still trying to avoid trampling Jezebel, the horses pushed back and forth, forcing one another to step on her in spite of themselves. Several times Jehu forced the sharp hooves of the chariot team over Jezebel's broken body, trampling her against the cobblestone street.

Suddenly, Jehu shivered as a cold chill went up his back and he was seized with a powerful sense of foreboding. The horses reared and kicked at their harness, trying to get away from some unseen danger. He pulled them back and looked around as though someone was watching him.

As Jezebel's body lay there, one of her legs twitched and her head jerked back and forth against the ground. Many times in battle he had seen the wounded, or the already dead, twitch like that. As he watched her die, he sensed a presence, something he had never known before, something evil. He knew the horses were sensing it too.

Jehu couldn't see what was taking place in the spirit world, as Jezebel suddenly found herself standing by her body. At first she didn't understand that she had died and that she was in her spirit body, invisible to Jehu. She walked in his direction. The next instant a tall young soldier in a blue tunic with a gold breastplate and a drawn sword appeared in her path. She instinctively paused and the soldier, an angel of Yahweh, nodded for her to look back. She looked, and, seeing her own body, realized that she had entered the plane where she believed the gods to dwell.

Movement near her body caught Jezebel's attention. Next to her body, the dirt was being stirred from beneath, falling inward like the sand in an hourglass, or the sand above the burrowing of a sand beetle. Unreasoning terror gripped Jezebel as she watched the circle become larger and larger.

Jehu's horses acted as though they were going mad, and he strained to hold them in place as they fought against their harness and bits. One, rearing onto her hind legs, snapped part of the harness and another kicked out to the side. They pawed and snorted and pushed away from where Jezebel's body lay.

Though he couldn't see what was unfolding before him, he knew that he was in the presence of an ungodly evil. The cold chill rushed through his body again, as fear seized him and held on for a long moment.

Jezebel watched as a brown hairy creature, two-thirds her height but much more massive, pulled his way from the surface of the earth. She turned and ran in the angel's direction, but he caught her by the shoulders and stopped her. He turned her around and said, "Your god, Baal Melkart."

The fanged demon approached them. "She belongs to me!" hissed the creature. The soldier released her without replying, as the creature wrapped his clawed fingers around one of her arms.

"Help me!" Jezebel pleaded. "Please help me!" she wept fearfully and tried to resist, as the creature dragged her toward the place where he first appeared, where the earth was sifting down like a funnel. The demon turned to look back at the angel, then at Jehu, who was still struggling to hold the horses. Jezebel seemed to have no more strength to resist than if she were a piece of cloth in the demon's massive arms and powerful grip. The creature snorted in the direction of the horses and they became even more violent. The mare on the end began to kick at the chariot. Jehu had never seen horses so violent.

"Be gone, demon!" the angel ordered. The demon, refusing to look into the angel's face, looked down as he turned to leave. Jezebel continued to scream until the creature shoved her face and head into the ground. Then it was as though something pulled her into the earth from the other side. When she was out of sight, the demon began to laugh as he followed her into the underworld.

Jehu, afraid to attempt any type of maneuver with the terrified team, held the struggling horses back against the chariot so tightly that they couldn't move or kick. Gradually they settled down enough for Jehu to step from the chariot and lead the wild-eyed animals away from the area.

After the team had quieted down, Jehu returned and stopped to gaze at the broken body of the once great Jezebel, Queen of Israel. Though he wasn't given to fear, fear gripped him again as he looked into the frozen eyes of the queen. He hurriedly passed her corpse and entered the palace.

Jehu ate the meal Jezebel had prepared for him. Not wanting to experience again the fear he had felt on the way into the palace, he sent the eunuchs out to bury Jezebel, but all that they found of her was the palms of her hands and her feet. Returning to Jehu, they exclaimed, "The dogs have eaten her!"

Jehu thought for a moment, then said, "It is the fulfillment of Elijah's prophecy. 'Dogs will devour Jezebel by the wall in Jezreel'."

"Yahweh is with me, I will fulfill the rest of the will of Yahweh." Then he hurried out to see for himself what the eunuchs had told him. As Jehu strode from the building, he was aware that something was different, something that he couldn't specifically identify had changed. He stopped and looked around. It was as though the sun was brighter. Rustling leaves in the nearby olive trees drew his attention, as if they were whispering to him. When he turned to look, they seemed alive and greener than he had ever noticed. Even the very air itself seemed alive.

Jehu took several more steps until he couldn't go further. He had to stop, for he felt his heart would burst if he didn't say something. Tears filled his eyes as the words poured out, "The Glory of Yahweh has filled all the earth."

The second time he shouted it, "The Glory of Yahweh El Shaddai has filled all the earth!" It wasn't like him to be uninhibited in worship, but he turned to see two of the eunuchs following him and he didn't care that they had heard.

"The God of Abraham has come down to visit his people," he said to them. He broke into a trot and followed the wall around to where he had left Jezebel's broken body lying. There were two young dogs sniffing the ground where some of her blood had spilled. Then the full realization struck him. She was gone forever, and he was King of Israel! Jehu ran up the steps leading to the top of the courtyard wall. "Yahweh has made me king!" he shouted.

Silence fell over him, as through clouded, tear-filled eyes, he saw Elijah standing before him. The prophet extended his arm, pointing for Jehu to look back across the valley.

Slowly, Jehu looked back to where Elijah was pointing and he saw a great army with thousands of luminous chariots lining the ridges above the Jezreel valley, stretching out across the plain of Jezreel as far as a man could see. Jehu knew that he hadn't been alone and he drank in the scene. When he turned back to speak to Elijah, the prophet was gone, and with him, the host of heaven disappeared also.

EPILOGUE

Though nearly half the army of Israel followed Captain Jehu, there was a sizable force still faithful to the house of Ahab and thousands were undecided about whom to follow. Those who backed the house of Ahab gathered in Samaria, where nine of the seventy sons of Ahab claimed the right to the throne. Before the elders, they disputed over who was the most eligible, while the city filled to overflowing with those who wanted to be on the winning side, and believed Jehu wouldn't be able to hold on to his claim to the throne of Israel.

Jehu knew the longer he waited the more powerful they would become and sent word to select a king from among Ahab's sons and meet him on the field of battle. The elders of the city, afraid of being defeated by Jehu and then having the inhabitants of Samaria slaughtered, conspired against the sons of Ahab and slew them before anyone could learn of their plans. As a sign of surrender and submission they decapitated them and sent their heads to King Jehu, in Jezreel. Thus the prophecy of Elijah against the house of Ahab was fulfilled.

Having conquered the whole of Israel, Jehu sent word throughout the land that he planned to worship the great Baal more than Ahab and Jezebel had, and proclaimed a great feast in Baal's honor. All the worshipers of Baal Melkart were invited to celebrate. He brought the priests of Baal and Ashtoreth together with the worshipers and supplied great sacrifices of oxen and sheep to complete his deception. As the sacrifices were being offered, he sent his men into the temple and slaughtered them all, then destroyed the temple of Baal, ending one of the darkest chapters in Israel's history.

Judah paid for King Jehoshaphat's disobedience to God in forming a pact with Israel. The pact stopped the war between the two countries and was economically advantageous for Judah, but Israel received far greater benefit from the alliance. Because of Judah's help, God's judgment against Israel was postponed for years. The alliance was sealed by the marriage of Ahab's daughter, Athaliah, to Jehoshaphat's son, Joram.

The sons and grandsons of Jehoshaphat paid with their lives. When Joram, the eldest of the king's sons, took the throne, he killed his brothers so there would never be anyone to contest his authority when he reversed the worship of Yahweh, which Jehoshaphat had promoted. To please Athaliah he allowed her to defile the house of Yahweh and to shut it up so no one could worship the God of Abraham there.

He built groves for the fertility worship of Ashtoreth and images of Baal and brought back the sacrifice of children. He reinstated everything that his father had abolished. And the wrath of Yahweh was kindled against him and smote him with an incurable disease of the bowels and he died.

In God's anger against Joram and Athaliah for following Baal, and defiling Solomon's temple, He sent the Philistines and the Arabians against Judah. In a battle for Jerusalem all of the sons of Athaliah were slain except the youngest, Ahaziah, named after his uncle. He was with King Jehoram of Israel in Jezreel after Jehoram was wounded in a battle to retake Ramoth Gilead. At that time Captain Jehu, in obedience to the word of God, rode against the king.

When Athaliah learned that her son had been killed by Captain Jehu, she had all the other sons of King Joram put to death except one, Joash, a year old infant. He had been hidden from Athaliah by his sister. When Athaliah thought that there wasn't an heir left, she took the throne and reigned over Judah for six years.

****

After many months of writing, Jehew the scribe laid down his pen and walked out into the sunlight. He stretched, reflecting on what he had just finished writing. His wish was that all who read his script could see as clearly as he, the life and exploits of Elijah, and the hand of Yahweh through it all. He took a seat beneath an olive tree as he wondered where, and at what time, Elijah might appear again.

****

"Jesus!" James called out as he half sat, half fell against the bank along side the steep path. As Jesus turned to look back, James spoke breathlessly, "I can't keep up this pace."

"Forgive me, James, I also am out of breath but I hardly noticed. I'm overjoyed at the prospect of seeing friends that I haven't seen in a very long time. We'll rest while we wait for John and Peter to catch up."

They looked back down the path at Peter and John. Peter, trying to convince John of his views as usual, got only one or two words out between hard breaths. James looked back at Jesus; "You're going to meet someone at the top of this mountain today? We'll be in the rain within the hour, judging from the clouds. I've seen it like this a thousand times and it always rains."

"I am glad for your sake that you are with me today, James."

When Peter and John were just a short distance behind, Jesus and James continued around the winding path upward. Peter and John lagged behind, more winded from trying to carry on a conversation in addition to the climb. Peter always had something to say, or some instruction for another. John was the best listener of all, taking everything in and weighing it against what he knew, never disputing, but quietly setting aside what he knew to be incorrect. As young as he was, nineteen, John could have been a teacher to those who taught him, except for Jesus, who had the answer to every question he had, and with patience answered them all.

Peter had many insightful thoughts that were unique to him alone though some were extreme, but they helped John see things in ways he never would have without Peter's help.

Jesus strode with purpose, a half-step ahead of James, as though he had an appointed time to be there and was late. James knew when Jesus was like this there was a reason he would understand only when they had arrived.

On the edge of the summit James collapsed to the ground. A minute later, the other two disciples arrived. Peter fell to one knee, panting for air. John took a seat on a rock, leaned forward and braced himself with his hands on his knees as he kept his eyes on Jesus, who continued over large rocks to the center and highest point of the mountain.

They rested as clouds quickly blew in from the great sea to the west, as they often did here. They became enshrouded in the mist.

"Peter!" John's voice was sharp with apprehension. Peter and James looked in the direction John was transfixed upon.

The ghostly outline of two men riding in the cloud passed them and came to stand by Jesus, where they began to take on a more solid form, with color and flesh.

Jesus began to radiate, like iron white-hot from the smith's fire. He embraced each man in turn as he spoke. "It is good that you came to strengthen me for the task ahead."

"The Eternal One and Father of us all has placed all judgment and redemption in your hands." The three disciples somehow knew that it was Moses speaking.

The second man spoke, "It all rests on you, Master."

Peter spoke quietly to James and John, "It is Elijah."

John interrupted, "Did you hear what he said? He called Jesus, Master. Elijah called him Master! Elijah, who was taken to heaven without tasting death, as great as he is, called him Master!" The three disciples fell silent, trying to fathom the significance of the statement.

Elijah spoke again, "We have been sent on ahead, to the time of the end, and will shut up the heavens, that there will be no rain on the nations that reject the word of your servants. Plagues upon the peoples who reject the salvation you are about to suffer for. The great hand of mercy will be lifted, and until he is cast into the lake of fire, Satan will devour those nations. We cannot leave until you descend into the bowels of the earth.

"And we cannot aid you in your time of suffering, but we will be close by, to bear witness of the injustice and of the redemption, and then you will have power over the earth. Praise be to Yahweh El Shaddai."

As Elijah was speaking, Peter timidly eased over to them. "Lord, it is good that we are here." Jesus turned his head to face him. "Allow us to build three tabernacles, one for you, one for Elijah and one for Moses."

No sooner had Peter spoken than he realized that he had said something wrong, again. A thick luminous fog moved across the rocks and silently wove its fingers around them as Peter waited for an answer.

"This is my beloved son." Emanating from every direction, the power of the voice shook them to the core. Peter dropped to his knees and bowed his face to the ground. When James and John saw Peter bow to the ground, they did likewise. "In whom I'm well pleased. Hear Him!"

Afraid to look up, they remained that way until Jesus walked to each, placing his hand on their shoulder and saying, "Arise, don't be afraid." As they rose to their feet, they saw that Moses and Elijah were gone. "Tell the vision to no one until I have risen from the dead."

Within a year Elijah and Moses, looking as normal as anyone, were standing among a large crowd staring up at Jesus and two other men on crosses surrounded by Roman soldiers. Many in the crowd jeered. The day had turned as dark as night on a quarter moon. An ominous presence electrified the air and sent chills over all who were present.

Elijah turned to Moses and repeated what Jesus had spoken earlier, "Father, forgive them, they don't know what they are doing." Tears streamed down his face and he could hardly get out the next words. "He is worthy to be seated at the right hand of El Shaddai." Suddenly Elijah realized that there wasn't a sound from the large gathering of people, and he remembered the stillness that had fallen on the people moments before the fire had fallen on the sacrifice at Mount Carmel.

From the sixth hour until the ninth hour, darkness came over all the land. About the ninth hour, Jesus cried out in a loud voice, "Eloi, Eloi, lama sabachthani?" which means, "My God, my God, why have you forsaken me?"

When some of those standing there heard this, they said, "He is calling Elijah." Immediately, one of them ran and got a sponge. He filled it with wine vinegar, put it on a stick, and offered it to Jesus to drink. The rest said, "Now leave him alone. Let's see if Elijah comes to save him."

When Jesus had cried again in a loud voice, He gave up the spirit.

At that moment, the curtain of the temple was torn in two, from top to bottom. The earth shook and the rocks split. The graves broke open, and the bodies of many holy people who had died were raised to life and came out of their tombs. They went into the Holy City and appeared to many people.

When the centurion, and those with him who were guarding Jesus, saw the earthquake and all that had happened, they were terrified, and exclaimed, "Surely He was the Son of God!"

****

Two thousand years later, the phone rings beside the bed of the president of the United States. The President recognizes the voice of the head of the Central Intelligence Agency, and detects the note of urgency in his voice. "Mr. President, we have an emergency."

"Go on."

"At 2:07, nine minutes ago, an aircraft of unknown origin entered U.S. air space. That is only an estimate, since we lost him over the Atlantic, before entering our airspace.

"We believe that this is a highly sophisticated stealth aircraft, and that he has penetrated our airspace. Estimated speed at last contact was approximately four hundred twenty miles per hour.

"He could be headed to any destination on the eastern seaboard."

"Today is May, 20th, isn't it?"

"Yes sir, it is."

The president remains silent, as he remembers the young televangelist, in a broadcast from Anaheim the previous November, predicting that God would send a second judgment of fire upon the United States in the spring if we didn't turn from our ungodly ways. He said it would begin May 20th.

"The plane is headed to New York," the president says quietly, as he remembers that was where the judgment was predicted to begin. This would be the eighth prediction that the Bible-thumping preacher from England had accurately made if the plane reached its target. Each judgment had been more catastrophic than the last. The prophet had even given the day and hour that Los Angeles was shaken to the ground, killing three hundred thousand people.

For nearly two years the president had him under surveillance, but what could he have done with him? The events that he had predicted were natural disasters until now.

Pensively, the president asks his Chief of Intelligence, "What can we do?"